About the Author

Lucia Nevai's short fiction has been published in *The New Yorker,* *Zoetrope,* the *Iowa Review, New England Review,* and other periodicals. She is the author of two collections of stories, *Star Game,* which won the Iowa Short Fiction Award, and *Normal.* Born in Iowa, Nevai now lives in upstate New York.

paisley hanover
kisses and tells

cameron tuttle

DIAL BOOKS

AN IMPRINT OF PENGUIN GROUP (USA) INC.

DIAL BOOKS
An imprint of Penguin Group (USA) Inc.
Published by The Penguin Group
Penguin Group (USA) Inc., 375 Hudson Street, New York, NY 10014, U.S.A.
Penguin Group (Canada), 90 Eglinton Avenue East, Suite 700, Toronto,
Ontario, Canada M4P 2Y3
(a division of Pearson Penguin Canada Inc.)
Penguin Books Ltd, 80 Strand, London WC2R 0RL, England
Penguin Ireland, 25 St. Stephen's Green, Dublin 2, Ireland (a division of Penguin Books Ltd)
Penguin Group (Australia), 250 Camberwell Road, Camberwell, Victoria 3124, Australia
(a division of Pearson Australia Group Pty Ltd)
Penguin Books India Pvt Ltd, 11 Community Centre, Panchsheel Park,
New Delhi - 110 017, India
Penguin Group (NZ), 67 Apollo Drive, Rosedale, North Shore 0632, New Zealand
(a division of Pearson New Zealand Ltd)
Penguin Books (South Africa) (Pty) Ltd, 24 Sturdee Avenue, Rosebank,
Johannesburg 2196, South Africa
Penguin Books Ltd, Registered Offices: 80 Strand, London WC2R 0RL, England

Illustrations copyright © 2009 by Alli Arnold
Book design by Jasmin Rubero
Text set in Centaur MT

Printed in the U.S.A.

1 3 5 7 9 10 8 6 4 2

Tuttle, Cameron.
Paisley Hanover kisses and tells / Cameron Tuttle.
p. cm.
Sequel to: Paisley Hanover acts out.
Summary: Paisley Hanover and her fellow unpopular friends picket the outcome
of the sophomore class election during a school year filled with rumors, rivals, love triangles,
and a plot to pull off the biggest scheme of the year.
ISBN 978-0-8037-3287-2 (hardcover)
[1. Cliques (Sociology)—Fiction. 2. Popularity—Fiction. 3. Individuality—Fiction.
4. High schools—Fiction. 5. Schools—Fiction.]
I. Title.
PZ7.T884Pb 2010
[Fic]   2009037940

Dedicated to the infinitely beautiful Fifteen-Year-Old—
UnCertain, UnNormal, UnPerfect, UnSane, UnPredictable,
and deservedly UnApologetic

chapter one
detention headache

There are *thirty-seven blue lines* on this page of notebook paper, 134 greenish flecks in the tile next to my right foot, and seven rock-hard chunks of dried gum stuck under this table. Gross.

I jiggled my knee, closed then opened my notebook. Closed it again. Then opened it.

Ergh!

I was trapped in the library, staring at a totally blank piece of notebook paper, feeling I-can't-believe-this-is-my-life. I might have been elected sophomore class president. Or I might not. The results hadn't been posted, but even if they had I wouldn't know because I was stuck in detention! *Detention!*

I flipped my notebook shut and slumped back in my chair.

I should have been writing about what I had done wrong yesterday and who it had hurt and why I had done it and what I would do differently next time. But the problem was—I wouldn't do *anything* differently next time. Are you insane? *Not* skip sixth and seventh periods with Eric Sobel, stretched out on the soccer field holding hands, watching clouds cruise by, and talking about the screwed-up social dynasty at our school?

But was Eric Sobel sitting next to me in morning detention?

No.

Of course not. Mr. Canfield didn't give Eric Sobel a detention because *he's* the star of Varsity Boys Soccer *and* the place kicker on the Varsity Football team. Total double standard. I mean, hey—I'm the star of Varsity Girls Soccer. Well, okay maybe not *the* star, but I am one of the top scorers. Why are the rules always different for guys?

I looked up at the clock. Ugh. Twenty-two minutes to go until freedom and finding out the future of my sophomore year fabulosity.

Because I had this feeling—this *totally crazy* feeling—that it had worked. Yes, I truly *was* destined for greatness! But, okay, so it might not happen until next week. I could wait. I scratched my chin and—whoops!—found a little dried-up toothpaste dribble. I casually rubbed it off. Yes, we'd thrown the election. Yes, we'd forced a class-wide do-over. Right? I mean, Hutch had voted for me. Even *Jen* had voted for me. Tons of people wrote my name in—I saw it! And well, of course, *I* voted for me.

I was so nervo-excited, it was like butterflies were doing Olympic water ballet in my stomach. I took a deep breath and started counting the number of fat red books in the reference section. I considered putting my head down on the table, but I didn't want to wake up in a puddle of drool and see a picture of it later on Facebook. Besides, who could sleep right now?

Instead, I folded my arms and watched dust particles sparkle and twist in a beam of sunlight while I tried to have a warm and fuzzy out-of-body experience.

Nothing.

I moved my notebook a little and—what was *that*? Holy shiitake mushrooms. Someone had carved *Big kiss, class dismissed!* into the top of the table!

While, of course, I would never condone vandalism of school property (Hi Mom! Hi Dad!), I couldn't help smiling inside and out. That was *my* line! Well, my line when I was writing as Miss UnPleasant. I lifted my notebook and looked for more. Oh. I tilted my head and smiled like an übery-goobery proud parent at *UnPop and Proud* etched carefully into the wood with a blue ballpoint pen.

I was sitting there thinking how cool it was to start a trend, especially among hardened student vandals, when—wait. What was th—? It was like a—

There it was again!

I popped straight up. Was I totally paranoid? Or was someone laugh-snorting at me?

Thwat!

Nope. Not paranoid—psychic. Eww. Something hit me in the back of the head. It was a wet, chewed-up wad of I don't-know-what. I flicked it to the floor, feeling a flood of embarrassment gush into my face.

I took another deep breath and calmly watched Ms. Whitaker, our school librarian and detention supervisor, carefully reorganize the magazine lounge. I could see her tattoo peeking out from under her short poofy sleeve. She was wearing this super-cute nerdy-girl dress with these sexy over-the-knee boots and a bunch of jangly silver bracelets. They were the only sound in the library aside from my screaming-hot face.

She glanced up at me and smiled, then disappeared into her office behind the counter.

Finally my cheeks cooled off. I casually turned around to get a good look at my fellow detention mates.

Yikes. Not my usual crowd. They *all* looked guilty.

It was like a lineup of Future Prison Inmates of America. This one girl looked like someone had outlined her whole body in black felt pen and then underlined her eyes, fingernails, and lips. I watched her, fascinated, as she obsessively trimmed her split ends with a pair of nail scissors. Wow. Clearly, she knew how to pass the time efficiently in detention. Next to her, this big guy in a leather motorcycle jacket was trying to set the table on fire with a silver Zippo lighter. OMG. Was he serious? I looked around for Ms. Whit, hoping to see her come out of her office—and that's when I saw them.

BS1 and BS2.

They were sitting at the table behind me, smirking as usual, and dressed like boutique sale-rack bookends, as usual. They waved their manicured hands at me and flashed matching tacky-fake smiles. Then BS2 held up a hollow ballpoint pen and twiddled it. OMG. Spitballs? Thanks a not!

BS1 air-kissed me. BS2 laughed and did the same. Genius.

SIDEBRA

You don't need to know their real names. Just call them Bratty Sasshole #1 and Bratty Sasshole #2—BS1 and BS2 for short. That's what I do. They look alike, dress alike, and think alike (if they think at all). They're juniors and popular and varsity Hornettes—Goooooo, Hornets! The talky one has straight dark hair. The other one, the blond one, just echoes her and nods. It's kinda sad.

BS1 and BS2 don't even know me, really, but I know they despise me because of the wildly popular (ha!) columns I wrote for *The Fly*, our school paper. Yeah, the ones written by my über-cool secret alter ego, Miss UnPleasant. Okay, well, not so secret anymore since Hutch outed me in front of the entire sophomore class a couple days ago . . . But hey, that's water under the fridge—it might still be there, or it might still not.

I smiled back, giving them my warmest, most sincere faux-real smile, and turned away. I wondered what they'd done to get a detention. Oh right. They'd cut off that girl's ponytail at lunch yesterday.

I opened my notebook and tapped the eraser end of my pencil. What to write . . . Hm . . . I could tell the truth and suffer the consequences (been there) or I could whip up some pious platitudes to get our terminally annoying vice principal off my back (done that—totally backfired). So I decided to embrace my principles: truth, honesty, and anything I can think of to infuriate Canfield.

Dear Mr. Canfield,
I cut two classes. It didn't hurt anyone.
I did it because not-in-detention Eric Sobel
was holding my hand, which obviously short-
circuited the wiring in my tender, vulnerable,
still-in-development frontal lobe and severely
impaired my good judgment. Next time, I may
have to cut three classes.
Sincerely,
Paisley Hanover
Sophomore
Pleasant Hill High

I leaned back, feeling defiant and proud—and a little psychic about my next detention.

A couple of scrawny freshman techno-nerds broke into a perfectly silent game of flick football across a table. I wondered if they were the ones who had hacked into Canfield's e-mail account and circulated that picture of him wearing tight lederhosen hot pants and not much else. Mr. Canfield is kind of chunky and *really* hairy. The photo wasn't pretty—but it was good for school morale.

And that's when I noticed a tiny plume of smoke twisting up from under the table.

I heard the sound of a lighter. Oh great. We were only completely surrounded by bookshelves loaded with *kindling*. Perfect. Pyroman, the missing link in human de-evolution, was going to kill us all before homeroom.

I cleared my throat kind of loudly. A few people glanced at me, but no one seemed to care about the smoke. And still no sign of Ms. Whit. I turned around.

Uh-oh. Pyroman was staring right at me holding up the flaming lighter. He looked like he wanted to set *me* on fire. I swallowed hard, gauging how far I was from the door of the library and how fast I could run for it in my cute new wedges.

But then his face softened into this weird curious grin. He wrapped his meaty fingers tightly around the lighter, making a huge fist. And then he said, "Power to the UnPops, baby."

BS1 and BS2 snorted, laughing. My stomach did a quick flip turn. Wait. Was he serious? Then—OMG! A few of Pyroman's future cellmates joined in, holding up their clenched fists and nodding at me. Were they all Miss UnPleasant fans? It was hard to tell. But then Split Ends smiled at me too. Oh my God. They didn't just like Miss UnPleasant—they liked *me*. I loved the Future Prison Inmates of America!

I smiled back and did my best I'm-cool-too wave. But then I had to look away and stare out the window because I couldn't stop smiling. And it wasn't just normal smiling—it was big, goobery, self-congratulatory, ain't-I-cool smiling. Totally *not* cool. But that was the moment I realized I had some very *unlikely* fans at Pleasant Hill High *and* that if I curled one leg under my butt and sat up really straight, I had a perfect view out the window into the sunshine of sophomore hall.

And then I stopped smiling.

chapter two
a winning personality

Everyone was out there, opening and closing lockers, gossiping—I'm sure—about who would win the elections, drinking lattes with cinnamon and three sugars (it was the new thing), and eating tacos for breakfast. Everyone was living their blissful, before-homeroom, high school lives. Everyone except Jen, Amy, and Carreyn.

They were parked on the bench across from our lockers, as usual—well, I should say, what used to be usual. But they weren't talking—definitely *not* usual. Jen was staring at her phone, Amy was staring at her Diet Coke, and Carreyn was holding up a compact, staring at her own reflection.

Whoa!

What was up with Carreyn's hair? It wasn't pink anymore (long story). It was kind of a mud-puddle brown but long and thin and bristly like a twig broom. Yikes. Carreyn was becoming a definite home-salon danger to herself. We might have to do an intervention before *all* of her hair fell out.

It looked like Amy was thinking the same thing. She sat at the far end of the bench, leaning against one of the poles under the covered walkway, just staring at Carreyn with this part-confused, part-grossed-out face. I watched her take a sip from her Diet Coke in one hand, then her latte in the other, then the Diet Coke, then the latte. I guess she figured if she kept her mouth full she wouldn't have to talk to Carreyn. I guess she was right.

And then there was Jen, looking super-cute as always. Wait. What was Jen even doing there? Normally she was off making googly eyes at her perfect, varsity superstud boyfriend Bodie Jones. Maybe this was her new idea of qual time with her *friends*. I'd give it three minutes—max.

And that's when Bean Merrill and Cate Maduro, my new best girls from Drama, rounded the corner, dressed like, I don't know what—ABBA groupies? Definitely something crazy from the seventies. Bean's blond hair was feathered and everything, spilling out from under this groovy floppy cap. She had on these striped hip huggers and platform shoes, which made her tower over everyone else in the hallway, even the tallish guys. She breezed past Peter Hutchison, who knocked her cap off her head and then stepped on it on purpose. Typical. Bean just picked it up, then turned and stuck her tongue out at him.

Cate had straightened her dark hair and stylishly sculpted her bangs across her pale forehead. She was wearing this, like, plaid schoolgirl jumper and a white blouse with this ridiculously long, pointy collar. I would have looked like a total kindergarten dropout wearing that. But somehow Cate could look foxy in *anything*, and make *anything* look foxy. It was like her superpower.

And then I witnessed the most beautiful thing.

Without hesitating, Cate plopped right down in the middle of our bench between Amy and Carreyn, while Bean stood in front of them telling a very animated two-handed story. Amy started laughing so hard, she bumped the back of her head on the pole, which just made her laugh harder. Even Jen laughed a little. Carreyn slowly inched away from Cate, smooshing her bony little butt right up against Jen's, like she was afraid she'd turn gay if Cate touched her.

Oh well. Not perfect. But even so, my heart was suddenly overflowing with cotton-candy luv fuzz as I watched my Pop and UnPop friends hanging out together like it was no big deal, like it was the most natural thing in the world. I wanted to hug them all and weep tears of joy.

"I'll take that!"

I turned to see Ms. Whit stepping out from the stacks right behind Pyroman. He groaned. "Thank you, Elliott," she said swiping the lighter out of his hand.

Elliott? What a strange name for the chairman of the Future Prison Inmates of America.

"I love skulls." She beamed, admiring it. "This will be a handsome addition to my lighter collection."

I heard a riot of voices and looked back outside.

Whoa.

All of a sudden, Peter Hutchison had scrawny Charlie Dodd in a headlock and was dragging him across sophomore lawn. Hutch. What a guy. Who *wouldn't* want him to be our class president? I waited for somebody to do something. But Hutch's varsity jerk buddies just gathered around, laughing and egging him on.

Poor Charlie. Public humiliation can be so painful—not that I'd know *anything* about that. I watched Hutch dragging Charlie around in a circle in front of the benches and smirked with karmic satisfaction. Yes, I knew I shouldn't be enjoying it, but whatever. Charlie deserved it. I'm sure he thought he'd be tight with the popular jocks after selling me out. Really, this couldn't be happening to a nicer, more unfaithful, backstabbing double agent.

Charlie had this amused look on his face like being humiliated in front of everyone was no big deal, like it was all cool. But then a couple guys wrestled his gangsta-nerdy XXL polo shirt up over his face and went for his belt. The hallway crowd slowly pulled away.

"Get off me! Get off!" I could hear Charlie's muffled high-pitched screams through the glass. He punched the air, kicking at the guys like a manic mascot at a football game. He finally pulled his shirt away from his face. His glasses went flying.

Hey! I stood up. Okay, that's enough. I was beginning to have this creepy déjà vu feeling. I looked around. Where was Ms. Whit?!

Charlie tried to fight. He really did. But he was no match for three big jocks. They stripped off his belt and used it to tether him and his arms to a pole under the covered walkway. He looked so pissed I thought his head was going to shoot right off his body.

Then Hutch went up behind Charlie and yanked his pants down to his ankles.

I heard a few gasps and turned. A bunch of Library Girls had gathered in front of a bank of windows. They were watching in silence, looking horrified. Charlie's XXL polo shirt hung on him like a dress. All you could see were his skinny legs and knobby knees.

Then my phone vibrated. I glanced at it quickly. It was a text from . . . *Jen?*

Need 2 tlk. U ther?

Jen had only been blowing me off for like the past month. She must be desperate, I figured. Whatever. It was her turn to wait. I flipped my phone shut

SIDEBRA

Silly me. I used to think Charlie Dodd was my friend. Who wouldn't? I mean, he was my campaign manager! When you're someone's campaign manager, doesn't that usually mean you're trying to help the person (me) get elected and not secretly sell the person (me) out to the enemy (Hutch) by videotaping the person (me) looking like a total criminal with nostrils so huge that the person's nose (mine) could be mistaken for a Smart Car garage?!!!

Do I sound mad? No, I'm not mad. I'm motivated—to get even. Step one: the silent treatment. Step two: not sure yet. Oh. Maybe I should send a letter of recommendation to all the Ivy League schools, raving about Charlie Dodd's superior skills as a traitor. Yeah. I'm sure Charlie only volunteered to be my campaign manager so he could slap it on his college applications. Moron. I hope he adds *betraying friends* to his list of extracurricular activities.

and looked back out the window. She wasn't at our bench anymore. See? That didn't take long.

Hutch walked back and forth in front of Charlie, laughing way too hard at his glorious accomplishment. A lot of people looked perturbed or embarrassed and walked away, but plenty of others were laughing right along with him. The past few days, I'd felt like Hutch and Charlie deserved each other. But now, I wasn't so sure.

Then Cate Maduro walked right up to Hutch, yelled something at him, and threw a huge cup of something in his face. Hard! Ice cubes and soda went flying everywhere. Hutch wiped his face with his sleeve, trying to act like it was funny, like he didn't care that he was drenched in ice-cold soda.

God, I so wished I was out there.

Cate was still all up in Hutch's face chewing him out when Bean and Amy went to Charlie's rescue. Carreyn just stood there looking at Charlie then Hutch then Charlie. Was her hair dye impairing her sense of right and wrong?

Charlie got his pants back up fast. He found his glasses in the grass, then marched over and yelled something at Hutch. I had no idea what he said. But whatever it was, he was obviously a dead man, and he knew it. Charlie ran for his life down the hall. Hutch pushed through the crowd trying to head him off at the corner, but Cate, Bean, and Amy lined up with their hands on their hips in this bad-ass human blockade.

I was about to whoop out loud when a folded-up note landed on the table in front of me.

I looked up and found myself watching the back of Eric Sobel's dirty blond hair, cut torso, and soccer-star-hard glutes walking away.

OMG.

Eric turned, pushing his hair out of his eyes, and shot me a quick smile over his shoulder. What a cutie. And did I mention his incredibly hot body? Yeah, I guess I just did. Ack. I'm so gross. Anyway, Eric smiled at me and then kept walking over to the library's magazine lounge.

I quickly unfolded the note.

> Hey—
> Bummer. Sorry you got busted. Here to keep you company. Can I perp-walk you out of detention?
> ES
> Btw: Looking forward to the dance Friday . . .

Looking forward to the dance? Yes!

I expected Eric to have his head buried in *Sports Illustrated*. But when I looked over at him, he was staring right at me—and he didn't look away. His green eyes were super-intense like he was trying to send me a mental message. It kind of freaked me out, but in a good way, I guess. My whole body took a big gulp. God, not again. I could feel my face turning bright red. I quickly looked down and pretended to reread his note a few times until I pulled it together. Then I scribbled a note in big letters and held it up for him to read.

> Thanks. Yes. Btw: Me too!

He nodded and smiled.

I was smiling too, imagining us slow dancing together, my head on his shoulder, our faces moving closer and closer and closer . . .

"Paisley Hanover? Can I see you in my office, please? Now."

Oh crap. Ms. Whit had her arms crossed and was giving me

the icy librarian eyes. She must have seen me flash the note—not acceptable detention behavior. Normally, Miss Whit really liked me, and I really liked her. She was cool, especially for a librarian. But the look on her face—definitely not cool.

I slid my chair back and glanced out the window just in time to see Mr. Canfield doing his fast waddle-walk down sophomore hall. He was wearing pilly polyester pants, belted tight over his lady butt. I couldn't help feeling sorry for his thighs, which were obviously rubbing together. I wondered if his pants ever started to melt when he had to chase someone down the hallway.

Wait. OMG!

Canfield was holding a roll of tape and a few sheets of paper. The election results!

He taped a piece of paper to a door halfway down the hall. A bunch of people swarmed around, clamoring to see who had won. I tried to read their faces. Who won? WHO WON?! I couldn't tell.

"Paisley? Let's go!" called Ms. Whit.

I nodded, still looking out the window. God, I had to get out of here!

I shot Eric a couple of look-out-the-window-now glances as I followed Ms. Whit across the library and into her office. She closed the door. Uh-oh. Not a good sign. I dropped down into a chair, slid both hands under my thighs, and waited.

Ms. Whit's eyes were bulging like she was about to blow—but then she suddenly broke into this mischievous grin. She leaned in. "I know I shouldn't be telling you this," she whispered, all excited. "I'll probably go straight to librarian hell. But when I saw you in detention this morning . . ." She looked at me like I should already know what she was going to say.

I sat straight up. "Telling me what?" I whispered back.

"Guess who got the most votes for sophomore class president?"

Was she torturing me? Was this a trick question?

"Miss UnPleasant!" she whispered. "In a landslide!"

Wait. How could my snarky pen name have gotten more votes than Peter Hutchison? Or *me*? "Is that even possible?" I whispered.

"It's not just possible—it happened! Everyone in the faculty lounge was buzzing about it." Ms. Whit did a stylish two-fisted air pound. "And you know what that means, don't you?"

I shook my head. Um. No.

"*You* won, Paisley! They have to give it to you. *You* are Miss UnPleasant!"

I jumped out of the chair. "Oh. My. God. Oh my God! I won? I won!"

"Shhhhhh. Library voices, please."

We happy-danced around in Ms. Whit's office giggling like total goobers. See? I *knew* it! Yes! My seven-point college-application action plan was back in action.

"I can't wait to call my parents," I whispered, followed by a quick burst of excited involuntary spastic jazz hands—but don't worry. The door was closed.

Then Ms. Whit got all super-serious. "Paisley, as a responsible faculty member, I must advise you not to tell anyone until it's official. Got it?"

"Got it. 'Do as I say, not as I do.' No problem. My mom tells me that all the time."

We both took a few seconds to pull ourselves together, and then I walked out doing my best I-just-got-busted face. I think it was pretty convincing, because Eric Sobel *and* Pyroman were looking a little sorry for me. I ignored BS1 and BS2 and plopped back down in my detention spot, using every ounce of willpower to contain my thrill of victory.

Two more minutes. Two more minutes till I saw my name on that list and it was official.

I looked around the library, gazing lovingly at my detention-mates, at the Library Girls working studiously around a table, at a couple of NILs—nerds in love—holding hands in front of a computer, and then at Eric Sobel, who looked up and smiled back. Had they all voted for Miss UnP? I felt like someone was pumping happy gas into the library ventilation system.

And then I made the mistake of looking back out the window.

chapter three
miss UnPlesident

Outside, Amy, Jen, and Bean were squashed up in front
of the list, along with a small mob of other kids. I couldn't see their
faces. Ergh! I couldn't see their faces! And then they turned . . . They
looked . . . They looked . . . confused. My heart fell into the heels of
my adorable wedges, which actually were starting to pinch my toes.

Then—finally!!!—the warning bell for homeroom rang.

Everyone but me jumped up and bolted for the door. I jumped
up and raced over to Eric—"Come on! The results are up!"—
grabbed his hand, and *then* bolted for the door.

We ran out of the library and down the hall, bobbing and
weaving our way through the morning traffic. Okay, so Canfield
had barred me from writing any more Miss UnPleasant columns.
Whatever. As class president, I could still use my newfound *underground* popularity to fight for UnPop rights. Right? Right. So why
did I suddenly have this icky feeling swishing around my stomach?

When we got to sophomore hall, I looked at Cate, Bean, and
Amy like *well?* They shrugged. I pushed past LG Wong and Bentley
Jones and a few other brainiac overachiever class-officer types, then
elbowed in front of Hutch to read the posted results. I scanned the
list of election winners and . . .

What?!

Next to Sophomore Class President, it said "TBD."

My brain felt queasy. Wait. That couldn't be right. Could it? A small wave of relief hit me. At least Hutch's name wasn't on the list. And then hot panic— Wait. Neither was mine!

"That's weird," Eric said. He was silent for a few seconds. "Hey, maybe the write-in campaign actually worked. Maybe you got it, and they're figuring out how to announce it . . ."

I stared at him blankly.

Hutch shook his head. "No way, dude." He had this funny look on his face. "I won. I have my sources."

I squinted at Hutch. What did he know? I squinted harder— then exhaled. Nothing. He knew nothing. He was totally bluffing.

Hutch started pushing through the crowd, but not before giving me a friendly smack on the arm. "Hey, Hamburger. What up?"

I rolled my eyes.

"So, how does it feel to be an unelected official loser?"

I chuckled, stalling. Relax. He's bluffing. Ms. Whit *told* me I won. Eric's probably right—Canfield just needed more time to count up all of my write-in votes, *plus* all the votes for Miss UnPleasant, and then read and reread the school by-laws. I felt suddenly fizzy and lightheaded. Ha! I was pretty sure this was an *un*precedented victory.

"Gee, Hutch," I said, smiling. "I don't know. How *does* it feel?" Then I pointed to the big wet spot on the front of his shirt. "Oh, did you spill something?"

A bunch of people laughed.

Hutch looked over at Cate. "Why don't you ask your little man-hating friend?"

"You deserved it," Cate scoffed. "Besides, you're not a man— you're a *Homo habilis* in a baseball hat."

"I don't give a crap what you think," Hutch said. Clearly he had no idea what she was talking about and, actually, neither did I, but it sounded scathing. "Nobody at this school cares about people like you, Maduro."

"Oh, well that really puts me in my place. Thanks, Hutch."

That one got roars. Amy and Bean were falling all over themselves. I suddenly wondered why Cate and Bean had spent so much time hiding out on the front lawn. They could work it right here.

Eric raised his hands. "Hey everybody, relax. Okay?" He looked around the group trying to calm everyone down with his team-sports leadership gaze. He gestured with his thumb toward the election results. "What's up with *this?* That's what I want to know."

"Don't worry, Pais!" Bean squeezed through the crowd and gave me a quick hunched-over hug. "I know you won. I'm picking up a very strong President Paisley vibe."

"From where? Outer space?" Hutch laughed. "Admit it, Hamburger. I won. You know it."

I put my hands on my hips, suddenly remembering the disgusting fact that Hutch had a secret, icky crush on me—and I had the locker-stalker notes to prove it. "I know a lot of things, Peter," I said, "but actually that isn't one of them. And you really shouldn't call me *hamburger.* People will think you can't read."

Amy guffawed and then quickly composed herself. "So, what does TBD mean, anyway?" she asked.

"To be determined. *Duh,*" Carreyn snapped. Where did she come from? I thought she'd left—OMG. I couldn't stop staring at her bizarre twiggy hair extensions.

"Are those extensions cut-

SIDEBRA

Homo habilis (Yes, I looked it up later. No, not a gay hillbilly.)
[**hoh**-moh **hab**-*uh-luhs*]
—*noun*
An extinct species of man. He had a really small brain and lived like two million years ago. You know in those *Evolution of Man* illustrations where the monkey walks his way to a standing upright man? Homo habilis is right next to the monkey.

ting off the blood to your brain?" Amy asked. "I know what TBD *stands for*, but what does it *mean*? Why don't we know who won yet?" She looked at me.

I shrugged. "I don't know."

Amy stared me down, then broke into a huge goobery grin. "You *so* know. Tell us!"

"Nice face," Cate added.

"What?" I said, but I really couldn't keep a straight face. Now Hutch was giving me the suspicious eyeball shakedown too.

Cate just laughed at me. "Remind me to play poker with you sometime—for money."

And then beyond Cate, cutting across the corner of sophomore lawn, I saw him.

Clint Bedard.

Was he coming this way? I so wanted him to, but I also didn't want him to. I glanced over at Eric Sobel, then back at Clint. He was striding across the lawn with that confident half smile, his dark, run-your-hands-through-me hair catching the morning sun, and I kind of forgot to breathe. Oh. I . . . Wow. He was still wearing the pink "I'D VOTE FOR PAISLEY" choker I'd given him. I closed my eyes, wondering if he slept with it on . . .

"Hey, Pains Me," said Hutch, looking over his shoulder, then back at me. "Know what TBD stands for?"

I smiled at him. "I'm thinking it stands for 'Too Bad, Dude.'"

More laughing.

God, that was close. Get a grip, Pais. No I'm-running-my-hands-through-his-hair flash fantasies in the middle of a heated debate!

"Right." Hutch smirked, nodding. He paused, making sure all eyes were on him. "But, no. It stands for 'Two Boyfriends, Donkey-Breath.'"

"That would be TBD-*B*, genius," I said. Wait—what did Hutch just say? I played it back in my head really fast. OMG! A weird noodle of fear wormed through my body.

How did Hutch know that? Did he read my notebook? Did he read my mind? I mean, not that either guy actually was my *boyfriend*, but I did have dates with both of them that coming weekend. I looked around in a sudden panic. Most people seemed kind of confused, especially Eric Sobel. I felt like everyone could read my mind, and it screamed, *Guilty! Guilty! Guilty!*

Then everyone started talking at once.

"What does *that* mean?"

"Lame."

"What does it have to do with the election?"

"Wait, who?"

Hutch folded his arms and grinned smugly.

Suddenly—no idea why—I had an uncontrollable urge to change the subject. I totally started talking like an over-caffeinated auctioneer. "Dude, you lost to a girl, a girl who wasn't even on the ballot, a girl who no one was even allowed to vote for. Face it, I have it in the bag, nobody wants you, they want me!"

Hutch's nostrils flared. He was all red in the face. "*Nobody* even likes you anymore, Hanover. Nobody that matters. You hate this school." He poked his chest right in the wet spot. "*I* love this school. I *am* this school!"

"Wrong!" I was still speed-talking like a total freak. "You're *not* this school—you're this school's biggest problem! And you're not gonna be president. I am. I *know* who won the election! I *know* because a faculty member told me! It's me! *Me!* I'm sophomore crass plesident!!!"

Shocked silence.

Whoops.

The crowd around us erupted, and the magnitude of my mortifying tongue-typo sunk in. The air was sucked out of my lungs. I couldn't breathe. Oh God.

When the hilarity died down, there was another, even longer, even more awkward silence as Hutch stared at me, blinking, fuming, and probably trying to figure out if I was telling the truth. And then—

"Right on, Plesident Paisley."

What?

Clint Bedard was standing on the fringe, nodding and clapping. I looked around. Everyone was staring. Before I could do anything, Amy had joined in, jumping up and down and doing this limp kind of cheerleader kick. "Right on, Plesident Paisley! Right on! Right on, Plesident Paisley! Right on!"

My face went even redder. What were they *doing*?

Then Bean and Cate and a bunch of other people joined in too. And all of a sudden it hit me. These were my friends. These were my friends, and Hutch was full of crap. I laughed. Oh well, so what if I couldn't talk? I'd won! I was going to be sophomore crass plesident!

I glanced over at Eric, hoping he had completely forgotten about the two boyfriends thing, and he looked . . . I don't know. Weird. I mean like *I* was weird—way too weird for him.

"We did it! We actually did it!" Bean screamed.

"You won? *Really*?" Cate looked amazed. "No way," she whispered.

"Yep. *Miss UnPleasant* got the most votes. In a landslide!" I caught Clint's eye. He tossed back his head and flashed me a lopsided smile.

Cate and Bean screamed, and a bunch of people started clapping.

"Yes!" yelled Amy.

"Amazing!" said Cate, grabbing my arm.

Cate, Bean, Amy, and I were all jumping up and down hugging, which is actually really hard to do.

"Am I dreaming? Are we living in an after-school special?" asked Cate. "This is *un*believable!" For a second, she looked like she was going to cry.

Hutch shoved both fists into the pockets of his letterman's jacket. He and his crew just stood there, watching us celebrate, looking royally pissed. Then Hutch opened his mouth.

"Throw the election?" he shouted at Eric, now standing off to the side. "*Throw the election? Great idea, Sobel!*"

"What, man? You didn't have to do it. You could've voted for yourself."

There was a crackling from the school intercom and the gravelly sound of someone clearing his throat. Everyone went quiet.

"*Good morning, Pleasant Hill High.*"

People groaned. It was Canfield.

"*Ahem . . . This is your vice principal, Mr. Canfield, coming to you live from the main office, where we have just finished conducting a last-minute recount of the votes for sophomore class president. . . . crackle . . . crackle . . . I now have a brief announcement to make.*"

His voice echoing through the halls usually made my head throb. But that morning, I couldn't stop smiling. This would make it official. I grinned at Peter Hutchison and tossed out my hands like *ta-dah!*

"*After a thorough recount and careful consideration, I am pleased to announce that the new sophomore class president is . . .*"

chapter four
homeroom insecurity

Crackle . . . crackle . . . crackle . . .

Just say it! Say it! *Just say my name!!!*

"*. . . Peter Hutchison!*"

I didn't even consider taking a breath. It was like I'd been plunged into this weird, silent, slow-motion dream. Amy did an exaggerated double take. Bean's feathered hair blew in the breeze. Cate's crazy long, pointed collar flapped slowly.

I was stunned.

I looked around with what I'm sure was a total freak-out face. My head felt hot. My nose started to sweat. There was a confused murmuring, and then Hutch and his rowdy cronies started cheering and high-fiving like dumb jocks, or jerks, or whatever.

"Aw, don't feel bad, Hamburger," Hutch said, draping his arm over my shoulder. "You got bad intelligence. It happens. But I'll find a place for you in my new administration. You can be Secretary of Homeroom Security. Bet you'd be *spastic jazzed* for it!" He laughed, and so did a bunch of other people.

Okay, Hutch was a complete shidiot. But I had to admit—that was a pretty good one.

"Doubt you'd have had time to be president anyway. You're so damn busy making sure *everyone* likes you." He laughed again and walked off.

I looked around for Clint. But he was gone. My heart dropped into my knees.

I wanted to crawl inside my locker and die. OMG. Could I do that? What if I didn't die but just got stuck? Oh God, how could this happen to me?! Why did I let myself believe that I'd won? Why did I have to announce it to *everyone?*

Amy crinkled up her face. "You were robbed, Pais, totally robbed!" She handed me her Diet Coke, I guess to make me feel better.

"*We* were robbed," said Cate. Now I think she actually *was* crying. I felt awful.

Carreyn looked at me like she might get a socially transmitted disease just by knowing me. She slowly backed away, turned, and ran off to homeroom.

I searched the shifting crowd for Eric Sobel. But the second I spotted him, he turned away, pretending not to see me. Was he so embarrassed for me that he couldn't even make eye contact?

Bean stood there limply, looking totally heartbroken. "Wait, what did Canfield say?" she asked slowly. "Something like *after careful consideration?*"

"Yeah. He meant to say *after a butt-full of favoritism,*" Cate snapped. "God. I hate this school!" she screamed between clenched teeth.

"Are you sure Miss UnPleasant got the most votes?" Bean asked me.

"Yeah. I mean, that's what Ms. Whit told me." I plopped down on a bench feeling a little dizzy and a lot mortified. But then my head started to clear. "Wait. How can he do that? Just *decide* who wins?"

Amy shook her head, all disgusted. "I guess you can't beat the man when the man is counting the votes."

"Counting *what* votes?!" Cate sounded like she was being strangled. "He didn't count any of *our* votes! This is outrageous!"

"Hutch was right." Bean sounded totally defeated. "Nobody at this school cares about people like us." She slumped down on the bench next to me. "Not even the faculty."

Nobody said anything for a few seconds while we watched the last few students darting into their homeroom classes.

"I do," said Cate. "I care."

"I do too!"

"I do three!" Amy said. No one laughed.

Cate looked at each of us. "Really? Do you? Okay. So, what are we going to do about it?"

"Move to Canada," I suggested.

"No." Cate shook her head like I was a total buttcap. "We're gonna get the word out. We're gonna start a petition demanding that Hutch resign. Fight for a recount!"

"And organize a huge protest!" Bean nodded. "With signs and drums and conga lines!"

"Maybe," I said, thinking out loud. "Or . . . maybe we need something a little more devious . . . a little more *t*expected?"

I jumped as my phone buzzed. Another text from Jen.

No jstice! Hutch = jrk!

I read it a couple of times. I couldn't figure Jen out. First she's on Hutch's side. Now she's on mine? But suddenly, I had a rather devious and unexpected idea. Or was it more of a psychic flash? Hard to tell sometimes. I opened my mouth to dish just as the final bell rang. I was late.

Great. I couldn't even hack Secretary of Homeroom Security.

chapter five
drama, drama, drama!

"But I don't get it!" said Bean, flapping her hands as we walked down the main hall to Drama later that morning. "Why would Ms. Whit tell you you'd won if you didn't win?"

"She didn't tell me I'd won. She told me Miss UnPleasant got the most votes. So they'd have to give it to me." I'd moved beyond stunned and was now totally, royally pissed. "And they *should* have. *I'm* Miss UnPleasant!"

"Yeah!" Cate said. "*You're* Miss UnPleasant—*you* won. Do the math, Canfield."

"I still don't understand how this happened," I said. "Bean, who did you vote for?" I asked.

"Paisley Hanover, duh."

"Yeah. Me too." I nodded. "Wasn't that the big plan?"

"Well, actually," Cate said, gently fingering the perfectly sculpted dark bangs across her forehead, "*I* voted for Miss UnPleasant. And obviously, I wasn't the only one."

I stopped cold in front of the doorway to Drama and grabbed Cate's arm. "What?"

She shrugged, giving me a sorry-but-not-really look. "Love knows no bounds—or big plans."

"Hey! You agreed to get all your Un supporters to write *me* in."

"Yeah. Before I read that little part on the ballot about no one's vote counting if you wrote in *Paisley Hanover*. Sorry, but I wanted my vote to count." She clenched her fists. "I still want my vote to count!"

"Hey! Hey you guys!" Charlie Dodd came barreling toward us from the opposite end of the hall. He stopped right in front of me, panting. "Any of you lovely ladies need mouth-to-mouth?" he asked, trying to sound all suave. What? The three of us just stared. He put his hands on his knees for a second, panting, then looked up and pushed back his glasses. "Yeah, I passed my CPR/First Aid class last night. I'm gonna include a copy of my certificate with all my college applications."

I groaned.

"Congrats, Charlie," said Cate, sounding suspiciously sincere. "FYI, do not resuscitate. I'd rather just die."

Charlie looked to me for help. I folded my arms and glared at him. I so clearly still wasn't talking to him.

"You okay?" Bean asked Charlie. "You know, after this morning . . . ?"

Charlie chuckled. "Oh, just a typical morning in the high school life of the small but mighty. Actually, it wasn't all bad. I got a number of quite flattering comments on my cute knobby knees from girls who normally would never even talk to me." He nodded enthusiastically, looking pleased. I gave him nothing but my chilliest cold front.

"Hey, um, really sorry you didn't win, Paisley." Charlie wiped a trickle of sweat off the side of his face. "Really. I never should have helped Hutch with his campaign. And I never should have helped him out you like that in front of everyone. Sorry. It was a serious lapse in judgment." He scratched his head nervously. "So, um, did you see who's sophomore class secretary?" He paused dramatically. "I won! Pretty awesome, huh? I mean, not that I'm surprised or anything."

"Traitor," said Bean coldly.

Cate folded her arms and cocked her head to the side. "Your little *Mr. Dodd pod* needs some Miracle Grow."

"That's fresh." Charlie smiled. "Never heard that one before. Seriously." He looked eagerly at all of us. "Hey, thanks for voting for me. I mean, if you did. Did you?"

None of us answered.

I couldn't believe him! What a tool—and definitely not the sharpest one in the shed. Finally, I said all über-calm, "I'm not talking to you, Charlie. Ever."

He nodded at me like he was expecting it. "Okay. No worries." Then he nervously scratched his nose and hoisted his overloaded backpack from one shoulder to the other. "So, um, I was wondering . . . Do you think you could talk to Hutch for me and ask him not to kill me until senior year *after* I get accepted to Princeton?"

I looked at him, like totally incredulous. "So um, *no.* I'm not talking *for* you either."

"Okay." Charlie looked a little scared but oddly at peace. "Well, it's been nice knowing all of you. Paisley, I'm sorry I let you down. I'll write up a will tonight. If I die, you'll get all my class notes plus the drafts of my application essays." He paused. "Pure Ivy gold."

Bean put her hand on his shoulder, looking for a second like she might actually miss him. "What'd you say to him after you got your pants up?" she asked.

"Called him a *crusty botch of nature,*" said Charlie, smiling proudly. "Shakespeare. *Troilus and Cressida!*"

"Sweet. An insult he couldn't even understand." Bean laughed.

"No wonder he wants to kill you." Cate smirked.

My phone buzzed again. I had a feeling I knew who it was.

C u @ r bench 10:45?

I sighed. If it would get Jen to stop texting me constantly . . .

ok

I hit SEND and opened the door to Drama. It sounded like a death match between the debate team and the A/V squad. I didn't really think about it until I heard a Library Girl shout—actually shout—"I DIDN'T VOTE FOR HUTCH! DID YOU?!"

"Okay people, quiet down," Mr. Eggertson called out from the front of the room. Everyone ignored him.

A bunch of people turned and stared at me, then went right back to their heated conversations.

"Yeah, but I didn't want my vote to *UNcount*!!" Mandy Mindel screeched to a motley crew of Drama geeks.

Mandy Mindel? Screeching? What was going on? Usually I love Drama class. It's fun. It's weird. All of the people are weird—in a good way. Even *I* get to be weird. And it's not just okay to be weird in Drama. Being weird actually counts toward your grade. But that day, Drama was *really* weird—and not in a good way. It was all drama, drama, drama. And all about me.

Mr. E. clapped his hands crisply. "The curtain is rising, people! Take a seat. Now!"

Finally, everyone sat down and the angry chatter died to an irritated murmur.

"Okay, people. Today we're going to start with a new concentration exercise. Everyone choose a partner."

Mandy Mindel raised her hand. Holy shiitake mushrooms. What was up with Mandy Mindel? This was the girl with no eyelashes who couldn't muster the courage to walk out to the front lawn alone?

"I *can't* concentrate!" she said, and lifted her chin defiantly. "I can't believe that thug is going to be our class president! *Is there no justice?*"

Cate stood up. "Yeah! Anyone whose vote wasn't counted was robbed."

Teddy Baedeker, who was Un way before it was cool, raised his hand like he was flagging down an airplane. "Hey Mr. E.! Did someone really get more votes than Hutch?"

"Well, yeah, Teddy," Cate said, exasperated. "Miss UnPleasant did!"

Mr. E. nodded. "That's what I heard as well . . ."

The room erupted again. I looked around, totally floored. Who knew that Mandy Mindel and the Library Girls could even talk that loud? Cate and Bean were both yelling too. Charlie Dodd just sat there clutching his backpack, looking sort of not well.

"Excuse me. Excuse me!" Svend, our totally cool, totally pierced foreign exchange student from Denmark raised his hand. Mr. E. called on him. "I have read that in America, this is how democracy works. Only some votes are counted. Have I been uninformed?"

Everyone in the room went nuts. Some people kind of laughed like yeah, that's pretty much it, but others seemed really pissed.

At that moment, the door swished open and there was Clint Bedard, looking more deliciously disheveled than usual. I clutched my chair. Just seeing him made my body do the wave. He grabbed a chair and dragged it over next to mine, then collapsed into it. I checked to make sure he wasn't wearing some other girl's sparkly lip gloss again (trust me, it happens) before I smiled at him. I was really trying to maintain a sliver of composure and cool. But then he pointed to his "I'D VOTE FOR PAISLEY" choker and winked at me. Melt!

"Glad you could join us, Mr. Bedard," said Mr. E. "Apparently, we are beginning a class discussion on politics. Why don't you lead off by sharing your opinion of the sophomore class election results."

Clint glanced around the room, trying to figure out what he had just walked into. "Um, yeah. Well, I usually just vote for the candidate with the best bling." He pointed to his pink choker, all gangsta cool. Everyone laughed.

A student messenger slipped into class and handed Mr. E. a piece of paper. He read it and walked toward us, talking. "Thank you, Clint. Very informative." He handed the slip of paper to me.

Dear Paisley,
Please stop by the library at morning break. I'd like to follow up on our conversation. I was mistaken to share what I'd heard with you, but all the same I do think that there has been some discrimination here.
Hang in there, Miss UnP!
Ms. Whitaker

Mr. E. turned to the rest of the class. "Okay people, how many of you voted in the class elections?"

Arms shot up everywhere.

I reread Ms. Whit's note. It *was* discrimination. I hadn't thought about it that way before.

"How many of you sophomores voted for Peter Hutchison for president?"

Nobody budged. Nobody. I turned and stared at Charlie Dodd.

Slowly, he raised his hand. "What?!" he asked, all defensive. "I thought he had the power."

"You had the power, you moron," I muttered. "The power to be an honest campaign manager and vote for the better candidate!"

"I thought you weren't talking to me, Paisley. Can we go back to that?"

I turned my back on him and passed Ms. Whit's note to Bean.

Cate stood up. "We should go to Canfield's office right now and demand to see the ballots."

Bean read the note and jumped to her feet. "This is discrimination! I demand a recount!"

There was a moment of silence. Then a bunch of people started talking at once.

"Yeah!"

"We should."

"Recount!"

"Let's go!"

"Right now!"

"Right on!" said Clint. "I'm up for anything that makes Canfield's day more exciting."

People rushed the door.

"Wait, wait, WAIT!" shouted Mr. E. "I encourage all of you to challenge authority—but not during my class. Anyone who leaves now gets a fast pass to the vice principal's office."

"How convenient," Cate said. "That's exactly where we're going!"

People started retreating to their seats. Then someone began to chant softly, "We count. Recount. We count! Recount!"

OMG. It was Mandy Mindel! Soon Cate and Bean and Teddy Baedeker and Clint and everyone else joined in, chanting like an angry mob. And then everyone started marching out the door.

I sat there watching. Was I allowed to protest for *me*, or was that tacky?

Then Bean ran back, grabbed my hand, and pulled me up from my seat. "Paisley, come on! This isn't just about you—it's about everyone who voted for you! UnPop Power!"

Charlie Dodd hadn't budged from his chair. Bean waved her

fingers at him as we passed. "Bye-bye, you little Hutch's Honey."
Charlie grunted and hugged his backpack tighter.

We marched out of Drama and up the main hall to Canfield's
office, chanting and cheering. Canfield's secretary was busy typing
with these huge, old-school headphones on that made her look like
Princess Leia.

When she finally noticed us, she looked around, totally flustered. She hoisted herself to her feet, waving and shouting, "Hello?
Hello?! Do you have an appointment?"

Canfield's office door was wide open, so we ignored her and marched
right in, chanting, "We count! Recount! We count! Recount!"

Mr. Canfield was sitting behind his desk, feeding paper into
a shredder. He looked up. "Welcome student activists! I've been
expecting you."

We all crammed into his office and, interestingly, everyone
avoided the torturous, wobbly Fink Fast Chair, everyone but Clint.
What courage.

"Hello friend," he said as he slid comfortably into it and leaned
hard on his left knee. My mouth fell open. So that's how you do it! I
made a quick note to self.

Cate jumped right in. "I did
not vote for Peter Hutchison,
and neither did any of these
people. We demand a recount
of the votes for sophomore
class president!"

Canfield seemed mildly
amused. But he didn't stop
feeding papers into the shredder. "On what grounds?"

SIDEBRA

The Fink Fast Chair is one of Canfield's
brilliant secret weapons. It looks like an
innocent office chair—but it's actually a
weapon of torture.
Distinguishing characteristics:
• Shorter than most chairs to keep you
feeling small and helpless
• Sticky non-breathable vinyl to make you
and your butt sweat while under interro-
gation
• One back leg is shorter than the rest
to keep you—the presumed guilty—off
balance.
(Yes, my small, sweaty, off-balance butt has
done time in the chair—but I didn't fink!)

We all looked around at each other as the paper shredder sliced and diced.

"On the grounds of justice and fairness," said Mandy firmly.

"Hello Mindy." Canfield smiled. "Do your parents know that you're cutting class today?"

She looked mortified. God, he couldn't even get her name right.

"We *know* that Miss UnPleasant got the most votes!" said Bean. "Not Hutch."

"Really?" Canfield asked, mashing his fish lips together in a smirk. "How could you possibly know that?"

"We have our sources," I said confidently. "Our *faculty* sources."

Mr. Canfield studied me suspiciously. "I'm sorry, Paisley, sorry for your loss. I know it can be very hard to accept that we're not as well-liked as we had hoped."

Yeah. I'll bet you know.

I took a step toward him. "Hutch may have won the popular vote, Mr. Canfield, but he didn't win the *un*popular vote," I said, suddenly imagining what it would feel like to win an Oscar and a Nobel Peace Prize.

"We want to see the ballots," Cate demanded. "Now."

"And count them ourselves," added Clint, casually crossing one leg over the other like he couldn't possibly be more relaxed. He flicked an imaginary piece of fuzz off his knee. "Of course, we'll need to do the recount in the presence of three *un*biased teachers and one janitor." He smiled at Canfield.

Canfield chuckled. "Well, that would require a petition with lots of names and signatures. Are you all willing to sign a petition?" Canfield asked.

"Duh!"

"Absolutely!"

"Bring it on!"

"Fine." Canfield scribbled "PETITION" across the top of a yellow legal pad and passed it around the room. "I should warn you that the recount process will be very time-consuming and very labor-intensive."

"We don't care," said Mandy. "We just want our votes to be counted."

And that's when the security guard arrived at Canfield's door, looking confused.

"Hi Dan." Teddy Baedeker waved.

Dan the security guard nodded. "Hi Teddy."

"No need to be alarmed, folks," said Mr. Canfield. "It's school policy to hit a silent alarm when the vice principal is in potential danger."

What a boob! My dad was so right about Canfield. "*You're* not in danger," I said, totally disgusted. "We are! We're the ones being discriminated against!"

"I'm surprised at you, Paisley. Surprised that you would end a sentence with a preposition."

"I'm surprised at *you*, Mr. Canfield," said Cate. "Surprised that you would end your career with a lawsuit."

Canfield did not look amused.

"Both my parents are lawyers, so I get a lot of free legal advice," she added casually. Trump!

Canfield rolled his eyes. "Okay, so has everyone signed the petition?" People nodded, and Mandy handed him the legal pad. He scanned the list of names, looking very pleased. "Super." Canfield counted the names on the petition. "This seems sufficient for a recount to me."

He walked behind his desk, took the lid off the paper shredder, and dumped its contents in a big heap on the floor. "Here are all the ballots. Recount away!"

Everyone was silent. The air vibrated. If Dan the security guard hadn't been there, I can promise you that Canfield would have been shredded alive.

"Thank you all for voicing your opinions. We value student involvement here at Pleasant Hill High. Now everyone back to class!" He waved us off like flies. "Oh, and thank you for signing this *petition*." He tapped the legal pad with his hairy finger. "I'll see every person on this list in detention next week."

What. A. *Pig*. We dragged ourselves out of Canfield's office looking like deflated buffoons. But I was brain-boiling mad. And so was Cate.

"This is not over!" said Cate to the group.

"This is *so* not over!" I agreed. "Flagpole on the front lawn at lunch. Be there or be unaware!"

chapter six
teen scream

At morning break, I skipped what was sure to be an awkward, not-so-sweet sticky bun with Amy, Carreyn, and Jen and headed over to the library to talk to Ms. Whit. I didn't really want to go. I mean, I love Ms. Whit, but what could she say? I figured I should just get it over with.

When she saw me walk into the library, she got this horrible look on her face, like she had just backed over my laptop with her SUV.

I started talking before she could say anything. "It's okay. Really. I mean, it sucks, but it's not your fault."

"I'm so sorry, Paisley. I was confident, given what I had heard, but it was wrong of me to say anything to you."

"No, I'm glad you did. It felt really good to be the winner, even if it was only for five minutes."

She smiled. "I think you should fight this."

"I tried, Ms. Whit. We went to Canfield's office and demanded a recount. But he just taunted us and shredded the ballots."

"Really?" Ms. Whit looked shocked. "That's not right. Glen Canfield is a . . ." Ms. Whit stopped herself and sighed. "Maybe there's another way." Then she suddenly got all excited and started digging through a pile of papers on the counter.

"I just got these this morning." She handed me a sheet of green paper.

It said *Teen Scene Reporter Wanted.*

I looked up at her, like, what is this?

"The county newspaper needs a student journalist to write about teen issues," she said. "You'd be great."

I sighed. I was glad Ms. Whit was still a fan, but what did this have to do with fighting the election results?

"You should write about what's happened here at our school—bring the facts to light."

Hm . . . Not a bad idea. That'd teach Canfield to abuse his power! I pictured a huge embarrassing photo of him on the front page of the *Seven Hills Herald* with the caption: "Vice Principal Canfield Gets Canned!"

I thanked Ms. Whit and walked out of the library feeling much, much better—until I passed Eric Sobel walking with Hutch down the hallway.

"Hey." Eric nodded with a shy smile and looked away.

"Hey." I smiled back at no one, feeling totally not sure. Eric seemed like a different guy all of a sudden. Uh-oh . . . I had this sinking feeling. Was he still totally embarrassed by me? Was he still thinking about the "two boyfriends" thing? I thought for a second, then sunk a little lower. Was our date for the dance still on?

"Well hello, Paisley," said Hutch all puffed up. "*Plesident* day we're having, don't you think?" He laughed like that was the funniest thing in the world.

I just kept right on walking. I was supposed to meet Jen at our bench.

But when I got there, Jen and *Bodie* were sitting talking. Actually, Bodie was sitting on the bench—Jen was sitting on Bodie's lap.

Typical. She can't do anything without him anymore. She can't even sit on her own butt.

"Hey Pais!" Jen waved, all cheerful. "Glad you got my text."

"Yeah. It's kinda been a busy morning. Where are Amy and Carreyn?"

"Cafeteria. The lunch ladies are giving out free samples of fried mac and cheese bites. Part of our school's new health plan, 'No Child Left With Small Behind.'"

Bodie laughed. So did I. Jen was funny. She'd always been funny, till she went to that stupid party over Labor Day weekend and turned into a crazy schizophrenic psycho. I stopped laughing.

Bodie nodded, flashing me his varsity smile. "Hey, really sorry to hear you lost the election."

"I didn't lose," I said, shifting my bag to my other shoulder. "Canfield just gave it to Hutch."

"Really?" Bodie asked, genuinely interested.

"Miss UnPleasant actually got the most votes."

Both Jen and Bodie looked surprised. "But Hutch got the gig?" Bodie asked. "That's not right."

"Well, I voted for you," Jen said. "And not because Peter Hutchison or anyone else told me to."

If she thought that was going to make up for weeks of weirdness, she was Pleasant Hill high.

"Do you want me to talk to Mr. Canfield?" asked Bodie.

See? Even when I *wanted* to hate Bodie, I couldn't. He was just such a nice guy—to everyone, not just me. And he didn't have to be. He was varsity A-list popular.

"If there's a problem," he went on, "maybe I can help out somehow."

"Thanks, Bodie. But it's too late. Canfield shredded all the ballots."

Before Bodie could say anything, there was a sudden swell of voices and a wave of movement heading down sophomore hall.

"I didn't say you had a crusty *crotch!*" screamed Charlie Dodd, sprinting past us in a panic.

"Come here you little turd blossom!" yelled Hutch, chasing after him.

I waved at Hutch's back. "Our new proud, fearful leader."

"Excuse me," said Bodie, lifting Jen off his lap. "I'll be right back." Bodie took off sprinting after Hutch. Did I mention he's an all-state sprinter?

"Don't you just love him, Pais." Jen stood there all googley-eyed, watching Bodie race off to save the life of another scrawny student. "I do."

Oh, God. First she acts crazy for weeks, then she tells me something happened at that pool party, then she runs off before telling me *what*, then she says she's going to come over to explain, then she stands me up, then she accuses me of becoming Miss UnPleasant *just to hurt her*, and then the first time we actually talk again, she has the nerve to gush about *her love for Bodie Jones?* Bodie Jones, blah blah blah, the greatest guy on earth—except, of course, when he plays on the varsity drinking team and kind of likes to *torture* scrawny students, just like the rest of the varsity jerks. God! I was such a sucker. I had to get out of there.

"I sure do," I said, smiling faux real. "Everyone does. But, um, sorry. I have to go . . . cram for an unpop quiz right now." I grabbed my American History book out of my locker and walked off in search of a quiet spot.

"Hey, when can we talk?" Jen yelled after me.

Ergh! She had some nerve. "Locker room. Before practice!" I hated myself.

I was wandering down the deserted main hall toward the front of the school when who do I see but Candy Esposito running in from the parking lot. It's so not fair. When Candy Esposito runs, it's like watching a slow-motion shampoo commercial. She was the last person I wanted to see at that moment. I leaned against the wall and stuck my nose in my history book.

She was about to run past me when she did a double take and stopped short. "It's you! God, Paisley, thanks to you I had to park way out in the boonies again today."

Did I mention that I wasn't getting *anything* I wanted that day? I lowered the book I was hiding behind. "What are you talking about, Candy? I don't even have a car."

"I know, but you do have power—*power to the UnPops.* Very impressive. Much better than a car, actually." She tucked a few wisps of her sun-kissed-honey hair behind one ear and checked out what I was wearing. "Cute shoes. But those *Up with Unpopular People* columns you wrote have given way too many weirdos way too much confidence. Now people I don't even know are parking in my spot."

"Well, Candy, it's not really *your* parking spot, is it?" I pointed out.

She didn't answer. She just tilted her head and slowly smiled. Obviously it wasn't her parking spot. But it was where junior Candy Esposito—beautiful, beloved, entitled, Pleasant Hill High Pop royalty—liked to park her new white Volkswagen Beetle convertible, no matter what time she got to school, and everyone knew it.

She leaned in to me and said in this soft breathy voice, "I want to give you some advice, Paisley, because I like you." Then her eyes got really big, or maybe it just seemed that way because she was standing so close to me. "Be careful. When you have power at this school, everyone thinks they know you. Everyone's *always* listening and *always* watching."

Um, what? What did she mean by that? I watched her expertly

can't act like you're on some tourist safari through Weirdo World."

"Okay, okay. Sorry. Cooling." She took a deep breath. "Cool."

When we arrived at the flagpole, a small group of Uns—mostly the core group from Drama—had already gathered around Cate and Bean. The two of them were standing on a step around the base of the flagpole. I could see their heads above the growing crowd and the free-range hair.

"And that's why we have to fight this!" Cate shouted.

"Even if we can't get a recount!" added Bean. She saw me and waved. "Hi Pais!"

Everyone turned to look at me. Clint. LG Wong. Mandy and Teddy. A few Library Girls. AV Geeks. Emos. Charlie Dodd—wait, what was Charlie Dodd doing here? Hm . . . Probably spying.

"Hey, everyone," I called, getting up on the stage, I mean, the step, and adding a semi-official little wave. "Thanks for coming. If you're here, you already know that Mr. Canfield shredded the ballots, so we can't actually do a recount—"

"Boo!"

"He sucks!"

"What a lederhoser!" yelled one of the scrawny techno nerds from detention, clearly enjoying his self-referential glory.

"But this isn't just about the election. It's about every student whose vote wasn't counted!" OMG. And when I said that, I totally gave myself the chills.

SIDEBRA

The Undigenous Species of the Front Lawn

Drama Queens: (can be male or female) often seen preening, performing, and rehearsing clever lines for the future

Emos: the chronically and stylishly depressed; typically found lying under a tree or bush too overwhelmed by the lunch menu to eat

Techno Nerds: anti-social but highly informed gadget geeks who would rather friend you online than in person

Library Girls: tend to travel in small editorial packs; too smart, shy, and/or acutely judgmental to fit in anywhere else

Foreign Exchange Students: highly prized for their exotic personal style and unique fashion sense until someone realizes that they're just from another country

SIDEBRA continued . . .

Bean smiled at me like a proud parent. In front of us, more and more people from all over the front lawn were trickling over.

"Hanover, nothing's gonna change," said LG Wong matter-of-factly, looking at me like I was an idiot. "This stuff happens all the time. Unlike *you*, we're used to being *un*visible." She blew her chopped-out, anime-girl bangs out of her face. "This is a waste of time." The Library Girls standing around her all nodded like brainy bobble-heads.

"It is not! We're gonna get the word out," I answered firmly. "Pressure Canfield to do the election over, or force Hutch to resign."

LG Wong rolled her eyes.

"Like that's ever going to happen," said Charlie Dodd.

"It should!" shouted Mandy.

"We're gonna make it happen!" Amy screamed, waving her arms. Wow, she caught on fast.

"Right on!" Clint yelled.

"Dream on!" some guy shouted from the back.

"So has everyone signed the petition?" Bean called out. Only a few people seemed to hear. Wow. This crowd was getting serious. "HAS EVERYONE SIGNED THE PETITION?" Bean yelled, louder this time.

A lot of people whooped and whistled and cheered, especially Amy, who started doing that weird limp cheerleader kick again. What *was* that? Her new signature move? Even the Butt Hut Commuters had stopped to listen. The area around the flagpole had turned into this amazing live mosaic of weirdness—

SIDEBRA continued

Butt Hut Commuters: smokers heading to or from the Butt Hut, and people trying to quit but desperately hoping to catch a whiff when the wind changes
NILs: (nerds in love) two not-so-attractives who, thankfully, found each other and fell in love; NILs are native to the front lawn because it offers safe cover for PDA w/o the threat of DOA
Mime Guy: (his own species) always wears a battered top hat and black cape; often gets beaten up; never speaks—no one even knows if he can

weird hair, weird clothes, weird body types. There must have been at least fifty or sixty Uns gathered around. Hey, there was Mime Guy! He stepped up to the front and stood poised to the side, wearing his usual cape and top hat.

"The point is," yelled Cate, taking over, "silence equals acceptance"—Mime Guy began acting it out, miming what she said for the hearing- and hair-impaired in the way back—"*our* acceptance of being treated like our votes don't count, like *we* don't count, like we're second-class citizens at this school!"

"That'd be an upgrade for me!" someone shouted from the back. It was this emo guy with perfectly styled disaster bed-hair and a studded belt triple-wrapped around his neck. Wow. A *lot* more people were here than I'd expected. I looked to the far back and—

OMG.

Eric Sobel. With his camera.

Wait. Was he taking pictures for Yearbook or Facebook or . . . Uh-oh.

And who was—? Holy shiitake mushrooms! What was *she* doing here? Standing next to Eric was—wait for it—Candy Esposito.

Ergh! I ignored them both and turned back to Cate.

"If we don't fight this," Cate continued, "the message is that it's okay to ignore us—that it's okay to discriminate against less popular students!"

"Hey! I'm not less popular than Peter Hutchison!"

Everyone laughed. OMG. Did I just say that out loud?

SIDEBRA

Before the first day of sophomore year, I loved getting my picture taken. But then tragedy struck! Eric Sobel captured me making a total fool of myself with his camera and cell-phone video thingy. Then he edited it all into this scario-hilario rap. And yes, my innocence was stolen when I made my YouTube debut in the now infamous Spastic Jazz Hands video. He apologized, saying it was like an *homage* to me. (I looked it up later. A tribute. The "h" is silent. It's a French thing.) But, can I tell you, it felt way more like a *fromage*— stinky cheesy. (Also a French thing.)

Oh, God. I totally did. I looked around in a panic. Everyone laughed harder. Oh. Oh no. Oh no! Oh . . .

Wait. Wow. Really?

Everyone was still laughing, but . . . they seemed to think I was *joking*. *Not* accidentally broadcasting my personal insecurities! I looked toward the back. Candy was staring down at her phone speed texting, but Eric was laughing behind his camera. My legs got all ramen-noodley for a second, but I quickly recovered and laughed along. I wasn't sure why Eric was there. But if he was taking pictures, I definitely wanted to look good in the action shots this time.

"Discrimination by the administration is unacceptable!" I yelled, regaining my activist's composure. "We have to make noise!"

The crowd cheered again, buzzing with excitement or sugar or maybe just ADD.

"Okay, people!" Bean shouted, referring to her notebook. "Here's the plan so far. Daily protests, signs, stickers, picketing, viral texts to get the word out. Any other ideas?" she called out to the crowd.

"Phone tree?" someone shouted.

"A locker-stuffing party!"

"Jam a banana up Canfield's exhaust pipe!"

A bunch of people laughed, followed by a loud chorus of *ewww*'s.

Pyroman! And guess who was standing next to him? *Split Ends.* "Hey, Elliott," I called.

He cocked his head and did this one-sided half smile like he was surprised I knew his name.

"I really like your outside-the-box thinking, *Elliott*, but let's keep this protest non-violent, okay? In honor of Dr. Martin Luther King Jr. and every student who's ever been bullied, taunted, beaten up, or peed on!"

Mime Guy was on a roll. Everyone was laughing.

Elliott nodded, obviously relating, but I wasn't sure to what.

"Okay. Our marketing team—so far Mandy Mindel in Drama and me daydreaming in American History—has come up with a couple of slogans." Mandy flashed me a big grin as I held my notebook up to the crowd.

We Count! Recount! CHANGE—YES WE CANfield!

"Other ideas?" I shouted to the crowd.

Nobody said anything. Then:

"Feel the burn in Pleasant Hell!" Elliott yelled, which made it hard for me to stop thinking of him as Pyroman.

"Get your *Un* on!" shouted Clint, doing a soulful but subtle little dance move.

"Get *Un*informed!"

Bean and I started scribbling frantically.

"Ignoring *Un*dividual Rights is Wrong!"

"Live Outside the Box!"

Charlie waved his arm. "Join the *Un* Crowd!"

"Go *Un*derground!"

"Join the *Un*derworld!"

"*Un*derwear is Wrong!"

Bentley Jones, Bodie's younger, equally superstar-ish sister, raised her hand. "Excuse me! Paisley! Paisley!" I pointed to her, relieved to get us out of underwear. She turned to address the crowd. "Bentley Jones, with *The Pleasant Hill Highlander*," she said, sounding all professional like she was reporting for CNN.

First Eric and Candy. Now Bentley Jones. How did the Yearbook staff find out about our meeting so fast?

"Paisley, are you expecting opposition from Pop rebels?"

"Um . . ." I hadn't even thought of that. I looked at Cate and Bean.

"Yes! Yes, we are," Cate answered like a zealot. "Which is why we're going underground. You won't know who we are, or where we're going to strike next."

Bean stepped forward. "Yeah, sometimes we'll be there," she said all mysteriously. "And sometimes, we were supposed to be there—but we weren't!"

Cate and I looked at her. Huh?

"*Vive la résistance!*" shouted Amy, sounding like an old French man.

Cate grabbed Bean and me. Really hard. "That's it! That's us," Cate whispered, all bug-eyed. "An Underground Resistance Movement. Like in World War Two."

Bean caught her breath. "Yes. Oh, yes please!" she squealed. "I can so see the fashion possibilities."

We turned back and faced the crowd.

"Paisley, Paisley! Just a few more questions." Bentley quickly checked her notes. She opened her mouth, but it was all wrong.

"Paisley, are you *this* in denial about everything in your life?"

The crowd went silent. Everyone turned to—

Hutch.

He bobbed his head, sporting this big nasty grin, and waved at me. "Let it go, Hamburger. Every protest is just gonna remind you and everyone else that you lost."

I could feel the blood surge into my face. I suddenly had this really bad taste in my mouth. Everyone turned and looked at me, waiting for my snappy response. OMG. Was Hutch right? I opened my mouth. I couldn't think of anything, but. . . . Oh God. What if he *was* right? I could hear the auto-shutter of Eric's camera clicking nonstop.

So much for the action shots.

sweeter than candy

In my afternoon classes, I kept polishing my doubt about the protest over and over in my brain until it was smooth and shiny.

Hutch was right.

Hutch was wrong.

We were right.

We were wrong.

No—we *were* right. We were definitely right. Our protest would remind people that Hutch *didn't* really win. Ha!

By the end of seventh period, I was back to feeling totally inspired by Cate's idea. Amy was too.

"Vive la résistance!" she grunted, running up behind me.

"Oui," I whispered back enthusiastically. It was the only French word I knew.

Then, on our way to soccer practice, you'll never guess who we saw in front of the gym—Eric Sobel and Clint Bedard standing around Clint's motorcycle, talking. To each other.

"Are they like friends now?" Amy whispered.

"I don't know." Uh-oh. "I don't think so." I watched Clint pointing to something on his bike while Eric listened, nodding.

"That's so cute, Pais. You brought them together."

"Yeah." Great. *Were* they like friends now? I really hoped they weren't talking about their plans for this weekend. My double-dating situation could get a little awkward for everyone. I wondered if Eric was even still willing to be seen with me at the dance.

Then, as if he could read my mind, Eric turned and looked right at me. He said something to Clint, then started jogging over to us. OMG. I looked around, suddenly panicked, then bent down to tie my shoe. Crap. I was wearing slip-on wedges. I straightened up way too fast and had to put a hand on Amy to steady myself.

"Hey," Eric said to me, digging through his pockets. "Hey Amy." He nodded, then looked back at me. "Heard what happened with the ballots. That really sucks."

I smiled, relieved. "Yeah. But we're not done. We're fighting it."

"*Oui,*" said Amy, still talking like an old French man.

He laughed and nodded. "Good," he said. "So, um, Paisley, give me your hand." His green eyes sparkled. "Got you a really expensive gift."

What? I slowly reached out my hand, trying to conceal my übery-goobery grin. He put something tiny in my palm and closed my fingers over it. Then he held it shut for a few seconds. His expression got kind of serious.

"Hey, um, if you want to talk . . . about anything, you know where to find me." He looked up and held my eyes for like an instant, then turned away.

OMG. I opened my mouth but nothing came out. My insides suddenly felt like warm chocolate syrup, melting down, down, down . . .

He jogged back over to Clint before I could even say thanks.

I looked at Amy. She had this puppies-playing-under-rainbows face.

I opened my fingers. Oh! It was a blade of grass, a big fat blade of grass, like from the soccer field. OMG. I got the chills and couldn't stop smiling.

"What *is* that?" Amy asked, touching the blade of grass with the tip of her finger.

"It's . . . it's from the listening spot." Amy had no idea what I was talking about. "It's this, this spot in the middle of the girls' soccer field where . . . where we kinda hang out and talk and hold hands and stare up at the clouds."

Amy clutched her heart with both hands like a soap opera actress. "No way," she whispered. "That is like the most romantic thing ever."

"I know." I smiled, all goobery and a little embarrassed.

"Pais, you are so lucky. Do you know how many girls at this school would—"

"I know."

We walked along in silence. I held the blade of grass gently in my hand, but I was feeling, I don't know, guilty . . . or greedy . . . or something.

I had two dates this weekend, and Amy hadn't had a real date since . . . since like never. And she was so great—it just didn't seem to translate to guys. Neither of us said another word.

But as we walked along, this doubt started nibbling away at the blade of grass in my hand. Had Clint seen Eric holding my hand? And what did Eric really mean anyway? *Talk . . . about anything?* Did he just want some qual time at the listening spot? Or . . . Or . . . OMG. Had he and Clint been talking? Talking about *me?* Talking about . . . Oh no. I could feel my face getting hot. Was it a hint? Did Eric want me to like confess about Clint—? Oh no. Oh no, oh no, oh no!

When Amy and I got to the locker room, everyone was rushing around screaming and changing into practice gear. Thank God. The noise was a perfect distraction. I pushed Clint and Eric out of

my head, changed, laced up my cleats, and went to the bathroom.
When I came out, guess who was standing in front of the sinks,
whispering? Jen and Candy Esposito.

They saw me and suddenly stopped.

"Hi Pais," said Jen like everything was totally normal.

"Hey Paisley." Candy smiled at me.

I fake smiled back, sweeter than Candy. Someone that perfect
could not be trusted.

Candy leaned in to Jen. "Hang in there, okay? Call me if you
need to talk."

What?!

"Have a good practice, you guys!" Candy waved and trotted off
in her perfectly white volleyball gear.

"Sorry I got all gushed out about Bodie at break, Pais. I really do
need to talk to you. I actually . . . I really need your advice."

"Looks like you have plenty of other people to talk to. What,
are you like BFFs with all the juniors now thanks to Bodie?"

She just stared at me.

"Hey you guys!" Carreyn bounded in, her hair gathered like a
bundle of sticks on top of her head. Amy followed her, holding her
shin guards in each hand, clapping them together. "Ready?"

I looked at Carreyn and then back at Jen. "Why are you guys dressed
for practice? You quit soccer to try out for *cheerleading*, remember?"

"I miss it," said Jen quietly. "I miss soccer. And I miss you guys."

"I *really* miss Coach Psycho," said Carreyn, giggling nervously.
Amy and Jen half laughed back, but I was in no mood to pretend
that we were all still the best of buds.

"We're going to beg Coach Sykes to take us back," said Jen.

"Yay!" cheered Amy. "We so need you."

I gave Amy a sharp what-gives glance, but she just shrugged. I
sighed. It was true. Whatever had gone on between us, we could

definitely use Carreyn and Jen—especially Jen—back on the team. But still.

"Whatever." I walked out of the locker room and jogged to the practice field.

And you know what? Coach Sykes didn't let them back on the team—even though Jen was one of our best players. It kind of hurt to watch her say no. But Coach Sykes was all about loyalty, and abandoning your team for a shot at being a bouncy, short-skirt-wearing Hornette was not loyal. I could totally see her point.

"If you really miss the team so much, prove it, ladies," said Coach Sykes. "We need a new water girl and someone to shag balls during practice."

Jen and Carreyn looked at each other.

"Are you joking?" Carreyn asked.

Coach Sykes put both hands on her hips. "Does it look like I'm joking?"

"I'll do it," said Jen without hesitating.

Everyone looked at her like she was nuts, especially Carreyn.

"Well, I won't. No way!" Carreyn said, all flustered.

"Fine. *Adios.*" Coach Sykes waved Carreyn off the field. "Three laps, everyone! You too, water girl."

During practice, Jen kept trying to talk to me. But just because she was now the water girl didn't mean I wasn't still pissed. The only thing that made me feel better was deliberately blasting balls over the goal post so that she had to run all over the place chasing them down. It was stupid but surprisingly satisfying. Jen just took it and never complained or even rolled her eyes once.

I thought I knew Jen better than anyone. But I couldn't figure her out at all anymore. Maybe I never would.

chapter nine
a school knight

After explaining everything—well, not *everything*—to my parents at dinner, I was too distracted to study. I twirled the drying blade of grass around and around as I played what Eric had said over and over in my head. I hadn't looked for him at the listening spot after practice. I was too freaked out. *Did* I want to talk to him about *anything*? I wasn't sure. But it did seem like he was trying to tell me something . . . or trying to get *me* to tell *him* something. Or maybe I was just being a total paranoid freak. That was always a possibility . . . I sighed. I kind of wished I could call Jen. A couple months ago I would have blabbed everything to her. Now, not so much.

I flushed it down my brain drain and tried to focus on that Teen Scene article thingy Ms. Whit had told me about. I so wanted to expose Canfield for the buttcap boob he was. But I just . . . I couldn't get into it. Why was it so easy for Miss UnPleasant to write? And why was it so hard for me? Ergh! I sat back and read what I'd written so far: *Teen Scene by Paisley Hanover*. Brilliant. I highlighted the whole line and hit DELETE.

So then I tried to concentrate on homework. But truthfully, I didn't care that much about my seven-point college-application action plan anymore. It didn't seem to matter. The only thing that did matter? Revenge! OMG. Did I just say that? What I meant was, figuring out a clever way to get Hutch out of the office that *I* had actually won. Forget Eric. Forget Jen. I turned on some music and curled up in my beanbag chair with Dyson—my cat, not my vacuum (that's another story)—to brainstorm the details of a plan.

It didn't take long for me to imagine Hutch belted to a pole with his pants down, surrounded by a mob of laughing Uns. I was even laughing to myself when I heard this thundering noise rumble into our driveway. I sat up quickly, which is hard to do in a big beanbag chair with a cat on your lap, and cocked my head to listen. The rumbling gave way to a series of loud *putt-putt-putts.* Then it stopped.

It sounded like a . . . like a . . . Oh God! It was a *motorcycle!*

I jumped up—also very hard to do in a beanbag chair—and quietly opened my bedroom door, then tiptoed-ran down the hall to one of the upstairs front windows.

OMG. Clint Bedard. Clint Bedard?!

He hopped off his bike and pulled off his helmet. As he walked toward the front door, he dug out some ChapStick and did two quick laps around his lips.

OMG. OMG! OMG!!!

I ran back to my room and looked in the mirror. Crap! My hair was in a messy ponytail, and I was still wearing my hooded sweatshirt from soccer practice. I pulled the band out of my hair and groaned at my reflection. Dyson yawned at me, totally disgusted.

Whatever. It was Clint Bedard!

SIDEBRA

When I was really young and naïve and thought I could control everything in life—like a few weeks ago at the beginning of sophomore year—I had this brilliant seven-point college-application action plan. I know. It sounds kind of silly to me now too. Anyway, my plan was to develop myself in seven different directions, each one growing out of me like spokes on a wheel so I could roll right into the college of my dreams. But then I hit a bump—or what I thought was a bump—but may actually have been a seed, a really huge seed, the seed of the new me. God, sometimes I'm so deep, I give myself chills.

I ripped off my sweat pants, grabbed a pair of jeans off the floor and pulled them on, hopping around like a freak. Then I heard a knock on my bedroom door and immediately flopped down into the beanbag chair, trying my best to look bored.

Mom poked her head in. "Someone's here to see you."

"Really?" I asked, not looking up from my notebook. "Someone who?"

"A boy." I looked up. "A cute boy on a motorcycle. It's Clint Bedard."

"Huh." I pretended to be über-blasé. "Wonder what he's doing here."

"He said he stopped by to cheer you up. He's quite the charmer."

"Uh, yeah. I know." I casually dropped my notebook on the floor.

"Even when he's not wearing that handsome Shakespeare costume." Mom raised her eyebrows and smiled.

"Mo-om! Gross." I had heard about Clint having that effect on some moms. I just didn't think it would be *my* mom. "Get a grip. Do I have to like worry about you?"

She rolled her eyes and smacked me in the shoulder with a small stack of—oh, no! It was our totally embarrassing old Christmas card photos.

"Mom, what are you doing with those? You didn't show them to Clint?" I asked, trying to grab them from her. "Please, tell me you didn't show them to Clint!"

"Of course not, honey. Why would I do that?" She glanced at the photo on the top of the stack, smiling. "Although you and your brother do look adorable. Look at you in your pigtails! And green is such a good color on you."

"Mom, hide those. Right now. Seriously. Parker will kill you. But I'll just secretly resent you for like ever!"

"The point is, honey, it's a school night." She smiled, giving Dad the agree-with-me-or-else glare.

He sighed. "Yes, right. My mistake. No, because it's a school night."

"Mr. Hanover, I don't know if this was true for you when you were in high school, but I often find that I learn the most important life lessons outside of class."

Oooh. That was a good one! Dad just stared at Clint, looking a little bewildered. Mom nodded, definitely amused.

"Today was a really rough day for Paisley, for all of us, actually. We saw a harsh side of reality." I nodded along, trying to keep the momentum going. "Not just prejudice, and not just bias toward male athletes. We saw . . ." Clint paused thoughtfully. "We saw Mr. Glen Canfield in action!"

Clint stood up and launched into a spot-on imitation of Mr. Canfield.

"There will be no recount!" Clint blustered like a pompous windbag, smacking his lips and poking his finger at my dad's face. "And if you challenge me, I will mock you! I will mock you in front of your friends and your enemies!"

Mom and Dad burst into hysterics. I was amazed. Clint was good. He was as good with parents as he was with girls. Maybe he was too good . . . ? I couldn't help wondering if this guy was out of my league.

Dad finally caught his breath and calmly said, "God, he's a boob."

"Such a boob he needs a bra," Clint added. "A varsity sports bra."

My parents screamed with laughter at that one. I looked from Dad to Mom, then back to Dad. Was it really *that* funny?

"I just want to cheer her up." Clint casually poked me in the shoulder with his thumb. "We won't be gone long. You have my word, my word as . . . as a young man with a motorcycle."

I casually looked at my parents, begging them with my eyes to say yes.

They stared at each other, doing a quick word-free parent conference.

"Okay, you two." Dad waved at us with the back of his hand. "Get out of here."

"Thank you! Good to see you again, Mr. Hanover." Clint reached out and shook Dad's hand. "We won't be out long."

"That's right, Mr. Bedard. You won't." Dad smiled, patting Clint on the back. "Back by ten, Paisley!"

And then Clint turned to my mother. "Always a pleasure to see you, Mrs. Hanover."

"Oh please, call me Vivienne."

OMG. My mother blushed! How disgusto embarrassing!

"Thanks, Dad! Ba-bye *Vivienne*." I waved. "Love to stay and chat. Gotta go."

It turned out I do like surprises—especially when they're Clint Bedard.

chapter ten
boyfriend or boy friend?

When Clint and I finally got outside, we didn't say a word. We just laughed. He tossed me a helmet, and I did my best imitation of a cool biker babe even though I had never been on a motorcycle before and had no idea how a cool biker babe would act.

The helmet smelled like stale girl, stale *pretty* girl. But everything else about the motorcycle was amazing.

The speed. The wind. The wrapping my arms around Clint's waist and holding on for dear life. The leaning into every curve along this back road. The way his shirt rode up a little after a few turns and I could feel the warm skin over his stomach muscles. It was *very* amazing.

When we finally slowed down and pulled over, my head and everything else was on a major guy-high. He cut the engine. The headlight faded off, and we were surrounded by soft darkness. It smelled like fall, like cold wet soil when you dig down a few inches.

I pulled off the helmet and ran my hand through my messy hair, waiting for my eyes to adjust to the dark. Thank God we just sat there for a few minutes, staring out at the night. I was pretty sure that if I had gotten off the bike right then, I would have taken a few wobbly steps and fallen over, delirious from my newfound love of . . . um . . . *motorcycles*.

In the distance, I could see yellow and white lights glowing and twinkling from the houses all the way down the valley leading to the center of town. I tried to find my house in all the lights, but I was completely disoriented by Clint's stomach.

"Nice view," I finally managed to get out.

"It gets better," he whispered. "This way."

Clint grabbed my hand and led me over the loose gravel toward a dim yellow utility light on top of a cyclone fence. There was a gate, locked with an old heavy chain and a padlock.

"What is this place?"

"Water storage tank." He flipped through a ring of keys, finally inserting one into the lock. "It was built in 1968. It's the only modernist water tank in the county." The lock popped open. "Love that sound."

It didn't look like a water tank at all. It looked like a huge concrete dome with open archways on the sides. I followed him through the gate, then looked back over my shoulder to make sure that he didn't lock us inside. I mean, it's not like I was paranoid or anything, but I still didn't know Clint Bedard that well. And hey, he did have a bit of a reputation.

I was relieved to hear the chain and lock hit the ground with a jingly thud. "So . . . what are we doing here?" I asked, doing my best imitation of nonchalant.

"You'll see." He ran ahead. "Come on."

"Hey wait!" I took a few steps after him, then stopped.

I watched him disappear into the shadows of an archway at the side of the dome. Where did he go? I couldn't see a thing in that archway. I stood there listening for a clue, but all I could hear was a lonely cricket and the faintest hum of cars on a freeway miles and miles away.

"Hey," I called out.

Nothing.

"Clint? Where are you?" I stepped slowly and carefully in his direction, the gravel popping under my shoes.

He laughed in that spooky haunted house way that echoed. Goose bumps crawled up the back of my neck. Oh great. What are we doing here? What am *I* doing here? I had no idea where we were or how to get home. I listened carefully, trying to engage my I-can't-see-a-thing hearing. But the only sound was my heart pounding in my ears and the soft hoot of an owl far in the distance—or maybe it was just Clint trying to scare me again.

"By the way, I'm not scared!" I shouted. "I'm not that kind of girl." I was totally that kind of girl. I inched toward the darkened archway. "Clint?"

I stopped in front of the archway. It was complete blackness. Something in the pit of my stomach said *U-turn!* Then I heard a strange growling coming from inside. Oh God. We were way up in the hills. Coyotes? A mountain lion? It had to be Clint, right? As the growling got louder and louder, I slowly stepped backward toward the open gate. I was about to run for it when I heard the most awful shriek of pain.

"Aaaaaaaaaah! He's got me!" Clint yelled. And then another, even louder shriek.

I screamed at the top of my lungs—and I am so not a screamer.

Then Clint jumped out of the shadows and grabbed me as I tried to run, laughing his head off.

"God! Don't you dare do that again! I thought you wanted to make me feel better!"

"I did. I do. Sorry." He took my hand again. "I couldn't resist."

"Jeez, I don't have the hiccups, okay?"

I wished it wasn't so dark, so I could see Clint's eyes. I couldn't figure him out. I wanted to stay mad at him or at least pretend to be mad for a few minutes. But I couldn't. I was too scared and excited and so dying to know where we were going next.

He held on to my hand and, it was weird—I was totally nervous, like I had never touched him before, like we had never spent weeks rehearsing that scene from *Taming of the Shrew* where he got to whip me around in his arms.

"So." I tried to sound confident, even cocky. "This where you bring *all* the girls you want to seduce?"

He chuckled. "Nope." There was just enough moonlight for me to see his grin. "Only some of them."

His hand was much bigger than mine, and his palm felt warm and a little sweaty. Or maybe it was my palm that was sweaty. Anyway, he led me away from the water tower. When we were about twenty feet away, he stopped and turned to face me.

"Ready?" he asked.

"For what?"

"Just relax and follow me, okay? You gotta go really hard and fast at first. But then it gets a lot easier. Trust me."

What?! OMG. What was he talking about? I tried to look cool, calm, and experienced, but my heart was pounding and my head was spinning. *He can't make me do anything I don't want to do,* I said to myself. *He can't make me do anything I don't want to do.*

Then he dropped my hand and took off, sprinting straight for the water tower. When he was a few feet from where the steep sloping side of the dome

SIDEBAR

The other week, Clint and I did a super-sexy scene from *Taming of the Shrew* for *Acting Out,* this night of onstage performances to show the best scenes from Drama class. Not to brag, but . . . it was hot! We were hot—especially Clint in his open-chested swashbucklerish shirt and tight pants. Me . . . well, I was hot too, I guess, but mostly because of my full-body blush from my mortifying wardrobe malfunction.

meets the ground, he took a flying leap at the sloped archway and began to run straight up. Just as he was losing speed, he crouched down and kept scrambling. And then, just like that, he was standing on top of the water tower laughing.

"See?" he yelled, panting. "It's easy. Come on!"

OMG. I'm such an idiot. I've been reading way too much Jane Austen. I shook my head, amazed at my vivid romantic imagination, and just went for it, sprinting as fast as I could. I leaped up the side of the sloped concrete and kept running, never doubting for a second that I could make it to the top—that is, until I stopped moving forward and slowly felt the pull of gravity.

"Grab my foot! Grab my foot!" Clint yelled, skidding toward me.

Just as I was about to fall backward and probably break my neck, I lunged for Clint's boot. He dragged me up a little, then reached down for my hand and pulled hard as I did a humiliating three-legged crab-skip up the last few feet. I ended up on top of him laughing my head off.

We finally stopped laughing and just lay there for a few seconds breathing. And then I realized . . . *I'm lying on top of Clint Bedard!* I suddenly scrambled to my feet, wandering over to the center of the dome, looking up as if I had developed an instant fascination with astronomy.

"Wow."

He came up behind me. "Yeah. Thought you'd like it. I dig this place at night, especially when I need to clear my head." He draped his arms over my shoulders and rested his chin on my head. "Thought it might help you clear yours."

"Can it clear the last forty-eight hours of my life?" Or maybe the last month?

"Come on, Red. It's not that bad. Do you really care that much about *student government?*"

God, that made me sound like such the über goober. But I wasn't just talking about the election.

"No! It's not that exactly." I thought about his question, looking out at the lights. What *did* I care so much about? "What bugs me is that nothing's fair at our school. There's a total double standard for some people."

He laughed at me.

"What?!" I pulled away and turned around to look at him. "I'm serious."

"Yeah. I know. Welcome to my world." He let out this disgusted snort. "I have to deal with this crap every day. I learned to ignore it a long time ago."

"Well, I don't want to ignore it. I hate it. It sucks. Hutch sucks. Canfield sucks. Canfield sucks the worst."

"Hutch is just an insecure dude with too much testosterone. Nobody really likes him, and he knows it, and it makes him crazy. Bet if he just had a girlfriend, he wouldn't be such an asshole all the time. Canfield, on the other hand, is simply a pathetic excuse for a human being. I don't hate him. I feel sorry for him. Look at his life. This is it. This is as far as he's going."

His voice trailed off and we stood there in silence for a minute. All I could hear were the crickets and the sound of his slow, calm breathing.

Clint was so not normal for my school. The way he talked about people, he was totally honest. It freaked me out a little. It was like he had emotional X-ray vision and could see right though Canfield and Hutch. Yikes. I wondered if he could see right through me. That freaked me out even more, so I immediately tried to distract myself and think about Mr. Canfield as a real person, not just as an annoying vice principal with a lady butt wrapped in polyester.

Clint was right. Canfield's life was pretty sad. I'd never thought about it before. Maybe Clint was right about Hutch too. Did Hutch just want someone to like him? Was it that simple? I started to shiver.

"You cold?"

"No." I shivered again. "I'm fine."

"Come here, Red. I'm not going to bite you." He pulled me over and opened up his leather jacket and wrapped me in it, holding me tight against his chest. I closed my eyes. Oh yes, I was *fine*. "I won't bite," he whispered in my ear, "but I might nibble on something."

His breath on my ear and neck made me shiver again. A warm chill melted down my body, but I was afraid to move a muscle. I didn't want to do the wrong thing, so I didn't do anything, except remember to keep breathing. God, he smelled so good. Thank God, he was holding me up.

My head felt a little spinny. A few weeks ago, I wouldn't have had anything to do with Clint Bedard. And now . . . now I was thinking of a lot of things I might want to do with him. But I had no idea what he was thinking about me.

"You know, I can see into the future."

If I had been thinking clearly, I might have thought that was kind of dumb—but no, I thought it was kind of dreamy. "Really?"

"It's true. It's a Bedard family thing. We learn to read the stars before we read a single word. And I'm very psychic."

"Come on." I laughed, kind of relieved by the distraction.

"Let's see, hm? What's in the stars for Paisley Hanover? Oh look!" He pointed straight above our heads. "There's Paisloony, crazy warrior girl. See the knife hanging from her fashionable chunky belt? Oh wait, that's not a knife, it's a pen. You will slay with words anyone who wrongs you or your friends."

"Wow. Cool." I laughed again.

"That bright wide streak over there? That's actually millions of tiny stars in a galaxy far, far away. Actually, it's called the Nutty Way. In the not-far-away future, I see you surrounded by many nuts. Fortunately, you don't have a nut allergy."

I laughed again, more because I was nervous than anything.

"Do you?" he asked. "Hope not."

I leaned back and looked up at him. "Oh my God! It's the Walnut Festival! Wow. You *are* totally psychic."

"Told you," Clint said. "Okay, one more. See those three bright stars over there?" He pointed up, over my shoulder. "That's the Bermuda Love Triangle." I turned, and there it was. "Soon you will travel with two others to this exciting romantic place." My mouth was beginning to get dry. "In this Bermuda Love Triangle, someone, but not you, will be lost and disappear without a trace."

Oh no. Oh God. I closed my eyes. He did talk to Eric. "That doesn't sound good," I whispered. I had this really bad feeling. Was this whole romantic field trip just to get me to come clean about Eric? I opened my eyes and looked up at him.

I could feel him looking down at me, even though I couldn't see his eyes in the dark. "Depends on who, I guess." He tilted his head. OMG. Was he about to kiss me? He *was* about to kiss me—at least I think he was about to kiss me. Was he really about to kiss *me*?! I quickly licked my lips.

SIDEBRA

The Walnut Festival is this annual event in the next town over. It's like this small-time carnival/festival/fund-raiser thing with games and rides and contests and a bunch of booths selling all this ridiculous nut stuff. Everyone goes. Everyone! Of course, the cool people only go at night—Saturday night—when they have the Nut-Packing Contest. It's insane. It's gotten so popular they have like a lottery now to see who gets to compete. (Yep. Most of us put our names in this year. We'll see.) When the Nut Festival was originally founded, it was a celebration of the annual walnut harvest. But now it's more like a celebration of the group date and the late-night make-out harvest.

"Thanks," he whispered.

I really hoped it wasn't for licking my lips. "For what?"

"For coming out here with me."

"Thanks for coming to get me and cheering me up."

"Hey, that's what friends do."

Friends?!

Am I just a *friend* to him? A friend like Cate Maduro, who just happens to be a girl? My mind started going around and around like a rattling hula hoop. Was I totally projecting? Can hot, throbbing, below-the-belt crushes be completely one-sided? Was that possible? Oh God, maybe my jeans are just too tight.

And then he kissed me softly on the lips. Mmm.

But it happened so fast— Wait. Was that a pity kiss? Did he just do that because he didn't want me to be the only girl on the planet to go out with Clint Bedard and *not* get kissed?

And then he leaned in—I think—to kiss me again, but I'll never know for sure because that was the exact moment I jumped and let out this embarrassing yelp. Yes, I actually yelped.

"What?" He jerked away. "What's wrong?"

"Um. Nothing." I giggled nervously, reaching for my pocket. "Sorry. My phone. My phone started vibrating."

"Perfect." He just laughed.

I considered not opening my phone, but Clint kind of shrugged and nodded, shoving his hands in his pockets so it seemed like he actually wanted me to. I guess my jumping yelp ruined the mood. It was a text from Amy.

Code Pnk!

"Whoa. Code Pink? I haven't gotten a Code Pink since Carreyn burned half her hair off with a hot iron."

"What's a *Code Pink?*"

"Emergency, mandatory meet-up in Amy's bedroom." I wondered what had happened—and who it had happened to. God, why now?! I sighed and looked up at him. "I'm really, really sorry but . . . I really have to go."

"Right *now?*" He sounded disappointed. But he couldn't have been more disappointed than I was.

"Um, yeah. My friends, we've got this pact thing." Clint didn't say a word. He just scuffed his boots against the concrete and started to walk away. "Hey." I grabbed his arm and held it tight with both hands. "Can we continue this on Saturday? I promise I won't yelp."

He stood there silently and finally said, "Yeah. Okay. Sure. But don't make a promise you can't keep, Red." I could see the silhouette of his head shaking. What did that mean? "So, do you want a ride to Amy's now?"

I thought about it for a sec. "I think it's better if you take me home. Then I'll sneak out and ride my bike over. I don't want you getting in trouble if I'm out half the night."

And, yes. I *was* out half the night.

chapter eleven
sexted!

I tapped on Amy's bedroom window, still panting from the frantic bike ride over from my house. At first, it looked dark inside, but then I could see a couple of candles flickering softly on the bedside table. Amy opened the window looking a little freaked.

"What?" I whispered. "What happened?"

She put her finger up to her lips and motioned me inside.

Jen was sitting on the side of Amy's big pink bed. Even in the candlelight, I could tell that Jen had been crying. Oh, God. Not again. I was really getting sick of Jen's crying.

"Thanks for coming," Jen whispered, wiping her nose with a wadded-up tissue.

I looked around. Where was Carreyn? Oooh . . . I couldn't help wondering if this was just another trap. "What's wrong?" I asked. "What happened *now*?" I turned on the lamp next to Amy's bed to get a better look around. Wow. The lampshade wasn't pink anymore. It was kind of a groovy aqua blue. Hey, Amy was branching out.

Jen let out a long heavy sigh. "This happened." She held her phone up for me to see. It was a photo.

I leaned toward it. "Oh my God!" I grabbed the phone to get a better look. "Jen! What's going on here?"

I looked at Amy, who was already looking at me.

Jen hesitated. "I'm . . . I'm not really sure."

I turned to Amy again. If this was another trap, I was so never going to talk to any of them again. But Amy seemed genuinely concerned. And Jen's neck was all blotchy, the way it gets when she's about to go ballistic. I don't think you can fake that kind of thing.

"Who sent this to you?"

Jen shook her head. "I don't know. Blocked number."

I kept getting a weird feeling. "Where's Carreyn?"

"She can't come." Jen sounded weirdly spaced out. "Family date night. She's having qual time with her mom."

Amy grinned. "Translation: A salon-quality toxic hair treatment at home!"

I looked at Amy, then back to Jen, scrutinizing her strange expression. I wanted to believe her. But Jen hadn't exactly been scoring trust points with me. So just in case, I looked under the bed. No Carreyn. I cocked my head and listened for rustling or breathing. Then I checked in Amy's closet too, just to be sure.

"Paisley, come on," said Amy.

"You guys come on!" I snapped back. "Trap me once, shame on you. Trap me twice, lame on *me*." I sat back down on the bed.

"This isn't a trap," said Jen, grabbing my knee. "Look, I know I've been acting weird lately." That was a huge understatement. "I'm sorry, Pais. Really. I . . . I don't know, it's . . . it's been a weird time for me. The divorce, moving, not playing soccer . . ."

"Don't forget"—I sat up defiantly—"dumping your real friends for your new boyfriend and his fabulous faux-real brat

SIDEBRA

Paisley Pointer #106:
The Importance of Trust.
Whenever you get a weirded-out feeling around your friends (or frenemies), trust it! Look, listen, and run for it if necessary. That's all I'm saying for now.
PS: *Always* look under the bed.
PPS: If you have to make a run for it, don't forget your shoes!

pack." I sounded as snotty as possible. I couldn't help it. I was still pissed.

Jen didn't respond. The blue-ish glow from the lamp made her look like a ghost. She just stared at me, blinking. Ooh, I hated that! Jen could make me feel so rotten and guilty just like that.

I looked away, sighing hard. I was glad Carreyn wasn't coming. I couldn't handle being pissed at two friends in the same room. I held the phone up to a candle and studied the photo again. It was a little blurry, obviously taken with someone's cell phone, but you could definitely tell it was Jen in Hutch's arms. Her head was tilted down a little, resting against his bare chest. Gross. The picture was taken from the side so you couldn't see all of Jen's face, but Hutch was turned, goofing for the camera with this stupid ain't-I-cool expression. And, yep, there was Jen's boob. *All* of it.

"Jen? What are you doing in Hutch's arms with no top on?"

"Nothing!" She looked at Amy and then at me. "I mean, I . . . I don't know." She curled up on her side in what I call the feeble position. "God, I feel sick."

Amy put her hand on Jen's shoulder. "Don't take this the wrong way, but . . . what do you mean you don't know? You were there."

"I *don't* know! It's . . . I know it's from that pool party over Labor Day weekend. We're in the hot tub, I think. See that, above my head?" She pointed to the corner of the photo. "That's the strap from my bikini top. Some shidiot is dangling it over my head."

Amy and I examined the photo again. "Oh yeah," I said. "I see it."

"I don't see anyone dangling your bikini *bottom*," said Amy. "So I guess that's a good sign."

Jen groaned. "You guys, what am I going to do?!"

"Come on, it's not that bad," I urged. "It's probably just some jerk's idea of a joke."

But she shook her head and started crying.

"Well, who took the picture?" I asked. "And what *was* going on with you and Hutch?"

She brought her hands up to her mouth, pressed her palms together, and slowly shook her head. "I don't know! I don't know!" she cried. "That's the whole problem! I don't know what happened or if *anything* happened. I heard a rumor weeks ago, about some incriminating photo, but I wasn't sure it really existed. Why do you think I've been so nice to Hutch since the beginning of school? Why do you think I was wearing one of those stupid 'I'm a Hutch's Honey' T-shirts? I don't *know* what happened. I don't know . . ."

Ugh. Those obnoxious "I'm a Hutch's Honey" T-shirts! I still couldn't believe Jen and Carreyn had worn them.

But now Jen was sitting here gritting her teeth and crying. I looked at her phone again. Whatever was going on in that photo, it didn't look good.

I put my arm around her and let her cry. I really wanted to believe her, but some little niggling doubt swimming around in my brain wouldn't let me. I just didn't *trust* Jen anymore. Since school started, she'd been acting like such a weird do-anything-to-be-more-popular freak, and this photo seemed a little too convenient. Did she really not know what had happened, or was she in on it? Maybe it was another Jen stunt—like quitting soccer to try out for cheerleading?

"Why didn't you tell me about this sooner?" I finally asked.

"I tried. But it was *embarrassing*. My whole life feels embarrassing now. And . . . it's like we've been in a fight the whole school year."

"Yeah. Well, we have."

"God, I feel so stupid," she said, wiping her nose. I watched her carefully, making sure her tears were for real. "I so wish I'd never gone to that party." She sighed.

I lifted up my arm so she could wipe her nose on my sleeve. Yeah, it was gross, but I got her to laugh a little.

"I should have known something bad would come from that creepy party," she sniffled. "I haven't told anyone about this, because I've been so paranoid, but there was a video camera. Hidden in the bathroom in the pool house." She paused, making sure we were following. We were. And then she lowered her voice. "Every girl who changed in that bathroom was caught on video."

"What?!" Amy asked, throwing her hands up to her head. "*I* changed in that bathroom!"

"For some reason," Jen said, wiping her nose, "I don't remember why now, I decided to change in the house. So I was looking for a bathroom and accidentally opened the door to Hutch's bedroom. That's when I saw it."

"What?" Amy whispered.

"A computer screen. The shades were all down, but I could see stuff moving around on the screen. So I went in."

"You snooped?"

"Totally." She nodded. "There was a live feed called, get this, *Summer Pool Potty.*"

"Ew, gross!"

"That'd be kinda funny," said Amy, "if it weren't so *totally* unfunny."

"Well, actually it was kinda funny—but still creepy. There were stills of every single person who had been in that bathroom. Girls putting on makeup, people smoking, making out, even some poor thing with frizzy hair stuffing something into her bikini top, and, yeah, guys peeing. A few guys were obviously in on it and kept flashing dopey faces right at the camera. Shidiots. But the funny part . . ." Jen raised her eyebrows. "In every shot, the only thing actually in focus was this pyramid of spare TP rolls on the back of the toilet. Everything else was a blur."

"Ha!" Amy howled, sounding more freaked than amused.

I didn't say this, but I was feeling *really* relieved that I had gone

with my grandmother to the spa that weekend instead of going to the party. I made a mental note to thank Grambo again for that massage and stinky mud bath the next time I saw her.

"What about me?" Amy cringed. "Did you see *me*? Even out-of-focus me?"

"Just the side of your butt. I only knew it was you because I recognized your swimsuit."

"Ugh. That *is* creepy," I said, feeling icked out.

"Beyond creepy," Amy agreed. "I hate those guys. How did my butt look?"

Jen and I both gave Amy the are-you-*insane* look.

"Okay," she said. "Never mind!"

"What did you do?" I asked Jen.

"Deleted them. All of them. And killed the feed." Amy let out a sigh of relief. "And then I went downstairs and out to the pool house and I went into that bathroom. I found the camera on the counter, hidden in this basket planter thingy with a little hole punched out." At this point, Amy and I were hanging on Jen's every word. "And, just in case, I spit out my gum and smashed it onto the camera lens. Cinnamon."

Amy laughed, totally relieved. Jen tried to laugh too but the reality of everything seemed to weigh her down. She squeezed her eyes shut and shook her head. "I didn't even want to stay late. I wanted to leave after I found that camera. And I really wanted to leave after the beer balloon fight. But that's when Candy puked in a planter by the pool, and Bodie—such the gentleman—offered to drive her home."

"You let him?" I asked, trying to imagine Bodie not drinking at a party.

"Let him? Are you kidding? What could I do? And besides, I trusted him." Amy and I nodded slowly. "So I stayed with Carreyn at the party and waited for him. But I felt kinda worried. I mean, even though Candy denies it, everyone says she wants Bodie back. And he was gone for a really long time. So . . . I did a shot of tequila." We looked at each other. Jen chomped on the ends of her white-blond hair, remembering the unfortunate details. "And then I did a few more shots and then, then I got drunk. *Really* drunk. FYI? Do *not* drink in a hot tub."

I nodded, making a mental note for six years down the road (Hi Mom! Hi Dad!). "Then what happened?" I asked.

Jen shook her head. "I don't know what happened. I can't remember. But I couldn't have done anything with Hutch, right? I love Bodie."

I suddenly wondered where Amy and Carreyn had been while Jen was drinking herself into a scandal. "Amy, did you see Jen doing anything weird with Hutch?"

"No. But I was in the garage playing with Eric Sobel."

"What?!"

"Playing *foosball.* Which requires a great deal of concentration!"

"Well, where was Carreyn?" I asked them. This was just so weird.

"Last time I saw her," said Amy, "being a beer babe for the guys." Amy shook her head. "Thank God I left right after foosball."

Jen looked miserable.

"Jen, you just have to *ask* Hutch what actually happened," I said. "As painful as that might be."

"Don't you think I have? I *have* asked him! I just came from his house. He acts all macho and cool like it's *funny*, but he doesn't confirm or deny anything."

"What a loser buttcap. I can't stand him," I said.

"I don't know what to do. If this picture gets out—and it so will—my reputation will be trashed. My parents are already emotional messes because of the divorce, and now I'm like auditioning for *Girls Gone Wild*? I'll never be allowed to leave the house again."

I hadn't even thought what this would do to her parents—or what they would do to her. Hm. Maybe I should ask my mom about all this. Wait. What was I thinking? Mom doesn't even get texting. She'll never understand sexting.

"And when Bodie sees this," Jen said, "it'll kill him. It'll break his heart. He really loves me, and I love him, I do. I really do. And Hutch . . . Hutch is supposedly his friend." She started to sob again. Okay, that was when I totally believed her. And I felt really awful for her.

Jen looked up as Amy handed her a sock off the floor. She blew her nose in it and handed it back.

I looked at Amy, alarmed. "Hope that was clean."

Amy smiled sadly.

"Should I just tell Bodie? Tell him I got so drunk, I don't remember what happened?" She winced and groaned. "God, that sounds just awful." She covered her mouth with her hand. "You guys, what am I gonna do?"

The three of us sat in silence for a few minutes in the cool blue glow, staring at the candle flame doing a slow dance on the wick.

"Don't tell him yet," I said, trying to be logical. I was still really pissed at Jen, but I wanted to help. I reached for Jen's phone. "He may never even see this. I think you should wait until you know what happened—or if *anything* happened—and then tell him." I looked at Amy. She didn't exactly look like she agreed with me, but she didn't say anything.

Jen stared at the flickering candle, biting her lip and nodding slowly.

I reached for the candle and dipped my index finger into warm melted wax. I slowly pulled it out and watched the wax covering the tip of my finger harden into a smooth purple shell.

And then it hit me, probably the strangest idea of my life.

Strange, but at the same time incredibly obvious. It was the perfect way for me to find out what had really happened. And to get my revenge.

"I have an idea," I said quietly, still trying to think it through. Jen and Amy looked up, the candlelight flickering in their faces as they waited for me to spill. "I can't tell you the whole plan yet, but to start, I'm going to act like I really, *really* like Hutch."

Neither of them said a word. They just stared at me like I was totally crazy.

And maybe I was.

chapter twelve
morning buzz kill

On game days, we have a tradition—go out to breakfast at Millie's Kitchen before school. It used to be all four of us, Amy, Carreyn, Jen, and me. Then, after Jen and Carreyn quit soccer, it was just Amy and me. But that morning, it was almost like old times. Jen went with us again even though she wasn't officially on the team anymore. But no Carreyn. And, frankly, I wasn't really missing her.

It was so packed that my dad, our invisible designated driver, had to sit with us. Even though he was reading the newspaper and constantly checking his BlackBerry, none of us dared to breathe a word about the sext message. But we had plenty of other exciting things to yak about.

All of us were totally pumped about the game, even Jen. Amy and I were first-string, so we'd both be starting, as usual. Jen joked that she was starting too, as the first-string water girl. It felt really good to have Jen back with the team. I watched her laughing with Amy and shoving a forkful of hash browns into her mouth. She must have really missed us and really missed soccer a lot to have volunteered to

SIDEBRA

Invisible Designated Driver (IDD)
—noun
Typically a parent or other semi-responsible adult whose only reason for living is to safely transport a carload of teenagers while pretending to be invisible, deaf, dumb, and blind to everything but traffic signals. Must often impersonate an ATM.

be our lackey water girl. I doubted that I would have had the guts to do that.

Maybe it was just the coffee we were drinking, but we were all buzzing about the upcoming weekend. And there was a lot going on—the dance, the Nut Festival, and all the gossip and emotional baggage to keep up with. I hadn't breathed a word to Jen about Clint and Eric. Maybe I'd tell her later—but I had to be sure I could trust her first.

We piled out of Millie's and into Dad's new Prius.

"Cool car, Mr. Hanover," said Jen. "My dad just bought this embarrassingly huge, totally fuel-inefficient sedan with no *annoying* stick shift. I call it *The Love Boat*," she said, trying to be ironic. But she kind of cringed.

"What's annoying about a stick shift?" Amy asked.

I turned around. Jen had lowered her chin and was staring solemnly at Amy. "Think about it."

Both Amy and I blurted versions of "Ew!" "Gross!" "That's disgusting!" at the same time.

"You're telling me." Jen shook her head, looking out the window. After a bit, she said, "Hey, Mr. Hanover?"

My dad was pretty good at being our invisible designated driver, so Jen had to ask twice. "Mr. Hanover?"

Dad looked startled and quickly glanced at her in the rearview mirror. "What? Who, me? Yes?"

"Promise me that if anything happens to Mrs. Hanover or to you and Mrs. Hanover that you won't date, okay?"

It was weirdly quiet as Dad looked at Jen again in the mirror. "I won't," he said like he really meant it. "I promise." He looked back to the road. "But I'll need to stay in touch with my friends, right? Hope I can keep my MyFace page."

Everyone but Dad burst into hysterics.

"What?" he asked sincerely, looking at me.

"Dad, you're such a total goober!" I screamed. "Thank God, only a hundred and eighty-two more days until I get my license—if I don't die of parental shame before then."

Fortunately, we were pulling into the parking lot of school. I mean, *MyFace*? Could my father be any more embarrassing? Oh wait. Of course he could! As we got out of the car, he yelled, "Good luck in the game today! Go, Lady Hornets!" waving his hand out the window and honking the horn wildly as he drove off.

"Your dad's so cute," said Amy.

"He's so *not*!"

"Pais, he is," Jen agreed. "He's sweet." The three of us were walking up to sophomore hall when I spotted Eric and a few other soccer players talking. He was looking right at me. Oh God. I quickly looked away like I hadn't seen him.

Jen went on, "My dad doesn't know enough about my life anymore to wish me good luck on game day. He doesn't even know I'm not playing soccer this year."

I didn't know what to say to Eric. Did he still want to *talk* about *anything*? Because I didn't. At least I didn't think I did. My brain was suddenly flooded with a noxious mix of confusion and . . . guilt. So I stared very intently at Jen as we passed Eric and his group. "Really?" I asked her. "He doesn't know? Why not?"

"I told him but, I don't know, whatever. He forgot or he wasn't listening. It's just as well. I'm sure he'd be very proud to know that his daughter is now the first-string water girl."

We kept walking, talking about what to wear to the dance, which, of course, didn't exactly help my guilt. And then our lockers came into view. Jen stopped. "Oh my God."

We all stared. Across the front of Jen's locker, someone had written "TRAMP" in huge block letters with a black Sharpie.

"Oh no." Jen sounded panicky. "I've gotta go. I've gotta find Bodie before he sees it." Amy and I watched her run off down the hall.

Amy tried to rub the letters off with the sleeve of her hoodie, but it turns out permanent marker is, uh, permanent. "I wonder who's seen that photo?" she asked.

"I don't know. But I hope just the creep who took it and sent it to Jen." I shook my head and started digging through my bag until I found a black Sharpie of my own. Not that I would ever use it for graffiti, of course. I stared at Jen's locker for a second. Then, with a few quick strokes, I transformed "TRAMP" into "I ♡ TRAM-POLINES!"

"Really? Are you serious?" Amy asked. "Who loves trampolines?"

"I don't know. Everyone. People in the circus? It was all I could think of!"

"Hey you guys!" Carreyn bopped up to us, holding her faux designer tote bag tight against her side.

"Hey!" Amy and I said at the same time. Wow. We both just stared at her trying to process. Fortunately, Carreyn's Miss Twiggy hair extensions were gone. Unfortunately, she was now sporting kind of a finger-in-the-socket 'fro, with overly confident highlights.

"Super-sorry I missed Code Pink last night." She hesitated, pushing a poof of her f-i-t-s 'fro out of her eyes. "What happened? What'd I miss?"

Amy and I exchanged glances. I debated for a second how much to tell Carreyn—if anything. Then I decided to savor the moment of my superior knowledge.

"A lot," I whispered. "It's bad."

"Really bad," added Amy.

Carreyn leaned in, looking genuinely concerned, like she was totally out of the loop. "What?"

"Last night someone sexted Jen this really gross photo of Hutch and her. From his pool party." Carreyn's eyes got huge. "And you can totally see Jen's boob."

"All of it." Amy nodded. "Full-frontal boobity."

Carreyn covered her mouth with her hand. "Oh no." Her fingernails were painted an electric blue and nibbled down to nothing. "Oh no. That's awful! Do you know . . . Do you know who . . ."

Before she could finish, a cluster of gossipy girls walked past us, whispering and laughing at Jen's locker. Amy and Carreyn and I looked at each other. Were we being paranoid? Or had other people already seen the sext too?

Carreyn looked worried.

"We're just being paranoid, right?" I asked.

"Sure hope so." But Amy didn't sound convinced.

chapter thirteen
locker talker

On my way to Drama, I took the long way and walked down
to the parking lot hoping to bump into Clint near his bike. There
he was, leaning against it talking to some senior girl with big eyes,
big hair, and . . . well, big everything. I didn't have the guts to go
over to them, but when Clint looked in my direction, I waved.

I waited for a second, clutching my notebook, then I turned and
made a beeline for main hall.

He didn't wave back. Not even the cool-guy head nod. My brain
started to fizz. Was he annoyed about last night? About the Code
Pink and me rushing off? I quickly moved along, staring at the
ground. Or was I blowing his cool by waving to him in public?
Or maybe he didn't even see me. Or maybe he needed glasses and
thought I was like a short redheaded tree waving in the wind. Or
maybe . . . Yeah. He probably didn't see me.

In the main hall, I met up with Bean and Cate, who were both wearing berets and looking amazing as usual. Cate was in a black one, pulled
tight over one ear, and a black turtleneck tucked into high-waisted pants
cinched with a belt. I don't know how she did it—it was like she had
fallen right out of a black-and-white photograph from the 1940s. Somehow she even looked French. Bean looked more like Bonnie from *Bonnie
and Clyde* and was dangerously cute.

"Love the resistance movement drag," I said, genuinely impressed and a little bit jealous.

"I'm not taking off this beret," said Cate, "until our mission is complete."

Bean waved a clipboard in front of me. "We already have twenty-three signatures on the petition—and that's *before* Drama. This will be a breeze."

"What *is* our mission, exactly?" I asked, feeling another jagged edge of doubt poking me in the brain. "Getting Hutch to resign? Forcing Canfield to do another election?"

"Yeah! Both. Kinda. I think?" Bean looked at Cate. "Wait. What was it again?"

"Forcing another election, a *fair* election," said Cate as we continued down the main hall to Drama. "That and making Canfield's life a living hell, every single day. So he *can't* ignore us." Cate pulled a piece of paper out of her pocket, waving it around like it was money. "I already have lots of ideas."

She read a few off her list. "Superglue his desk drawers shut. Fill his office with live chickens. Put a diaper filled with mashed potatoes, gravy, and Raisinets on the brass hornet in the quad. Do a little rewiring so that every time someone makes copies, his phone rings . . ."

Bean was laughing. I nodded along but wasn't really listening. I was lost in my own headspace, thinking about seeing Clint in Drama—and this time *him* seeing *me*. Would he come up behind me and whisper something in my ear? Ooh, chills! Or would he act all cool like nothing had happened last night? Should *I* act all cool like nothing had happened? Could I?

When we walked into Drama, Charlie Dodd and Svend came right over to us.

"Hi Svend." Bean smiled, all flirty like she had a naughty secret she couldn't possibly keep. She shifted the petition clipboard from one hand to the other.

"*Hallo* Miss Bønne Bean." He gave her a quick kiss on the cheek, then whispered something in her ear. She giggled *and* blushed.

Charlie stared up at them with his mouth half open and a painfully pinched forehead. Somehow his expression made him look even shorter and skinnier than usual.

"Hey Svend." Cate stepped in close to him. "Do you know anything about electrical wiring?"

He shook his head, then asked innocently, "Oh, pardon me, *whose* electrical wiring?" Bean, Cate, and I laughed, then Svend joined in.

Poor Charlie just stood there trapped in some sort of male competition coma. Finally, he rallied. "Hey, ah . . . Bean, would you like my *John Hancock* on your petition?" he asked.

I rolled my eyes. Bean shrugged, handing the petition over to Charlie. Svend gave Charlie an inquisitive look.

"A *John Hancock* is an American colloquialism for a person's signature," Charlie explained, trying to sound all History Channel. "It refers to one of our Founding Fathers, who wrote and signed the Declaration of Independence."

"Oh, I see." Svend nodded, pretending not to understand. "In my country, a John Handcock is something very different."

Bean giggled again.

Charlie nodded seriously, considering the possibilities. Then he blushed sunburn-red.

Served him right. I turned away and looked around the room. No sign of Clint yet. Mandy Mindel was surrounded by Library Girls and AV geeks, all chattering away. I walked over to her. She and Teddy Baedeker were passing out *We Count Recount!* signs.

I picked one up. "Wow." Each sign was handwritten on a paper plate with a wood paint-stirring stick as a handle. "These are really nice."

"Yeah." Mandy nodded matter-of-factly, continuing to hand them out. "I couldn't sleep last night, so I made a bunch." She pointed to the back of one. "See? The handles won't fall off. I used a hot glue gun."

I stared at her. Something was different. OMG. Were her eyelashes starting to grow back? I smiled inside, handing the sign back to her.

"No, keep it." She nodded again. "I want you to have one."

She smiled like she was actually feeling it. I hoped she'd forgiven me for not sticking up for her and Teddy that night. It seemed like she had. I smiled back. "Thanks."

Clint never showed up for Drama (ergh!!!), so I had a lot of time to practice acting cool—like nothing had happened—while listening to Mr. E. go on and on about the fourth wall. But I couldn't stop thinking about Clint and replaying the details from last night, especially the kiss. Even though it had happened really fast, I kept doing it over and over in my mind, really, *really* slowly. It was starting to feel like we had actually made out for like twenty minutes.

My lips were getting chapped from all the action. I smiled as I applied lip balm in my mind. So where *was* he?! I replayed the last twelve hours in my mind, flashing on Clint's face as he dropped me off last night, and his vacant look when I waved to him this morning. I closed my eyes. Oh, groan. Was Clint avoiding me?

On the way to fourth period, I bumped into Jen at our lockers. She looked awful. But she didn't say a word.

I opened my locker, trying not to think about Clint, and grabbed my American History

SIDEBRA

Miss UnPleasant was the secret lovechild of Hutch's bullying and my shame. Shame because I didn't do anything to stick up for Mandy and Teddy when Hutch and a bunch of his beer-buzzed varsity jerk buddies totally harassed and humiliated them after a football game. It was pretty awful. Mandy tried not to cry and Teddy . . . well, Teddy cried—and for good reason. I just kind of watched, like some lame-o wussy buttcap. The only good thing to come out of it was Miss UnPleasant, and the Underground movement that her columns ignited. But I hate being a wimp. And I still feel really crappy about not doing anything that night. And I probably always will.

book. "How's Bodie?" I finally asked like I was afraid to ask—because I totally was.

She shook her head. "I couldn't find him. I feel like I could throw up."

I pictured the huge western omelet she had eaten at breakfast and reached for my lunch bag, quickly dumping it out in the bottom of my locker. I folded it up. "Here. Take this, just in case."

"I'm serious!" she said, all flustered.

"I know. So am I."

In fourth period, I pushed all thoughts of Clint and Eric and Jen out of my head. It was like pushing a boulder. Hey, I'd never actually pushed a mental boulder away before. That was progress, right? The point is, I had work to do.

All through class, I looked extremely attentive like I was writing down every single word Mr. Yamaguchi said, because, basically, I *was* concentrating really hard—just on the details of my big plan. I knew I had to learn more about Hutch, and fast. I knew I had to get him to trust me. I knew he secretly had a crush on me—or at least he used to—a crush I could probably reactivate if I killed him with kindness and maybe even flirted a little. Ick. And then, just as Mr. Yamaguchi was launching into a spiel about early American dialects, it came to me. I had to speak Hutch's language, his *socially stunted* language.

Locker notes!

Okay. So maybe it wasn't a big plan . . . yet. But phase one was devious—designed-by-Peter-Hutchison-to-hook-Peter-Hutchison. Brilliant. Where do I get these ideas?

I flipped past three pages of groan-worthy Teen Scene false starts to a clean page of my notebook. Then in generic all capital letters, I wrote my first locker stalker note to Hutch.

♦ ♥ ♡ DO YOU LIKE SURPRISES? ♥ ♡

I doodled cute little hearts all around the words. And then I sprayed it with breath freshener. Before folding it up, I looked it over a few times, picturing Hutch reading it with a completely bewildered look on his face, then looking up and down the hall all curious, wondering if he was being punk'd or pursued. I smiled. This was going to be fun.

And then I got a twinge of psychic niggling. Could this backfire on me? No. No way! Ridiculous. No one in a million years would really think I liked Hutch—except maybe Hutch.

I shrugged off my niggles and carefully folded the note up tight, slipping it into my back pocket. When Mr. Yamaguchi finally stopped lecturing and gave us our reading assignment, I asked for the hall pass to go to the bathroom.

I casually jogged over to sophomore hall, trying to look relaxed like I had just forgotten something that I really needed for class. When I spotted Hutch's locker, I slowed to a walk. And then, checking in both directions to see that the coast was clear, I pulled the note out of my back pocket and slipped it through one of the vents in Hutch's locker. Easy as pie.

I turned to head back to class and—

Oh, crap. You'll never guess who was walking right toward me, looking really perturbed.

Hutch.

Had he seen me? I wasn't sure. *Just act normal, just act normal*, I said to myself, trying to look innocent, walk, and ignore the thundering of my heartbeat all at the same time.

"Hey Paisley," Hutch mumbled, passing by me.

"Hey."

"Forgot my French homework in my locker. Least I hope it's in my locker."

"Yeah. Hate that."

"What are *you* doing out of class?"

"Uh." Oh crap! "I um . . . I . . . I was . . . I was having a low-blood-sugar moment in American History and, um, I needed to get a . . . a cupcake from my locker."

"Really? A cupcake? Can I have a bite?"

Unbelievable. "Sorry. Ate it already."

Hutch looked disappointed. I made a mental note: *food*.

He scratched his nose with the back of his fist. "No hard feelings about the election, right? I mean, you had to know I was going to win, right?"

I wanted to scream. *Hutch, you didn't win, you stupid narcissistic egomaniac!* Instead, I thought of Jen and took a deep breath. Then I harnessed every bit of personal strength to smile and stay on message. "Yeah, sure. No hard feelings. You deserved it, Hutch. And you know, something tells me you're going get a lot more of what you deserve."

"Really? Hey, thanks."

I waved at him and headed off down the hall. But then I realized this was my chance.

"Hey, Hutch!" I called after him.

He turned, looking a little surprised as he took a swish of mouthwash from a mini Listerine bottle. Typical. Bet he's always thinking about getting some action. Ew. Did he swallow it? That's gross. I mean, I like fresh breath too, but . . . ick.

"Hey, can I interview you at lunch?" I asked, walking back over to him. "I'm researching a . . . a science fair project on . . ." Um, um, um! "It's this project called . . . I'm thinking of calling it . . . 'Emotional Global Warming.'" Yes! My plan was going global.

He smiled. "Cool. Yeah, we could use some of that."

"Yeah." I sighed, feeling relieved. "I'll just need to ask you a few questions about yourself and stuff, okay?"

"Yeah, sure." He nodded. "Just come find me."

I nodded. That was easy. By lunch, I'd have Hutch eating cup-cakes out of my hand.

But instead of going straight back to class, I took another lap around the halls trying to think of good to-catch-a-creep ques-tions. I wandered down into the main hall, heading toward the quad. That's when I saw a stack of brand-new issues of *The Fly*, our school paper. I grabbed one and flipped through it as I walked—

And I stopped cold.

I was staring at a full-page ad with this huge close-up picture of me—or more accurately, a huge close-up-my-nose picture of me. OMG! How did they get a still from that video?! Ergh! Charlie Dodd. Hutch! I could kill them all over again. The giant head-line read: "Boycott Paisley Hanover!" And underneath that, it said: "(Our very own Miss UnPleasant)." And underneath *that* it said:

UnKind,
UnInformed,
UnPatriotic,
Un–Pleasant Hill High,
UnDeserving,
And most importantly, UnDatable.

Yours pleasantly,
three Pleasant Hill Patriots

Unkind? Uninformed? *Undatable?*
"What?!"

chapter fourteen
freedumb of speech

I bolted for the girls' bathroom. I needed a place to hide out and think before everyone in school read this and my life was over (again!). Get a grip. Get a grip! I pushed open the bathroom door, went straight for the handicapped stall at the far end, and locked it. It smelled like cigarettes. Gross.

Who would do this? Who? WHO?! I held my head with both hands, pacing back and forth in the handicapped stall, which is actually really hard to do.

Boycott. . . . Boycott? Wait, what does that mean exactly? Ignore me? Don't shop with me? What was I going to do? Wait. Think. Think!

I stared at the ad again, rereading it. Undatable? *Undatable?!*

Oh God!

I dropped the lid, sat down on the toilet seat, and texted Jen, Amy, and Carreyn.

Confrnce stall now!

Why *Boycott?* That's weird. *Boycott Paisley Hanover?* Maybe boycott doesn't just mean what it normally means—maybe it's also some secret coded message to all guys? It could be, right? Am I crazy? I *am* crazy. Yes. That's it. Crazy.

Okay, breathe. Breathe.

The bell for lunch rang. Crap. Mr. Yamaguchi was going to kill me for not going back to class. Actually, that could be a good thing, I realized, chewing on my cuticle.

Finally, there was a knock on the stall door. I flipped the lock. It was Amy, red-faced and panting. "What? What happened?" she said, bursting in.

I shoved the ad in front of her and locked the door. Her face did this quick shuffle of emotions as she read it. She pushed it down. "This is such crap! You are *not* unpatriotic."

"Amy! Come on. What am I going to do?"

"Um? I dunno! What would Miss UnPleasant do?"

Before I could answer, there were three quick pounds on the door. I unlocked it. Jen slipped in. Tiny beads of sweat glistened across her nose. She looked terrorized, like she'd just been chased down to the bathroom by the school band.

"Is it out?" Her eyes darted back and forth between us. "Have you seen it? Did you get the sext?"

"No. Jen. Relax." I put my hand on her arm. "It's not the photo."

She studied me hard, then exhaled with relief. "Thank God."

"But have you seen *this?*" Amy asked her.

All three of us leaned in to each other and read the ad.

Jen's eyes got very intense. "Oh wow," she said, looking both confused and pissed. "This is so nasty. This is *personal*. Who would do this?"

"I don't know." I slumped against the wall. "But I'm gonna find out."

"I do." Amy looked up from the ad. "The same kind of people who hide video cameras in bathrooms."

"Shidiots," said Jen under her breath.

I nodded. "One guess where they got this photo?"

Amy looked at the ad, then at me. "Charlie," she breathed.

"Or Hutch," said Jen, curling her lip in disgust.

"Or both." I pressed my palms into my eyes.

We were all silent for a few seconds picturing the likely suspects, listening to the whir and click of the overhead fan.

My phone started vibrating. A text. From Carreyn.

omw! Brnging m&c bts!

"M and C bits?" I held up my phone so they could read it.

"Mac and cheese bites!" said Amy like she hadn't eaten anything all month.

Jen made her disgusto face. "Gross."

"You guys, what am I going to do about this?" I held up *The Fly* like I was about to swat a huge one.

There was a nervous tapping on the stall door. We ignored it.

"Nothing," said Amy confidently. "Just act totally normal, like it never happened."

What? Was she kidding? I mean, how could I just *ignore* it? Everyone in the whole school was going to see this and think I was un . . . *un*-everything!

Jen was silent for a few more seconds, tapping her fingers against her lips and looking at me. "Actually, I have a better idea," she said, her eyes full of wicked fun. I felt a sudden rush of gratitude and relief. This was the old Jen—the Jen I knew.

"Act like it's a compliment," she said, "like you're totally flattered that three *Pleasant Hill Patriots* care about you so much—no—are so *afraid* of you that they'd do this, that they'd spend money to do this. And go around showing the ad to everyone, bragging." Amy was nodding along, smiling. "We'll put the word out that you want to thank them for honoring you and Miss UnPleasant with this great, hilarious ad."

"And then I find out who it is"—I was smiling too, starting to picture it all—"and I clobber them over the head with a super-cute chunky shoe!"

Jen and Amy laughed.

"Something like that." Jen smiled, nodding.

There was another series of quick taps on the door. "What?" I blurted out just as I opened it. Oops. It was a girl on crutches with a big cast on her leg. She looked like she really had to pee. "Oh, sorry," I said.

I marched out of the bathroom and headed up toward sophomore hall with Amy on one side and Jen on the other. I don't know if I felt honored exactly, but I definitely felt . . . *something*.

"Look!" said Amy, pointing, as we walked past the cafeteria. Carreyn was right at the front of the line for mac and cheese bites. Figures. Food over friends.

Amy peeled off in Carreyn's direction, waving good-bye.

"No more fried mac and cheese bites!" I yelled after her. "They're a gateway drug!" She just held up her hands, like *what can you do?*

Jen and I had brought our lunches, but we hadn't even made it to our lockers when Charlie Dodd ran up to me, his heavy backpack thudding against his skinny body.

"Paisley, have you seen this?" He waved a copy of *The Fly*. "Great press. I mean, in a, you know, *there's no such thing as bad press* way. People actually hate you enough to advertise! That's awesome power. Admissions officers will be extremely impressed."

I clenched my teeth and ignored him.

Jen nodded. "See?" she said to me.

"What are you gonna do?" he asked, skipping along next to me, trying to keep up. "Move? Home school? Never date?"

Ergh! Either he or Hutch had given that humiliating up-my-nose photo to the three Pleasant Hill High *shidiots*. I so wanted to stomp on his foot and demand answers. But I had committed, as a serious actor, to my I'm-so-flattered façade. So I just waved my hand in his direction. "Not talking to you." I stopped in front of my locker and calmly turned the combination lock.

"Fine," Charlie said, and stomped off, walking right into Bean. His face basically smashed into her boobs. He looked up at her. "You smell good." And then he turned beet-red. "Sorry. Sorry."

Bean and Jen and I watched him flee down the hall.

"What was that?" Bean asked.

I just shook my head.

"Better question," she said. "What is *this?*" She waved her copy of *The Fly* at me.

I opened my locker. "Oh, just a little Pop propaganda," I said, tossing my books inside and reaching for my sandwich on the bottom of my locker. Then I caught a look from Jen and added, "Yeah, isn't it great?! Way flattering!"

Jen nodded and leaned in. "Less sarcasm," she whispered, tucking her white-blond hair behind her ear.

Bean wrinkled up her face. "Flattering?" she asked.

I was trying hard to feel honored, honestly, but I still managed to slam my locker door so hard, it bounced back open. I slammed it again.

Bean opened her mouth to say something but was suddenly distracted by the enormous heart on Jen's locker. "Oh, Jen, wow," she said sweetly. "I heart trampolines too." Then she did this little clapping thing under her chin.

Jen shot me a look, then smiled at Bean. "Yeah. They're fun." Then she smacked me on the butt. "Thanks, Pais. Huge improvement. I *have* been acting kinda *jumpy* lately, haven't I?" She barked like a seal until I seal-laughed with her. Oh . . . this was my Jen. A lump of cotton-candy luv fuzz got stuck in my throat.

Bean just stared at us, looking concerned for our sanity.

"There she is!" someone yelled.

We all turned.

Cate was pointing right at me, walking toward us with Bentley Jones, who was looking like a mini Michelle Obama. In her beret, Cate blended in like a black beauty mark on a baby's butt as she and Bentley weaved their way around pods of people eating on the lawn. So much for going underground.

"Hi Paisley," said Bentley, holding up a small audio recorder. "Can I get a quote from you? I'm writing a special for *The Fly*. What's your reaction to this ad?"

I stared at the ad again, then down at the red blinking light on the recorder. Then I took a deep breath. I looked Bentley in the eye, and I smiled with faux-real confidence. "This ad is . . . such an *unexpected* compliment," I gushed, accessorizing my performance by placing my hand on my heart. "I'm so delighted and touched to know that Miss UnPleasant has had such an impact on so many people. I am honored. Truly honored."

Wow that sounded good. Even I was buying it.

Cate and Bean looked at me like I had totally lost it. Jen nodded approvingly.

Bentley tilted her head. "Hm, I'm surprised," she said, then went on with the poise of a pro. "In your opinion, Paisley, is there a difference between this ad and the harsh columns that you wrote under the anonymous *nom de plume* Miss UnPleasant, categorically condemning the popular students at our school?"

I hesitated, not sure what to say. Actually, I wasn't quite sure what the question was.

Bentley looked at me, waiting.

"Well, um . . . This is . . . This is a good start. You know, because not everyone can write like Miss UnPleasant. I mean, whoever wrote this has clearly been influenced by her irreverence and her ironic sense of . . . irony . . . and her unusual sense of humor, and creative spelling . . ." I looked around wondering if I was making any sense. "Bottom line, I'm flattered."

Jen jumped in. "It's certainly not as funny as what Paisley wrote. But I think we all appreciate the effort."

Cate stared at her, incredulous. "Is it funny at all?"

"Is it supposed to be funny?" Bean asked. She stared at the ad again.

"Oh yeah, *I* think so," Jen answered. "It's *trying* to be funny. Actually, I think it's a really nice tribute to Paisley and to Miss UnPleasant." Jen leaned close to the recorder. "Jen Sweetland, sophomore."

Everyone laughed, even Bentley.

"Do you have plans to respond?" she asked.

"Does she ever." Cate smirked.

"Oh yeah, Bentley. Lots of plans," I said, nodding. Of course I had absolutely no plans, except . . . Wait. "For starters, I want to thank them. Actually, I'd love to meet all three patriots so I can thank them in person."

"Any idea who they are?" Bentley asked.

"Nope. Do you?" I was trying to sound as innocent as possible.

"Not yet, but I'm on it." She clicked off her recorder and looked at me. "I'll just ask Bodie. He'll know. He knows everything that goes on at this school."

I glanced at Jen. She looked like she'd just swallowed *The Fly*.

chapter fifteen
red hairing

"With Bentley Jones on this," said Cate, holding a rolled-up copy of *The Fly*, "it should take about a minute and a half to find out who they are. And then . . ." She raised her eyebrows seductively. "Then we bring them down."

"*Vive la résistance!*" Bean whispered. "We are so *Prêt à Porter!*" Then the two of them darted off to handle some business for the Underground Resistance Movement, which had quickly been renamed the Underwear Resistance Movement, which made me wonder if any of us understood what we were resisting.

Jen and I just stood there for a second watching them maneuver down the hall like spies.

She shook her head. "They're nuts," she said, smiling.

"I know. Aren't they great?"

She nodded, then pulled out her phone. A text. From Bodie. She stared at it for a long time, frowning.

"What? What?!" I whispered. "Has he gotten it?"

"No. Don't think so. He's acting totally normal." She tucked her hair behind her ear and spaced out for a second. "Unless . . . unless he *has* seen it and he is just *acting* totally normal." She looked a little freaked.

I grabbed her arm. "Uh-uh. Bodie can do a lot of things, but he can't act. Remember that don't-do-drugs skit with the dwarf last year?"

She nodded. "Oh right. Good point."

"Stay calm, okay? I'm on it." I pulled my notebook and a pen out of my locker. "I'm interviewing Hutch today at lunch for my quote-unquote science fair project, 'Emotional Global Warming.'"

She smirked. "Nice."

"I'll get some info. I promise." I looked around sophomore hall for Hutch—

"Hey Pais!" Charlie Dodd yelled. *Pais?* He held out his cell phone in my direction. "Check this out! Have you gotten it yet?" Oh no. I glanced at Jen, who looked like she wanted to die. She turned away and stood there staring into her locker.

I approached Charlie's phone slowly, pretty sure what I was going to see.

But guess what?

It was a photo of Canfield in his lederhosen with a jack-o'-lantern on his head! I laughed way too hard.

"What?" Jen asked. Charlie held up his phone so she could see it. She laughed so hard, she doubled over and came up with tears—and relief—in her eyes.

"Yeah. It's pretty hilarious," Charlie said, trying to sound all cool. "I Photoshopped it last night and sent it out to some people during third period. Have you gotten it yet?"

I shook my head. I still wasn't talking to Charlie.

"I'm sure you'll get it soon," said Charlie, barely containing his excitement about the possibility of going viral.

"Freeze Dodd, you little rectal-rooter!" Hutch yelled at Charlie from the far end of sophomore hall.

Charlie looked up, then dropped his backpack at my feet with a thud. "Whoops. Gotta run!" He took off hurtling over our bench, doing the fifty-yard dash for his life through groups of people eating on the lawn. In one day, Charlie had become Pleasant Hill High's very own personification of *survival of the fittest*.

Then from out of nowhere, Carreyn stepped in front of Hutch, tossing a glance over her shoulder in Charlie's direction. She cocked her hip and posed seductively for Hutch, cupping one side of her f-i-t-s 'fro. "Hey handsome, can I buy you lunch?"

Wow. Carreyn was good. I mean bad. Wait! Was she horning in on my plan? Did someone tell her about it? I turned to ask Jen. But she was already walking away down the hall. I squinted after Carreyn, watching her lead Hutch off toward the cafeteria, swishing her tiny little hips. Hm. Maybe I needed to start thinking like a Hutch's Honey. Oh my gag!

I inhaled my sandwich in front of my locker and was about to go down to the cafeteria to look for Hutch. But then I spotted Charlie's huge backpack. It was sitting on the ground next to my locker like a boulder. I couldn't just leave it there. So I picked it up and hoisted it over one shoulder. OMG. It weighed a ton. It was a miracle Charlie didn't have scoliosis.

I couldn't find Hutch inside, so I headed out to the front lawn. A bunch of Uns, wearing more black than usual, had gathered around the base of the flagpole. Overhead, the sky was getting gray and cloudy.

"Not a word," Cate was saying to the crowd. "Not a single word!" Everyone nodded, slowly fanning themselves with Mandy's

SIDEBRA

I guess I should explain. So, right before the class election, a bunch of flirty sophomoronic girls started wearing these tight little yellow (and obnoxious!) "I'm a Hutch's Honey" T-shirts, helping with Hutch's campaign, and totally sucking up to him. Yeah. Including Jen and Carreyn, my supposedly best friends. Okay, so after Code Pink I get why Jen did that. But what was Carreyn's excuse? Just imitating Jen? So sad. Anyway, the whole Hutch's Honey thing was insulting. And not just for me—for them. I mean really, who would want to be a Hutch's Honey? Disgusting! Oh wait. I do. But only because of my plan. Seriously.

paper-plate signs. Cate pulled a few rolls of duct tape out of her bag and passed them solemnly to Bean.

Duct tape? What for? I wondered, watching Bean handing them out to the crowd. Were they going to kidnap Canfield and force him to eat fried mac and cheese bites until he agreed to another election or his polyester pants split? Hm . . . Not a bad idea.

I looked around the lawn, hoping to see Clint. Maybe he wasn't just avoiding me. Maybe he was out sick. Maybe he was *really* sick. Maybe he was like in the hospital or dead or dying and would have to cancel our date.

I was feeling sorry for myself somehow going from two dates to totally UnDatable in like twenty-four hours, when I spotted Charlie Dodd pushing through the double doors from the main hall. I waved to him and then awkwardly lifted his backpack with both hands. He wandered out onto the front lawn heading vaguely in my direction. His shoulders were slumped down, and he had one hand over his face. Then I noticed blood running down his chin and the sides of his wrist.

And then he fell over.

I dropped his bag on the ground. "Charlie, are you okay?!" I asked, running over to him. His nose was really swollen. "Oh my God. What happened?" Crap! Forgot I wasn't talking to him.

Charlie looked up at me, still holding his nose, and rolled his head from side to side. "I hit a pole."

Yeah, right. That was a funny name for Hutch's fist. But he sounded all congested and nasally. And he'd been crying. I opened my mouth to say something, but couldn't figure out what.

He sat up and wiped his face with his XXL polo shirt, which fortunately that day was black.

"Should I get you some ice or something?" I offered.

"No. I'm good." He stood up slowly. "I'm gonna go to the

nurse's and impress her with my CPR skills. Maybe I'll score a codeine sucker." He tried to chuckle, but I could tell he was in major pain. "Hey, thanks for keeping my backpack."

"Sure."

I watched him walk away along the edge of the front lawn out toward the boonies. He dragged his backpack by one strap, moving slowly, like his head weighed ten times more than usual.

As he disappeared around the corner, I had to wonder. A pole? No way. But why would Charlie lie about that? It's not like I was going to fink on him.

I thought about it for a second. If Hutch really did this to him, after Charlie helped him out and, by the way, sold *me* out in the process . . . I shook my head, suddenly overwhelmed by this unbelievable surge of teen superhero justice. I was so going to bring Hutch down—any way I could.

I turned to head back to Cate, Bean, and the protesters, but they were gone.

All of them.

I turned in a circle. The only things left behind were a few empty rolls of duct tape scattered around the grass where they'd been standing. They'd all left, and I hadn't heard a sound.

chapter sixteen
high school of protesting arts

The Underwear Resistance Movement would be fine without me—wherever it had gone. I wanted to be in on the protest, sure, but my top priority now was the hunt for Hutch. If I moved fast, I could still sting him with a few tranquilizing questions before the end of lunch—and maybe soften him up enough to spill something about that photo.

On my way to the quad, I bumped into Carreyn. She was pacing around in front of one of the four entrances—and she was holding a copy of *The Fly.*

Great.

"Hey Carreyn," I called to her, like I was truly delighted to be *Un*Datable

"Oh. Um. Hi . . . Pais." She looked a little frazzled. I think it was the new hair. "Have you . . ." She raised her copy of *The Fly* and cringed. "Have you seen this?"

"Oh yeah. I've seen it," I said, peeking through a window in the main hall and scanning the jock corner of the quad. There was Hutch on a bench, looking uncharacteristically pensive. "Isn't it great?" I tried not to sound too sarcastic. "I'm so flattered to get this kind of attention."

"You are?" Carreyn looked baffled. "You're not . . . you're not like mad?" I shook my head, smiling faux real. She looked back down at the boycott-me ad like maybe she had missed something. "That's . . . wow. I mean . . . I'd be freakin' furious."

"Well, the photo could be better. But it's the thought that counts."

Carreyn nodded vaguely.

I wanted to change the subject. "Carreyn, were you just flirting with Peter Hutchison?"

"No! I mean, yeah, but no. Not for real." She stepped back and forth a little like she had to pee. "I was just trying to . . . to help Charlie." She made this goofy face. "He's always getting pounded, and he's so sweet. Have you noticed he's getting taller?"

OMG. Carreyn had a secret crush on Charlie Dodd! I nodded and tried not to smile as I looked back out into the quad. It was strangely dark out there. I glanced up at the sky. Fat heavy rain clouds *loomed ominously.* (Right? I think that's what you say in a novel when something bad is about to happen.)

I took a deep breath and let it out through my clenched teeth. I wasn't exactly thrilled about going into the quad at lunch. The last time I'd done that— the *only* time I'd done that—it wasn't pretty. Actually, it was pretty humiliating. *And* I was sure those "three Pleasant Hill Patriots" were out there somewhere. I wasn't in the mood for a verbal smack-down.

But there was Hutch. This was my chance. I had to do it.

SIDEBRA

The Quad: Our Centrally Located Pit of Social Quicksand
To the unsuspecting eye of a new student or clueless freshman, the quad is the perfect spot to enjoy a sticky bun, lunch with friends, or—surprise!—a near-death experience. Basically, if you go in there at break or lunch and you're *not* an upperclassman or one of the über-popular Varsity Jocks, Poms, or BPs (Beautiful People), you're dead.

In the middle of the quad, there's an eight-foot-tall bronze hornet (our mascot) standing proudly in a boxer's stance with gloves on four of his six legs. Yes, it's a ridiculous statue—but it's *our* ridiculous statue. So we love it (even though most of us never get to see it up close).

"I'm going in," I said to Carreyn. "You coming?"

"Um . . . No, that's okay." She tried to smooth down her f-i-t-s 'fro. "I think I'll just . . . I'll just watch from out here."

Poor Carreyn. She tried to act so confident. But it was all just a discount-fashion façade. "Okay. If anything happens to me," I said in what was definitely a stress-induced flash of generosity, "you can have my locker." I gripped my notebook and pen and boldly entered the quad.

It was packed with people—*packed*. But something was . . . It was the freakiest thing . . . The quad was *quiet*. Eerily quiet. And kind of dark. There were groups of Pops standing around as usual, talking—wait, whispering? Why were they whispering?

OMG. OMG! My butt puckered. I looked around. I knew it! They were all reading about me in *The Fly!* Oh, wait, no. Never mind. Hardly anyone was reading *The Fly*—because *everyone* was staring at the Uns.

They were everywhere.

Uns sitting crossed-legged on the ground. Uns standing on the benches. Uns gathered around the base of the big brass hornet, silently holding up signs.

We Count Recount

UN Visible, not Invisible

We Can't Spare CHANGE

Wow. A bunch of them were even sitting right at the feet of the Pops, right in the middle of their conversational clusters!

And the coolest thing? They all had strips of silver duct tape over their mouths.

The silver silent treatment. Nice.

I was really impressed—and really, *really* relieved that something way more interesting was going on today than that dumb ad in *The Fly*.

Most of the Pops were looking around, like totally baffled. Should they move out of the way or hold on to their prime real estate? Candy Esposito stood solemnly like she was in church and this was some fascinating new prayer service. Of course, BS1, BS2, and the other varsity Hornettes pretended to ignore the Uns, just whispering, eating, brushing their hair like this was the High School of Protesting Arts and this kind of thing happened three times a day.

I heard shouts behind me and turned. A bunch of rowdy varsity jocks were laughing and hooting, pointing at the protesters. Bodie looked like he was trying to get them to quiet down. He kept raising and then lowering his hands.

Then I spotted Bean and Amy standing on a bench along the far side of the quad, each holding up the ends of a big yellow banner that screamed:

YES WE CANfield!

They stood there, arms raised, looking like beautiful, proud, duct-taped Statues of Liberty. I barely even recognized Amy with her mouth shut.

A big lump of sugary pride stuck in my throat as I gazed at this silent army of courageous *Un*known Soldiers. OMG. I was making myself weep.

Mandy, Teddy, and LG Wong, silver tape stretched over their mouths, moved silently through the quad like zombie activists,

handing out flyers to the Pops. LG Wong stopped and handed one to Hutch.

He read it, shaking his head, then crumpled it up and threw it at the ground.

Cate zombied over in my direction and handed me a flyer. Her mouth said nothing, but her eyes said *Is this cool or what?!*

I nodded at her vigorously, trying to say *cool* and *or what!* back. Then I looked at the flyer.

One Wrong Does Not Erase All Students' Rights!

Every student at this school counts.
So every vote must be counted.
We demand—and deserve—another vote
for sophomore class president.
If you support our cause, stop talking now.
Silence = Strength

I felt someone looking at me and glanced up. Eric Sobel. He had his camera to his face and was shooting pictures—of me. Gulp. I guess there was no avoiding him now. I smiled and waved, but he just hopped up on a bench and started taking shots of the quad. Uh-oh. Would my picture end up in the yearbook or in a book of mug shots of juvenile-delinquent two-timers? I was kind of kidding, but kind of not.

I watched him moving through the crowd, working his camera like a pro. I waited a long time for him to look back at me. He never did.

Oh . . . a wave of realization hit me.

He'd probably seen the Boycott Paisley ad. Now I wasn't just a minor embarrassment to him, I was a major social liability! Or . . .

another huge wave rolled over me. Or maybe he went to the listening spot yesterday and he was really pissed at me for not showing up. Or maybe *he* never showed up. Or . . . maybe I was completely soaked in self-doubt by now. Maybe he thought *I* wasn't interested anymore?

I suddenly got this like bad seaweed taste in my mouth. Eric and Clint had clearly talked about the weekend and . . . I mean, they were both acting weird. Were my dates still on or not? Silent Unprotest scream! This was ridiculous. I decided I was just going to ask Eric point blank about the dance.

I took a deep breath and started walking toward him. He was making his way down the other side of the quad. As I carefully stepped around the silent protestors, I tried to make eye contact with him, but he wouldn't look at me. Ergh! He kept hiding behind his camera. I followed the line of his lens to . . .

Hutch.

Hutch was standing there with both hands jammed in his jacket pockets, sort of pacing like a caged animal. I stopped. I had completely forgotten about my hunt for Hutch! What was wrong with me?

Just then Cate walked past Hutch, handing out more flyers.

"Get a life, Maduro!" he yelled. "Or should I say, get a *wife!*"

A bunch of Pops laughed.

Cate flipped him off.

"What'd you say?" Hutch yelled again. "I can't hear you!"

Cate ignored him, so he threw the crumpled-up flyer at her. And another. Eric kept snapping pictures. Suddenly, dozens of Pops were throwing balls of flyer at Cate.

"Hey!" I ran toward her, raising my hands in the air, trying to block the incoming barrage. "Stop! STOP IT!" I yelled.

Cate looked right at me and put her index finger up to her taped lips. Then she lifted her head toward the sky, closed her eyes, and took it—like she enjoyed it, like she was feeling a soft rain on her face.

And then Craig Delaney threw the end of a burrito at her. What a jerk! She ducked just in time, and it splattered against the bronze hornet. Unbelievable—and yet, totally predictable. A bunch of people laughed. And then more Pops threw more food. What pigs. But the Uns hung in there, and Cate stood her ground in the middle of the quad. She was awesome. And Mandy's paper-plate signs made surprisingly good shields.

Just as it started to rain, Mr. Canfield, led by some brown-noser, quickly waddle-walked into the quad to investigate. He was wearing his old coach's baseball cap and his Hornets team Windbreaker. Yes, Canfield had been a JV coach and a lousy science teacher before he had been promoted. Go figure. He whipped out his coach's whistle, blowing it like an insane referee. No one paid any attention to Canfield, but the flying food eventually died down under the weight of the rain.

Hutch turned and stomped out of the quad. The other Pops quickly cleared out, covering their heads with books or jackets and stepping around all the sitting protesters. But the Uns stayed— undaunted by the hailstorm of food, paper flyers, and rain—and triumphantly took possession of the quad. Everyone clapped when Teddy Baedeker climbed up on the bronze Hornet and slapped a piece of silver duct tape over its mouth. All the paper-plate signs were getting soggy and hard to read, but no seemed to care.

Eric was one of the last Pops to leave the quad. He took a few more pictures of the drenched, deliriously happy protesters, then covered his camera with his shirt and ran for the main hall. Nope. He never even glanced at me. Not once.

I stood there in the rain getting drenched in self-pity.

Then Cate pulled off her tape and let out this screaming loud *"Whoop!"*

The Unknown Soldiers all hopped to their feet and started jumping and hugging and dancing around in the rain. I couldn't help smiling. That would have been a great shot. I know I should have felt like celebrating too, but I didn't. I really just wanted to get out of there. Might as well do what I came to do.

So I followed Hutch.

chapter seventeen
scario hilario—i'm a hutch's honey!

I had to jog to catch up. Hutch was headed over to the small courtyard next to the gym. And he was by himself. I guess he wanted to get away from everyone too. I slowed to a walk just as he sat down on the edge of a brick planter under an overhang.

He saw me coming and put up one hand. "Not in the mood, Hanover."

I stopped, wiping the rain off my forehead. This was going to be harder than I thought. I took a few more steps and swallowed hard.

"Hey there . . . *handsome*," I said all perky, ducking under the overhang. Ew. Gross. Puke in a purse!

He stared at me like he had no idea who I was. Then he finally said, "Hey." He didn't sound at all perky. Actually, he sounded mad. I guess the protest really got to him.

"That was weird," he said. "What was that crap?"

"Yeah. Weird." Hey, I had to agree with him. It *was* weird—good weird. But I didn't say that part.

"Man, why are they doing this to me? Calling *me* wrong? This sucks." He winced.

OMG. Doing it to *you*?! What a big bully baby.

"What do you want anyway? I'm not talking about the election," he said, glaring at me.

"Fine. No problem."

He seemed suspicious.

I ran my fingertips over one eyebrow, then smiled. "I was just wondering . . . Can I ask you a few questions for my science fair project?"

"Um, yeah." He winced again. "But now's not a good time."

Ergh! I tapped my notebook nervously. "Really? I'm kinda up against a deadline."

He didn't seem the least bit fazed.

"Actually, I'm kinda way past my deadline." I fidgeted with my wet bangs, then pushed them to the side.

He just stared at me.

Crap. I knew I didn't have a lot of time and started to panic. "Could we do it later *today?* Come to my soccer game. Please? Oh, *please?* Our uniforms are really cute. We can do the interview right after. It'll be super-fun. I promise!" OMG. Suddenly I was channeling Carreyn. This was scary.

He gave me a funny—funny-strange—look. "Did you just get hit on the head with an apple?"

I laughed faux real. "Hutch, you are so funny." And I am so Hutch's Honey! Focus, Paisley. Focus. "It's just that . . . well, now that the election is behind us, I think it'd be kinda fun to hang out."

"Really?" He didn't sound at all convinced.

I nodded.

He dropped his voice. "Really."

"That . . ." I motioned back toward the quad. "That wasn't my idea. I didn't even know about it." Which was totally true! "So, yeah, really."

It had stopped raining, and the sun was beginning to peek through the clouds.

He stared at me. I could see his jaw muscle flexing and unflexing. "Yeah, okay. I'll come by after practice. Hey, do you have any Advil or something? Don't all chicks have that stuff in their bag?"

No. But I've got you in the bag, *dude*. I smiled inside. It was only a matter of time.

In my desperate attempt to act desperate, which was spooky easy, I hadn't even noticed that Hutch's right hand was resting in the planter in a plastic bag filled with ice. He moved it farther out of view. I got a bad feeling.

"What happened to your hand?" I asked, all innocent, as if I didn't already know.

He hesitated. "Nothing. I mean . . . it was an accident." He lifted his hand out of the bag. It was all red from the ice. Then he flexed his swollen fingers and tried to make a fist a few times. "Yeah. An accident. It just kinda happened. No big deal."

"What happened?" I asked, pressing him, trying to sound concerned.

"Um . . ." Hutch looked away in the direction of the parking lot. "A car door. It got slammed in a car door." He said it like he couldn't quite believe it himself.

"Really? Ouch. That sounds so painful." I tried to sound sympathetic as I thought of Charlie, and all the Uns, and Jen, and, of course, myself. I wondered how elaborate a lie I could get out of him. "Whose car door?"

He looked down at his shoes, probably doing a quick mental shuffle of who even has a car. "Don't say anything, okay?" Then he looked me in the eye. "Bodie. Bodie's car."

What? Suddenly, a weird worm of doubt wiggled through my brain. I pictured the sext. OMG. Was it possible that Hutch was telling the truth? Had Bodie already seen the photo?

chapter eighteen
field goal!

By the afternoon, the rain had cleared. It was blue and warm with a fall breeze that sliced the air. Before our game, I walked with Amy and Jen out to the girls' soccer field telling them all about Hutch's hand. They both stopped in their tracks and stared at me with big eyes.

Jen didn't say anything. She just ran her hand nervously through her hair a few times, thinking. In the distance, the fields were already buzzing with the sounds of balls and whistles and shouting voices.

"Wait," said Amy, wrinkling up her nose. "Would Bodie even do that?"

Amy and I looked at Jen.

"That doesn't sound like Bodie," she said.

"I know," Amy and I said at the same time.

"But . . ." Jen turned to me, a little worried. "I've never seen him really angry either."

"Maybe it *was* an accident?" I tried to sound hopeful. "It's possible, right? Or . . . or maybe Hutch is just lying."

"But why would he lie?" Jen asked.

"At lunch today"—I paused, wondering how much to tell them—

"Charlie Dodd told me he ran into a quote-unquote *pole*. I'm pretty sure his nose was broken. It was bleeding everywhere."

"Wow." Amy's eyes darted from mine to Jen's and back to mine. "That's so wrong."

Jen grabbed my arm. "Pais, that's suspension material."

Then Amy asked exactly what I was thinking. "Even for a class president and football star? I dunno."

We started walking again, considering the possibilities as we cut past the guys' practice field. I looked for Eric, but then a whistle blew, and the varsity soccer players all jogged for the sideline. I quickly looked away.

"We'd need proof," I said. "And if we got it, Canfield would still probably give Hutch VIP varsity athlete treatment."

Jen was about to say something, when she looked over my shoulder and stopped. I turned. Eric Sobel was jogging up to us.

A surge of nervous ick pounded through me. *Oh, mighty Crisis!* I thought, trying to prepare myself for the worst.

"Paisley, got a minute?" he asked all shy, shifting his water bottle from one hand to the other.

"Hey. Uh, yeah. Sure," I said, not at all sure I wanted to hear what he had to say.

Jen and Amy walked ahead. After a few feet, they both turned and smiled, flashing me gooey *Eric-loves-Paisley* faces.

If they only knew. I waved them on. "Catch up with you guys in a sec!"

Eric wiped the sweat off his face with his shirt as we walked along in silence for a few seconds. I had one eye on Jen and Amy just to make sure they kept a safe distance ahead.

"Hey," he said at the ground, kicking along a piece of gravel.

"Hey," I said again. Silence. Was I supposed to start the conversation? I mean, I would have if I knew what we were talking about.

We walked a little more.

"Hey, sorry about that boycott thing in *The Fly*."

I licked my lips nervously. "Yeah. Me too."

"It's really lame. You know whoever did that's just jealous of you, right?" Yeah right. I scratched the tip of my nose. "But you showed them with that great protest in the quad." He nodded, grinning.

Was he kidding? That great protest when he wouldn't even look at me? "That wasn't me," I said to the side of his face. "It was Cate and Bean and Amy, really—and Mandy Mindel. Can you believe that? Mandy talks—she talks loud!" Wait. What am *I* talking about? "But, yeah, not during silent protests, of course." *Duh?* OMG. Why do I always sound like such a blabbering über-boob around him?

Eric rubbed his fingers along his chin and jaw a few times. "Yeah, well . . . I got some great shots for Yearbook. So, um . . ." He finally looked at me. I know because I was still staring at him, admiring the profile of his nose and chin and jaw and . . . everything else, and feeling bummed that I'd already probably blown it with this amazing, gorgeous guy.

Maybe I should just tell him about Clint, I thought. I looked at the ground, scraping the bottoms of my cleats as we walked. But what would I say? *I really like you and I also really like this other guy who maybe likes me, but I'm really not sure.* Oh yeah, brilliant plan.

"How's ah . . . how's Jen doing?" Eric looked ahead. "Does she . . ." He hesitated, so I jumped right in.

"She *hates* being the water girl. But she's hanging in there."

Eric mashed his lips together and nodded a few times, like he understood. "So, hey, about tomorrow night . . ."

My little heart sighed and sank like a stone. I looked down at the ground. It was off. Our date was off. I knew it.

"So, um, I'd really like to pick you up for the dance on my *bike*."

What? The dance? OMG. The dance! Wait. *What did he say?* On his *bike*? I kept walking, staring at the ground. Was he kidding? Was this some kind of Clint trap?

Finally, I looked at him. But he was smiling sweetly at me, fidgeting with his practice jersey.

OMG. He wasn't kidding! I looked back at the ground, trying to act cool, like I hadn't already spent tons of time thinking I'd dance all night with my girlfriends—except for the occasional romantic slow dances with Charlie Dodd and Teddy Baedeker.

"But unfortunately, my bike's a ten-speed." He shrugged and gave me his double-dimple smile. God, he's so adorable! "It's a very impressive ten-speed. But if I did, you'd have to ride on the handlebars. And then, you know, I'd probably crash into a ditch or a tree or something." I couldn't help laughing. "So how about we just meet there, okay?"

OMG! Was I the biggest paranoid freak on the planet? Yes!

"Okay," I managed to croak, staring at him with this totally gooberish smile. "I mean, yeah, sounds great," I said, pulling myself together.

He seemed excited, like he was really looking forward to the dance again. "Hey, wanna talk after your game?"

OMG. He probably *did* just want some qual time with me at the listening spot. But then I got all weirdo Frigidaire on him. Poor guy. No wonder he was acting chilly. "Yeah. Definitely."

"Cool." He nodded, grinning at me. "Have a great game."

I couldn't stop smiling as I watched him jog off toward the guys' field. *Yay!* My heart cheered. *Date on!*

We did our stretches and warm-up drills, and then Coach Sykes called us into a huddle and pointed out the other team's top players. Finally the ref waved to us. It was time. We all put our hands into the middle of the huddle and cheered, "Go, Lady Hornets!"

Out on the field, I kept clenching and unclenching my hands

as we waited for the whistle to blow for the kick-off. I was totally pumped. For starters, *I was going to the dance with Eric Sobel!* It was really happening! I did the happy dance inside my head. *And* I had compiled an excellent list of strategic Emotional Global Warming questions for Hutch. *And* Jen was back with the team—even if she couldn't actually play on the team. *And* Clint—well, I'd leave Clint off my happy mental checklist for now.

The crowd was amazing. It was our usual fans and parents plus this cool mix of totally diverse UnPop fans, and I'm pretty sure that most of them had never been to a girls' soccer game before. They were looking around all wide-eyed like they were about to witness a school-sanctioned girls' mud-wrestling match.

And they were *loud*.

Cate had sent out a text urging all Uns to attend our soccer game, and announcing a temporary suspension of the silent protest as a sign of support for Miss UnPleasant's alter ego—me.

So the bleachers were really packed. Everyone was there—Mandy Mindel and Teddy Baedeker, Carreyn, Bentley Jones and Charlie Dodd, Svend, LG Wong and some of the other Library Girls, and even Ms. Whit and Mr. E. OMG. Miriam Goldfarb, esteemed (for an Un) editor of *The Fly*, and her cute-slash-weird boyfriend-slash-assistant-editor, Logan Adler, were directing the Dumbe Blondes like passionate conductors, leading an orchestra of crazy cheering lunatics. I watched them screaming their usual nonsensical cheers and waving big signs that said things like: "Field Goal!" "*Un*Coordinated & Proud!" "Go Lady Hornets! Kick Their Balls!" Hm . . . I suddenly remembered Miriam Goldfarb had been one of Miss UnPleasant's biggest fans. Maybe I could get her to help me with my Teen Scene article. *She* obviously didn't have writer's block.

Then Bean and Cate waved at me. They stood front and center, looking foxy in their black URM retro wear with the addition of platinum blond wigs. And they both wore these bright yellow beauty pageant sashes. Bean's said: *I'm an Athletic Supporter!* And Cate's said: *I Love Girls in Uniform!*

I couldn't help laughing. Wow, I have such cool weird friends. How did that happen?

Mom and Dad waved like they hadn't seen me in ten years. I tried to hide my smile. How could I have such weird, uncool parents? Oh yeah, Grambo—that explained a quarter of it. She looked so tiny and sweet and innocent standing next to my dad in her pearls and one of her many tasteful, plaid Chanel suits. Her red, flood-ready rain boots really brought the outfit together.

Meet The Lady Hornets' Athletic Supporters
Usual Fans: Herr Dunkelberger, our German teacher, who tells everyone he once played for the German National Team; half of the German class sucking up to Herr D.; people secretly crushing on players but pretending to have developed a sudden fascination for soccer; Coach Sykes's girlfriend; people too stoned to realize that they're watching girls playing soccer
Parents: Insanely devoted parents, insanely competitive parents, parents with nothing better to do but pretend to be insanely devoted or competitive, recently divorced parents looking for other recently divorced parents.
UnPops: Unpopular students and a few edgy popular students who were fans of Miss UnPleasant (me!).
The Dumbe Blondes: A student protest group fighting for the school arts budget and infamous for their dumb misspelled signs. (See name of the group.) Hm . . . Maybe we *do* actually go to the High School of Protesting Arts?

She pointed at me, then tapped her matching red purse a couple of times, smiling. We both knew what that meant, but I'm way too embarrassed to tell you. I smiled back and did a few quick quad stretches so I had a good reason to look away. I scanned the sidelines again.

Wow. Just about everyone was there . . . everyone but Clint Bedard. I wondered where he'd been today—for real. I knew he wasn't dead or dying. What I *didn't* know was if *we* were dead or dying. Or if we were *anything*. I kept hoping I'd hear his bike rumble into the parking lot, but I never did. Not like Clint was into Lady Hornets' soccer or anything . . . I just thought . . . Never mind. Maybe I really was just one of the many blips—or should I say lips—on his social radar.

Then it hit me like a soccer ball cleared at my head. Um, social radar? Mine—if I even had any—was totally off. Shouldn't I *know* which guy I was more into? And which guy was really into me? Wait. Maybe that was more like emotional radar . . . I'd have to think about this—but not until after the game.

Not to brag, but I was awesome! From the opening kickoff, I played like a rabid pit bull, slide-tackling girls twice my size, fearlessly going up for head balls, and passing sharp daisy-cutters right through the defenders. And the weirdest part, for the first quarter or so, every time I saw the ball, it looked just like Canfield's jack-o'-lantern head. That really helped my game.

About fifteen minutes into the first half, Amy cleared a ball down the sideline. I chased it, stripped it from this huge fullback, then did a little stutter-step head-fake, beat her to the right, dribbled past another defender, and chipped Canfield's head over the goalkeeper's outstretched hand and into the upper left corner of the net. Whoosh!

Yes! The crowd went nuts—and so did I!

I was doing my dorky little happy dance for real until (whoops!) I spotted Eric Sobel and—*Clint Bedard?*

They were standing next to each other at the far end of the field. What was Clint doing at my soccer game?! Nope, he didn't look sick at all. Actually, he looked pretty healthy. He had two fingers jammed in his mouth and was making this loud, shrieking wolf whistle. Eric held this super-big camera up to his face, taking pictures. I gave them a casual DL wave in between high-fives as I ran back to our half of the field. I couldn't help noticing that Eric was drenched in sweat. He must have just gotten out of the second half of practice to take photos for Yearbook. I watched him lift the bottom of his shirt to wipe the sweat off his face, and OMG—I ran smack into Amy, who was running to give me a hug.

I know I shouldn't say this, but . . . Eric Sobel had the most beautiful body I had ever seen—seen from a distance, that is. He looked like some perfect Greek statue. But the best thing about him? He had no idea how gorgelicious he was, which, of course, made him gorgelicious inside and out.

OMG. I totally missed the kick-off!

We continued to dominate through the end of the first half, but we couldn't finish and put the ball in the net. Ergh! Every time I was on the side of the field near our fans, I got don't-mess-with-me crazy from adrenaline, and the crowd kept roaring *Go Paisley!* I could hear Grambo screaming like some rowdy World Cup fan. I felt like I had Mountain Dew pulsing through my veins.

At halftime, we all jogged over to Coach Sykes on the sideline. It bummed me out to see Jen handing us all water bottles. Jen! Star-of-our-team, first-team, all-district-her-freshman-year Jen! But she acted like being our water girl was a huge honor, her reason for being on the planet. And that made me appreciate her even more. Coach Sykes delivered her usual pump-up-the-pressure halftime talk while we all ate orange wedges. Amy kept smiling at me with bright orange-rind teeth.

After Coach Sykes finished, Jen came over to me and lowered her head. "Pais, I think the stopper has a bad ankle or something. She hesitates going right." I nodded, listening carefully. "You have an awesome left foot. Body fake right, then go hard left, get by her and take the long shot. You'll have time. I guarantee it."

I nodded again. "Okay, I'll try. Thanks." I gave her a big hug.

"You stink," she said, pushing me off.

"You're just jealous you don't." We both laughed, but then it was kind of awkward and I looked away.

Yikes! Eric Sobel was speed-clicking a bunch of pictures of us. I tried to ignore him and looked away again. Bean and Cate waved at me from a distance. Clint was with them. He was wearing a long blond wig that he'd probably just swiped off some poor freshman's head. Wow. He even looked hot in drag. I swallowed. A little trickle of dread bubbled up. I pushed it back down and stomped on it with my soccer cleat.

"Nice goal, Pais!" Bean yelled. "You're such a stud out there."

Jen and I laughed.

Then Cate whistled at me and yelled, "I do *love* a girl in uniform!"

"Me too!" yelled Clint, trying to sound like a girl. He waved and blew me a kiss.

What a goober . . . a sexy, irresistible goober. Jen and I both laughed again. "Your Drama friends are funny," she said.

"Funnny weird or funny haha?"

"Both." Suddenly, Jen's eyes got all big. "Oh crap." She turned away.

I twisted to see what she was looking at. Hutch was walking right toward us, straight from the showers. They must have had a light practice before the big game tomorrow. I took a deep breath.

"*Hola, chicas,*" he said, doing the cool-guy head nod.

"What are you doing here?" Jen asked.

"Hello, Jen." Hutch was smiling, but it sounded a little like an insult. "Actually, Paisley requested the pleasure of my company at this game, right?" He looked at me. Then Jen looked at me. I nodded, kind of wishing I hadn't invited him. "And hey, hot sweaty chicks? Running around in shorts? All bumpin' into each other?" He nodded, grinning like a total perv. "Know what I'm sayin'?"

"You're disgusting," Jen snapped.

"You know you love me, Sweetland."

I rolled my eyes at him. "Jen," I whispered, dragging her away. "I got him here so I could *interview* him after the game."

"Oh," she whispered back, getting it.

"Yeah, I actually called him *handsome*." I made a gagging sound.

"Ew," she said, all grossed out. Then, playing along, she turned and waved. "Love you too, Hutch!"

"Hanover!" screeched Coach Sykes. "Get your gluteus maximus out there!"

"Gotta go."

I ran back onto the field, running sort of sideways so I could still watch what was going on between Hutch and Jen. I couldn't tell what they were saying. Jen seemed disturbed and walked away. He followed her over to the other end of our bench, laughing. Then the whistle blew, and the ball was in play.

By the time I had a chance to look back over at them, Hutch had moved away from Jen down the sideline and was standing, talking to Eric Sobel. They were really into some deep conversation, probably about football.

And then my head was totally back in the game—dribbling, passing, and crossing when I had the ball, moving to the open space when I didn't.

The other team came back hard after the half. It was pretty tight for a long time, and no one scored. I followed Jen's advice. Every chance I had to go one-on-one with the stopper, I did a flashy or sometimes totally lame fake, then went hard to my left. Jen was right. I did have time to get off a few shots. The first one went wide. Their goalkeeper made an amazing save on the second one, punching my shot over the crossbar.

And then the other team scored on a corner kick. Our keeper went up to make the save but the ball popped out of her hands and spilled to the ground. Then there was this fierce flurry of kicks as everyone went for it. The ball bounced around in the traffic, ricocheting off of players' shins. There were so many people mobbing the goal that our keeper couldn't even see the ball as it trickled slower than slow across the goal line.

Ergh! The other bench cheered and hooted like it was the most awesome goal in the world.

Whatever. It was a total garbage goal that never should have gone in. But in soccer—and in life—even garbage goals count.

The third time I got a shot off, the crowd exploded with cheers as the ball soared through the air. It *so* looked like it was going in—but then (boing!) it hit the crossbar. The crowd fell into one big group groan. But for some strange reason I was following my shot, which I know I'm always supposed to do but I usually don't. The ball had bounced out hard, but the sweeper didn't see it and spun around for a second. She didn't know whether to go for the ball or for me— and that was all I needed. I soft trapped the ball and did a little flick forward right past her. I was sprinting around her, about to blast another shot into the corner of the goal at point blank range, when she caught my foot and I went flying headfirst into the turf.

That was the bad news. The good news was it happened in the penalty box! The whistle blew just as I hit the ground and skidded across the torn-up grass on one palm, a shoulder, and the side of my face. Ouch.

I lay there for a few seconds wondering if I should lie there for a few *more* seconds and really milk it.

Some woman was yelling at the top of her lungs, "Foul! Foul! Red card!" I sat up. Oh God. It was Grambo again. Now you know how she got her name.

The ref ran over and made sure that I was okay, then walked over to the girl who had tripped me and gave her a yellow card. Go, Grambo! I smiled as I watched him write down her jersey number and then set up the ball at the top of the box for a penalty kick.

"Hanover!" Coach Sykes pointed at me. "You!"

I took the time to catch my breath, rub the mud off of my cheek, and enjoy the moment. "How much time?" I asked the ref.

He checked his watch. "Four minutes."

The score was 1–1. Pressure was on. I had to get the ball in the net. I walked up to the ball and repositioned it slightly. Some girl yelled, "Go Paisley! Field goal! Field goal!"

It was Mandy Mindel. She and Teddy Baedeker and Cate and Bean were jumping up and down and yelling like authentic crazy soccer fanatics. And then they suddenly disappeared. What the—?! A line of varsity football players filed in and stopped on the sideline next to Hutch. I couldn't believe it! The jocks stood there right in front of the UnPop cheering section, completely blocking their view!

What a bunch of shidiots! I watched the tops of the UnPop signs peeking over the heads of the line of big beefy football players. Ergh! I wanted to blast the ball at them and take them out, one by one.

And that's when it hit me. Those people didn't even notice the UnPop students—they didn't even *see* them.

I took a few steps back from the ball and stared down the goalkeeper. Hard and high to the corner? Or crisp and low? I decided on crisp and low, the *un*likely and more difficult choice. The crowd was crazy. It was like this wall of sound crashing down onto the field. Everyone was cheering and yelling my name, and all the varsity jocks were pointing and yelling, "You! You! You! You!" And then I had this endorphin-induced epiphany right there in front of everyone.

It was so obvious. My UnPop friends could maneuver *un*noticed under Hutch and his Pop friends' radar like stealth bombers. They could probably do anything without being seen—definitely deliver my locker stalker notes. And who knew what else?

I took three quick steps toward the ball and kicked it hard, right into the goalkeeper's hands. Ergh!

chapter nineteen
emotional global warming

We ended up tying the game, which wasn't what I had hoped for, obviously, but it was a lot better than losing. A bunch of people came up to me afterward and congratulated me on my goal and stuff.

"Wow, Paisley. Wow," Mandy said. "You're so . . . coordinated." Teddy Baedeker just stood next to her, nodding nonstop with this big grin on his face.

"Hey, sweet pea," my mom called out. "Great game." Mom and Dad gave me hugs while Grambo was off yelling at the ref. Oh, Grambo.

"Remember," Dad said, "you're still a winner even when you don't win."

"Thanks, Dad." I put my hand on his shoulder and picked the mud out of my cleats. "But I'd still rather be a winner who *actually* wins."

"Nice goal," said Eric, reaching in to give me a quick hug. "Perfect placement—really."

"Yeah," said Clint, still wearing his long blond wig. "*Red alert* in the penalty box. Field goal!" I don't think he had any idea what he was talking about, but he was definitely enthusiastic.

Grambo marched away from the ref, shaking her head. "What a mental mini marshmallow! I told him to man up and use the red card!"

I looked at Eric and Clint, a little mortified. "Thanks Grambo," I said.

"My pleasure!" And she meant it. Then she paused for a second, looking at me, then Eric, then Clint, then back at me. Was that a tiny smile?

Clearing her throat, Grambo snapped opened her red leather purse. She pulled out a crisp new one-dollar bill and handed it to me, pretending to be discreet. (See? I told you! Embarrassing!) I smiled, doing my best to look very appreciative.

Eric and Clint exchanged amused looks as she reached out and held my face in her tiny little hands. "I love you very much and I want to keep you motivated." Oh, Grambo. Then she kissed me on the cheek, gave me a knowing squint, and marched off across the field after my parents.

The three of us watched her stomping away in her red rubber boots, feeling a little awkward. Or maybe I was the only one feeling awkward.

"What a sweet lady," said Clint, flashing his lopsided grin. "If I give you a dollar, can I kiss you too?"

OMG. My cheeks gushed red-hot. I glanced at Eric. Thank God my face was already red from the game.

Eric snapped Clint with his towel. "Back off, man!" he said, laughing. Eric snapped him again, pretending to attack him. Clint hopped out of the way a few times, then grabbed the towel and pulled. They went at it and both ended up on the ground laughing. Oh wow. They really were friends. I smiled watching them, but inside, that weird trickle of ick bubbled up again.

"Hey Grambo!" Jen waved as she jogged over to us. Grambo turned, waving back, and kept on marching. "Pais, you were awesome," Jen gushed. "I so wish I'd been out there with you."

"Me too." I wiped my cheek on my shoulder, feeling kind of embarrassed. Fortunately, Amy ran up just then and gave me this full-body-slam hug, and the group broke apart. I was starting to cool down, feeling the wind against my sweaty uniform, so I walked over to get my sweats from the bench.

That was when Logan Adler, the assistant editor of *The Fly* and founder of the Dumbe Blondes—a guy I barely even knew—grabbed my shoulder. He glanced around suspiciously. Then he stared at me for a second, looking a little weird. I mean, weirder than usual.

"You're tight with Jen Sweetland, right?" he asked. I nodded. "Bummer. You should see this." He slowly passed me his phone.

My stomach dropped. It was out. The photo was out!

I looked around in a panic trying to look like I wasn't in a panic. Had everyone else gotten it too? But the crowd seemed normal, just doing the usual post-game stuff. Jen was talking with Amy and Bean and Eric. Clint had taken Eric's camera and was shooting pictures of Cate vamping around like some forties pinup. Parents were schmoozing with other parents. A bunch of Dumbe Blondes tried to kneel on top of each other, practicing their *Recommended Food Group Pyramid*.

Everything was still . . . normal. Maybe only a few people had gotten it. I let out a breath I hadn't realized I'd been holding and handed Logan back his phone. "Who sent this to you?" I asked.

"I dunno."

"Don't send it to anyone or show it to anyone else, okay?" He nodded. "Thanks," I said.

"No problem. Just thought you'd want to know." He gave me a

small salute, then ran over to the pyramid and tried to climb to the top over Miriam Goldfarb. Everyone fell down in a laughing heap.

I spotted Hutch standing with both hands jammed into the pockets of his letterman's jacket. Carreyn was casually talking to him—but her body language was saying so much more. Wait. I thought she was crushing on Charlie. I waved to Hutch. He nodded back but seemed distracted. I ran over to my duffel bag and quickly grabbed my notebook, a pen, and a frosting-stained brown paper bag.

I had an interview to do.

"Hey, Hutch?" I called. "Can we do it now?"

"Take a number, Hangover!" he yelled at me, laughing. His buddies and even Carreyn joined in.

I rolled my eyes. "Can we do the *interview* now?"

"Sorry. I'm boycotting you. You! YOU!" he said, pointing at me. Everyone in his crew laughed again.

I wanted to dump a huge cooler of ice water over his head. But then I got a better idea.

"Hey, how's your hand?" He looked right at me. And he wasn't laughing. "Are you gonna be able to play in the game tomorrow?" I called.

He started walking straight toward me. "So, what'd you want to ask me?" he said, sounding impatient and totally over it.

"Well, I have a lot of questions, actually." I held up my notebook. "Let's go over to the dugout."

"I don't know." He looked annoyed. "I've got stuff to do."

Then I held up the paper bag. "I have cupcakes?"

I quickly scanned my notes as we walked over to the baseball diamond. "So, um, what's your favorite color?" I asked, once we were settled on the bench.

"You're kidding, right?" He took a huge bite of cupcake.

"It's an *ice breaker*. I'm just trying to warm you up a little."

"Whatever. Yellow and black."

Not exactly *a* color, but yes, our school colors.

"That ad in *The Fly* today was harsh," he said out of the blue, wiping crumbs from his mouth.

"Tell me about it. Any idea who did it?" I asked.

"Nope."

"Really. So you weren't the source of that flattering, nose-worthy, I mean, newsworthy photo?"

"Hell no. I beat you. I don't need to smear you. Maybe you should check with my little buddy."

I scrutinized his face. Yeah, right. The little buddy he belted to a pole and pantsed? But he seemed to be telling the truth. It must've been Charlie. I was so going to kill him. I looked back to my notebook.

"What's your favorite food?"

He shoved the last bite of cupcake into his mouth. "Pizza. Cold. For breakfast."

"Ah," I said, nodding like this should have been obvious. I scanned my notes again. Then, trying to sound official, I asked, "How many people are in your household?"

"Which one?" he asked like it was no big deal. "My mom's or my dad's?" Oh, right. His parents were divorced.

We sat down on the home-team bench a few feet away from each other. It smelled like dusty dirt and Ben-Gay. I turned to him, lifting my feet to sit cross-legged on the bench. "Both."

"In my mom's, two. In my dad's four, not counting me. And trust me, over there, I don't count."

Hm . . . I made a quick note. *Dropped on head by divorcing parents.*

"Do you believe in God or some other higher power?"

"No." I drew a little box in my notebook and checked it. Then he added all cocky, "Why would I? I got the power."

Yeah, the power to lose friends and *un*-influence people. What a delusional thug.

But did I say that? Nope. I just smiled and nodded sweet as a Hutch's Honey. "What's your opinion . . ." I couldn't resist. It just popped into my head. "What's your opinion on videotaping people in the bathroom without their consent?" I looked at him like that was the most normal question in the world.

His nostrils flared. His face flooded with red-hot guilt, then clenched up all mad. "I didn't do that!" He punched his index finger at me in the air. "That was Delaney and Fiest. I had nothing to do with that." Tiny beads of sweat had broken out across his cheeks and nose.

"Okay. All right. I didn't ask if you *did* it." I scribbled. *Jumbo chip on shoulder.*

"Yeah, well I didn't."

"Sorry," I said, not because I meant it, just because I wanted to calm him down. Then I read him my next question. "If you, or someone you know, were wrongfully elected to public office, would you resign?" Oops.

He folded his arms. "I wasn't *wrongfully* elected, Hanover. I won! Deal with it."

"Jeez, Hutch. Take a relaxative. You can't blame me for asking. You've heard the rumors too."

"Yeah. Whatever. They're *rumors*."

I flipped through a couple pages of notes, hoping I hadn't already blown it. I decided to keep it light, and I offered him another cupcake.

"Who's your biggest hero?"

"My dad." I made another note. *Yawn. Typical father worshipper.*

"Who's your biggest enemy?"

He thought about it for few seconds, peeling the paper wrapper thingy off the cupcake. "My dad."

Huh. What did that mean? I scribbled *Dad: Hero and enemy???*

"If you could have dinner with anyone in the whole world, alive or dead, who would it be?"

He thought about it for a long time. Finally, he said, "My dad." He nodded, kinda half smiling, but he sounded sort of sad.

I couldn't believe he said that. I mean, it's not that I couldn't believe it—I just couldn't believe he said it to *me*. I studied his face. Should I act like it was no big deal . . . ? I pretended to read my notes. Finally, I was like, "Really?"

He nodded, then wiped frosting off his lip and licked his finger. For a second, he looked sweet, like a little kid. I could hardly believe it, but I almost felt sorry for Peter Hutchison.

Then he slapped his hands on the bench between us.

"Kidding, Hanover!" He laughed a little too hard and threw a crumpled-up cupcake wrapper at me.

Almost felt sorry for him.

"Got you, sucker! Okay, for real? Tiger Woods."

Yeah right. I was about to ask more about his dad, but I didn't want to spook him. I changed course.

"So, um . . . if you really liked someone, would you: A. Ask her out? B. Slip a note in her locker?"—I was totally afraid to take my eyes off the page—"or C. Send her funny texts until she liked you?"

"C," he said really quickly. "Send texts."

I scribbled *C. Send texts* like three times before I looked up at him. But he was staring at his sneakers, kicking around baseball dust. His shoes were worn and dirty, but they had these bright white new laces.

He tossed the other wrapper out into the infield. It didn't go very far. "What's this for again?" he asked, giving me a strange look.

"Science fair project," I said without skipping a beat. Okay, I thought, here goes. "I think *I'd* slip a note in the locker."

He stared at me like I had just spoken in Japanese. "Really? Why?"

"I don't know. It's sweet."

His face totally changed. It was the weirdest thing. Everything got kind of soft and warm—his cheeks, his eyes, his mouth. He smiled at me. *"Really."*

Uh-oh. Crap! I was being way too direct. "Maybe. I don't know." I backpedaled fast. "I'd probably just ask him out. Yeah. Definitely."

He smiled again and looked me hard in the eyes. Then he slowly leaned in toward my face. OMG! Was he . . . Was he going to *kiss* me? No. Ick. Gross. Abort. Abort! ABORT!

"You've got something . . ." He brushed his cheekbone underneath his eye with a finger. "I think it's an eyelash."

Oh man. What an idiot. Not the eyelash part—the kissing part. I frantically wiped my fingers under both eyes like my cheeks were covered with eyelashes.

"Yeah. You got it."

I tried to change the subject fast. "Hey, are you going to the dance?"

"Probably. Depends on how the game goes." He looked at his hand, which was still swollen and starting to bruise. "And don't say anything about the hand, okay? Bodie already feels really bad about it."

"Okay. Hey, I'll look for you at the dance. Maybe we can—" I stopped because he got a strange look on his face.

Suddenly, he reached into his jacket pocket, pulled out his phone, and flipped it open. I watched him staring at the screen, blinking slowly like he wasn't sure what he was seeing. Then he laughed nervously. And then he got pissed.

"What?" I asked. But I knew it was the sext.

"Damn it! I told them . . ." He exhaled hard and stood up. "I gotta go."

Told *who*? I wondered, watching him kicking up infield dust as he quickly walked away. I wrote "them" in my notebook and underlined it a few times. I watched Hutch walk back over toward the soccer fields, which were pretty much deserted by now.

And then I remembered—oh no! I stood up, my notebook sliding off my lap. I totally forgot about meeting Eric!

chapter twenty
suspect profiling

The minute I got home, I texted Amy and Jen. I had to tell Jen the sext was beginning to circulate.

Code Pnk?

I waited for a response. One Mississippi, two Mississippi, three Mississippi . . . Nothing.

I paced around for a bit, thinking. Okay, if I were Jen, I would want to know that the photo was out, that I—not Jen-me but me-me—had actually seen it. Definitely. But Jen wasn't me. Her life had been rough lately . . . maybe she'd rather *not* know. You know? So she could have a few more hours to be happy before her life was ruined? No. She'd want to know. Definitely.

My phone buzzed. Uh-oh. A text from Eric. Crap. I should have just called him and apologized. But I didn't know what to say! Again! Sorry I blew you off? I totally forgot? I was having such a good time with Hutch in the baseball dugout? Yeah, that sounded great.

Wher wur u?

I stared at the screen, chewing on my lower lip. I knew it was going to sound weird to Eric, but I also knew I had to tell him the truth, at least part of it.

Rlly sry! w/ Hutch.

???

I groaned. I took a deep breath and slowly released it through my teeth.

Its complic8d. Mor 2moro.

I stared at my phone waiting for his next text. Nothing. Then finally:

OK But u o me big! Paybacks @ the dance!

I smiled inside and out. That sounded like fun—whatever it meant. I got undressed really slowly, trying to imagine what it was going to be like dancing all night with Eric Sobel. OMG. How did I get so lucky? I dropped my sweats and stinky soccer uniform in a big pile next to my beanbag chair. I pulled on my favorite faded flannel robe and checked my phone *again*. Still nothing from Jen, so I jumped in the shower. I let the warm water run over my head and smiled, picturing everyone who had shown up for my game. Then, right in the middle of shampooing my hair, I suddenly had this warm, lightheaded, *life is great* moment. I breathed in the scent of my clementine zest shampoo and replayed the highlights of the game—yes, that included Eric and Clint—smiling as I rinsed out my hair. Eric. Clint. Eric and Clint. Eric or—

Aaah! Soap in my eye!!! I pushed my face into the water. It burned. It really burned!

What was I *doing?*

The water flowed over me for a while, clearing my head. Wait. What's the big deal? So I was going to the dance with Eric tomorrow, and going to the Walnut Festival with Clint on Saturday night. Big deal! Whatever. I wasn't exclusive with either of them. I wasn't even officially going out with either of them.

Them.

Them . . . ?

Who was the *them* that Hutch had told? And *what* had he told them? Whoever it was, it definitely wasn't just the one person who had taken that photo. But who else was involved in sending it around? Who would want to trash Jen's reputation? I couldn't think of anyone. Jen was a lot like Candy Esposito in that way—everyone liked her. Or so I thought.

After my shower, I snuggled into my soft, fleecy, totally unsexy pajamas and searched for my fuzzy slippers. Then I checked my phone again. Finally, I had a text back from Amy.

Not hom @ pza w/ fmly. Wht up?!!

Okay, no Code Pink. I texted back.

OK l8r t8r

So I plopped down at my desk and hunkered over my biology homework. My little desk lamp was the only light on in my room, which helped. I couldn't see anything else. I spent a long time drawing this giant cell using a bunch of colored pencils, then going over the cell lining with black ink. I got kind of neurotic about the details, but in the end, it looked cool. And then I diagrammed the Krebs Cycle—not nearly as fun.

I finished my homework and checked my phone. I flea-combed Dyson and checked my phone. I picked up all the clothes on the floor of my room, threw them behind my beanbag chair, and checked my phone *again*.

Nothing!

I sent Jen another text.

Nvr mind. OK 4 now.

Why rush to give her the bad news, I figured. If she didn't already know, at least she could have one more good night's sleep. And hey, there was nothing I could do now anyway, except stick to the plan: turning up the emotional heat on Hutch until I squeezed the truth out of him—and the Uns and I squeezed him out of office.

I opened my notebook and started scribbling ideas for more locker stalker notes. After some A-plus brainstorming with Dyson, I had a good list of juicy, semi-provocative notes sure to drive Hutch nuts with curiosity.

I rewrote the winners in robotic all caps so my handwriting couldn't be traced. I even used one of the "Fighting Hornets" black ballpoint pens that you can buy in the vending machine in our cafeteria, just to be safe. Hey, I'm not stupid—I watch *CSI*.

I LIKE SURPRISES—
AND YOU SURPRISE ME BIG-TIME

STRONG, SENSITIVE GUYS TURN ME ON

SAVE ME A SLOW DANCE

I THINK YOU'RE SUPER-SMEXY!
[SMART AND SEXY!]

I'M PSYCHIC. I SEE US TOGETHER.

Cheesy, yes! But as they say, know your audience.

I cut each note into a thin strip of paper and folded them in half for delivery tomorrow. Then I sat back and admired them, sort of. I mean, I wanted to. But they all looked so small and insignificant. I kept stacking and restacking the little pieces of paper. How could these notes smack down that icky photo?

I turned the sexted photo over and over again in my mind, trying to come up with clues. Jen's boob loomed large. Even if *nothing* happened between her and Hutch, this was so bad. Everybody in school—and probably half the faculty and *all* the parents—would be talking about Jen and her boob.

I stood up and paced around my dark room. I wanted to do something right now. What? What?! WHAT?

Oh! I got an idea. I grabbed my laptop, sunk down into my beanbag chair, and signed in to Facebook. No new friend requests or juicy wall posts. Ugh. Sometimes I hated Facebook. I went to Hutch's profile.

He friended me a while back, and of course, I confirmed and immediately put him on my Frenemy list. But I'd never really looked at his profile. It was the usual stuff on his Wall. Dumb-ass comments from other football players on (drunken) party pix and fans of blah, blah, blah. But then I clicked on his photos and started snooping through his albums. Football action shots. Basketball action shots. Hoping-for-action party shots. And then I found something really interesting. Pictures of his family. They were in two albums, one labeled "Old Family" and the other "New Family." Huh.

I clicked on "Old Family" first. It was a bunch of cute, back-in-the day shots of little Hutch with his parents—blowing out candles on a birthday cake, wearing super-baggy jeans and sunglasses pretending to be a rock star, doing cannonballs with his dad into a pool, Hutch in a hammock with his mom and a yellow Lab that was bigger than he was, standing on his dad's shoulders trying to dunk a basketball.

There was this one picture I couldn't stop looking at. It was black-and-white, and Hutch was probably around nine or ten, just staring right into the camera, not smiling, just sitting there. His eyes were sweet and trusting. He was really cute with this mop of curly blond hair, and he hadn't quite grown into his front teeth yet. It was hard to believe that *this* had turned into the Hutch I knew.

Then I went to "New Family." There were only a few photos. One was like a Christmas-card type shot of Hutch's dad with, I guess, his new wife, who was really pretty and looked a lot younger, and two super-cute little kids. There was a picture of Hutch arm-wrestling with his dad, also a really big guy. And then there was a pretty recent shot of them on a vacation, I think. All of them had big smiles on their faces and seemed really happy. Well . . . I looked more carefully—except maybe for Hutch. He was smiling too, but it was all wrong. He looked like this stiff cardboard version of himself.

I clicked back on the black-and-white photo of little Hutch and stared at it, thinking. Little Hutch was still in there. I knew it. I'd seen it for a second when we were talking after the game. His ten-year-old self was there, just like stuck in time or something. I leaned back in my beanbag chair feeling a little . . . I don't know. I had planned to post a message on his Wall, but then I had another idea.

Cute pic. Were you ever really so sweet?

I deliberately phrased it as a question, so he'd be more likely to comment back. Then I double- and triple-checked my spelling and hit COMMENT on that black-and-white photo.

I wondered if a part of Jen would get stuck because of her parents' divorce. Maybe she already had. I went to her Facebook page. I saw her latest profile picture and felt this pinch of sadness. It was Jen in Bodie's arms, laughing. That probably wouldn't be up for much longer.

A hot surge of guilt rippled through me. I leaned back nervously, feeling totally uncertain all of a sudden. Was I doing the right thing by not telling Jen the sext was out? Maybe I should call her right away? Maybe I was completely delusional to think that I could protect her from it. No. This was ridiculous. It was late. Let her sleep.

Dyson jumped up and curled beside me on the beanbag chair.

I scratched his head and chin as I clicked through a bunch of Jen's photos—soccer pix from last year, pictures of us posing beside the pool at her old house, skiing with her family before her parents split up, Halloween shots of the four of us dressed up like glam beauty pageant contestants representing the stages of grief. I smiled. Carreyn's sash said *Denial*. Mine said *Guilt*. Amy was *Anger & Bargaining*. And Jen proudly wore the *Acceptance* sash.

It was all Jen's idea—maybe she's psychic too. We wore them to school that day and then we went out trick-or-treating that night just for kicks. Parents really laughed. Oh man, did we get a lot of candy! And only a couple bad looks from adults who thought we were way too old to beg for candy.

I clicked around through some other albums. Ugh! Pictures from that skanky pool party. I sat up straight and examined them closely, trying to see who else might have been there around the time of Jen's topless hot tub photo. I looked for suspicious-looking *thems*. There was one of Bodie and Jen with Carreyn leaning in, mugging for the camera, one of Jen and Candy Esposito making goofy faces, a shot of Eric holding Candy in his arms, about to throw her into the pool. Ergh! I looked at that one for a while before finally tearing my eyes away. And a couple giggly shots of Carreyn in the hot tub sitting on a few guys' laps—Bobby Fiest, Craig Delaney, and, yep, Peter Hutchison.

I looked at the photo again.

Wait. That was weird. I closed my eyes and stared at a poster-sized image of the sext photo on the wall of my headspace, then I looked back at the photo of Carreyn and the guys in the hot tub. Hm . . . The sext photo looked really similar. I was pretty sure the camera angle was the same, and the lighting seemed pretty much the same, and . . . I leaned back and closed my eyes again.

This was Jen's Facebook page. These were *Jen's* photos taken with *Jen's* phone. Could the sext photo have been taken with Jen's phone too? I opened my eyes and rubbed my fingers between my lip and nose, thinking. OMG. If it was, then there would be a record of it in Jen's phone—*and* a record of whose phone it was sent to.

(Sorry—I really hate ending a sentence with a preposition, and I really, *really* hate ending a chapter with a preposition. But, hey, sometimes life is messy.)

chapter twenty-one
UNconditional love

The next morning in carpool hell, a few kids were talking about yesterday's silent protest—the ones who didn't have duct tape over their mouths, that is. Wow. I hoped none of them were super-congested. I kept my mouth shut in a show of solidarity and leaned against the side of the minivan with my eyes closed in a show of I'm tiredness.

And then my phone started vibrating. I pulled it out of my bag. It was a text from . . . *unknown caller.* I covered the screen with my hand to make sure no one else could see and cringed. Yep. It was the sext. I studied the photo for a few seconds. My first thought: Hutch is such a pig. My second thought: Yep, it looks exactly the same as the other photos taken with Jen's phone. Even the, whatever you call it—pixel somethings—looked the same.

I immediately started texting.

First, Amy.

I got the sext. Did u?

She texted me right back.

No! ☹ I so losr.

I texted her back.

LOL But NOT fny!

Then I texted Eric. I definitely wanted to explain at least a little

more about Hutch and smooth things out before the dance. And
maybe he'd heard something about the sext.

Listng Spt @ lunch?

He texted right back.

Cant. Make-up Bio tst.

Hm. Was that the truth? Or was it code for he's secretly pissed at
me for not meeting him at the listening spot after the game? Ergh!
I guess I'd find out at the dance tonight.

Charlie Dodd got into the van with this big bandage on his
face—it looked like a nose saddle—and he had two black eyes in
the works. Ouch. If I had looked like that, I would have totally
stayed home. He sat behind me and kept trying to read my texts
over my shoulder. So I turned sideways and held one hand over my
phone. Sure, I felt sorry for him, but not *that* sorry.

Next, I sent texts to five of my favorite Uns—Cate, Bean, Mandy
Mindel, Teddy Baedeker, and LG Wong. LG was still unconvinced
that protesting would change anything at our school. But she
couldn't resist the opportunity to inflict psychological torture on
Canfield and Peter Hutchison. I knew she'd want in.

Flgpol @ break. Tell no 1.

As I walked up the main hall, I glanced at Mr. Canfield's official
framed photo next to his office and laughed. Someone had changed
his title—inside the frame—from Vice Principal to *Principal of Vice*.
Gee. Who in the world could've done such a thing? I wondered
what else Cate had in the works.

Heading up to sophomore hall, I passed more and more people
with silver and black duct tape over their mouths. OMG. *Trés* cool!
LG Wong nodded slyly as I walked by her. She was wearing a black
beret and this bitchin' vintage black leather jacket, belted. Nice! In and
in fashion. She flashed me a sign she had written on binder paper:

NO TAPE—BUT NOT TALKING!

(I HAVE SENSITIVE SKIN.)

I nodded back with approval. Then I spotted Split Ends, walking toward me with a few Future *Women's* Prison Inmates of America. She smiled as best she could behind clear packing tape and waved enthusiastically. OMG. Wow. It was official then. Silent Protest. Day Two.

And then I noticed something even more bizarre. BS1 and BS2 were standing in the middle of junior lawn talking to . . . Carreyn? I slowed to watch them. Then I stopped behind a pole and casually hid. Well, as much as you can hide behind a four-inch pole. Carreyn was all animated and chatty like she was telling some amazing story. Why was Carreyn even talking to them? Or more to the point, why were *they* talking to *Carreyn*? BS1 whispered something, and they all burst into hysterics like they were BFFs. Maybe it was some secret hair and makeup club?

Jen ran up behind me, smacking me in the butt. She had a huge grin on her face.

"Hey, sorry. I didn't see your texts until this morning." We kept walking toward sophomore hall. "I was at Bodie's last night, *studying.*" She said it in a way that made me wonder what exactly they'd been studying. "So, Code Pink. What happened?"

Um? Uh-oh. Should I tell her? Or protect her from the inevitable crush of pain and humiliation? She seemed so happy. I just didn't have the heart to tell her. "Oh, no big. Grambo joined Facebook and

SIDEBRA

Carreyn's mom, Brandi, owns this salon in town called *Brandilocks*. They mostly do hair, but they also have this Beauty Bar with tons of makeup and other mysterious beauty treatments and tortures. (Mom has warned me to stay far from The Bar. It's a bad habit.) Carreyn works there as a receptionist in the summers and has always had her birthday parties there too. My favorite was the year we got to do hair-scare makeovers. It was hilario! (Actually, I think that might have been where *hilario* and *scario* were born.) Anyway, girls are always hitting Carreyn up for discounts on stuff. She acts like it's totally annoying. But I know she loves it.

PS: Don't ever call Brandi a hairstylist. She's a *Personal Improvement Entrepreneur.*

started poking me and all my guy friends. I kinda freaked out."

Jen laughed. "I love Grambo. I'm totally gonna friend her." A pack of duct-taped Un protesters glided past us silently. Jen dropped her voice. "Wait. Should we be talking?"

I nodded. "Just whisper. Oh, man!" I stopped and pointed toward my locker up ahead. From way down the hall, I could see it was plastered with strips of silver tape that said in huge letters, *UnKind, UnInformed, UnPleasant Hill, UnDatable!*

I sighed. What shidiots, stealing the duct tape idea. At least they didn't write in permanent marker on my locker.

Jen shook her head, totally disgusted. "God, I hate these people," she whispered. "What's their problem?"

Neither of us said a word as we walked down the hall to our lockers and silently started pulling off the tape.

"Everything okay with Bodie?" I casually whispered, wadding up *UnDatable* into a tight sticky lump.

"Yeah, great. I mean, he's nervous about the game tonight, but that's normal."

"Did he say anything about Hutch's hand?" I asked.

She thought about it for a second, pulling the strip of *UnKind* off my locker. "Nope."

Hm . . . I was hoping for at least a clue from Bodie. "Hey, can I see your phone?"

"Why?"

"Well, I have an idea . . . actually, more like a hunch." She stared me down. "About that photo?" I whispered. "I could be wrong— totally wrong—but . . . can I see your phone?"

She reluctantly handed it over.

I went into her text messages, then clicked SENT MESSAGES, and started scrolling back, way back. Jeez, Jen had sent a ton of texts in the last month or so—and not a lot to me.

I kept scrolling until I caught sight of Amy out of the corner of my eye. She jogged up to us with duct tape over her mouth, then stopped and ripped the tape off.

"Ow!" She rubbed her finger back and forth over her upper lip, then looked at the sticky side of the tape in her hand. "Ew. I gotta start waxing."

"Silence please," I whispered, giving her the don't-say-another-word face.

She looked at Jen, then me, and nodded.

The warning bell for homeroom rang. Crap.

"Jen, can I keep this till break?" I asked.

"Yeah, uh . . . okay." She sounded a little bewildered. "So, see you guys for our sticky bun?"

I nodded, heading off to homeroom, dragging Amy with me.

"Don't say anything to her about the sext yet. Okay? I told her that Code Pink was Grambo gone wild on Facebook."

Amy almost smiled. Almost. But this was serious. "Okay," she whispered, still rubbing her upper lip.

In homeroom, Mrs. Hollet basically ignored the silent protesters—about half of the students in her class. So I listened to her droning lecture with one deaf ear as I scrolled through all of Jen's sent texts under my desk. Yes! I got to the date of the party—Labor Day.

I scrolled and scrolled. I was getting so close! And then—ow!

The arthritic claw of death chomped down on my shoulder, followed by a wave of hoots and laughs all around me.

Crap!

Mrs. Hollet stood behind me with her hands on her bony hips, sneering. "Do you think you're special, Miss Hanover? You're not." She reached out her hand. I sighed, putting Jen's phone in her shriveled, wrinkly palm. "You can pick this up at the end of the day."

Jen was so going to kill me. "But . . . but it's . . . it's not my phone," I sputtered.

"Oh, it's not? Really? Then where is yours?"

I dug frantically through my bag on the floor, pulling my phone out like a prize.

She snatched it from my hand. "Thank you. I'll take this one too. See you at three oh five."

When the muffled and unmuffled laughter had died down, I groaned, sliding low in my chair, feeling like the total loser I was. If only I could get *everyone's* phone confiscated—that would save Jen's reputation.

I was sitting there feeling sorry for myself, when Canfield's voice started droning over the intercom. Oh Great. Just what I needed.

"Good morning, people."

. . . *crackle* . . . *crackle* . . .

Canfield cleared his throat a few times. *"I hope we're all feeling Pleasant Hill High this morning!"* Huh. Really? A bunch of people laughed. *"This is Glen Canfield coming to you live from the main office."* That's weird. He never used his first name. *"I just wanted to apologize to all the sophomore students whose votes were not counted."* My mouth dropped open. *"I feel like such a boob . . . a total boob."*

OMG. OMG! It was Clint! I was laughing until I noticed a blur of polyester out the window. Uh-oh. Canfield was racing down the hall, doing his best waddle-sprint for the main office. Oh no. Clint, get out of there!

Mrs. Hollet looked very confused, like she was hearing voices and should probably retire immediately.

. . . *crackle* . . . *crackle* . . .

"The people have spoken, and I have listened. We will be scheduling another vote for sophomore class president next week. Stay tuned—and stay clean!"

Homeroom erupted with voices all talking over one another.

about half of the other people in class all had duct tape over their mouths. Charlie's piece of tape had a white straw sticking out of it. He looked like some sort of industrial plastic alien. I guess it was the only way he could be in on the protest and still breathe. And when had Charlie gotten in on the Un protest? My psychic powers told me that *pole* was strangely persuasive.

I scanned the room again. Where was Clint? He wouldn't miss school two days in a row, would he?

Bean laid a big tape-to-tape smacker on Svend. He blushed. Then she did the same to Cate, who pretended to swoon lovingly. They both giggled behind their tape. Teddy tried to do it to Mandy, but she pulled away, all pink-cheeked. Then Mandy caught my eye and gave me this subtle finger across the nose signal. I guess that meant she'd gotten my text and was in.

Cate kept her distance from me, probably because that was some strict French underground resistance movement rule. I gave her my nice-prank face. But she shrugged, pretending to be all innocent. Then she tapped her wrist with her finger, winked, and nodded once. Cate was in on the meeting too.

I was contemplating whether or not it was even worth stuffing Hutch's locker with notes when someone came up behind me, wrapped his arms around my stomach, and whispered in my ear, *"Vive la résistance, baby!"*

I got the chills and quickly turned around, trying not to blush. "Hi. Wow." Clint had on a tight black turtleneck and black beret pulled down on one side. *"Vive . . .* is right," I stammered trying to keep it down. "Oh. My. God. That was . . . You were so . . ."

He put his index finger up to my lips and smiled. Oh right. I nodded.

Then he pulled something off my back. Tape. He held it up for me to see. *UNdigested Barf.* That's why those seniors were laugh-

The silent protesters around me started pulling off their tape and cheering. It was awesome. You could even hear cheers coming from other classrooms.

"We did it!"

"It worked!"

"Recount! *We* count!"

Everyone looked a little freaked, like they couldn't quite believe it, but totally excited too. I just smiled and kept my mouth shut.

The cheering had barely died down when the intercom started crackling again.

"This is Mr. Canfield, your vice principal. Please disregard the previous announcement. I seem to have had a technical malfunction . . . er . . . rather the intercom seems to have had a technical malfunction. Thank you."

Everyone groaned. The protesters slapped their duct tape back over their mouths. I sighed. Oh well, it was fun for a minute. Mrs. Hollet was the only one in the room who looked relieved.

On my way to Hutch's locker after class, I noticed that the halls were much quieter than usual. Even people who weren't taped shut were keeping it down in a show of *Un* solidarity.

Bentley Jones started walking along next to me. I nodded at her. She handed me a note.

> The Boycott Paisley ad was paid for with a personal check—a check with pink pandas on it. The name on the check: Candy Esposito.

I stopped. "No way!" Bentley nodded, looking disappointed. "Are you sure?"

Bentley nodded again.

Bean glided past us, putting her finger up to her taped mouth.

Oh Bean. She had drawn a big smiley face on her piece of tape.

"How did you find out? Bodie? What did he say?" She shook her head. "Then how do you know?"

Bentley's eyes got all big, and her nostrils flared. She carefully peeled back one end of her tape. "I *asked* them"—she whispered out of the corner of her mouth—"the editors, of *The Fly*."

Oh. That was all? I looked at the note again. I couldn't believe it. Candy Esposito? But the other morning she said she liked me, right to my face. What a two-faced . . . I just shook my head.

"Still planning on thanking them?" Bentley whispered.

I could barely find the energy to shrug lamely. "Thanks, Bentley."

She nodded. Then she leaned forward and whispered, "I might write about this incident for my Teen Scene article. If I do, would you be willing to sign a waiver?"

Uh, Teen Scene? Crap. I'd totally forgotten. "Sure. I guess." I nodded, not at all sure what a waiver waives. So Bentley Jones was competing for the student journalist job too. Great.

"Thanks," she whispered, and walked off.

I'd worry about Teen Scene later. Right now I had to process my latest social crisis. Candy Esposito? I scratched behind one ear, then ran my fingers through my hair. Candy Esposito *hates* me? I looked up and sighed. Oh, perfect.

Hutch was bounding toward me with a few of his buddies, including Eric Sobel. All of them—except Eric—were wearing their letterman's jackets, as usual, in their unique expression of individuality. I didn't feel like talking to Hutch anymore—or talking to anyone. The *supposedly* nicest and most popular girl in school hated me so much, she had to advertise it? I wanted to crawl inside my bag and curl up in a ball for the rest of the year.

I tried to hide behind a group of softball players lumbering down the hall and then duck into the library, but it was too late.

"Hey Hamburger," Hutch said really loud. "Nice nos
The Fly!" The other jocks snickered and jeered as if it was
yesterday's news. I glanced over at Eric, planning to smi
was staring at the ground. Then the other guys peppered
nasty comments and questions in between the rowdy laugh

"How's that *Un* thing working for you, Hanover?"

"Totally UnDatable. I could've told you that," said Cra
ney, smirking.

"UnDatable? More like UnTouchable," Bobby Fiest chin

I tried to say something snappy and insulting back, but th
this gross sour taste holding my mouth shut.

"Hamburger, were you cyber-stalking me last night?"
asked as the laughter died down.

I sighed—I was doing *a lot* of sighing that day. At least it un
my mouth. "No."

"Think you were. I read your comment. You crushin' on
He poked me in the arm and laughed along with a few other va
jerks. I looked at Eric again. He wasn't laughing. He had this p
zled look on his face. Then Hutch patted me on the back. "W
congratulations on another big day of loser protesting!"

I rolled my eyes. This was hopeless. I was starting to have seric
doubts about my brilliant plan. No amount of niceness or emotion
warming would ever get through to Hutch. Actually, it seemed t
be turning him into a bigger jerk than ever. I didn't say anything.
walked off, feeling like I was wearing Charlie Dodd's backpack.

On the way to Drama, a bunch of seniors passed by, suddenly all
talking and laughing at the top of their lungs. I was sure they were
all laughing and pointing at me. "It's not about *me!*" I shouted at no
one in particular. That just made them laugh harder.

Drama was as quiet as the library's supposed to be. You could
only hear a few whispers. Cate and Bean and Teddy and Svend and

ing at me. I sighed—again. Hutch! God, *all* of him was only ten years old! My locker stalker notes were *so* worth it! So what if they didn't make him open up? They would make him suffer trying to figure it out—and boy did he deserve to suffer. I wadded up the piece of tape, crushing it tight into a little ball, imagining I was crushing Hutch's head. Then Clint gave me another hug, and I got all distracted.

"Vive l'amour," Clint whispered with a nice French accent, followed by a naughty smirk. Okay, I didn't speak French, but even *I* could figure that one out. I totally blushed hot pink.

"Yeah, me too," I blurted through a little snort-laugh. OMG. Did I just say that out loud—with a *snort*? OMG! I totally did! But Clint didn't seem to mind. He just smiled at me.

Yikes! I wanted to kiss him right there in front of everyone. I looked around feeling a little self-conscious. Cate was staring at us with one eyebrow raised and this knowing little duct-taped smirk. Charlie's industrial plastic alien eyes were huge, like he had never before seen PDA among earthlings.

So it seemed like a good idea to change the subject fast. "Um . . . so, thanks for coming to my game."

He flashed his flirty grin. "My pleasure. Who knew you were such a scoring threat."

I tried not to smile, but it was hopeless. I still wondered if he'd been avoiding me, though. I couldn't shake it off. And who was the girl he'd been with in the parking lot? I wasn't about to let on that I saw. "I didn't see you all day yesterday. Were you sick . . . or something?"

"No more than usual." Clint smiled. "Just setting up some *action* for a . . . for Saturday night."

Saturday night? Wait. What? What about our date?! My heart folded up tight like a little origami. I swallowed hard, trying not to look too disappointed.

"Wait. You have . . . you have plans for Saturday night?" I asked casually, hoping I had misunderstood.

He nodded, raising his eyebrows seductively. "Oh yeah. Big plans." Then he leaned in close and whispered, "A blow-out house party." He laughed mischievously, like he was invited to some super-cool, super-secret party and I wasn't.

A house party? I looked at him for a second, waiting. Then I looked away. I could feel my head getting hotter and hotter. OMG. What a total jerk. He's going to a party! And not even inviting me! Had he totally forgotten about our date? Had he already lost interest because I was such a friggin' goody-goody? Or did he just get a better offer? From like that trashy lip gloss girl in the parking lot? Ergh!

I considered feeling totally humiliated but instead I felt totally pissed—and no way was I going to let on. So I did my best imitation of couldn't-care-less. "Well, have fun at the party with your . . . your like girlfriend of the week," I blurted. "I have big plans for Saturday night too."

He looked at me a little funny. "Good. Glad to hear it." Then he smiled and nodded all cocky. "Girlfriend of the week. I like the way that sounds."

Ergh! What a pig! But before I could say anything else, Mr. Eggertson walked out into the center of the room, clapping his hands. "Good morning, people!" He gazed around at everyone with this amused look on his face. "Something tells me that today would be a brilliant day to work on communicating with our bodies." He gestured grandly. "The *instrument*."

There were muffled laughs.

"Just nod if you agree." Everyone nodded. I just stood there, wanting to cry.

chapter twenty-two
secret agents of change

At the end of Drama I bolted right out of class and ran
back to sophomore hall, looking for Jen. I had to break the news to
her about her phone. And I didn't want to look at Clint for another
second. What was *wrong* with him? Jen was sitting on our bench
whispering to Amy, who had a strip of tape back over her mouth.

"Hey, you guys," I whispered, wearing, I'm sure, my I'm-so-guilty
face. "Jen, I have some really bad news."

She looked at me, biting the inside of her lip. Then she slumped
back against a pole. "Oh no."

"No, no, no!" I grabbed her shoulders. "It's not that," I kinda-
sorta lied, well not really, I mean, that wasn't the bad news I was talking about. "I got your phone confiscated till the end of the day."

"Paisley!"

"I know. Sorry." Jen looked really mad, so I quickly changed the
subject. "Hey, um, guess who did that nasty ad in *The Fly*?"

They looked at me like *well?*

"Candy Esposito."

"What?!" Jen sat up. "She wouldn't do that. No way!"

Amy jumped to her feet, throwing her hands in the air, like
what? Then she made the hand signal for *movie*, like we were playing charades.

Jen shook her head at Amy. "You've got to be kidding."

"Movie," I said quietly. "One word."

Amy's eyes got huge, like her head was going to explode.

"Mad," I said. "Pissed."

"Angry. Furious. Furious George!" Jen shouted, all excited.

Amy rolled her eyes and started over. She threw down her hands, twisted up her eyebrows, and got all pink in the face.

"Pissed. Angry. Rage," I whispered. "Raging Bull!"

Amy put her hands on her hips, dropped her head, and frowned at me.

"Sorry." I shrugged.

Then she did it all again, only this time she put her hand to her mouth and then tossed it out.

"Barf! Vomit!" Jen was really getting into it. "Puke! Puke in a purse!"

LG Wong walked by us and whispered, "*Scream*. You know, the movie?" without even slowing down. She pointed with her head down the hall. Oh right. I had to get out to the front lawn for my *tell no 1* meeting.

Amy jumped up and down, pointing to her nose. Duh. Well, yeah. I guess it *is* hard to scream with tape over your mouth. Jen and I just looked at each other like Amy was crazy because, well, she was.

"I can't believe Candy would do that. Are you sure?" Jen asked.

"Bentley Jones told me the ad was paid for with a personal check from Candy Esposito."

Jen exhaled. "Wow."

"I know."

Amy jumped up and folded both hands open, the charades sign for *book*.

"Nope. Sorry." I held up one hand. "Gotta go. I'm on a mission."

I took a few steps down the hall. "Hi you guys!" Carreyn called, fast walking toward us and carrying a sticky bun like it was her beloved baby. Her f-i-t-s 'fro had been tamed into cute little piglet tails. "Pais, don't go," she gushed. I stopped. "This is *so* beautio. The four of us sticky-bunning together again!" Carreyn sat down on our bench and carefully sawed her baby into four equal quarters with a plastic knife.

Amy eagerly held out her hands, and Carreyn plopped a gooey quarter into one palm. Amy stared at it, looking frustrated all of a sudden, realizing her mouth was taped shut.

"Jen?" asked Carreyn, holding out another quarter.

"No thanks."

"What's wrong?" Carreyn sounded genuinely concerned.

"Nothing's wrong!" Jen snapped.

"Okay, sorry." Carreyn tugged on one of her piglet tails, looking from Jen to me to Amy and back to Jen. "Is everything okay with Bodie? Do you want to talk?"

Jen shot her a look and shook her head, nervously twisting her white-blond hair. "Everything's fine. I'm fine. Really. Thanks."

The reason for last night's aborted Code Pink filled my head-space. I glanced at Amy, who was now wearing her tape like a giant mustache, slipping bits of sticky bun under it into her mouth.

"Well, if you ever do"—Carreyn stuffed a big piece of sugary, squishy dough into her mouth and kept talking—"I'm here for you."

"We all are," I added, sticky-bun-sweet, giving Jen a huge squeeze-hug till she smiled.

"Pais?" Carreyn offered me a quarter of sticky bun.

"Sorry. But I really have to go." I ran off down the hall, glad to have something more important to do than sweet talk with Carreyn. When I got out to the front lawn, I could see my handpicked stealth bombers sitting around in a lopsided circle under the flagpole.

"Hey guys," I whispered, sitting down next to them. "Thanks

for coming." The tape was off. All of them, except LG, had pink irritated skin around their mouths. I pulled my folded-up locker stalker notes from my pocket and handed one to each of them. "Okay, your mission: The note in your hand must be slipped into Peter Hutchison's locker—today. It's locker number two thirty-seven. And *no one* can see you do it."

They all looked at me weirdly, then down at their notes.

Mandy read her note and blushed.

LG Wong opened hers and read it out loud. "I think you're *smexy*—smart *and* sexy?" She looked at me with this disgusted face. "Hanover, are you insane?"

"Yeah, well . . . I know this might seem a little strange. But I need you to trust me."

Teddy read his note out loud too. "Save me a slow dance?" He broke into nervous giggles. "Hutch would never slow dance with me."

"Teddy, no," I said. "It's not *you* saying this to Hutch. I am. You're just delivering the message to him. Okay? No one will know it's you." He nodded, looking extremely relieved.

Cate opened her note and rolled her eyes. Yep. She got the *Strong, Sensitive Guy* note. She held it up for all of us to read. Everyone leaned in, then quickly recoiled, releasing variations of "Ew!" "Gross!" and "That's disgusting!"

I just smiled.

"Pais, is this about the boycott-you ad?" Bean asked. "'Cause I don't think anonymous locker notes are much of a payback."

"No, it's . . . It's not that." I pulled out a few pieces of grass in front of me. "Hutch wasn't behind that ad. This is for something else."

"That ad was so mean," said Mandy, scratching her nose. "If someone had done that to me, I would've died."

"And friggin' cowardly," added LG. "When you find out who did it, Hanover, you have to retaliate."

I sighed, trying to exhale my feeling of dread. How does anyone retaliate against Candy Esposito, the most popular, powerful, perfect person in school?

"We're going to, right?" Cate asked me, raising her eyebrows and sounding very motivated. "I've got *good* ideas. And by good, I mean bad."

"I just found out." I slumped forward and looked around the group before turning back to my blade of grass. "It was Candy Esposito's ad."

Bean gasped, all bug-eyed.

"Oh no," whispered Mandy, covering her mouth.

"I love her." Teddy sounded a little dreamy. "She's so nice to me and so pretty." Mandy made a snorting sound.

"Bummer, man." LG made this scary face. "Scratch that retaliation plan. You're doomed if Candy Esposito hates you. Trickle-down hate-onomics, Hanover. Everyone will hate you soon."

"Thanks for your support, LG."

Cate sat up straight, looking indignant. "No way! Even Candy Esposito can't get away with crap like that."

We all sat there silently tugging at the grass in front of us. I could hear the flag above snapping in the cool wind. I'd be willing to bet that all of us were thinking exactly the same thing—Candy Esposito could get away with anything.

"Well, I've already decided, I'm not gonna do anything," I said to the ground. "What's the point?"

Nobody said anything for a few seconds.

"Are you sure?" Mandy asked. She sounded kind of disappointed. "Miss UnPleasant would definitely do something."

I looked at Cate, who was nodding with her whole upper body. Ugh. The last thing I wanted to do was think about the difference between bad-ass Miss UnPleasant and the real me.

Fortunately the warning bell rang just then. I popped up onto my knees. "Okay *Un*Visible secret agents, we need to move fast. All the notes have to get into Hutch's locker by the end of school today. Locker two thirty-seven. Got it?"

They all nodded.

"Wait. If this isn't about that ad, then . . ." Cate wrinkled her nose. "What *is* this about?"

"It's . . . it's complicated. Basically, I'm trying to get Hutch to think I like him so he'll tell me something . . . Something that's . . . kinda private."

Cate raised one eyebrow, looking impressed by my devious strategy. Mandy just looked deeply concerned for my mental health.

"Hey, Hanover." LG waved her note at me. "What if Hutch starts to think that you really *do* like him? Have you thought of that? I mean, how far are you willing to go to get him to talk?"

I actually hadn't thought of that. I looked at Bean and Cate for backup, but they both had these equally grossed-out expressions on their faces. Well crap. How far *was* I willing to go?

chapter twenty-three
holy fashion icon!

That disturbing question was still icking me out as I was getting ready for the dance that night. Oh God. What if Hutch actually asked me to dance? Gross. What if he asked me to *slow* dance! Ew. Silent library scream! What if he . . . No, it was too disgusting. Just the thought of it made me want to puke in a purse.

Wait. But what if he didn't even realize that the notes were from me? Was that possible? No. He had to know, right? I mean, I dropped a hint the size of the bronze hornet on him while we were talking in the dugout. He knew. I was sure he knew. But I wasn't sure what he was going to do about it. Was he still secretly crushing on me? Was that possible after our little public smackdown over the election? I sure hoped so. I mean, don't get me wrong—only so I could get him to admit his heinous crimes, or admit that nothing had even happened.

I chewed on my lower lip as I put on mascara and a little eye shadow—just enough to look more glam than my everyday ordinary self but not so glam that Mom would clear her throat and point me back to the bathroom for a total undo-over.

Could I dance with Hutch? I guess I'd have to if he actually asked me. Eric would understand. And then I had a terrible thought. What if Clint was at the dance with sparkly lip-gloss girl? Ick.

I bent over to blow-dry my hair, brushing it down to achieve maximum volume with minimum product. While I was staring at my knees upside down, I wondered what Eric would be wearing tonight. Something cool and nice, I was pretty sure, because he *is* cool and nice. Not like *some* guys I knew.

I stood up. Clint. Ergh! I was *not* going to think about him, I told myself as I massaged Lavender Love Potion lotion into my freshly shaved legs. Ow. It stung. Of course, trying *not* to think about Clint just made me think about him more.

I didn't get it. I really didn't. I thought for sure Clint liked me. At least it felt that way. Even the way he came up to me in Drama today . . . Had he just been playing me? Or was he just such a player that he moved through girls in like a week? Where was the guy from the water tower who was so honest and had that awesome emotional X-ray vision? I reached for the dress hanging from a hanger on the back of the bathroom door. Oh . . . Maybe this *was* that guy—that guy seeing right through me. And seeing me with Eric at the dance.

I should try to talk to Clint, I realized, looking at myself in the mirror, tying the little belt off to one side. I had on this super-cute wrap dress with a V-neck and a kind of crazy pattern. My mom called it like a Poochie print or something. But like I was saying, I should talk to Clint and tell him I didn't have time for him anyway. I smoothed the dress over my hips.

Forget it. I'm such a bad liar.

Maybe I was better off with Eric. Maybe much better. I unscrewed the top of my extremely *un-sparkly* lip gloss and dabbed it on my lips with my pinkie. Then I smooshed it around a little. Yeah. Eric's gorgelicious. And sensitive. Not some player. He's not mister *manfident* and all cocky all the time. Eric's sweet. Everyone likes Eric, *everyone*—even Clint.

Crap. I blew a big puff of air out my lips. I kept trying to slam the mental door on Clint. But he kept finding an open window and climbing back in and *flirting* with me. Ergh. Would he be at the dance? God, I hoped not. I really didn't want to have to watch him slow dancing with hot little Lip Gloss all night.

The doorbell rang. Yikes! Thank God I was having qual time with my girls before the dance so I could pull it together.

Okay. I took a few deep breaths, then tucked my hair behind both ears and smiled faux real at myself in the mirror. Wow. I looked almost kind of hot. *Take that, Lip Gloss!* I strutted out of the bathroom and into my bedroom, stepping in time with the music blaring from my speakers. I found my shoes under a big pile of clothes, slipped them on, and ran to get the door.

But before I got halfway down the stairs, Cate, Bean, and Amy burst in—all looking Friday night fab. Bean's mother, Mrs. Merrill (aka Wendi the Wonder Mom), followed them in, making a beeline for the wine. I mean, for the kitchen.

"Whoa Pais, sexy-groovy dress!" Bean squealed with genuine amazement that I was wearing something retro cool. "Is it vintage? I'd so wear that!"

OMG! That was the ultimate compliment, coming from Bean. She looked great in this super-cute little embroidered Mexican top and I don't know what on the bottom. And she had this striped poncho blanket thing over her arm. Sounds weird, I know, but she totally pulled it off.

"Bean, are those like really short pants or two longish skirts?" I asked. We all stared at her legs for a second.

Bean shook her head, obviously pitying me and my fashion ignorance. "Pais, they're *gauchos*. Inspired by the wandering cowboys of Argentina and a really scary fashion trend in the seventies. Cool, huh?"

Cate approached me with big, bulging eyes like she was possessed or something. She slowly reached out to touch my dress. "No. It's not a . . ." She caught her breath. "It is! Oh God. It's a Diane von Furstenberg vintage wrap dress?" She put her hand up to her mouth. "Holy fashion icon. Paisley, this is a classic! You know there's one of these hanging in the Smithsonian."

Bean nodded, eyes wide.

I glanced over at Amy, who was wearing a simple scoop-neck top with contrast stitching over black pants and these high platform shoes. They looked like a super-cute wipeout waiting to happen. She and I shook our heads. "Uh, no."

Cate looked amazing as always. Her dark hair was swept up in a tight bun to one side. She was wearing this black swishy forties-style dress with a thick belt that showed off her figure and a tiny red silk scarf tied around her neck. Her beauty mark was on. And yes, she still had on her black beret too. Over her shoulders, she had draped this vintage black suede jacket with a faux fur collar. Like I said, amazing.

Cate's eyes sparkled like my dress was made of 100 percent machine-washable gold and diamonds. "You gotta tell me where . . . Where did you *find* this?"

"Um . . ." I looked at Amy again. "In the back of my mom's closet. The way back . . . the way-back-in-the-day *way* back."

"God, that's so not fair." Cate shook her head wistfully, somehow managing to sound bitter and dreamy at the same time. "My life is just so sad, so tragic. The only thing I ever find in my mom's walk-in closets—lawyer suits, tailored shirts, cedar balls, and pumps so ugly, a drag queen wouldn't wear them."

Bean and I giggled, then nodded in solidarity, sharing a silent moment of profound faux sadness with Cate.

But Amy had this uncertain look on her face like she was trying to figure out where to put Cate in her mental address book—under "F" for Friend or "E" for enemy or "C" for competition. Amy was used to being the funny one in our group. Or at least she thought she was. But now that our group was expanding in *un*expectedly humorous ways, Amy seemed a little off her game.

Amy looked at me and smiled, breaking the silence. "Wow, Pais. Who knew your mom was ever so *sexy-groovy?*"

"I know." I shrugged, feeling relieved. "It's freakin' me out!"

Amy and I laughed.

"I heard that!" Mom called out from the kitchen.

Then we all laughed.

"Mothers," I whispered, cocking an eyebrow, "should neither be seen nor heard."

As everyone followed me into the kitchen, Amy asked under her breath, "You invited Carreyn, right?"

"Twice," I whispered.

Amy nodded. "Good. She seemed bummed that you didn't stick around for her sticky-bun fun."

We piled into the chairs around the kitchen table and started dishing the pizza onto paper plates. I poured glasses of diet soda from a huge bottle. Nobody said anything until Mom and Mrs. Merrill finally went into the other room carrying their wineglasses and the cheese board.

"So, who else is coming?" Cate asked, delicately shoving a slice into her mouth.

Before I could answer, the doorbell rang. We all looked up. Then the front door slammed.

"Hellooo!" Jen called, bounding into the kitchen like it was her house. Actually, that made me feel pretty good, since that's what the old Jen would have done. "Sorry I'm late! I would have *called*, but I don't have my phone!" She folded her arms, dropped her head, and stared at me like I had taken her off of social life support and left her for dead.

Yeah. Whoops! I guess I kind of did. I'd totally forgotten to get our cell phones after school. And by the time I remembered, Mrs. Hollet was gone. I found a note taped to the door of her locked classroom.

> Dear Paisley,
> Have a nice, quiet weekend! You can pick up your phones on Monday morning.
> Mrs. Hollet

I slumped back in my chair, chewing. I swallowed. "Jen, I said I was sorry."

"I know, I know. But that doesn't mean I'm not going to torture you about it all weekend, just a little." She smiled and leaned against the kitchen counter. "Cute dress, Pais."

"It's Diane von Furstenberg," said Cate, pouring sparkling water into a tilted glass like it was champagne.

"Vintage," Bean added.

Jen looked at them weirdly, then at me.

"Jen, dahling, surely you know that this exact dress is hanging in the Smithsonian," said Amy, oozing attitude and fake fashionista knowledge.

We all looked around at each other. It was . . . yeah, uncomfortable. Then Amy laughed. Alone.

Jen suddenly threw her hands up dramatically. "No Amy, *dahling*, I didn't know."

Silence.

Cate and Bean exchanged perturbed glances. Cate leaned back in her chair, arms folded. Bean looked down at her plate.

At my school, the Friday night dances are a big deal. So are the Friday night football games. But we pretty much knew our football team was going to get destroyed by the Cougars, so I'd decided to skip the game and have a little pre-dance pizza party at my house instead. It was the first time I had tried to mix all of my friends together outside of school, and I was beginning to think it had *not* been a very good idea.

"Jen, want some pizza?" I asked, shoving a plate at her.

"No thanks. I'm not hungry," she said. "I haven't been hungry for days."

"Why not?" Bean asked nicely, wiping pizza grease from her chin.

"Can I have your slice? I'm always hungry," said Amy. "God, I'd be eating all the time if I were you."

"I kinda doubt it," said Jen coldly.

Amy looked a little hurt and stared down at her pizza. Cate and Bean looked around trying to figure out what was going on, but nobody said a word.

"It's really stressful," Jen continued. "I feel like I'm waiting for a bomb to go off! It could happen any second." She looked right at me. A fist of guilt grabbed my stomach and twisted. I glanced at Amy, who was picking at a piece of pepperoni. "There's a photo," Jen said, turning to Cate and Bean, "and it's not pretty. If it gets out, then everyone's gonna be gossiping about me and speculating on my hookups." Jen closed her eyes and shook her head. "You guys have no idea."

Cate put down her slice. *"Au contraire,* Sweets."

Jen shot her a who-you-callin'-*Sweets?* glare.

Wow. Cate had shortened Sweetland to Sweets in a mere five minutes. How come I'd never thought of that?

Now Cate and Jen were doing a serious alpha-girl stare down. Uh-oh. Bean and I exchanged worried glances.

"Actually, I know *exactly* how you feel." Cate smiled at Jen in this knowing way, like they shared a secret. "Last year, when that senior girl kissed me at the dance, every horny guy and snotty girl in school was talking about me for months."

"Oh . . . yeah," said Jen, slowly remembering. She shook her head sympathetically. "That got kinda nasty."

"Wait. I heard *you* kissed *her*," said Amy, nibbling a piece of pepperoni with two hands like a tiny hamburger.

Cate waved at Amy. "See?"

Amy's eyes got all big as she lowered her pepperoni. "*What?* I'm not snotty! How do you know I wasn't concerned about *you* or—or something?"

"I didn't mean *you* were snotty," Cate said. "It's just . . . some people were so . . ." This strange look flashed across her face. "Whatever." She laughed. "You would've thought we were getting gay married at prom or something. God, we just kissed. Big friggin' deal." Cate handed Jen a slice of pizza. "You shouldn't lose weight over this. Believe me."

Jen reluctantly accepted the slice but didn't take a bite. She put it down on a napkin and let out this heavy sigh. "No one thinks being a slut is cool. Not even the other sluts." She tried to laugh, but . . . Well, she tried.

"Whoever wrote that on your locker doesn't know you," I said.

"Yeah. That was just stupid, ugly gossip," Amy added. "But now it's a confession of trampoline love." She tried to start a wave of laughter, but it didn't catch on.

"Obviously they don't know me." Jen shrugged. "That almost makes it worse. I just wish that photo didn't even exist. God, I so hate people talking about me!"

Cate leaned back and smiled at Jen, tracing her hairline with a finger. "Hey, Sweets, look on the bright side. My dad always tells me it's a lot better to be talked about than not talked about. At least you know people care enough about you to trash-talk you."

Jen and Cate stared at each other. It was weird. It was like someone whispered the punch line to some joke in their ears at the exact same moment. They both started to laugh. And they kept laughing. Then they looked at each other and laughed even harder.

Amy and Bean and I exchanged glances.

Jen started talking with her hands the way she always does when she gets excited. "Cate, Cate! We should start an exclusive club— you have to be trash-talked to join." She laughed. "We could call it Gossiped Girls or Scandal Sistahs."

Cate smiled. "Jen, I'd be honored to be trash-talked with you."

"Hey, I want to be trash-talked too!" Bean squealed.

"No. You. Don't!" said Jen and Cate at exactly the same time. Then they looked at each other and burst into hysterics again. Wow. I didn't see that one coming. Jen and Cate were totally bonding. I slumped back in my chair and picked at a piece of pepperoni.

"So Jen, do you think Bodie's gotten the sext yet?" I blurted. The room got quiet really fast. Everyone turned and stared at me. Uh-oh. Did I just say that *out loud?* Gulp. I totally did. "I mean . . . I mean, I hope he hasn't gotten it yet."

Jen just stared at me. All she said was, "Me too."

"Don't worry," I assured her, furiously backpedaling. "I'm on it. I'm wearing Hutch down. He's gonna spill any day—maybe even tonight," I lied. Well, it was possible.

"I don't get it. Why don't you just ask the person who took the picture?" asked Bean, sounding uncharacteristically logical. I sighed inside. If only it were that simple.

The doorbell rang.

"Got it!" Mom called from the other room. "But we should be leaving soon, girls!"

"I don't know who took the picture," said Jen, trying to be calm. "But whoever it was, when I find out, I'm gonna kill him."

"Hey you guys!" Carreyn buzzed into the room.

My jaw dropped. Whoa. Where did her hair go?

"So super-sorry I'm so super-late!" Then she noticed Cate and Bean and stopped in her tracks. "Oh." She looked around the table awkwardly, like maybe she had just walked into the wrong pizza party. "Hi."

"Oh. Hi, back," said Cate with hardly any attitude.

Bean just smiled and waved in a trying-to-be friendly way.

"Pizza?" Cate held the box out to Carreyn.

"Yeah, thanks." Carreyn leaned over me to grab the last slice. She took a huge bite and kept right on talking. "I had this major fashion crisis and this minor hair scare. But as you can see"—she paused and turned her head to both sides so we all could fully appreciate her handiwork—"I got it under control. Pretty sick, huh?"

We all just smiled and nodded, afraid to say anything in case she was serious.

Her hair extensions were gone—like most of her hair. Seriously. She looked like a science lab explosion survivor with eyeliner and lipstick.

"Yeah," I managed to say. I mean, I didn't want to hurt her feelings. "*Really* sick!"

"Sick and *sassy!*" Jen added. Carreyn beamed.

"Yeah." Amy nodded. "And . . . and think how much you're gonna save on shampoo."

"Well, maybe not." Carreyn pinched and twisted a few of the greasy, spiky niblets of hair. "My new styling secret—*mayonnaise.*" She giggled like it was some genius invention.

We all exploded into hysterics, howling with laughter until most of us were wiping away tears with greasy napkins. I almost peed in my Smithsonian-worthy DVF wrap dress.

Even Carreyn was laughing, totally not getting it. "Yeah, mayonnaise. It really holds."

"Girls, check the time!" my mom yelled as she and Mrs. Merrill walked back in carrying the bamboo cutting board and their empty wineglasses. "You're going to miss half the slow songs." Mom winked at us.

"Mo-om! God! Can you please leave us alone and grow up!"

She looked at me, pretending to think hard. "No. And . . . probably not."

We all laughed. Ergh! I so hate it when she does that—makes me laugh when I'm trying to be disgusted by her.

"*Definitely* not," added Mrs. Merrill. She hoisted her hands onto to her hip bones and shook her head, obviously amazed. "Can I just say, you girls all look fabulous. Fabulous! Such foxy style."

Bean looked like she wanted to die.

"All of you, *all of you*, are gonna get lots of action tonight!"

"Mom!" Bean looked mortified. "That's totally inappropriate!"

"What?" Mrs. Merrill threw her hands up. "Action on the *dance floor*. All I mean is, the boys are going to see you girls, get excited, and want to dance with you."

Bean raised her hands and closed her eyes. "Mom. *Please*. Stop."

We all piled into my mom's SUV, feeling high on life and diet soda. Mom was our IDD (Invisible Designated Driver) that night. Unlike Dad, Mom was horrible at being invisible, so she brought Mrs. Merrill along to distract her from our conversation. Even though the car smelled like bad mayonnaise, everyone was buzzing with excitement, talking over each other and laughing, and talking louder and louder.

When we pulled up to school, there were already a lot of people gathered in front of the entrance to the gym. Tight little clusters of girls and loose, sloppy groups of guys mingled outside trying to decide if it was cool enough yet to go in.

We gracefully spilled out of the car, and only one of us hit the pavement. Yep, Amy. But she looked super-cute as she fell. I know. I was the last one out of the car and helped her up.

"Eleven o'clock, right?" Mom asked before I could close the door.

"Mom, I'll call from Amy's phone, okay?"

"Eleven o'clock," she repeated firmly, giving me her serious I'm-the-mom face.

"Okay!"

I slammed the car door really hard and turned to face the gym. The music sounded surprisingly good. I spotted Eric talking with Bodie and a few other football guys next to Bodie's car, this vintage cherry-red BMW 2002tii that he had paid for himself.

Amy was right. I was *so* lucky to be going to the dance with Eric—Eric Sobel! He looked really handsome and really . . . clean. Obviously he had just come from the showers. He smiled at me. I smiled back and did this kind of excited silent squeal inside. Then I got this tingling magical feeling and this crystal clear sense that something truly unbelievable and amazing was about to happen to me.

Have I mentioned that I'm psychic?

That was the exact moment my mom pulled away from the curb, pulling my wrap dress with her. It happened so fast—I didn't have a second to react. I felt this sudden tug that practically yanked me over, then I got whipped around in a circle like a wobbly spinning top. And then, there I was—standing in front of the whole school in my underwear.

"Aaaaaaaaaah!" I screamed, trying to cover myself.

Everyone else screamed too, except for the guys and all the other people who were too busy gawking and/or laughing hysterically. I turned in a panic toward our car and yelled "Mom!!! Stop! STOP!!!"

But the car kept going—with my sexy-groovy retro wrap dress flapping in the wind. Cate looked after it with this sad, heartbroken face.

Then chaos ensued. (I'm definitely sure that's what they say in novels when things get really crazy.)

Cate and Amy threw themselves in front of me trying to shield me and my underwear from the crowd. Jen and Bean took off running after the car, waving frantically. Poor Carreyn just stood there with her mouth open, too mortified to move.

I started waving frantically too, jumping up and down with one arm over my bra. Bean stopped running after a few yards, but Jen kept sprinting for a good fifty. But when my mom's arm popped out the window waving back, I stopped jumping and Jen stopped running. And then—I swear to God—over the music seeping out from the gym, I actually heard my mom yell, "Have fun, girls!" as she drove out of the parking lot and out onto the road.

SIDEBRA

Paisley Pointer #399:
The importance of wearing matching bras & panties.
On a good day, if you're lucky, no one but you will see you in your underwear. But let's face it. We all have bad days. So I totally recommend wearing a super-cute matching bra and panties whenever possible. Then if you're ever caught in an unnatural disaster or suffer a wardrobe malfunction, you're covered. Literally! And if nothing freaky happens, then you'll go through the day filled with a sense of confidence and inner beauty—or what I like to call *inner booty beauty*.
PS: If your bra and panties match, it's so much easier to find your underwear in a rush while skinny dipping at your friend's house and your friend's parents suddenly show up. Not that I would know anything about that, of course.
PPS: No need for matching sidebras & panties.

I couldn't believe it. I was going to have to kill her. Kill her! Poor Dad would be very sad, but I was sure he'd understand.

Bean and Jen jogged back to us, panting and looking horrified.

"Good try, Sweets." Cate put her hand on Jen's back. Everyone stared at me, speechless. Finally, Cate said seductively, "Wow, Paisley. Have you been working out?"

Jen started it, trying not to laugh. But then Cate and Bean joined in. Jen lost it. By the time Amy and Carreyn realized it was safe to laugh at me, everyone was howling.

"Not funny!" I screamed, feeling my body temperature shooting up despite the chilly night air.

But my friends kept laughing—all of them. Not in a mean way, just in a you-really-make-me-want-to-pee-in-my-pants way.

Finally, I started laughing too. I mean, what else could I do? Fortunately, I *had* been working out, playing soccer every day. And hey, what's the big deal, really? The only difference between me standing around in my underwear and me standing around in my bikini is sunscreen. SPF 45.

Okay, but that didn't occur to me then. It took months of therapy.

"Bean! Poncho! Poncho!" I shouted in a panic. She looked at me totally confused. Was I was speaking in tongues? "Your poncho. Give it. Give it!"

She finally understood and quickly ripped off her poncho, tossing it to me like a hot potato. Jen and Bean helped me wrestle it over my head and down over my—thank God!—very cute matching bra and panties. Phew. I took a few quick breaths, feeling a bit better but still sweating like a pig that had just run the fifty-yard dash over hot coals.

I looked down at Bean's groovy striped thrift-shop poncho. Wow. It was kind of cute. But it needed something. I looked around at what everyone else was wearing and pointed at Cate's wide black belt. She whipped it right off and wrapped it around me, fastening it while Bean artfully arranged the folds of poncho fabric.

Amy and Jen watched with big eyes, seeming quite impressed by Cate and Bean's impromptu styling skills. Carreyn looked a little scared and confused, like she was watching a horror movie in Japanese with no subtitles.

Finally, Bean and Cate stepped back, smiling, and admired their work. They fussed a little more, then both nodded proudly.

"Not bad," said Cate.

Jen nodded too. "Yeah. Not bad. Kinda—"

"Not bad?" Bean threw up her arms, smiling enviously. "I wish I'd thought of this. You look *muy caliente*, Pais."

"Really?" I asked.

Everyone—even Carreyn—nodded. I wiped the nervous sweat off of my forehead with the back of my wrist and took a few more deep breaths. "Okay, then. Let's . . . go." There was this loud group sigh of nervous energy.

I turned around, and guess who was standing right there grinning at me with his delicious double-dimpled smile?

Eric Sobel.

"Quite the entrance," he said. Then he reached for my hand, ignoring the fact that I was wearing a belted poncho and basically nothing else. "Come on. Let's go for the whole enchilada."

chapter twenty-four
buzz factor

It was quite the entrance. Legendary, in fact. And yes, people were definitely talking. "Talk," it turns out, would be the theme that entire night.

I walked along with Eric in a state of semi-shock, holding his hand and holding my head high. But I was totally out of my body, watching us from like twenty feet above. I must have nearly died of embarrassment and floated up toward that soothing white light you read about. I was sure I looked a little wobbly as I walked beside him. Maybe it was my shoes—but it was probably just me trying not to pass out.

My poncho dress was an immediate hit. It was unreal, like the poncho suddenly had its own fan base. Of course, some Pops laughed and pointed as I walked by. But most people and all of the UnPops clapped and cheered. And trust me, they were clapping for the poncho—not for me. But I didn't mind. The poncho was my friend.

Cate, Jen, Amy, Bean, and Carreyn followed behind us in a loose bouquet of styles, keeping a safe distance. I checked out the social and fashion food chain as we made our way to the entrance to the gym. LG Wong, still wearing her beret and fab black URM outfit, was walking next to Bentley Jones.

"Nice save," said Bentley, as if I had just saved someone's life.

"Yeah." LG nodded. "Good thing you didn't take that *underwear* resistance thing too seriously."

We all laughed.

Elliott and Split Ends gave me two thumbs up as I walked by them. OMG. I tapped Bean on the arm and pointed. Split Ends's strapless dress was made entirely out of black duct tape! And Elliott's vest and hat were made of silver duct tape. Very *Un.*

"Cool," whispered Bean. "You know, there's one of those hanging in the Smithsonian." She arched her eyebrow and smiled. Then she spotted Svend standing with a few techno geek guys from Drama and trotted over to him.

Then Jen peeled off toward Bodie, who was leaning against his car. She approached him slowly, stopping to get a read on his mood. Bodie looked up and flashed her his gleaming movie star smile. Jen's whole body seemed to exhale. Then she walked up and gave him a kiss and a hug.

Phew.

Cate, Amy, and Carreyn were left standing together like the corners of a spreading isosceles triangle. Cate and Carreyn kept glancing awkwardly at each other, clearly realizing that they had nothing but Amy in common and absolutely nothing to say to each other—if they even spoke the same language.

Carreyn searched the crowd anxiously. She micro-waved at Charlie Dodd, who was still wearing his huge white nose saddle with two full-on black eyes. He looked a little surprised, like a raccoon stuck in a cat door, but then he smiled and waved back. Carreyn happily bounded off in his direction.

Finally, I was back in my body and managed to squeak out something to Eric. "So, um, how was your game?"

He laughed in that it's-anything-but-funny way. "Painful. We got *destroyed*. Bodie played great, and I . . . I kicked a couple of field goals," he said like he was embarrassed to have put points on the scoreboard. "But Hutch, man, he dropped almost every pass."

I flashed on Hutch's swollen, bruised hand. "Really?" I looked around, wondering if I would see him. "Is he here?"

Eric looked at me kind of weird. "Haven't seen him yet. He may not show—his dad ripped him a new one in front of everyone after the game."

"What? Why?"

Eric just shrugged and shook his head. "His dad's got some anger issues. The whole thing was pretty . . . awkward."

As we inched toward the entrance to the gym in what was now a small mob-ish line to get in, I wondered about Hutch and his dad. Their relationship seemed complicated. Or maybe it wasn't complicated at all. Maybe it just sucked. I probably shouldn't have been thinking about myself, but I was. Actually, I was thinking about my parents. Yeah, they could both be major über-goober embarrassments but they weren't *that* bad. I mean the worst thing either of them had ever done was leave me in the school parking lot in my underwear.

Eric and I showed our student IDs to Mr. Canfield, who was dressed up in his finest Friday night polyester suit.

"Lookin' sharp, Mr. Canfield," said Eric, somehow managing to sound sincere.

"Thanks, Eric. You too. By the way, nice game tonight. Those kicks of yours—outstanding!" As we walked by him into the gym, he patted Eric a few times on the back and gave me this lame half smile. Then, when we were way past him, he called after us, "Oh, Paisley, nice goal yesterday!"

Nice afterthought, Canfield. "Thanks," I said over my shoulder. Was Canfield trying to get back on my good side? Wait. He was never *on* my good side. Maybe he thought if he was nice to me, I'd persuade Cate to shut down the protesters, make them all disappear and fade back into the oppressed-slash-depressed student body. I made a mental note to talk to Cate about that right after she super-glued all his desk drawers shut.

Eric and I walked a safe distance away from the door and then stopped, waiting for our eyes to adjust. It was pretty dark in there, and the music was loud. Red and yellow and blue strobe lights screamed back and forth across the gym ceiling.

The gym, aka the *Hornets' Nest,* was cavernous. At the far end, two soft yellow lights glowed above the entrance to the bathrooms, girls' on one side, boys' on the other. A few faculty chaperones stood near the bathroom, leaning against the wall, talking.

The bleachers along the far wall had been pulled out so people had a place to park their stuff and sit and try to make out before getting laser beamed by a chaperone. There were already a few bunches of non-dancers—Emos, Library Girls, and, I don't know, band geeks with no rhythm?—sitting together up and down the bleachers. I spotted Logan Adler, Miriam Goldfarb, and the Dumbe Blondes up near the top in one corner. A lot of them still had duct tape over their mouths and were holding signs that said: *Here the Music!* and *Get Down & Booger!* and *Will Dance for Respect!* Miriam Goldfarb stood on the bleachers in front of them doing some sort of free-form *unterpretive* dance, her smarty arty glasses and her curly mop of hair bouncing crazily.

The DJ was spinning up in the announcer's booth, and the music was groovin' and the people were moovin', except for Eric and me. I stood next to him feeling awkward—and not because of my poncho dress. How long were we just going to stand there? I couldn't help kind of moving my hips a little with the music, watching the other people out there *getting down and boogering.*

Finally, Eric tapped me on the shoulder. "Wanna dance?" he shouted.

I nodded, following him deep into the middle of the dance floor. I quickly felt like a total dork, dancing like I was trying way too hard. It always seems to take me a few minutes to relax and actually remember how to dance. What's up with that?

But then I stopped thinking about my every little move and watched Eric instead.

OMG. Eric was a sick dancer. Not in that practice-at-home-in-front-of-the-mirror way—but in this sexy, easy, relaxed way, like every muscle in his body could hear the music and knew exactly what to do. Just watching him move made me smile uncontrollably and unconsciously start to imitate him. Of course, I probably should have practiced at home in front of the mirror beforehand—but oh well. I did my best. And I was so having fun.

Eric danced for a while, getting into it and groovin' to the music, basically ignoring me. And then he started dancing at me, then toward me. He smiled. I smiled back, putting on my best cool dance face and going for it. He laughed sweetly, mirroring a few of my more creative moves—the dork and slide, the open-mouth-goober-faced shimmy, and—my fave—the butter-churner backbend. At one point, Eric had to dance around and look away, he was laughing so hard.

When the song ended, he came up to me and put both hands on my hips. "Hi," he whispered. "You're fun."

I laughed and shook my head, pointing to him, because I was too embarrassed to say anything.

Jen and Bodie came over just as the next song started.

"Hey!" Bodie nodded at us, quote-unquote dancing with Jen in our direction. Incidentally, Bodie is not that great of a dancer. I'm sure he saves all of his best moves for football, basketball, and track.

I waved at them, and Eric nodded back. The four of us danced together for a while as the floor filled up. Jen looked really pretty and really happy. I was so glad I hadn't told her about the sext. She grooved up close to Bodie and threw her arms around his neck. He put his arms around her waist. I watched them as their hips moved together with the music. They both had matching I-totally-dig-you grins on their faces.

I turned away doing my best attempt at a slow soulful spin—yes, with my super-cool dance face on. I spotted Bean dancing with Svend, pretending to be runway models or something. Cate and Amy stood off to the side, watching us, trying not to broadcast that they'd rather be dancing than watching us dance. Charlie Dodd and Carreyn kept leaning into each other trying to talk over the music. Good thing Charlie couldn't smell anything. Near them, LG Wong and her Library Girls stood in a tight pack, arms crossed, all scowling at us dancing fools.

No sign of Clint.

I turned back around to Eric and watched Bodie and Jen some more. It was hard not to watch them. They weren't just in love. They had so much fun together. You could see it. They both kind of glowed. I looked back at Eric wondering if I would ever feel that way, the way that Jen felt, about any guy—or would any guy ever feel that way about me?

Eric danced toward me, moving easily with the music. He gave me this cute little smile as he put his arms loosely around me. I draped my arms over his shoulders, and we danced like that for a while. At first, I had a hard time keeping up with the beat because I was trying to manage a surge of feelings.

His body was . . . I don't know. So . . . so . . . *there*.

It wasn't that I wanted to rip his clothes off with my teeth or anything. It was different from that, more like I wanted to fold into him, just relax into his arms, his shoulders, his chest. We could get to the clothes-ripping part later, right? Like after we've dated for a few years and graduated college and had a long and tasteful engagement and gotten married. (Hi Mom! Hi Dad!) Anyway, so I was almost feeling safe enough to relax and really let go.

But then the song ended.

I swallowed hard. We both stepped away from each other a little awkwardly. Thank God it was dark in there, because I was pretty sure I was blushing big-time, and I was definitely feeling a little overheated. Eric and I stared at each other like we had a secret. Then we kind of laughed and both looked away.

"Hey you guys!" called Candy, walking over to us with Bratty Sasshole #1 and #2, joined at the hips like some fashionably dressed, six-legged monster. Great. My three unfavorite people. But I was not going to let them get to me.

I was giving them my confident, don't-mess-with-me face when Carreyn ran up to them like they were her new best friends.

"Hey you guys!" She waved all cheery. "Frozen yogurt later?"

What? That was weird. Jen and I exchanged glances. She definitely wasn't talking to us. Candy looked at Carreyn like she didn't quite recognize her. But BS1 and BS2 shot her these catty smirks.

"Love the new hair," said BS1, elbowing BS2. "Very . . ." She focused hard on Carreyn's short spiky niblets trying to come up with the right words. "Very lemon meringue pie."

Practically everyone laughed. I didn't. I was too busy thinking *Poor Carreyn*. Her bright cheery smile collapsed into a mortified fish face, and she slowly slunk away. I would have gone after her, but I had bigger fish to fly. I turned and gave Candy my best tough-girl stare-down face, which apparently wasn't very tough.

Candy broke off from the six-legged monster and gave Jen a quick hug. "Hey, Bodes. Eric. Hi Paisley." Candy smiled right at me.

Un-frigging-believable! I smiled faux real right back. Jen folded her arms, cocked a hip, and glared right at her. But Candy didn't seem to notice. I watched Bodie and Eric walking off to get a drink and really hoped Candy would go away too.

"I'm so impressed you're here," said Candy earnestly. "Not hiding at home after that unpleasant rant about you in *The Fly.*" I looked at her. Was she kidding? "That shows real courage." No. OMG. She's evil!

"Yeah, that was too bad," BS1 added, all fakey fake, while BS2 nodded along.

"Who would do that to you?" Candy asked.

"I have no idea," I said like a talking Bambi. "But it's obviously three people who are very afraid of my . . . *power* at this school." I smiled smugly.

There was an awkward silence.

"Paisley, wow! Your dress is *fabulosa*," blurted BS1, sneering at me.

BS2 jumped right in. "Did you like get that at Target in Mexico?"

My first thought was—OMG! BS2 actually said something original. My second thought was—I'll bet Target in Mexico has really cool stuff.

"Yeah, actually I did." I nodded cheerfully. "So, ah, sorry! *You* can't buy one."

BS2 cocked her head to the side, looking like she wanted to bite off a baby bird's head or something. But it was obvious she couldn't think of anything to say back.

"Whatever. Who would want to?" snarled BS1, grabbing BS2's hand and pulling her off to safety.

"*Adios!*" I said cheerfully, waving at their bratty little retreating butts.

"Don't listen to them, Paisley. You look great. Really," Candy said. "I think your outfit is inspired." Wait. Was she like *psycho*? Jen and I exchanged quick glances. Then Candy reached out and touched my shoulder. "Oh, and hey! I have the same matching bra and panties!"

I winced inside. Great. Even Candy had seen my not-so-grand entrance. Eric came over and handed me a paper cup filled with water. I chugged it so I wouldn't have to say anything back—I *so* could not figure her out. Fortunately, the next song started just then.

And you won't believe this—Candy started dancing right next to us! And she even had the nerve to ooze more than her usual shameless confidence by not noticing that she was dancing alone. But what could I do? Nothing! So I just tried to ignore her.

But she certainly didn't ignore Eric.

Candy kept doing her sexy little get-down groove-sistah steps right at him. At first I just smiled, pretending my heart was open and full of love for all living things—even two-faced things like Candy Esposito. But she kept doing it. Was I invisible?! Was I not even there?! I had to reclaim my dance territory. So I started doing my own sexy little groove-sistah moves right at Eric.

Candy pointed at me, grinning. "So cute!" she yelled. "You dance just like your brother Parker!"

OMG. What an insult.

But I would not give up that easily. I cranked it up a notch and really went for it. Get out of my way—I'm gettin' down with my bad self! Candy and Eric burst into laughter. What? Well, yeah. Apparently my version was more ho-down than get-down. Ergh! What was her problem? I wanted to spray Candy in the face with a blast of back-it-up.

The next song got everyone out on the dance floor doing our school's version of, basically, fourth-generation Soulja Boy. We called it The Buzz Factor after some cheerleading routine because . . . *Uh-huh! Right on! We're the Hornets!* Clap. Clap. *Uh-huh! Right on! We're the Hornets!* Clap. Clap.

And I mean *everyone* was out there poppin' it—even Ms. Whit and a few other cool faculty chaperones. Amy and Cate danced up to us and joined our line. Bean and Svend danced over. Carreyn pulled Charlie out and they started dancing next to each other. Cute! She's going for it. Through the crowd I could even see Teddy, Mandy, LG, and a few Library Girls off together doing the spastic jazz hands spazz-dance version. I smiled.

And then . . . I saw Hutch.

He grabbed Carreyn away from Charlie and pulled her over in our direction. Uh-oh.

"Hey! What up?" yelled Hutch. "Sick tunes, man!" He danced around, hopping and bouncing and punching his arms out like some crazy, out-of-control boxer. His version of The Buzz Factor had a whole different meaning.

Yeah. Obviously, Hutch was drunk.

Either Carreyn didn't notice he was drunk or she didn't care because—hey, she was dancing with all the varsity football players! She kept dancing next to Hutch, barely bobbing and ducking out of the way of his air jabs as she did her flawless Buzz Factor steps with cheerleader enthusiasm. Her body was shouting *Look at me! I'm so happy!* But her eyes were kind of scanning the dance floor. They swept the whole gym. Finally, she saw something and stared. It was Charlie Dodd sitting near the top of the bleachers, leaning hard on both fists. She smiled at him and did a little wave. Then, still looking at him, she dialed her Buzz Factor moves up a notch.

Before I had a chance to process all this, Hutch started doing body slams against Eric and Bodie and a few other guys from the team. Then he bumped into me, almost knocking me over.

"Hutch, come on!" yelled Eric, helping me stay on my feet, and at the same time, pulling me away from Hutch.

Hutch regained his balance and tossed up both hands. "Sorry! Sorry, man!" he said to Eric—not to me.

Then he yelled at Eric, pointing at me with his thumb. "Has she asked you those weird Emotional Warming questions yet?"

Eric had no idea what Hutch was talking about and just shook his head. But then Hutch looked at me all flushed and smiled in this open, whoops-I-left-my-inhibitions-in-the-trunk-with-the-beer kind of way. Then he patted Eric on the back a few times, still smiling at me.

"Dude, does she think you're *smexy* too?"

Oh God.

Eric looked at him, frowning, then he looked at me. I shrugged on the outside and cringed on the inside. Eric turned his back on Hutch and took my hand, basically spinning me around and away from him. Hutch just stood there for a while, looking rejected, watching us.

He quote-unquote danced back over to Carreyn, who didn't look happy to see him coming, then he started lurching around the dance floor. He punch-drunk boxed over behind Jen, imitated her for a few beats, and smacked her on the butt. Hard. What a shidiot. She turned and yelled something at him, looking like she might hit him. But he just laughed in her face. Bodie calmly stepped between them. He put his hand up to Hutch and protectively ushered Jen off to a different part of the dance floor.

The Buzz Factor song blended smoothly into a slow song. There were a few quick seconds when most people glanced around hopefully. Then it was like someone had dropped a *Don't even think about touching me! Oops. I mean, I really have to pee!* stink bomb in the middle of the dance floor and half the people cleared out.

Eric stepped into me, giving me a dose of his double dimples and putting his arms around my waist. I rested my arms on his shoulders as we swayed slowly with the music. Wow. Eric's shoulders were rock solid. I was discreetly admiring them with my pinkies when Charlie Dodd ran up to Bean, standing off to the side of us.

"Hi!" Charlie rubbed his palms down his thighs a few times, looking around for Svend. "So, um, wanna dance?" Man, Charlie could be totally annoying, but he really had guts to ask Bean to dance sporting a honkin' nose saddle and two black eyes. I noticed his feet and smiled. I doubt Charlie realized he was actually standing on his toes.

Bean looked down at him sweetly. "Thanks, Charlie, but I'm here with someone."

Charlie dropped down off his toes, looking disappointed. But he wasn't giving up. "You know, my dad is *really* tall, over six foot three, almost six three and a half." He pushed his glasses back up his nose saddle with a finger. "And . . . and you should know that I've already grown five-eighths of an inch since the beginning of the school year."

Bean smiled at him—but probably not the way that any guy wants a girl to smile at him. Svend walked up to them, wiping water from his mouth with his sleeve. When Charlie saw him, he twisted his face up, not looking happy. But then Bean whispered something in Svend's ear. He nodded.

"Hey, I'm gonna take a breather of fresh air, okay? You two"—he pointed at Bean and Charlie—"you should dance." Svend smiled and headed off toward the bleachers.

Bean nodded to Charlie, who broke into this ridiculously happy grin, until he seemed to realize that he'd be staring right at her boobs the entire dance. Suddenly he looked like he was afraid to make a move. Bean took charge. She stepped up, casually resting her arms on top of his shoulders, like dancing with a guy a foot shorter was the most natural and most enjoyable thing in the world.

OMG. Bean's the nicest person ever, I thought. I wished I could be that nice. She should get some national high school humanitarian award. They were talking about something while they danced, but I couldn't tell what.

I was trying to read their lips when Eric pulled me tight against his body, putting his hands around my waist right above my butt. Oh, hello. I laced my hands behind his neck. It took like all of two seconds for me to become totally aware of the fact that Eric Sobel's body was only a poncho away from mine. I started feeling warm inside—really warm—and then I started to sweat, and my mouth got really dry. *Breathe. Breathe.* I held on tight to the back of his neck, mostly because I didn't want to fall over in the middle of the dance floor.

Eric pressed the side of his head against mine for a while, holding me close as we danced. He smelled goooood. I could feel his chest rising and falling and his warm breath just behind my ear. Then he softly ran his lips down the side of my neck, pausing just above the edge of my poncho. OMG. That totally sounded like a line from a Mexican soap opera! But that's what happened.

Oh . . . Oh, wow.

I closed my eyes. Wow again. I got the chills and a below-the-belted-poncho rush.

I held my breath for a while, then I slowly exhaled.

Did I mention that Eric was a really, *really* good dancer? Yeah. So, whatever he lacked in verbal communication skills, he was more than making up for with his um . . . non-verbal skills.

I had always thought of Eric as my above-the-belt crush. You know, because he's the kind of guy I thought I *should* be with. But as we danced, pressed up hard against each other, I could hear my own breathing—and I was definitely rethinking my whole crush organization system.

I opened my eyes and blinked a few times. I was looking right at Bean. She smiled at me over Charlie's head and winked. I smiled back. It was one of those moments when you look at a friend and have this flash, both knowing it's a special moment in your life— even if it's special for completely different reasons.

And then Bean disappeared behind the side of Eric's head as we danced, and my view shifted. I could see Jen and Bodie through a break in the crowd. Something was wrong. I lifted my head off of Eric's shoulder to get a better view. Bodie was just standing there with his arms crossed not saying anything. Jen looked really freaked out and kept throwing her arms down like she was pleading with him.

Then Bodie turned and walked toward the exit. Uh-oh. That's not good.

Jen's arms fell to her sides, and her shoulders sank. She stood there for a few seconds, watching him leave. Then she ran for the girls' bathroom.

Oh no. I pushed away from Eric. "Hey, um sorry. But I . . ." He seemed confused, like he had done something he shouldn't have done. "No. It's not you—it's—"The look on his face . . . Instantly, my brain flooded with feelings, and I didn't know what to say. All I knew is that I wanted to kiss him right there and it kind of freaked me out. So I ran for it. I had to find Jen.

chapter twenty-five
pity potty

Finding Jen was the easy part.

I pushed open the door to the girls' bathroom, squinting and blinking a few times from the sudden burst of light reflecting off of everything shiny. I could hear Jen sobbing in the far stall. Fortunately, the bathroom was empty except for two perky freshmen leaning close to the mirror applying lip gloss and whispering back and forth. They both watched me in the mirror as I walked past them.

I was just about to give them my best guy-crisis-clear-the-room! face, when suddenly, they both got all big-eyed and nervously glanced at each other. They slowly turned around and faced me. They seemed, I don't know, guilty or something. The short one with the frizzy scare-hair held her phone up and nodded. The tall one with the long shiny nose slowly pointed toward the sound of the sobbing and mouthed *Jen Sweetland?*

Great. This was way worse than really bad if freshmen girls like that had already gotten the sext. I nodded, pushing past them.

Jen's kind of famous at our school—and not just because of dating Bodie or because of her naked boob. Everyone knew her because of soccer and because of her personality and because, let's face it, she's gorgeous.

Both girls looked like they were in big trouble and bolted for the exit. OMG. They'd probably sent it on to other people. Unbelievable.

I knocked on the stall door. "Jen!" I whispered. "It's me. You okay? What happened?" Yeah. Dumb question. I guess it was obvious.

She stopped sobbing for a few seconds. But then it all swelled up again and more tears crashed through.

I listened to her crying for a little more, then knocked again. "Come on, Jen. Open the door. Please."

I waited, looking over my shoulder, hoping that no one would come bursting into the bathroom. Finally, I heard the lock slide over. But she didn't come out. I waited a few seconds more, then slowly pushed open the door and peeked in.

Jen was leaning against the tile wall with her eyes closed. They looked red and puffy. At least she was wearing waterproof mascara. I reached out and touched her arm. She looked at me with these sad, heavy eyes. I didn't know what to say. Then she covered her mouth with both hands and kept crying.

"Bodie just got the sext?" I whispered.

She shook her head and groaned. "I'm such an idiot."

Wait. He didn't get it? "Jen, you're not an idiot. Just tell me."

She pushed her hands from her chin out to her temples. Her mouth hung open before she said anything. "He's crushed. Devastated. He wants to know why I didn't just tell him." She sniffled hard, trying not to cry. I handed her a few squares of toilet paper, and she wiped her nose. "Why didn't I just tell him? I should have just told him. And now . . ."

I didn't know what to say, especially since I was the one who had the brilliant idea *not* to tell Bodie. Oh God. I really hoped she didn't remember that little detail.

"You didn't know. You didn't know. That's all," I said.

"He's known about that stupid photo for *days*. Eric told him." She threw her head back against the wall and sort of growled. "He's been waiting for me to talk to him about it."

Wait, what did she say? Eric? Eric told him? I scratched the side of my jaw anxiously, trying to backtrack in my head. Oh, God. Oh no. Was *that* what Eric wanted to talk to me about? My stomach twisted into a nasty knot of ick. I leaned back against the stall door, staring at the toilet flusher. Eric hadn't wanted romantic qual time with me. He'd wanted me to warn Jen! God, *I'm* such an idiot!

"What about the Hutch part?" I asked, cringing.

"Bodie didn't even mention that. I mean, he knows Hutch. He knows *me*. God, I hope he doesn't think anything happened. I don't think so. But he's really worried about me—and . . . and he's really hurt." She looked at the floor and sniffled, slowly shaking her head like *could this get any worse?*

I didn't want to think about the answer to that question, so I handed her more toilet paper.

She blew her nose, then wiped it a few times. "Crap! I should have talked to him before the whole school got this. Now everyone is gonna think Hutch and I hooked up—which so isn't the point!" She pounded air with both fists. "Everyone in this whole friggin' town has probably seen my boob and thinks I'm a huge slut."

I felt a little sick but I wasn't sure why. Was it because of what I did do? Or because of what I didn't do? I honestly didn't know.

"Not everyone." I tried to sound super-positive. What was the point of telling her that even I'd gotten the sext? It would just make her feel worse. The only thing that might make her feel better now was me getting the truth out of Hutch. "I mean, I doubt *everyone* has seen it."

A toilet down the line flushed.

I looked at Jen, but she was too upset to even notice.

"Come on, let's get out of here," I whispered, leading her out of the stall.

She walked over to the sink, landing on the counter with both hands like she hadn't slept for days. I watched her splash water on her face and felt this crazy shuffle of emotions—from massive guilt that I didn't tell her the second I knew it was out to secret relief that it wasn't *me* in that sext.

Someone came out of a stall a few doors down. I turned. LG Wong nodded to me.

"Hey Jen," said LG, running water over her hands at the other sink. "Don't cry. At least you *have* boobs."

What?! I glared at LG like *you didn't really just say that?!*

Jen looked at LG, then at me, throwing up her hands. "See?" she growled, and burst into tears again, leaning against the tile wall, then sliding down it until she landed on the floor. She dropped her head. Her shoulders shook as she cried.

"Oh . . ." LG looked at me, then back at Jen. "Sorry." She ripped a paper towel from the dispenser and darted out of the bathroom.

I followed LG to the door and leaned against it until it closed all the way. Then I kicked down the little door stop that the janitors use. Someone tried to push the door open.

I pounded on the door. "Hold it, okay?!"

I slid down the door and sat on the floor across from Jen, careful to get the bottom of the poncho under my butt. We stared at each other across the bathroom floor for a while. Finally, Jen stopped crying. I think she was just too tired to keep going.

"What else did he say?" I asked.

"He's worried about me. People can get *arrested* for sending photos like that! But I didn't send that photo. I didn't. And he's just hurt, really hurt." She picked at a loose thread on her skirt. "And disappointed. He said if I really loved him, I would've trusted him and told him about it."

I didn't say anything. Oh man, she should have just told him. Why did I tell her not to say anything?

"I do, Pais. I do really love him . . ."

"I know."

There were three crisp knocks on the bathroom door. Crap.

"Just a sec!" I yelled.

"Open up, girls. Now!" shouted a voice from the other side of the door. "This is Ms. Whitaker. Open the door *now*." Double crap.

I jumped to my feet and kicked up the door stopper thingy, then stepped out of the way. A bunch of girls rushed in, pouring into each open stall. Ms. Whit followed them in.

She put her hands on her hips as she looked at Jen sitting on the floor with puffy red eyes, then at me, then back at Jen.

"Sorry," I said lamely. "It was an emergency, kinda."

I expected Ms. Whit to ream us, but she didn't. She didn't even seem mad. She walked over to Jen and squatted down in front of her. They whispered some stuff that I couldn't hear, Jen nodded, and they whispered some more stuff. Then Ms. Whit helped Jen to her feet, and the toilets started flushing.

I stood next to the towel dispenser just watching like some unskilled bathroom attendant.

Ms. Whit leaned against the counter and cleaned her glasses with the bottom of her cool hobohemian frayed top while Jen washed her hands. Then Ms. Whit whispered something else in Jen's ear.

Jen started laughing. OMG.

Ms. Whit nodded, watching her with a growing smile. I had no idea what Ms. Whit said to Jen, but whatever it was, it made me like her even more.

I decided to make myself useful and started ripping paper

towels out of the dispenser and handing them to each girl who left the sink area.

Jen wiped a finger under each eye and took a few deep breaths. Then she smiled at her reflection. That was when I looked at my own reflection.

OMG. My poncho dress was totally cute! I pulled my hair back with both hands so I could fully appreciate its dramatic flattering neckline. *Muy caliente* was right!

Jen smiled at me and grabbed my hand, pulling me out the door. Ms. Whit followed us. As we walked, she put her hand on my shoulder.

"Paisley, Teen Scene," she whispered.

I looked back at her like *what?* Was this really the time to be reminding me about my terminally unwritten Teen Scene article? "I hope you'll consider writing about this for your sample column," she whispered. "This is important stuff. This is real."

Ohhh. I nodded, finally getting it. It wasn't a bad idea, actually. Writing about this would definitely make my Teen Scene submission stand out. But I'd have to worry about it later.

By the time we got out of the bathroom, the music was long gone, and the lights were up in the gym. I looked around for Eric, but I couldn't find him anywhere. There were only a few clumps of people left standing around talking and a few brown-nosers and stoners helping the faculty chaperones clean up.

Jen and I slipped out the back exit fast. The cold night air grabbed us. We had to walk quickly to stay warm as we cut across the courtyard toward the parking lot. I felt even crappier than I should have because neither one of us could even call for a ride, thanks to brilliant me.

Amy was standing with Carreyn and Charlie and Bean and Svend near the pickup spot in the parking lot. A line of cars driven by IDDs inched along as groups of kids piled in. Amy spotted us, waved, and trotted carefully on her platform shoes in our direction.

"Check this out!" She held something up in both hands. "Cate and Clint made them. They're out there in the dark slapping them on all the cars right now!"

Huh? It was one of those obnoxious *Proud Parent* car stickers. But wait. I read it again and laughed. OMG. It looked exactly like the real deal but it said:

> **PROUD PARENT**
> **OF A PLEASANT HILL HIGH**
> **HORNY STUDENT!**

Canfield was going to freak in his polyester pants.

Amy stopped suddenly a few feet away. I could tell that she could tell that something was really wrong. So I threw my arm around Jen and gave her a squeeze. I was about to say something when I realized that Amy wasn't looking at Jen. She was staring at something behind us.

I looked over my shoulder to the far end of the courtyard just in time to see Eric walking past the bleachers onto the darkened football field with Candy Esposito.

chapter twenty-six
gathering nuts for winter

"Ouch!" I yelped, grabbing at my back. Mom poked me with a pin *again*.

No, it wasn't some voodoo doll thing. It was worse—way worse. It was the second Saturday in October, the day of our annual family Christmas card photo.

I was standing on this upside-down milk carton crate staring at myself in a full-length mirror watching Mom let out the back of my elf costume. I wanted to kill myself. How could I have agreed to do this *again?!*

"Oh Paisley, you are going to look even *more* adorable this year," Mom gushed out of the side of her mouth, careful not to spit pins at me.

I tried to smile, but it felt more like a painful wince. Fortunately, Mom didn't notice. She was intently focused on the expandable panty hose panel she was adding to the back of my little red elf vest. Yes, it was all very sad.

Our Christmas photo started out as a fun little Hanover family tradition, featuring Mom, Dad, my older brother Parker, and me in cute costumes lovingly sewn by Mom way before she realized she hated sewing and totally sucked at it. I should clarify—the costumes *used to be* cute, when I was like four. But now they were just ridiculous and really tight. Our fun little family tradition had morphed into an unfun huge annual nightmare.

Parker, always the reindeer in our photo, had been rebelling for years. He'd tried everything. It was an insult to all reindeer-kind, a redheaded reindeer was biologically impossible, he would never get a girlfriend, never get married, and end up living at home with our parents for the rest of his life until he lost it and went on a homicidal shooting rampage that would, of course, be attributed to his formative years as a reindeer. Nothing worked.

So this year, Parker not only refused to wear the reindeer costume, he also refused to come home from college. We were going to have to Photoshop him in. But I was stuck—in my elf costume. I still needed food, shelter, and a decent clothes allowance.

I sighed, shaking my head at my glittery red and green reflection. How did my life turn out like this? It's so not fair. And it wasn't like I was feeling good *before* the elf costume. All morning my brain had been hitting the replay button on the disastrous mix known as my sophomore life.

Eric—my brand-new below-the-belt crush—ditched me at the end of the dance and snuck off to do I-don't-even-want-to-know-what with *Candy Esposito!* What, was it like her life's mission now to ruin *my* life?! And Clint—my long-standing below-the-belt crush—had totally blown me off for our big date tonight. Just the thought of our conversation in Drama made me sick to my stomach. Maybe I needed a new belt—and I wasn't talking about my elf costume.

"Too tight?" asked Mom.

"No," I said glumly to my reflection. "Too elf."

Mom ignored me.

Worst of all, I'd completely failed Jen. I was nowhere near saving her reputation! Thanks to me, our phones were spending a nice relaxing weekend locked in Mrs. Hollet's desk. So I couldn't even investigate my big theory that the sext had actually been taken with Jen's phone until Monday morning.

And Hutch? I had no clue. But it seemed way more likely that he'd barf on me before he'd spill the truth about that photo. So much for my "big plan." And thanks to my brilliant relationship advice, Jen had managed to crush the heart and soul of Bodie Jones—the most confident guy at our school. What else . . . Oh, right. Pleasant Hill High darling Candy Esposito hated me so much, she had to advertise it. *And* the whole school had seen me in my underwear. Other than that, life was great.

I stared at my reflection feeling sorry for my overgrown elf self. Well, at least my green sparkly hat and jingle-bell earrings still fit perfectly. Maybe I could fake my own death and go off to join the Elf Capades.

"Okay, all done!" Mom smacked me in the butt, which made my stiff red flannel micro-mini with glitter glue trim suddenly pop up in the front. Perfect. Mom stood up, admiring me proudly in the mirror. "You have the cutest little legs."

"Mom. How would you know? I'm wearing green tights with a droopy crotch that hangs below my skirt!"

"Honey, don't be negative. It imprints on your brain and leaves a scar."

"Oh, right, sorry." I rolled my eyes. "We wouldn't want *that* to happen—which reminds me . . . maybe I should just wear my elf hat and my underwear for the photo this year."

Mom winced, and I instantly felt bad—but it quickly passed.

"Oh honey, I'm so, *so* sorry." She covered her mouth, looking genuinely remorseful for a second. "I feel just awful. How can I make it up to you? I could give you private driving lessons?"

I looked at her like she was nuts. "Uh, no thanks."

"What about a big party? A shopping spree? A new computer?" Now she was laying it on thick.

"I dunno." I gazed vaguely in her direction, trying my best to appear scarred for life. "I'm still a little in shock. But when I can fully assess the depth of my emotional damage, I'll give you a list." I was determined to milk the wrap-dress debacle for as long as possible.

"Anything, Paisley. Anything," she said with mock desperation. I started to open my mouth. "Except the Christmas card photo, of course." She reached out and lovingly stroked the back of my elf hat.

Mom reached for Parker's clip-on brown fuzzy antlers on the counter and shook her head, gazing wistfully at them. "I'm so disappointed in Parker. Everyone loves him as the reindeer. Everyone." She sniffled softly. "It won't be the same this year without Parker in his antlers and cute little black nose."

I stared hard at her from across the room. "Mom, are you *crying?*"

"No, I'm weeping. There's a difference."

The day went downhill from there.

Dad went for a long run in his embarrassingly short shorts. Mom pouted and stitched, and pouted and unstitched, and pouted and re-stitched my elf vest. I sat at the kitchen table doing my homework and hoping to forget about my miserable life.

When I'd finished, I tried to pound out a draft of my Teen Scene article, but—surprise!—I didn't know where to start. So instead I just typed random thoughts and observations about school and double standards and this whole sexting thing. When I reread it, it was a total rambling mess. I stared blankly at the computer screen. What was I trying to say? I couldn't find the right voice for non-Miss-UnPleasant me. And besides, how could I finish anything about the sexting drama if I didn't know how or why the whole thing started? I slumped back in my chair and sighed.

After like three hours, Mom *finally* got the expandable panty hose panel just right. She raced upstairs to change into her Mrs. Claus costume.

"Ho, ho, ho, everyone!" she said, making her big entrance.

Dad looked up from the bills he was sorting at the counter. "Well hello, Mrs. Claus." He winked at her and smiled.

I stared at Mom, wrinkling my nose and blinking. Wait. Something was . . . not right. Had Mom gained weight? Had her costume shrunk? OMG. Why hadn't I ever noticed this before? My mother didn't look like Mrs. Santa Claus—she looked like a varsity North Pole dancer!

Ho, ho, ho was right. OMG. How totally embarrassing!

Dad, still wearing his running stuff, sprang into action. "I'll be right back," he said to Mom, all flirty, jogging toward the stairs. "After I slip into something . . . a little more comfortable—and dazzling."

I rolled my eyes. "Please. You guys are really grossing me out!"

I looked back at my laptop, but I couldn't concentrate anymore. I really wanted to call Jen to see how she was doing, but I couldn't. Her house didn't have a landline—part of their post-divorce new economy—and I didn't know her mom or little brother's cell numbers. So I closed my Teen Scene file and went online. I was just about to write Jen an e-mail when . . . OMG.

Eric Sobel sent you a message on Facebook . . .

I held my breath and clicked open the e-mail.

Re: Hey, PH.

Where'd you go last night?

What? I read it again searching for hidden meaning. That's it?

That's it?! *PH, where'd you go last night?* No apology? No explanation? Unbelievable! Jeez, ES. Where'd *you* go last night?!

So that's basically what I typed.

> Hey, ES.
>
> Bathroom. Where'd you go last night? And what'd you do with Candy?

Guys are such jerks—even nice guys! All they care about is one thing. I sat there fuming, trying not to imagine what he and Candy had done after the dance on the dark football field. I was just about to hit SEND when I thought of something.

The sext.

I tapped my fingernail against my upper teeth, thinking. Eric must know something about that photo, because he had warned Bodie about it a few days before it started circulating. But what? I stopped tapping. Had Eric actually seen something at that party? Or maybe . . . maybe Hutch had confided in him and actually told him what went down. Ergh! Why hadn't I just met him at the listening spot?!

I quickly revised my message.

> Hey, ES.
>
> Bathroom. Jen really needed me. You know anything about the Jen/Hutch photo that's going around? Jen's crushed. Bodie dumped her. Hey, where'd you go last night?

As I was rereading my note for like the fifth time, a chat window popped up. It was Jen.

> Jen: U there?
>
> Me: Yep. U ok?
>
> Jen: No. BoD wont tlk 2 me.
>
> Me: Bumr! giv him time.
>
> Jen: Doubt it. Sext buzz all over FB. ☹
>
> Me: Crp!

Jen: anyting frm vrsty buttcap Hutch?

I hit SAVE on my note to Eric. I'd deal with him later.

Me: Not yet. Im on it. 2nite 4 sure!

Jen: wht dif dos it mak now? 2 late.

Me: Not tru! Nut Fest 2nite?

Jen: Cant. Grounded til senr yr. Mom hrd abt sext
& freakd! Dad 2.

Me: Dbl crp! mayb I wont go ethr.

Jen: yeah . . . Miss my phon!!!!

Me: sorreeeeeee!!!!

Jen: whyd u wnt it anywy?

Me: i thnk sext was takn w/ ur phon!

Jen: wht?! why?

Me: looks lik othr pix u took. Look at ur pix albms
frm that wknd

There was nothing new from Jen for a few minutes. So I just watched Dad in his Vegas Santa costume setting up the tripod in front of the fireplace. He started a fire and turned on Christmas music really loud to get us all quote-unquote in the mood.

Yeah, in the mood to convert to Islam.

Vegas Santa wore sunglasses, a glittery red dinner jacket with black tuxedo pants, and the traditional hat and a long white beard. It was kind of a Dean-Martin-meets-ZZ-Top-on-an-eggnog-bender look. I had no idea how Vegas Santa started. And frankly, I didn't want to know.

Mom and Dad started dancing together to this super-sultry version of "Santa Baby"—the original Eartha Kitt one—like it was the most normal thing to be doing in the middle of October in front of their impressionable child. Silent library scream!!!

Finally, Jen started typing again. Thank God.

Jen: weird! yeah. c wht u mean. but who?!!

Me: dunno yet. Who u thnk? membr any 1?

Long pause. I waited.

"Okay, everyone, places please!" Dad called out, buttoning his red dinner jacket and pulling his beard into place. "Come on! We're about to lose our light."

The bells on my slippers jingled as I trudged over and stood in front of the fireplace. I just wanted to get the whole thing over with so I could get back to Jen and solving the mysteries of my pathetic life.

Mom gave me a quick once-over, tugging down my fitted vest and brushing the pigtails sticking out below my elf cap. "Adorable!" she said. "Oh, wait. Wait! Lip gloss!" She ran over to her purse and came back dabbing a little gloss on her lips, then on mine.

Dad double-checked his camera settings and directed us into our places in front of the crackling fire. "Leave enough room for Photoshop Parker, okay?" I stepped a little to the left. Then Dad pushed the auto thingy and ran toward us shouting, "Ho, ho, ho! Smile, everyone!"

My face went on auto-smile just as the auto-shutter started going off like crazy.

When it stopped, Dad ran back over to his camera. "Okay, now let's do the leaping one for backup," he said, totally seriously. "Ready?"

That's when the doorbell rang.

"I'll get it!" I couldn't wait to get out of there. I trotted toward the front door jingling all the way. My face was still on auto-smile when I opened the door—until . . . OMG!

Clint Bedard was standing on my doorstep holding his motor-cycle helmet.

missed connections

Clint smiled. "Hey Red . . . and ah, *green* and . . ." He scratched his upper lip with his fingers, obviously trying not to laugh. "So, am I . . . am I *early*? Or . . . two months late?"

This wasn't really happening. It couldn't be! I slammed the door shut and tried to think, but I was panting way too loud, and my brain circuits felt totally morti-fried! Please, no. This *couldn't* be happening. I turned and looked through the peephole.

Yep. There was Clint Bedard in a black T-shirt and his stylishly beat-up leather jacket, waiting patiently, looking extremely good and extremely amused.

I opened the door a few inches. "What are you *doing* here?!"

He pulled back and squinted a little like I was blowing smoke in his eyes or something. "I kinda thought we had a date tonight. You know, the Nut Festival?" He looked down at something written on his palm and nodded. "Yeah, I'm sure we had a date."

What?! OMG. OMG! I was totally confused, but all I could do was stare blankly at him and shake my head like a bug-eyed escapee from the island of misfit toys.

"Oh, I get it." He grinned. "*Nutty.* You're already in character. Cool. Right on."

"No!" I kept shaking my head. "What happened to . . . Where's Lip Gloss?"

"Who?" Clint seemed completely confused.

"Your *girlfriend of the week.*"

Clint ran a hand through his dark messy hair and tilted his head. "Um . . . Red, wasn't that you?" He frowned, then smiled at whatever dorky expression I was making. "Hey, I'm cool to take it one week at a time."

OMG! Why was I such an idiot? Why was I so sure Clint had blown me off? God, now I couldn't even remember! He'd said he was going to some party!!! Didn't he?

"Paisley!" Mom called from the living room. "Hon, who is it?"

"It's nobody! Nothing! I got it!"

"Red, you didn't forget about tonight, did you?" Clint looked at me, trying to get a read. "I called you twice today."

Groan . . . "My phone's at school, in lockup . . . And no! No, I didn't forget. But I . . . I sorta thought . . ." I shook my head again. "Never mind. Just . . . No."

"Good." He leaned casually against the doorjamb, raising his eyebrows. "'Cause I've got some fun stuff planned for tonight."

I immediately went from constantly shaking my head to constantly nodding.

"I dig your crazy little outfit." He smiled, taking in all of my micro-mini elfish glory.

I winced. "I'll be right back."

"Hey," he called after me. "You don't have to change. I like your fashion deviant side." I turned back to look at him. "Heard about that poncho thing last night." He smiled wickedly. "Sorry I missed it."

OMG! My cheeks burst into flames. Yep, I was sure owning the name *Red.*

I laughed nervously, then sprinted up the stairs, pulling off my hat and vest and kicking off my jingle-bell slippers like a total spaz along the way. OMG. I had to change clothes before Clint saw my insane parents and changed his mind.

I got back down the stairs in like forty-five seconds, wearing boots, jeans, and a cute fitted thermal long-sleeve tee. Clint was waiting for me out by his bike. I smiled calmly, trying not to pant as I caught a glimpse of myself in the mirror next to the front door. Oops. Pigtails! I yanked out both elastic bands and shook my hair loose. Uh-oh. I had serious elf hat hair. Oh well, I shrugged.

"Bye, Santa! Bye, Mrs. Claus! Off to the Walnut Festival with Clint!" I waited for like half a second for a response, then slipped out the door.

I held on to Clint for my crazy life as we screamed down the frontage road on his bike. I couldn't stop smiling. OMG. Clint and I were actually going out! I wondered what people would think when they saw us together. Whatever. Who cares! Then I started to laugh. It was one of those weird exhilaration-fueled, uncontrollable laugh attacks. I just laughed into the wind for the longest time.

But then, whatever had seemed funny suddenly wasn't funny anymore.

For some strange reason, I all of a sudden couldn't stop thinking about Eric Sobel. Ergh. He could've at least apologized for ditching me! What a major buttcap. If he wanted to be with Candy Esposito instead of me, then fine. Whatever! No. Not fine. Who was I kidding? But I wasn't going to throw myself at him like Candy. And I refused be one of those pathetic, clingy girls who just hang around waiting for some guy, any guy—even Eric Sobel.

I so didn't need Eric Sobel. Hey, I was on a date with Clint Bedard! The motorcycle accelerated hard. I tightened my grip around Clint's waist and leaned against his back. I smiled. His worn leather jacket felt soft against my cheek and smelled really good.

If Eric was at the Nut Festival, I decided, I wasn't going to talk to him. I'd just ignore him. Yeah, see how that feels, dude. Wait. Oh, crap in a hat. I can't ignore him. I have to find out what he knows about the sext!

I thought about it for a few blocks and totally changed my mind. If I saw Eric, I was definitely going to talk to him. I wanted to know about the sext *and* I wanted to know about last night. I wasn't gonna let him off that easy.

I closed my eyes and rested my head against Clint's back. Oh boy. This was all getting very confusing.

chapter twenty-eight
whack-a-mole

When Clint and I hopped off his bike, it was just beginning to get dark. The sky was an electric blue behind the darkening silhouettes of the highest rides, the Ferris wheel and the Zipper and the Super Loop. The lights at the top of the Zipper looked almost like stars. It still smelled like summer, but it felt cool like fall. I hugged myself, wishing I had brought a jacket instead of just a hoodie.

People were spilling out of cars and minivans and SUVs everywhere, heading to the entrance in loud excited packs. I looked around the parking lot but I didn't see anyone I knew, which was weird. Just about everyone in our whole school—in our whole *town*—goes to the Nut Festival every October. Since it only happens once a year, it's a pretty big deal—and an excellent, parentally approved reason to get out of the house. And stay out late.

I pulled off my helmet. Wow. The air was popping with unsupervised excitement, ringing bells and buzzers, and crazy-weird carnival music. A carload of screams poured down from the top of the Super Loop.

Inside the gates, it smelled sweet and dusty like straw and dropped corndogs. Clint and I cruised around for a while, not really talking, just wandering along the rows of crowded booths, taking it all in:

nut bread, nut pies, nut candies, nut sculptures, nut jewelry, nut key chains. Yep, it was exactly as advertised—*nut*rageous!

And it was already packed. Groups of kids moved like screaming sugared-up amoeba blobs down the rows of booths, absorbing smaller groups, then splitting and splitting again as people stopped to roll a wooden ball up a chute or toss Ping-Pong balls or shoot a stream of water into a clown's mouth until its balloon brain exploded and set off a jackpot of bells and flashing lights.

Clint and I stopped at the water pistol clown-killing booth and watched. He had his hands stuffed in his jeans pockets. I leaned against a post, looking around and casually trying to smooth out my elf-hat hair.

Groan. There was Hutch.

I moved my head to get a better look at him past the hanging stuffed animals. He was pitching baseballs at a stack of dented silver bottle-shaped thingies and was surrounded by some of his jock crew and a few squealing girls. No sign of Eric. Yet. Every time Hutch threw a pitch, there was an explosion of clinking metal, and everyone standing around him cheered.

I shook my head. Jen was at home by herself, grounded, because of that stupid sext, and Hutch seemed more popular than ever— with guys *and* girls. Ugh. I so didn't get it.

I was thinking how totally unfair it was when a small group of Uns with black duct tape over their mouths walked by all wearing black T-shirts. It was Mandy Mindel and Teddy Baedeker, Bean and Amy, Svend, LG Wong, and a few Library Girls. I waved, but they didn't see me. I watched them carving their way around and through the groups as parents and kids from other schools stared and pointed, trying to figure out what was up with the tape. I smiled. Then the weirdest, coolest thing happened. The Uns stopped near the baseball booth, standing in a loose cluster right behind Hutch and his crew. Then slowly they moved into a line with their backs to me and—OMG!

When they all lined up, the backs of their shirts read:

PRESIDENT HUTCH DID NOT WIN

My jaw dropped. "Clint. Clint!" He was way into the water pistol clown-drench-off going on next to us. I grabbed his shoulder. "Look at this!" But when we turned back to the Uns, they were innocently standing in a group again. Their message was gone.

"Wait. No," I sputtered. "That's not . . ."

Clint looked at me funny. "What? Hutch has a bunch of groupies . . . ?"

Did I just dream that? "No, wait. Keep watching."

When Hutch wound up for another pitch, the Uns quickly moved back into another formation. I grabbed Clint's arm and squeezed. There it was again—but different—in big bold yellow letters!

HUTCH IS NOT MY PRESIDENT

"Look!" I whispered. Each shirt had a word—or part of a word—slapped across the back in yellow tape.

Suddenly there was another eruption of clinks and flying metal bottles. Hutch pumped the air and his groupies cheered and clapped. The Uns stood motionless in their fomenting formation. I laughed, suddenly filled with this giddy euphoric *un*thusiasm. The guy working in the booth tossed Hutch a big stuffed pink pig. Ah. Perfect.

Hutch turned around, holding his pig in the air. He had a bright yellow cast on his left hand. Wow. That was new. He started to give the pig to BS2 but then jerked it away and held it up above her head, teasing her and trying to get her and the other girls to jump for it like little dogs leaping for a bacon treat. Gross. Pig was right.

Hutch looked around all of a sudden and frowned. He took a quick step forward, thrusting out his jaw. He must have seen the faces of protesting Uns with tape over their mouths. Good thing he couldn't see their backs. Before things got ugly, the Uns calmly dispersed in different directions and disappeared into the crowd.

I exhaled slowly. "Wow," I breathed. "Nice UnVisible protest."

"Next round?" Clint asked casually, pointing to the clown game.

I turned to him, gesturing to where the Uns had been. "That was so cool! Very . . . *creative.*"

Clint looked weirdly innocent, which made me so sure he was guilty.

"Was that . . . was that your idea?"

"What are you talking about?" he asked, shrugging. But he had this huge lopsided grin on his face as he pulled me toward the counter of the booth. "Get your head down."

"*Was* that your idea?" I asked again. He shook his head. "Was it Cate's?"

We sat down on these sticky vinyl stools in front of the mounted squirt guns. He leaned in. "You'll never guess."

I looked at him like *and?*

He smiled wickedly. "It was the deviant brainchild of one Mandy Mindel."

"No way!" I practically shouted.

"She loves you. They all love you. Well, they love Miss UnPleasant you."

I should've just smiled and soaked up the warm glow of group love. Instead I kind of freaked out. "But I can't *be* Miss UnPleasant anymore!" I blurted.

Clint studied me for a second. "Sure you can." He shrugged again, reaching for his water pistol. "You *are* her. You just can't hide behind her name anymore."

He made it sound so easy. Sure, be fearless, be honest, and don't give a crap what anyone else thinks. But I wasn't sure how to do that. *Could* I even do that? I leaned my elbows on the counter and gripped my water pistol, aiming at the grotesque clown head in front of me. I waited for the starting bell. How was I supposed to be Paisley Hanover *and* Miss UnPleasant at the same time?

The bell went off like the start of a horse race. I gave my clown a good face-drenching before my stream of water found his mouth. But then I was on it. The more I stared at that mocking clown face, the more it looked just like Hutch. I so wanted to drown it. My clown's balloon got bigger and bigger. I was sure I was going to win. But then I looked over at Clint's clown and sprayed my guy in the nose again. Crap! Clint must have been having the same problem, only worse. He started whooping and trying to distract me. And then he turned and sprayed me in the face.

"Hey!" I yelled. But I didn't break my focus. A second later, my clown's balloon brain exploded.

"Yeah, baby!" I jumped to my feet, wiping water off the side of my face, and did my happy spastic jazz hands dance right in front of Clint. He shook his head, trying not to appear impressed at my superior squirt-gun-slinging skills.

We started to walk off, but then the guy in the clown booth called to us. "Hey lady, you are wiener!" Huh? I turned around and he held out this little stuffed frog. Oh, right.

"Thank you," I said, grabbing my goofy green trophy. As we walked down the row of booths, I waved it in Clint's face. "I am wiener. I am wiener!"

"No, lady," he said with a funny foreign accent. "You are corndog! Very cute corndog!" He laughed, grabbing me, and then he whispered something in my ear.

I leaned back into him. "What?!" I couldn't hear. There was so much going on around us, it was like we were walking inside a giant pinball machine.

Clint tilted his head and smiled at me for a second. His expression was definitely not a typical Clint look. "Nothing!" he said. "Tell you later." And we kept walking.

What did he say? What did he say?! I wanted to yell, *Tell me now! Tell me now!* But before I could mortify myself by screaming it out loud, Clint said something else.

"What?" I called over the noise.

"There're more!" he shouted.

"What?"

"All over."

"More *what* all over?"

"You'll see." I looked at him. For real? He flashed me a devilish grin. "Wherever Hutch goes tonight, the painful truth will follow," he said.

Huh. I had no idea what that meant, but I smiled, ready to be awed and inspired by Cate and Bean's Underwear Resistance Movement. Then I felt a pinch of guilt. I should definitely be doing more for the cause.

Before I could say anything, an eruption of screams from a nearby booth caught my attention. I turned to see Candy Esposito speed-pounding a big round hammer, ferociously playing whack-a-mole. She was surrounded by cheering friends and fans. And guess who was front and center? Carreyn! She was jumping up and down like Candy Esposito's new biggest fan. I couldn't believe her. Everyone was screaming and cheering—except for Cate, Split Ends, LG, and a few Library Girls standing nearby, suspiciously quiet in a cluster of black T-shirts.

Wow. Candy was scary fast, and her hand-eye coordination was deadly. You could tell that her dad used to play professional baseball. I wondered whose face she was seeing on the mole's head. Probably mine. I tugged on Clint's sleeve, pulling him along, hoping to slip through the crowd without being seen. Candy was the last person I wanted to deal with tonight.

"Hey Paisley!" Candy yelled. Gulp. I kept my head down and kept walking. "Paisley! Paisley, wait up!" I glanced quickly over my shoulder to see her hand her Whack-a-Mole hammer to Bratty Sasshole #1, who, by the way, was horrible. Then Candy bounded gracefully in our direction.

I stopped and turned to face her. My stomach prickled. This could get ugly. First that stupid ad, then date-napping Eric, and now rubbing it in my face?! I felt ick-to-my-stomach watching her run over. *Oh, mighty Crisis!* I shouted inside my headspace, trying to summon my inner warrior girl.

Candy jogged up to us. "Hey, Paisley, how you doin'?" she asked.

I didn't say anything. What, was she like my new best friend? Now that we were dating the same guy? On the same night?! Ergh!

She smiled at Clint all friendly. "Hi, Clint."

"Hey, Cindy." He nodded.

She gave him a strange look. "Candy," she said, correcting him.

"Oh right, sorry, Candy. I thought you were someone else."

Candy looked surprised and a little wounded, like no one had ever confused her with someone else before in her entire life. Ooh. Clint was good, and by that I mean *bad*.

"So how's Jen doing?" She pressed her perfectly pouty, glowing-with-gloss lips together, looking sad.

OMG, what nerve!

"I keep trying to call her," Candy went on, "but she never picks up, and her voicemail's full."

I stared at her hard. "How do you *think* she's doing?"

Candy shrugged awkwardly. "Well, just tell her I'm thinking of her, okay?"

I nodded, then I was blown back a little when this booming, cheesy voice came crashing down from the loudspeakers.

"Welcome to the sixty-third annual Walnut Festival! Be sure to visit the pie pavilion to taste the finalists of this year's nut-off recipe contest."

SIDEBRA

The Nut-Packing Contest was insanely popular—and not just because you almost always got on the eleven o'clock news. If you won, you also got to be Nut King or Nut Queen for a whole year. It brought great prestige to your school and came with tons of perks, like getting out of class a lot and riding in limos to all these official city events, and the big gold "I'm Nut Royalty" lawn sign (which was tacky, but still), and a $1,000 cash prize, and best of all, you got to star in a real TV commercial with the dancing Nut Crackers.

A few years ago, Logan Adler's older sister Adelle was Nut Queen and this talent scout saw her commercial and discovered her and now she's on *All My Children*. True story. So now, practically every teenager in town tries to enter. There's a lottery to see who actually gets to compete. And no, I didn't get in this year—but Amy did!

Clint and I looked at each other. Not likely.

"And don't miss tonight's main event, the Nut-in-Cheek Nut-Packing Contest at seven thirty in the Nut Dish Amphitheatre!"

Clint pointed up at the loudspeaker over our heads. "We're there."

I nodded. "We're so there!"

"Oh, I'm there too!" said Candy. "I'm entered this year! I got in!"

I had to fight the urge to roll my eyes. What else did she have to try to win?

"If I'm Nut Queen," she gushed, "I'm going to donate the cash prize to orphans in Zimbabwe."

OMG. Was she for real?

"Good luck," I said lamely.

"Thanks." Candy smiled her warmest sun-kissed-honey smile. "Hey, don't miss it, okay? It's going to be fun. Really."

"Oh yeah." Clint nodded with a smirk. "It's going to be *unbe-lievably* fun."

chapter twenty-nine
performance anxiety

Candy waved and ran back to finish clobbering a poor defenseless rodent.

I looked at Clint. "What did you mean by *un*believably fun?" I asked.

"You'll see." He flashed his flirty grin and grabbed my hand. He held it the whole time we walked along, weaving our way through the crowd. I felt a little tingly nervous. What would everyone think if they saw us together? What would Eric think? I glanced over my shoulder a few times. This so wasn't how I wanted Eric to find out about Clint.

I looked up at him. He brushed one hand through his hair, seeming totally relaxed, like it was the most natural thing in our social universe to be walking through the Walnut Festival holding hands. So I tried to relax too, but first I offered a quick silent prayer to Svetlana the sweat goddess. *Svetlana, Svetlana, dry and cool, don't let me be a clammy fool.* I glanced at Clint, doing my best imitation of confident, composed, unclammy me.

"Hey, check out the Bouncy House," he said, pointing at this giant red inflated castle filled with happy, shrieking kids.

"Oh, I always loved the Bouncy House!" I squeaked.

Clint nodded with this funny smile on his face. He must have had really good Bouncy House memories too. I stared wistfully at the big painted sign near the entrance.

If You're Taller Than Mr. Walnut (Sorry), YOU'RE TOO BIG TO BOUNCE!

"We're too big." I sighed. "Forever."

Clint shook his head. "When did we get taller than Mr. Walnut?" he asked, sounding weirdly earnest. "When did life get so . . . complicated?" He turned and looked at me.

Wait. I tried to get a read on him. Was he kidding? He had to be. I smacked him with my stuffed green frog, which, of course, just made him laugh.

When we turned the corner, a big whiff of fried dough and cotton candy hit us in the nose. Yum! We headed straight across the fried food court, basically a bunch of white trucks parked on a big patch of dirt, and got in line. I was standing there listening to the hum of generators when I suddenly got this weird feeling. I turned to Clint. He just smiled and squeezed my hand.

Then I saw a pack of Pleasant Hill High varsity letterman's jackets coming our way. I immediately turned and pretended to read the illuminated menu on the side of the truck. There were dead bugs trapped inside it. I glanced over my shoulder after they had passed by. Yep, Eric was with them. I quickly turned back and stared at the dead bugs. Holy shiitake mushrooms. When *did* life get so complicated?

"Hey, what do you know—it's the queen of the *undesirables!*" I turned. Hutch was standing right behind us. He gave Clint the cool-guy-head-nod greeting while Clint gave him the don't-mess-with-her face. "Where's the tape over your mouth, Hanover? You too good for your own protest?"

I felt my neck go hot and was about to tell Hutch what I *really* thought of him when—

"Easy there, dude," said Clint, raising his hand. "You're not on the football field. You're talking to a lady."

Hutch forced out a raspy laugh.

I smiled. *A lady?* I liked how that sounded. But I could take Hutch myself. "Hutch, I told you—it's not *my* protest. It's all the people whose votes weren't counted—who, by the way, voted for *me*, not you."

"Whatever," Hutch groaned. "It's annoying. Come on, it's the weekend, Hanover. Give it a rest."

"Hey man, don't take it personally," said Clint, in this like confidential way. "It's nothing against you—it's really about Canfield. You did a cool thing, voting for Paisley instead of yourself, and sticking it to Canfield. People dig that about you."

Hutch was nodding along and almost smiling. Wow. Clint was . . . I didn't even know how to describe him. He was like Mr. UnPleasant—fearless and honest and . . . totally like . . . *sexy-manfident.*

Clint turned to me and stared deep into my eyes, like he was discovering a secret truth, the secret of . . . of true love. He put his arm around me and pulled me close. God, he felt good and he smelled good too. And it wasn't just his beat-up leather jacket. His eyes sparkled with mischief or . . . or—what was it?—as he raised one side of his mouth in a sexy smile. He finally tore his eyes away from mine and looked back at Hutch.

"But dude, you should man up and just resign," Clint said casually. "No one really believes you got more votes than this brainy babe."

I blushed in 3-D.

SIDEBRA

After Canfield had printed up the election ballots with this nasty little paragraph about how anyone who wrote in Paisley Hanover (me!) for sophomore class president wouldn't get their ballot counted at all, Eric Sobel had a genius idea. *Everyone should write me in!* Because if *everyone* wrote me in, we could throw the election, and Canfield would have to accept that I was the people's choice for sophomore class president. And it worked! Well, kind of. Okay, well, not really.

Hutch looked a little disappointed, but then he nodded earnestly. "Yeah, man. You're right. I'll do it on Monday."

What?

"Next!"

I looked around, totally startled. Clint was counting some bills. Hutch was puffing out his cheeks like a doofus staring at some girl's butt.

Whoops! Major flash fantasy.

"Next!" yelled the puffy, sweaty lady trapped inside the truck. She had wisps of cotton candy in her hair. "Step up, please!"

Clint stepped to the window and ordered. Hutch and I stood there awkwardly for a few seconds, not looking, then looking, then not looking at each other.

"Hey, are you doing the Nut-Packing Contest?" he asked.

"No. I entered but I didn't win the lottery thing."

"Too bad. You'd make a foxy Nut Queen." He chuckled but then looked away. "I'm in it this year. In it to win it! I've been training hard." He puffed out his cheeks really big and made this goofy face. And I laughed, like for real. It was weird. I was kind of horrified.

"It was . . . it was fun dancing with you last night," he said, scratching the back of his neck.

What?! I nodded vaguely. Did he really think we had danced together?

He glanced over at Clint still standing at the window. "Hey, wanna go on some rides later?"

Uh-oh.

"Yeah, I would but . . . I mean, I do want to talk and stuff . . . But I'm, you know, here with someone."

He nodded and sort of smirked at me. "Playing it cool, huh? No worries. That's how I like to play it too." Inside, I totally cringed. *Ick!* Clint joined us holding a huge poof of cotton candy. "So, see you guys at the contest later?" Clint nodded. "And, Paisley, keep those cards and letters coming!" He chuckled.

I smiled faux real. But OMG. What had I done? I'd created a monster. I had to find a way to talk to Hutch about the sext before this locker stalker thing blew up in my face.

"What cards and letters?" Clint asked as we watched Hutch lumber off into the crowd.

I shrugged. "I don't know. Probably some jock talk, varsity letterman thing." I winced inside.

"He's a funny dude."

"Yeah." I changed the subject fast. "Hey, thanks for sticking up for me."

"But of course," he said in his Shakespearean accent, "'tis what a gentleman does for his lady."

Clint could make my heart blush. It was the strangest, most wonderful feeling. I nervously grabbed a piece of cotton candy and kept walking.

"Hey Red, let's win a giant stuffed animal together," he said, twirling the white paper wand as I tugged off another pink tuft of sugar. "We can give it a loving home and raise it together or . . . or if it's really rotten, put it up for adoption."

What?! I stuffed a big wad of cotton candy halfway into his mouth.

"Mmm." He nodded, trying to wangle the last bit past his lips. "Should I take that as a yes?"

I suddenly felt all embarrassed like a total dorkasaurus and looked away, trying to figure out what to say to that. Fortunately, I didn't have to. I pointed over Clint's shoulder with this huge goobery smile. "Hey, check it out."

Yay! It was the fundraising booth for our Drama class. A big banner hung across the front of it. *Support Pleasant Hill High's Performance Anxiety!* Finally, some people I wanted to see.

"It's not just the Drama booth," he whispered as we walked over. "It's headquarters for the Underwear Resistance. And just so you know my personal level of commitment, I'm not wearing any!" He raced off toward the booth. I tried to catch him but he was surprisingly fast for a non-athlete who had probably spent more time cutting P.E. than attending.

Charlie and a few other Uns were manning the booth, all with black tape over their mouths and wearing matching black T-shirts: *Show the Arts Some Love, Date a Drama Student!*

"Hey, Paisley! How's it goin'?" asked Charlie. "Wanna buy a shirt?"

Wait a second. I looked at him closely. It wasn't black duct tape over his mouth—it was black greasepaint, theatre makeup. It was greasepaint on all of their mouths. It just *looked* like tape. Huh. Cool trick.

Just then, Bean, Svend, and Amy strolled casually up to the booth. But they were panting, all with flushed red faces.

"Hey, you nut jobs!" I called out. "Impressive UnVisible work out there."

"Yeah, way to get the message out," Clint added.

"I love this!" said Amy with a huge grin. "This is the most fun I've ever had at the Walnut Festival ever!"

"Me too!" Bean squealed. "Did you see his face? Hutch looked like his head was going to explode all over the food court!"

Amy and Svend nodded, trying to catch their breath.

"That was a close one." Svend wiped sweat off his face, careful not to smear his black "tape." "He's very sure on to us."

Mandy and Teddy jogged up behind us. They looked completely

exhilarated. I'd never ever seen Mandy looking so . . . so flushed and glowing—and not from embarrassment for a change.

"Operation *Watch Your Back*—all systems go," said Mandy with this devil-girl face, her eyes sparkling and naughty. OMG. I hardly recognized her.

Teddy giggled. "Yeah! Mission accomplished."

Cate and LG strolled up casually, followed by a string of not-very-innocent-looking Uns.

"Nice shirts, you guys," I said.

Charlie held up a Drama shirt. "Twenty dollars and this one is yours!" He sounded very cheerful despite the nose saddle and double black eyes. Charlie had been working overtime to get back on my good side since the ad. He smiled at me all salesman-y. "All proceeds go to the Pleasant Hill High Drama program!"

"Yeah. I'll take one." Clint reached for his wallet.

"Does it come with a subliminal morphing message on the back?" I asked Charlie.

"Nope," interrupted Mandy, sounding quite proud. "Those shirts are a limited edition. I have a silk-screening machine in our garage. I can make anything," she whispered.

I smiled, genuinely impressed. Who knew that Mandy Mindel was so arts-and-*crafty*?

"Hey Pais." Bean waved. "Wanna buy a twelve-pack of dark chocolate Hor*nut* clusters?"

Svend, chewing a Hornut cluster, gave me two thumbs up.

"The antennas are edible," added Cate with salesgirl enthusiasm. "And it's for a really good cause. Us!"

"Slick presentation, you guys. But sorry." I shrugged. "I'm a dork. I forgot to bring money. Cate, by the way, love those *Horny Student* stickers."

"Thanks," she and Clint said at the same time. Then Cate pulled us in close. "Last night, we mobilized almost thirty people to slap stickers on cars in the parking lot," she whispered. "Over three hundred—*smack!*—in like ten minutes! By Monday morning, Canfield's phone will be ringing off the hook."

"He'll be going *nuts!*" said Bean, leaning in with crazy Charles Manson eyes. "And ready to negotiate with us."

"Or resign in shame!" added Amy.

"That's when we deliver our little message." Clint nodded. He stood up straight and got all dad-like. "Dear Mr. Canfield, We accept your *un*biased decision regarding the results of sophomore class president election—along with your resignation. Sincerely, about six hundred names lifted off the parents' club donor list."

"Wow," said Charlie in total awe. "Strategic *and* devious. I'm truly impressed."

I looked at Charlie, then at Clint and Cate. "That's kinda harsh, don't you think? I mean, I hate the guy, but I don't want him to lose his job."

"He won't lose his job," said Cate, like I was a total moron. "But we're fighting to win. We have to be ruthless! Paisley, the battle for equality and human rights is never pretty."

"*Oui,*" Bean whispered. "*Vive la résistance!*"

"*Apropos* to that!" Clint smirked, with clearly no idea what he was saying.

"Cate, you're pretty good at this. Maybe *you* should run for class officer."

She rolled her eyes. "Yeah right. *I* wouldn't even vote for me."

Amy pointed up, looking all excited. "Listen. Listen!"

"*That's right, folks, just three minutes until the main event, The Nut-in-Cheek Nut-Packing Competition located in the Nut Dish Amphitheatre! Better get cracking. You'd be nuts to miss it!*"

We all groaned at the pun *punishment.*

"I'm nervous," Amy admitted to everyone.

"Don't be." Cate put her arm around her shoulder. "There's no reason to be nervous. You're so doing the right thing. And we really appreciate your personal sacrifice."

"Yeah!" Bean nodded. "*And* you're going to be famous!"

Cate handed Amy a roll of black duct tape. I looked suspiciously from Amy to Cate to Bean to Clint and back to Cate. "What's going on, you guys? Tell me."

"We thought it would be better if you didn't know," said Cate, examining her short, blood-red fingernails.

"Yeah, it's for your own good," Amy agreed. "And we also didn't want you to say no," she mumbled.

I looked at Clint like, *Should I be worried?*

He smiled. "Don't worry. It's gonna be a trip. *You're* gonna be famous too."

"Actually," said LG with this sly grin, "we're all going to be famous."

Amy nodded, still looking a little nervous. "Wish me luck. It's *showtime!*" She flashed us some first-rate spastic jazz hands, then ran off in the direction of the Nut Dish Amphitheatre.

"Everyone's going to be famous but me." Charlie sighed, working his two black eyes for all they were worth. "I'm stuck in the booth. Why do I always pick the short edible antenna?"

"Charlie, you're in charge of headquarters," said Mandy. "We're just field agents."

"We'll report back soon!" Bean waved. The rest of us waved too as we walked away from the booth.

"Hey Paisley!" Charlie yelled. "Almost forgot, Eric Sobel's looking for you!"

Clint and I exchanged quick looks of . . . I don't know . . . understanding? Or more like not understanding. So I decided to just go for it. I grabbed his hand and held it as we walked along. I turned and smiled at Charlie. "Okay. Thanks!"

But I suddenly had this cold, creepy feeling, like there were a dozen live Hor*nuts* crawling around inside my stomach.

chapter thirty
nut in cheek

"Poor Charlie," said Bean sweetly as we all walked
along in a loose group.

"Poor Charlie's nose," said Mandy.

"Yeah. What happened to his nose, anyway?" asked Teddy,
feeling his own nose like he was checking to make sure it wasn't
broken.

"He got hit in the face with a trumpet case," said Mandy, wincing. "It was an accident."

"That's funny," I said, not thinking it was funny at all. "He told
me he ran into a pole. I saw him right after it happened."

"Really?" LG scrunched up her face and pushed up her glasses.
"He told me a fat reference book fell on him from the top shelf.
Something about the *De-evolution of Mankind*." The other Library
Girls nodded in agreement. At least he got his story straight with
one group.

I looked over at Bean, who was already looking right at me with
an unusually serious face.

"Why would he tell everyone different stories?" Mandy asked.

LG threw up her arms, shrugging. "Why does Charlie say anything? He's just Charlie being Charlie."

"I don't think so," Clint said, scuffing his boots along in the dirt.

I was still holding his hand. He looked up. "I think he's freaked out. He's just throwing people off the trail."

All of us looked at Clint.

"Off the trail of what?" Teddy asked.

"Ted, I can't just tell you now, can I?" Clint patted him on the back a few times. "That wouldn't be cool, especially after Charlie's worked so hard to keep it on the down low."

"Oh, you mean who hit him?" Teddy asked.

No one said a word as we turned into the Nut Dish Amphitheatre. We got there just in time, wedging our way toward the front of the crowd. The place was packed with kids from our school and other schools in the district. The Evening News 7 cameras were there with hot lights shining on our local celebrity news anchor Monty Montego as he delivered his Walnut Festival intro coverage, flashing his dazzling white TV teeth.

Bentley Jones stood next to him, looking like a camera-ready reporter, writing notes in her long skinny notepad. She was only a sophomore— was she already interning for the news? Or maybe she was just covering the contest for Yearbook or *The Fly*. Or . . . Oh no. I hoped she wasn't researching her Teen Scene article. No way I could beat the eleven o'clock news.

Suddenly, I wondered who else was competing for the Teen Scene job. Miriam Goldfarb? Logan Adler? The entire staff of *The Fly*?

Twelve nervous teens from three different high schools were standing behind a long table on

SIDEBAR

Monty Montego wasn't just our local celebrity news anchor. He was also a Pleasant Hill High alum from like a million years ago. Somehow, he always managed to make the news about himself. Yep. His name underneath the ridiculous boxing bronze hornet that he donated to the quad is *huge*. Guess he didn't want anyone to forget him. But the funny thing is, anyone who remembers him from high school would picture a total dweeb with bad skin, bad teeth, and greasy, already-thinning hair. Amazingly, he now has no wrinkles, perfect, blinding white teeth, and a thick head of expensive hair. I guess that's just the healing power of being on TV.

the middle of the stage, which was basically a big raised platform on the grass. On the table in front of each nut-packer was a brown paper bag filled with walnuts and a big counting bowl to spit the nuts into at the end. Gross.

Candy Esposito stood front and center, smiling and waving to people in the crowd like a prom queen on a mellow Cheetos high. Hutch was standing a few spots down, pumping air into his cheeks over and over again. And . . . Wait. Where was Amy? I was up on my tippy toes searching for her when Bean grabbed my arm.

"I know what really happened to Charlie," she whispered. "He told me last night when we were dancing." I looked at her. What? "After that crusty crotch comment, Hutch tried to grab him around the neck. But Charlie ducked, and Hutch's left hand smashed into a pole right behind him. Then Hutch was so pissed—and probably embarrassed—that he pounded Charlie in the face three times."

I looked at her again. Holy shiitake mushrooms. Way worse than I'd thought—and total grounds for . . . "Suspension," I said out loud.

"I know." She nodded with super-big eyes. She glanced over her shoulder at the stage. "I gotta go and get into position." She paused, then rubbed her hands together. "Get ready for some crazy fun!"

A jolt of adrenaline shot through me. I suddenly felt nervous again, but I didn't know why. I stared at Hutch up onstage. What a shidiot. And this was our class president? I had to get Hutch out of office. For Charlie. For the Uns. For myself. For everyone. I could be honest. I could be fearless. I could be . . . Wait.

I looked up at Clint. "Where's Amy?"

He smiled and pointed at the stage. I turned. Amy was moving into her place at the table—with black tape over her mouth! What?! I felt a huge goobery grin spread across my face.

The announcer came out wearing a tacky brown velour tuxedo that barely buttoned over his belly. The shoulders stuck out way too wide, and the sleeves were at least an inch too short. He looked pretty ridiculous, and that was before I noticed his hat. It was kind of a bowler hat that I guess was supposed to look like a giant walnut but it looked more like a big dried-out prune brain.

"Welcome all you nuts to the festival's big event!" he said, all carnival-cheesy. "We have here twelve fearless big-mouths for this year's Nut-in-Cheek competition!"

The crowd whooped and cheered like it was the biggest deal in the world.

Then the announcer turned to the contestants. "Excuse me, folks, what are you, cracked?!" He guffawed, slapping his knee and playing to the cameras.

The crowd groaned.

Then he noticed Amy's tape. "Excuse me, miss." He turned to face the cameras. "You're trying to get nuts in, not keep them out!" The audience laughed uncomfortably, clearly wondering what was going on. Amy's eyes darted around. She looked nervous. What *was* going on?

"At the sound of the first buzzer, you'll have sixty seconds"—he pointed his microphone up at a big clock behind the stage—"to pack your cheeks and mouth with as many nuts as possible. When the second buzzer sounds, kindly expel your nuts into the bowl in front of you. Remember, folks, nuts expelled *before* the second buzzer will not be counted. The guy and girl with the most nuts in his or her bowl, wins a host of prizes and the honor of being crowned this year's Walnut Festival King and Queen!"

Everyone went wild. Clint and I dropped hands so we could clap like nuts for Amy.

"Hey, you guys!" Charlie pushed in right next to me. "I got a freshman to cover the booth. Couldn't miss this."

Clint reached his arm around me and smacked Charlie on the back. "Good call, Chuck. Glad you're here."

The three of us leaned together, watching the announcer pace around the stage while he waited for the crowd to quiet down. "Okay, folks, are you ready?" he asked the contestants. They all nodded, looking a little ill, especially Amy. "You sure?" he asked her. She nodded violently. The announcer shrugged. A murmur drifted through the crowd. "Okay then, five seconds to buzzer."

The audience quieted down. Then someone yelled, "Hey Hutch! Grab the small nuts!" Everyone laughed. I looked around. OMG. It was LG Wong. She waved at me. I smiled, then looked over her shoulder and flinched.

Eric.

He was standing near BS1 and BS2 and the other jocks in the Hutch and Candy cheering section. But he wasn't cheering. He was looking right at me.

My heart did a quick little super loop. I swallowed hard, but I didn't look away. And then I remembered I was mad and folded my arms, really *trying* to feel mad at him. But I couldn't. I felt too . . . I don't know. It was weird. I wasn't sure what I was feeling, but it definitely wasn't mad. But Eric . . . Eric looked pissed. *Really* pissed. At *me*. His back was weirdly stiff, and his eyes were hard and cold. Wait. What did *I* do? My brain flashed on Clint just as the buzzer sounded. The crowd and all of the nut-packers went, well—nuts! I had this panicky fluttering in my chest and turned away from Eric, trying to focus on the action.

Most of the contestants were frantically stuffing nuts into their mouths, both arms flying as fast as possible. A few of the more experienced contestants calmly picked through their paper bags, collecting the smaller nuts, then packing them in like they were packing the trunk for a long family vacation.

Amy stood perfectly still. She was intently focused—total game face behind her tape.

Hutch obviously had no strategy, but his mouth was so big he probably didn't need one. He held the bag steady with his cast like a big yellow paw and shoveled nuts in one-handed. His lumpy cheeks kept getting rounder and rounder, and his face got redder and redder. It looked like his cheeks might explode. It was freaky. And he wasn't the only one looking like that.

Candy kept stuffing in more nuts and trying not to laugh. She looked beautiful even with big fat lumpy cheeks! Ergh!

I glanced back over at Eric but he was focused on the action. Rooting, I'm sure, for Candy friggin'-perfect Esposito.

The announcer walked up to Amy. "Sweetie, you're not going to win with tape over your mouth," he said, mocking her.

Right then, she pulled something out of her back pocket and held it up in front of her chest. It quickly unrolled. It was like a window shade or something with words written on it.

FIGHT THE UNFAIR

TREATMENT

OF UNs AT

PLEASANT HILL HIGH!

"Well, hello!" the announcer barked. "Apparently, folks, we have a protester tonight! How exciting. Isn't America beautiful?!"

That was when the first protest pod stormed the stage. Mandy, Teddy, Bean, Svend, and LG Wong lined up in front of the nut-packers doing their best to get their message on camera.

PRESIDENT HUTCH DID NOT WIN

The competitors couldn't see what was going on, but the crowd sure could. The cheers shifted into murmurs as the audience looked around, baffled. But Clint whistled and hooted like he was watching his new favorite sport. Charlie tried to whistle, but it sounded more like a tire losing air.

Then there was a quick Un shuffle of protestors.

HUTCH IS NOT MY PRESIDENT

Clint clapped a few times and threw his arm around me, laughing. And Charlie jumped up and down clapping like a happy seal. The audience went quiet, then erupted in a whole new sound wave of reactions ranging from wild annoyance to wild enthusiasm. I looked around and saw a lot of kids from school—and a lot of UnPops. The Future Prison Inmates of America were there, both male and female contingents. Pyroman had his lighter raised in the air. Mime Guy too, just, you know, without the lighter. A group of Emos were slumped against the sound booth looking slightly less depressed than usual. A bunch of Library Girls lined the back rim of the Nut Dish Amphitheatre. Up in front, Logan Adler and Miriam Goldfarb in full flowing faux-blond hair-wear swayed along with the rest of the Dumbe Blondes.

It was like the front lawn of Pleasant Hill High had overtaken the Walnut Festival. And everyone was going crazy. Soccer moms and car-pool dads looked around, totally freaked. Kids from other high schools had no idea what was going on. I caught sight of BS1 and BS2 with some of the other cheerleaders and wanna-be's, scowling like they were getting AP credit for it. Where was Carreyn? Wasn't she like Candy's biggest fan now?

Meanwhile, the nut-packers were looking around, a little confused, but still packing away—except for Hutch, whose eyes and cheeks were bulging like an angry chipmunk, and Amy, who stood there solemnly, holding her window-shade protest scroll.

"Down in front!" someone in the audience yelled.

"Yes. Down in front. Shoo! Shoo!" said the announcer, trying to be funny as he swatted at the protesters like flies.

I checked the clock. Eighteen seconds to go.

The announcer darted around the stage like he was dancing barefoot on hot coals. "Fifteen seconds to go, folks! Isn't this fun! Look at those nut-packers go!"

Then the Un protesters unshuffled and shuffled again as Pyroman, Mime Guy, and a few other Uns joined the human billboard.

MY PRESIDENT IS MISS UNPLEASANT

A roar went up from the Un crowd. Charlie elbowed me twice. My jaw might have hit the ground. I'm not sure. But somewhere deep in my headspace, this proud little voice said, *Oh! Hey, that's me!*

The rest of the audience rustled anxiously, murmuring with questions and a few boos, but they were quickly drowned out by a rolling wave of Un cheers. Even kids from other schools were getting into it a little, howling and clapping, even though they had no idea what was going on or who Miss UnPleasant was.

"Write on, Miss UnP!" Clint yelled, cupping his hands around his mouth.

The TV lights got brighter off to the side of the stage as Monty Montego began reporting live from the Walnut Festival. I couldn't figure out where to look—there was so much going on at once. A few middle-aged alpha-dads were getting hostile, yelling at the protestors to get off the stage. But the Uns were still screaming and cheering like lunatics. Miriam Goldfarb screamed at the top of her lungs, "Right on, peoples! Feel the anarchist burn!" Up on stage, Hutch started throwing walnuts at the Uns. Then a bunch of Pleasant Hill varsity jocks scrambled up and tackled them, hauling them off the platform.

"Bullies!" Charlie said, spitting mad. "Ignorant varsity bullies!"

A rah-rah type from another school started to gag on her mouthful of walnuts and almost puked. She immediately stopped trying to stuff and grabbed the table, spitting her nuts into the bowl in front of her.

Before I could figure out what was going on, I nearly got knocked off my feet as another protester pod made its move for the stage. They jumped up and scrambled into their lineup, standing proudly with their backs to the crowd. OMG. Now what?

BOYCOTT CANDY ESPOSITO MEAN OF QUEEN

Someone in the crowd shouted, "What's a mean of queen?" A bunch of people laughed. A dad with a little kid on his shoulders looked totally pissed. The kid looked totally freaked. Then the announcer pulled off his dried prune-brain hat and threw it at the protesters. The crowd's murmur swelled to a roar.

OMG. I had to help. I pushed past the crowd toward the protesters, wildly pointing with both hands like a good Samaritan trying to direct traffic to avoid an accident. "Queen of Mean! Queen of Mean!!!" I yelled, trying to get them in the right order.

Cate and LG and Split Ends turned back to me looking confused.

"Wrong order!" I yelled again. "Candy. Esposito. Queen. Of. Mean!" I yelled, pointing to each word. I caught Eric Sobel's intense green gaze for a second—he did *not* look happy—then I snapped back to the protest. The Uns quickly scrambled into the right order, ducking as Hutch pitched walnuts at them.

The announcer ran in one direction then the other trying to avoid Hutch's fast-pitch nuts. Then he began the countdown, wiping sweat from his forehead as he watched the big clock above the stage. "Seven, six, five—"

Hutch and the remaining contestants all stood there, waiting with grossly distended lumpy cheeks and varying degrees of I-will-not-puke! determination. But Candy looked like she wanted to cry. Oh no.

Poor Amy couldn't stand it anymore. She dropped her scroll, ripped off her duct tape, and shoved two huge fistfuls of nuts into her big mouth. And then she reached for a third.

"Two. One!"

The final buzzer cut through the cheers and laughter. All of the remaining contestants reached for the bowls in front of them, spitting out nuts like machine-gun fire—all the contestants but Candy.

Her mouth opened and closed a little like a fish out of water. A bunch of walnuts dribbled out, bouncing onto the table and down to the ground.

Oh, no. Oh, no.

Suddenly no one was laughing or cheering. The amphitheatre fell quiet as everyone watched Candy try to cough. Even Monty Montego had stopped talking. Hutch turned to her, wiping his mouth on his sleeve. Then he slapped her on the back a few times.

That clearly didn't help. She collapsed onto her elbows, leaning on the table, and staring out—I swear to God—right at me, looking desperate and scared.

Oh my God. Candy was choking. Candy was choking? Did I— Oh my God! Did I do that?

Somebody screamed. Someone else yelled for a doctor. The announcer hopped around anxiously like he didn't know what to do. Hutch slapped Candy on the back again.

And then a bunch of people started yelling. "Doctor! We need a doctor! She's choking!"

Oh. My. God. Candy's really choking? I turned around and screamed, "Charlie!"

chapter thirty-one
mouth-to-mouth
(part one)

"Charlie!" I screamed again, pushing my way back through the crowd to him. "Charlie! Charlie!"

He looked at me like I was crazy. "What? What'd I do?"

"CPR! Come on!"

He stared at me, shaking his head and looking totally scared. "I'm not a doctor. I should defer to the medical professionals."

I grabbed him by the neck of his XXL T-shirt and literally pulled him toward the stage. "Candy. Is. CHOKING!" I yelled through panting breaths. "Get up there!"

I jerked him forward and pushed him toward the stage. Then I scrambled after him onto the platform. There was this huge crowd around Candy. Everyone was yelling advice. Two alpha-dads were having an I'm-not-a-doctor-but-I'll-fake-it face-off while Eric pounded her on the back. It didn't look like it was helping. She was turning blue and reaching for her throat. She still couldn't breathe.

"Everybody out of the way!" I yelled like a quarterback calling a play.

Charlie stood there for a second, not moving. I gave him a nudge and he looked up at me, wild-eyed.

"Go," I panted.

Without a word, he slid in behind her, hoisted her up onto her feet, and immediately began the Heimlich maneuver, popping his fists with a hard thrust up and under her rib cage. I watched, my lungs burning, and tried to catch my breath. *Come on. Come on!*

Nothing happened.

"Come on, Charlie," I whispered. "Come on."

Charlie tried it again. Still nothing. I put my hand over my mouth. My arm was shaking. Girls were starting to cry, like Candy was already dead. Eric and I exchanged scared glances.

Charlie tried again, grunting as he pulled his fists back hard.

A walnut came flying out of Candy Esposito's mouth. Charlie fell backward onto the ground, and Candy went with him. She landed on top of him, coughing and gasping for air. Charlie popped up onto his knees next to her. "Okay Candy, now I'm gonna do mouth-to-mouth on you!"

Candy raised her hand, shaking her head slightly. "I'm okay," she gasped, coughing. "I'm okay."

And then she smiled, looking around. "Did I win?" she croaked, trying to be funny. Everyone laughed with relief—except for Charlie, who looked really disappointed to have gotten so close to Candy's legendary lips. He sat back on his heels, exhausted.

Everyone was hugging Candy, and then Candy was hugging Charlie, and then Charlie was hugging Candy back. I slowly backed into the crowd, hoping to blend in with all the innocent people who hadn't almost killed Candy Esposito.

That's when I spotted Carreyn dashing into the Nut Dish Amphitheatre holding a big pink helium balloon and looking really concerned. It was one of those personalized balloons they made in a booth by the entrance. It said *Queen Candy Rules!* I cringed. For more than one reason.

The announcer stepped forward. "She's fine!" he shouted, searching for the ON switch to his microphone. "She's fine, folks! Everything's fine! Just fine! The night is young. Let's have some fun!"

Eric reached for Charlie, patting him on the back, and gave him
a one-armed guy-hug. "Thanks, man. Really."

"Way to go, dude!" said one of the rah-rahs from another school,
slapping Charlie on the back and shaking his hand.

Carreyn's pink balloon, hovering above the crowd, was making
its way to the stage in fits and jerks.

"You're the man, little man," Hutch yelled. "Awesome save."
Hutch reached out to pat him on the back. Charlie flinched.

"Charlieee!" BS1 ran up to him. "Thank you soooo much! You
saved my best friend's life." Just as Carreyn made it onto the platform, BS1 gave Charlie a big full-body hug. Then BS2 joined in.
Charlie seemed to levitate, floating on a little cloud of varsity cheerleader love. Carreyn started to join in, like she really wanted to hug
Charlie too, but then she stopped a few feet away, looking totally
crushed—in both ways—and just watched, gripping the string of
her balloon tight in both hands.

A bunch of people, who before that moment would never even
have admitted to knowing Charlie Dodd, were suddenly lining up
to hug him and thank him and pat him on the back. Monty Montego approached with cameras rolling and launched into an on-the-
spot interview with Charlie and Candy.

Carreyn just stood there, shoulders slumped. I heard someone
groan and realized it was me. OMG. I felt awful for her. Carreyn's
private crush had suddenly become everyone's public love—before
she'd even found the guts to say anything to him. Then her big pink
balloon slipped out of her fingers and quickly disappeared into the
night sky.

I watched it for much longer that I could actually see it, wishing I could disappear too. Then I took a few more steps backward. So much for being fearless . . . I had to get out of there. I looked around for Clint, but he was gone.

And so were all the other Un protestors.

chapter thirty-two
double nut standard

I wasn't sure where to go so I just walked, feeling like I had a pound of fried dough in my stomach and bags of pink sugar spinning in my head. Oh my God. I almost killed Candy Esposito. If only I'd kept my mouth shut instead of trying to like . . .

Oh . . . Holy . . . OMG! Did I somehow do that *on purpose*? Was my yelling that out some kind of under-the-mental-radar retaliation? I tried to swallow but only gasped. Had my like mean evil twin taken over? Because of that ad? Because she date-napped Eric? I felt ick-to-my-stomach and put my hands on my knees, breathing deeply. No. That's ridiculous. That's completely ins . . . Eric. Ooh. What nerve! How could he stand there being all pissed at *me*? He ditched me! Why *wouldn't* I be holding Clint's hand? Or anyone's hand! Still . . .

I almost killed Candy Esposito.

And then it hit me. I didn't have to worry about Eric anymore. I was sure he totally hated me now. I sagged. I guess that meant I could hold hands with Clint, or anyone else, or *everyone* else I wanted. I looked around. Where *was* Clint anyway? I felt this sudden flood of warm wet emotions rising up in the back of my throat. Why did I even come to the stupid Nut Festival? I could have been home lounging safely in droopy green tights and an elf hat. I crumpled down on this grassy mound and sat by myself, watching the action on the stage from a safe distance. It looked almost cheerful from over here.

The announcer tapped his microphone a couple of times. "No worries, folks! No lawsuits either! Ha, ha, ha! It's all good—and all good fun at the Nut Festival! That's right. You never know what's going to happen next—yes, it's *nut*rageous! And now it's time to celebrate!" He nodded a little desperately. Then he seemed to pull himself together and gestured grandly. "Ladies and gentlemen, I am proud to introduce this year's nut-packing winners and the sixty-third Annual Walnut Festival King and Queen, Peter Hutchison and Amy Myles, our own little naughty, nutty activist! And both are students at Pleasant Hill High!"

Amy and Hutch rushed the stage. Wow. Amy won! After all that. Strong finish. I tried to feel excited for her.

The audience clapped politely as the announcer guy placed a big gold crown made of nuts on Amy's head. It was spray-painted to match her gold *Walnut Queen* sash and totally tacky, but Amy seemed to be loving it. Hutch played to the crowd, parading around in his Nut King sash and crown like he had won the gold at the nut-packing Olympics.

There was a little more applause and a few sharp whistles and hoots as Amy and Hutch did a victory lap around the stage. It got quiet pretty fast, though. I guess people weren't really in the mood to celebrate much.

Then Hutch grabbed the mic from the announcer. "Thank you, thank you! Thank you very much!" He waved. "Of course it's a great honor to be named Nut King, but"—he paused dramatically—"I want to pass my crown and all the perks to this year's real Nut King. Charlie Dodd! Get up here, little dude!" Hutch clapped a little too enthusiastically.

Wow. Unbelievable.

Charlie jumped to his feet, looking around, totally surprised and excited and then a little cautious, like *was this a trap?* But everyone cheered for him and started pushing him toward the stage. He scrambled onto the platform and the whole Nut Dish Amphitheatre cheered for him like crazy. Crappy as I felt, it was pretty cool. Charlie's smile was so big, you hardly even noticed his nose-saddle and two black eyes.

The crowd cheered for Charlie. And for Hutch—what a guy. Was I the only one who knew the real reason Hutch gave it all to Charlie? Well, I'm sure Charlie knew too, but he wasn't going to tell anyone . . . at least that's what Hutch was banking on. I pulled myself together and made a few mental notes for my Teen Scene article.

As I watched Amy and Charlie parading around, I felt a little better about the whole Un protest. It hadn't been a *total* near-death disaster after all. Only a partial one. And amazingly, both the Nut King and Queen ended up being proud Pleasant Hill Uns! Very cool. I smiled at Amy mugging for the crowd. She got the Uns' window shade message out there, probably on TV even, *and* she still won! I got to my feet, brushed myself off, and headed for the Drama booth to tell everyone.

When I got there, though, they were all in this heated debate. I couldn't get a word in. Clint didn't say anything, but he put his arm around me.

"It wasn't mean!" said Cate. "It was pointed. There's a huge difference."

"It *was* mean," said Mandy defiantly.

"It was kinda mean." Teddy nodded.

"And ha, ha," Bean added. "That's what we were protesting, right? Candy being mean."

Clint and Svend just stood there listening.

"It was a completely fair and just retaliation." Cate was not budging. "Candy Esposito ran an ad in a school newspaper—in print. We just lined up in T-shirts for five seconds."

"But she could have died," said LG matter-of-factly.

Cate threw up her hands. "We didn't know she was gonna *choke!* That wasn't part of the plan. She wasn't even supposed to see the body billboard."

I looked at my boots. "Uh . . . She didn't see it." Everyone turned and stared at me. "I yelled it at her."

Silence.

"Oh Pais," said Bean sympathetically. "You were just trying to help us."

"It's not a protest when it gets personal!" Mandy sounded really exasperated. "That's where we crossed the line. We got personal. That's just picking on someone. Trust me—I know." Teddy and the Library Girls nodded.

Everyone was suddenly quiet. Cate chewed on the inside of her cheek, thinking. Finally she said, "Yeah, I guess you're right." Then she looked around the group. "Mandy's totally right. Sorry. I screwed up."

Nobody said anything for a while.

"*We* screwed up," LG declared. Everyone nodded and murmured. Thank God it wasn't just me.

Then Clint broke in. "Hey, look on the bright side. The Un protest definitely made the eleven o'clock news."

Everyone laughed weakly.

"And guess who's Nut King and Queen?" I piped. They all looked at me, waiting. I milked it for a second or two, I'll admit. Then I announced grandly, "Amy Myles and Charlie Dodd!"

"Charlie?" Bean asked.

"Well, Hutch actually won, but he gave it all to Charlie."

She flashed me this I-can't-believe-him face. At least one more person knew why Hutch was so incredibly quote-unquote generous.

"That was really good of him," said Svend, sort of doubtfully.

"Oh man." LG sighed. "We're never going to hear the end of this from Nut King Charlie."

Bean shook her head, disgusted. "I'll bet it was all *very* touching."

"Very." I rolled my eyes. "You guys wanna get out of here and get something to eat?"

Everyone looked at Clint. He checked his watch. Then Cate checked her watch. Then LG checked her watch. When did everyone start wearing watches?

Clint smiled at me. "We can't leave quite yet."

Just then Elliott walked up with Split Ends. They both had motorcycle jackets on over their Un protester shirts. No need to attract *un*wanted attention, I guess. "Dude, are we on?" Elliott asked Clint.

Clint nodded. "Snip snip."

"Cool." Elliott and Split Ends walked off, smiling.

"Yay!" Bean did this little clap under her chin like an excited little girl. "I can't wait!"

Cate started applying a deep red lipstick. She did it like a pro without even looking.

"What's going on?" I asked, feeling totally out of the loop— and not for the first time that night.

Svend turned to me. "Didn't you get the text?" I threw up my hands. Ergh! Mrs. Hollet!

Clint's eyes were hopping with wicked fun. "Okay. Ladies, work your magic." Cate and Bean winked and waved as they walked away, swinging their hips. Something told me their magic wasn't the only thing they'd be workin'.

Clint checked his watch again and then his phone.

"Clint, come on. What's going on?"

He smiled. "You'll see. Just wait . . . a little . . . longer." He looked up, surveying the crowd. Then he pointed over to the Bouncy House. "Red, check this out."

chapter thirty-three
mouth-to-mouth
(part two)

I followed the line of Clint's finger to the Bouncy House. Cate and Bean were talking to the bouncer (ha-ha!) guarding the entrance. I couldn't tell what they were saying but it looked sort of like they were doing a scene from Drama or something. They gradually moved away from the Bouncy House, step by step, drawing the bouncer guy with them. And then they both started yelling and flinging their arms at each other like a catty stage fight.

Cate chased Bean as she ran off screaming like a lunatic, checking over her shoulder a couple of times to make sure that the Bouncy House guard was running after them.

LG Wong suddenly darted out from behind a booth and slapped something on the Mr. Walnut sign. Hordes of teenagers swarmed the entrance to the Bouncy House, kicking off their shoes and climbing inside. Little kids scrambled out as wild-eyed parents pulled them away from the entrance.

Then Amy ran up with Charlie Dodd, both wearing their gold walnut crowns and sashes. Carreyn pulled up behind them looking almost shy. Then BS1 and BS2 and Candy showed up with a bunch of jocks, and Bentley Jones and Logan Adler and Miriam Goldfarb, and Mandy and Teddy and . . . I turned to Clint.

"What's going *on* in there?!"

Clint had this big grin on his face as he held up his phone. I read the text.

BOUNCY HOUSE PARTY @ 8:12 pm.

"Flash mob, baby," Clint said with a bad-boy grin.

"You did this?" He nodded proudly. OMG. A Bouncy House party! Genius. I loved this guy! I grabbed his hand. "Let's go in!"

"Wait, wait. There's one more thing. Look up."

Clint stood behind me pointing up at the bright yellow sign above the inflatable castle. It said BOUNCY FUN HOUSE!

"What am I looking at?"

And then suddenly, the F went out, and the sign said BOUNCY UN HOUSE!

I caught my breath and then I laughed, looking at Clint then back up at the sign. By the way, he looked quite pleased with his accomplishment. I stood there staring at the sign with this huge smile but, deep inside, I kind of wanted to cry. Clint was just so . . . I don't know—so different. I just wanted to be around him. I never knew what was going to happen next.

"Come on, Red!" he yelled, totally pumped. "Let's get sweaty! Until we all get busted!"

We pulled off our boots in front of the Mr. Walnut sign, which now said—

If You're Taller Than Mr. Walnut, WELCOME TO THE BOUNCY HOUSE PARTY!

I shook my head laughing as I watched Clint dive in, and then I pretty much did the same.

Inside was like a giant human popcorn popper. People were screaming and bouncing and flying all over the place. It was packed with people from our school, and—OMG—everyone was laughing hysterically. It was like this big spontaneous laugh-attack party.

And amazingly, we were all in it together whether we wanted to be or not. There just wasn't enough room for anyone to pull away into their usual little groups.

I couldn't stop laughing as I watched Teddy and Mime Guy doing bouncing chest slams with Svend and Elliott and Split Ends. I did a half turn in midair. Eric and Candy were bouncing together. Ooh! I quickly looked away. I felt this blenderized not-so-smoothie mix of emotions. I was still pissed, but now I also felt ick-to-my-stomach guilty and . . . and jealous! Ergh. Jealous?! I looked back at them. I hate feeling jealous! I looked away again and watched LG with Bentley and Mandy literally bouncing off the far wall, laughing. Hutch and Carreyn and Charlie and BS2 were holding hands all bouncing in a circle together. BS2 was wearing (barely) Charlie's gold walnut crown. It was all very surreal.

I looked around for Clint but I couldn't find him anywhere. Instead I spotted Bean and Amy and Cate doing somersaults in a corner and started bouncing in their direction, getting smacked a little along the way, but I didn't even care. I was just so Bouncy-House high, like my headspace was filled with helium.

That's when Hutch saw me.

Great.

He did this sloppy diving somersault right at my feet and popped up. "Hey, Paisley!" he yelled at my face.

"Hey!" I yelled back mid bounce, trying to see past him to Bean, Cate, and Amy.

He bounced in front of me a few times, grinning. "Did you see me win?" I nodded. We bounced a few more times. "Got your notes!" he shouted. "You don't have to play it so cool!"

"What?!" I yelled leaning toward him.

"I think you're *smexy* too!" he yelled in my ear as we both hung in the air.

Oh, crap in a hat! I pulled back.

He had this funny look on his face as he put his hands on my shoulders, I mean his hand and his cast. Ew. Hutch was touching me. I tried to smile. This was the plan, right? This was what I'd wanted so he would open up and talk, right? I smiled harder. We bounced in sync a couple of times, then he kind of smirked at me. "Life is short! *Carpe diem*, baby!"

OMG. Hutch was trying to be deep, which, to his credit, is really not easy to do while bouncing. I looked around for backup or an escape or something. But I was trapped in the middle of total chaos bouncing with Peter Hutchison. I took a deep breath. *Carpe diem* was right. So I just went for it right there.

"What happened with Jen?!" I yelled at him. "In the photo!"

"What?" he kept bouncing with me. His cheeks were all flushed, and his face was covered with tiny beads of sweat.

"What happened with you and Jen?" I yelled in his ear. "At the party?! That photo?!"

"Nothing!" Someone smashed into Hutch from behind and he kind of fell against me. I quickly got back up and started bouncing again. Then he did too. "Is that what you think? That we hooked up?"

"That's what *everyone* thinks! Isn't that what you wanted? Who sent that stupid sext around?"

"I didn't! I don't know!" He started to laugh.

"It's not funny!" But before I could ask him another question, the most amazing, beautiful thing happened.

It started raining caramel corn!

I swear to God. I looked up and there were these giant bags suspended above the top of the Bouncy House, pouring sweet sticky caramel corn onto everyone.

We all went ultra double nuts! People started screaming and

giggling and squealing like five-year-olds. Caramel corn was everywhere. Yes—I laughed so hard, I almost peed in my pants.

OMG. Clint was a genius. But where *was* he? I looked around trying to find him. All I saw was Hutch's yellow cast flying right at my face as he got tackled by a couple of jocks.

"Ow!" I grabbed my lip. Ooh. That really hurt. I put my fingers to my lip. It was bleeding.

"Hey, sorry!" Hutch yelled up from the bouncy floor. "You okay?"

My eyes started to water as I held my mouth and nodded. Then Hutch was mobbed by a bunch of girls and he disappeared under this big bouncy-girl dog pile.

I didn't want to leave without seeing Clint, but I could taste blood and figured I should probably find the exit. Then I felt someone's hand on my back right above my butt. I turned right into Eric Sobel.

God, his eyes are so green.

He didn't say a word. He put one arm around my shoulders and held his other arm out, clearing the way for me to the exit so I wouldn't get smacked again. We tumbled out of the Bouncy House and right back into reality. Three tubby security guards with big flashlights were jogging straight at us. Eric tugged me, and we rolled to the side, quickly crawling out of the way. Then we ran around to the backside, laughing.

When he caught his breath, he said, "You've got caramel corn in your hair."

"So do you!" My lip was throbbing big-time. I pulled my hand away, checking for more blood.

Eric leaned in close to get a good look. He winced a little. "Ouch. There's a cut. Want me to get you some ice?"

I licked my lip, but it was hardly bleeding anymore. "It's okay. I'm fine. Really."

Eric tapped me on the arm and pointed. Security guards were pulling people out of the Bouncy House and making them line up in front of the entrance. We did this casual sideways walk in our socks moving far enough away so we wouldn't get busted too.

Eric brushed both hands wildly through his hair a few times to shake loose any incriminating signs of caramel corn. I couldn't stop grinning, even as I watched the Bouncy House slowly deflating and starting to lean a little to one side. The security guards were making everyone sign something before getting their shoes back. OMG. Two freshmen in the lineup were wearing belted poncho dresses! Hello! I was a wardrobe-malfunction fashion trendsetter!

"That was close," Eric whispered. He plucked a piece of caramel corn from my hair and ate it.

I snort-giggled shamelessly. "Yeah," I gasped.

We stood there for a minute in the moonlight, giggling beneath the carnival-colorful spray of lights and sounds. Then I suddenly realized that I was standing alone with Eric Sobel, eating caramel corn out of my hair. I didn't know what I was feeling for him after last night—or what to say. So, of course, I started blabbing. "Wow. That was so awesome. Wasn't it? Wasn't that amazing? How did he do that? I hope Clint doesn't get in trouble."

"Very cool. Very Clint. He won't. He's probably long gone by now."

I nodded. "Hope so."

Then Eric turned and stared at me like I owed him something, something he really wanted.

"What?" I asked.

He hesitated, fiddling with the zipper on his sweatshirt. "Why'd you leave last night?"

"I didn't leave."

"Yeah you did. You left me on the middle of the dance floor and you never came back. I thought . . . I thought we were having a great time. Then you ditched me."

What? OMG. How could he think that? I *explained* in my e— Oh, no. Oh no, oh no, oh no! I never sent that e-mail! "No! I was with Jen. In the bathroom."

He shook his head like he didn't believe me. "I looked *everywhere* for you."

"You looked *everywhere*?"

He nodded.

"Yeah?" I felt insane all of a sudden. I was totally icked out by it but I couldn't stop myself from talking. "Apparently even on the *football field*. In the *dark*. With Candy Esposito! What kind of creep goes on a date with one person and then leaves with someone else?!"

He opened his mouth to say something, but then he just looked away, shaking his head. "Oh, man."

"Yeah," I said, trying to sound cold. "I saw you guys."

"She's a *friend*. That's all!" He sounded really frustrated. "And not," he said coldly, "the queen of mean."

Ouch. "Whatever." I folded my arms and looked away, knowing I kind of deserved it. God, why did I even bother with guys? Why did I even care at all? I gritted my teeth, blinking away tears. "Whatever. I don't really care what you do."

He grabbed both my shoulders and held me there looking . . . I don't know, pissed or something. I'd never seen Eric look like that before. Behind us, I could hear the *click click click* of a roller coaster starting its slow, steep climb.

"You don't get it, do you?" he asked.

"Get what?!" I sounded all annoyed and confused and hurt because, yeah, I was. And I honestly didn't know what he was talking about.

His green eyes got even more intense for a few seconds. And suddenly, it was like someone turned off the volume on the carnival sounds all around us. And then . . . and then I got it. Whatever he was feeling came shooting into my body like some warm electrical current. For a second, I felt kind of terrified.

Then he kissed me. Gently at first like he didn't want to hurt my smashed lip.

And then . . . OMG.

Eric could *really* kiss. And I . . . I kissed him back, and it didn't even matter that my lip was throbbing. I have no idea how my lips knew what to do. But boy did they. It was like magic. Suddenly, I had Candy Esposito lips and mouth and hips—and whoa! I didn't feel terrified at all. I felt like, I don't know, this explosion of warm tingly fireworks inside.

We pulled apart, and I caught a few breaths, and then we stared at each other.

He put his hands on the back of my head and pulled me toward him. "Hi," he whispered all sweet but kind of serious too.

"Hi."

"Do you get it now?"

I nodded slowly. I mean, I think I did. Yeah. I did. Definitely. I got it.

OMG. OMG! I'm such an idiot! Eric didn't ditch me. I ditched him! He didn't like Candy Esposito—he liked me. For real! My heart was having its own private Bouncy House party. I had no idea what to say and I was kind of afraid of what might come out of my new uncontrollable Candy Esposito mouth, so I quickly turned back to watch the Bouncy House action, and—

Oh no. I caught my breath and blinked a few times.

My smile fell, and my excitement fell harder. Clint was standing there behind the deflating Bouncy House, holding a ladder and staring right at us.

Oh, no. Oh please, no.

Clint stood there for the longest time, then he slowly lowered the ladder to the ground and walked over to us.

"Hey," Clint said, smiling and nodding.

"Hey," said Eric, sounding a little embarrassed or something.

Clint just nodded. He stared at me, looking pained. I tried to swallow but it felt like my mouth was filled with dry dirt.

When Clint flashed his hey-don't-worry-about-me face, I was way more than worried. I felt like I had just stomped on his heart. "We always figured you'd choose, right?" He looked at me then at Eric, but Eric was looking at his socks. Clint shoved his hands in his pockets. "Hey, Red, can you catch a ride home?" He pulled his phone out and held it up. "I gotta . . . a call. Sorry. I gotta go."

Oh no. Oh no! Oh NO! I screamed inside my headspace. But I just nodded lamely. What else could I do?

"Oh, yeah." Clint pulled on something tucked into his belt and handed it to me. "This was for you." He smiled and walked off.

It was a girl's black T-shirt that said:

Show the Arts Some Love, Date a Drama Student!

I grabbed my head. It was spinning like I had just gotten off ten rides on the Zipper. I felt awful, like I might throw up.

Eric looked at the T-shirt, then at me, then at Clint walking away. "Oh, man," he whispered, shaking his head. He turned away and stared up at the dark sky. "I'm an idiot." Then he let out a long sigh and turned back to me. "I'm . . . I'm really sorry. I . . . I didn't know you were here with Clint."

"No, *I'm* sorry." I felt like I needed to sit down. How did everything go so wrong so fast? "I should have said something, I guess. It just . . . I . . . Everything happened so . . ." I felt too depressed to finish the sentence.

"God, I'm such a royal jerk!" He tried to laugh, but it sounded more like . . . I don't know, like he was disgusted with himself.

"It's not your fault. It . . . it just happened."

Eric dropped his head but didn't say anything. He just kicked at the dust with his socks as he walked around me in a small circle. Finally, he stopped. "You know, Clint's a friend." He kept walking. Then he stopped again. "Look, if you and Clint are . . ." He couldn't even say it.

"What?"

"If you're . . . anything." He shrugged and started kicking the dust again.

Were Clint and I anything? After the look on his face, I didn't know. But yes, I so wanted to be *anything* with him! I wanted to be *everything* with him too but I had no idea what that was exactly. And the worst part was, I wanted to be anything and everything with Eric too. But all I said was, "I don't know."

He stopped and turned to me. "I gotta do the right thing. I gotta . . . Till you figure it out, I gotta do it."

I nodded. I had no idea what the right thing was, but I was pretty sure I wasn't going to like it. "Okay," I said softly.

"I'll just, you know, I'll . . . I'll step back." Eric nodded like he was trying to convince himself. "I don't want to, but . . . but it's the right thing." He took a long deep breath and looked me in the eye. "Look, let's just act like nothing ever happened tonight, okay?

Okay?" I nodded limply, getting a lump in my throat. "But . . . we can still be friends, right?"

Friends? My mouth slowly dropped and my heart followed. Like nothing-ever-happened *friends?* I closed my eyes and tilted my head up at the night sky. All I saw were blinking carnival lights. Friends. That word ripped through me. It sounded like some cruel form of torture. My lips sure didn't want to be *friends.* I was pretty sure the rest of me didn't either. What did the rest of me want? I looked into his eyes but I couldn't say a word. I didn't have to—a carload of screams from some scary wild ride behind us seemed to pour out of my open mouth.

chapter thirty-four
the mourning after

The next morning, I woke up and lay there for a second in my happy, sleepy, cozy I-just-woke-up fuzz-bubble watching this little black spider crawling across my ceiling. And then I remembered. Everything.

I closed my eyes. I wanted to die.

How could I have lost Clint, Eric, and my favorite pair of boots all in one night? Oh yeah, and I almost killed Candy Esposito too. I wished for the thousandth time that I'd never even gone to the stupid Nut Festival.

I *am* UnDatable! Candy was right all along. I wanted to die all over again.

So I did the next best thing. I tried to go back to sleep. But I couldn't. I couldn't stop thinking about what I could've-should've said or should've-could've done or . . . OMG. My eyes popped open. Charlie's nose. Hutch really *did* hit him—three times!

That woke me up fast. It was really bad news. But it was really good news too, I mean, kind of. Hm. I sat up. I had to call Cate and Bean and Jen and Amy ASAP to tell them. I reached for my phone for like the fiftieth time that weekend. Ergh! Crap. Duh, no phone.

How did people even function before cell phones?

I grabbed my laptop and typed an e-mail:

Subject: The Nose Knows

Jen,

Hope you're doing ok. The Nut Festival was . . . NUTS. More soon.

Jen/Cate/Bean/Amy,

Hutch DID punch Charlie in the nose! (Thanks Bean!) Total grounds for suspension. Which means adios president Hutch!!! Go Uns!!! I can taste the victory. But how do I get Charlie to talk?

Pais

PS: ES kissed me! ☺ It was amaaaaazing!

PPS: CB saw. ☹☹☹

CONCLUSION: I am totally UnDatable. ☹☹☹☹☹☹☹

I waited for a response. Nothing. I brushed my teeth. Nothing.

E-mail is so slow! But it was still kind of early. I sat down on my bed. Typing all those sad faces had totally bummed me out all over again. What was I going to do? How was I going to fix this? Would Clint ever talk to me again? Could I stand to be Eric's . . . *friend*? Until I made up my mind . . . But that was the whole problem! I couldn't. Ergh! I wanted to throw something! I looked at Dyson. He blinked at me slowly, like *don't you dare*.

I flopped back onto my pillow and thought about getting dressed, then thought better of it. Dyson eyed me, disgusted.

"Fine."

I changed out of my sleeping sweats and into my lounging-around-on-the-weekend sweats. I considered wearing the T-shirt that Clint had given me but I didn't want to torture myself with tragic irony. So I pulled on an old beat-up soccer practice shirt and a sweatshirt.

I checked my e-mail again. No response. Hm. I went to Facebook. Maybe I could find someone there to distract me from my depression.

As soon as I logged in, my screen was filled with a stack of little smiling Candy Esposito perfect profile photos. Yikes. Guilt surge! Wow. She had already posted three status updates this morning. Oh, God. What was she saying?

> **Candy Esposito** has seen the light, eaten pancakes, and
> found her life's calling.
> Sun at 10:33 am
> **Candy Esposito's** heart is open and full of love for every
> living thing.
> Sun at 8:48 am
> **Candy Esposito** is so happy to be alive!
> Sun at 7:22 am

Man, I was happy she was alive too. But this was really weird. Should I post a comment? I wasn't sure. Did everyone know what I'd yelled at her and how it made her choke? Would everyone think I was psycho? Probably. But . . . No. It would be like a public apology. Kinda-sorta. Right?

> So happy you're alive too!

I hesitated for a second, then I hit COMMENT. I hoped it wouldn't make her feel too bad about that nasty ad in *The Fly*. I mean, I didn't want her to get all choked up. Ha! OMG. I was so gross.

I checked my ONLINE FRIENDS. Nobody. Not even Jen. And she was always online. Her mother must have grounded her Internet connection too.

I reread Candy's posts, trying to figure out what she was talking about. I had no clue. But I was pretty sure that if I'd had a near-nut-death experience, I wouldn't be sitting around living my life on Facebook.

I scrolled down. Oh, poor Jen.

Jen Sweetland can't sleep and is so depressed, she doesn't even need to be grounded.
Sun at 4:12 am

Jeez. I sighed. I scrolled down some more. Oh great.

Bentley Jones stayed up half the night finishing her coverage of the Nut Festival for her Teen Scene sample article!
Sun at 2:58 am

Ergh! How could anyone compete with Bentley Jones? Didn't she know anything about writer's block?! I sighed. If I didn't finish my Teen Scene article today, I'd totally miss the deadline tomorrow. Did I say finish? I meant start. Because after the horror of last night, I kind of had a new angle. Kind of. I think.

I was about to log out when Hutch's little grinning face popped up in a chat window.

Hanover? R u there?

I leaned in, examining his goofy trying-to-be-tough-in-a-baseball-hat mug shot. Crap. What should I do? *Was* I there for Hutch? I tapped my foot nervously under my desk. No. Definitely not.

But wait. OMG. My plan was working! I started typing.

Me: Yeah. What up, dude?

Hutch: That's Mr. Incredibly Generous Nut King Dude to you.

I rolled my eyes. Was he really going work that generous and nice thing? I waited.

Hutch: Wanna talk.

Me: About what?

I waited. Hutch was typing for a while. But then he must have changed his mind and deleted a lot.

Hutch: stuff

I waited again. I wasn't going to bite that easily.

Me: wht stuff?

Hutch: imprtnt stuff.

Me: Ok. When?

Hutch: Noon.

Me: I'm there. Talk soon. Over and chill out.

I jumped up, grabbing my shoes. I was wearing him down. Hutch was ready to spill the truth about the sext. Finally! At least one thing was going right this weekend.

"Bye! Going to Jen's house!" I yelled at my mom, who was in her Martha-Stewart-on-a-gardening-safari outfit. She waved and I waved back as I jumped on my bike and pedaled off for Hutch's house. I cruised down the road, passing trees and tall hedges and designer mailboxes and that evil storm drain (long story), trying to figure out my strategy. I couldn't be too direct—that would freak him out. And I couldn't be too flirty—that would freak *me* out.

When I cruised into the Hutchisons' driveway, I dropped my bike on the lush green lawn, and quickly walked up the stone path to the front door. I took a few deep breaths and rang the bell. It was one of those grand three-chime doorbells. Stuff-ee!

"Come on in!" called a woman's voice from inside. "It's open!"

Huh? Okay. I pushed open the front door and looked around. No one was there. I took a few steps inside but still didn't see anyone. Uh-oh. I hoped Hutch wasn't going to be like dancing around in his underwear singing into a banana or anything. I slowly walked into this big room attached to the kitchen. It had high ceilings and a huge flat-panel TV on the wall next to an even huger stone fireplace and these super-cushy-looking big sectional sofas, but classy sectionals. The house was really nice but it gave me the creeps a little, like no one actually lived there.

"Hello?" I called out tentatively.

I could hear a TV playing somewhere a few rooms away. It sounded like cartoons. OMG. Does Hutch still watch cartoons?

I looked through the double sliding glass doors to the pool area. Wow. It looked a little like a movie set out there. Swank. And there was the infamous hot tub. A little tickle of ick ran up my spine. Even though I hadn't been at that party, I kind of felt like I had.

I heard the sound of a woman's high heels on the hardwood floor coming my way and quickly turned around. A really pretty woman, middle-aged-ish, probably about thirty-three, came rushing into the room.

She looked at me, surprised.

"Hi." I waved.

"Oh, I'm so sorry," she said, clapping her hands together. "I thought you were Hailey, the babysitter. Can I help you?"

"Hi. Yeah. I'm Paisley Hanover. I'm in Hutch's class, I mean, Peter's class. Is he . . . is he here?"

She smiled warmly. "No, no he's not here," she said, clicking into the kitchen on a pair of extremely-fashionable-and-high-for-a-mom boots. They were expensive. I could tell. "Paisley, would you like something to drink, water, lemonade, juice box?"

Juice box? What am I, five? "Oh, no thank you, Mrs. Hutchison. I was just hoping to talk to . . . Peter. We were supposed to talk at noon. Do you know when he'll be back?"

"Oh sweetie, Peter doesn't live here anymore. He lives with his mom now." She smiled big, nodding like that was a really good thing.

"Oh. Right." I tried not to look surprised even though I totally was. "I forgot that. Sorry."

"Would you like that address?" she asked. I nodded. She clicked across the kitchen on a pair of typically-fashionable-and-high-for-a-*step*-mom boots and reached for a pen and paper. "Here you go. Tell him Sheila says hi!"

"I will. Thanks."

I took the paper and smiled. I couldn't get out of there fast enough. Wow. Hutch really meant it when he said he doesn't count here anymore.

When I got back outside, I looked at the address on the paper. It was downtown, near Jen's house, Jen's *new* house where she lived with her mom and her little brother since the divorce, the *rental* house behind Savemart.

I pedaled away wondering when Hutch had moved out. Was it before or after that party? Maybe he had gotten kicked out because of that party? Or maybe he hadn't even officially been living there when he'd had it? I wished I'd asked his stepmother something instead of just pretending I knew.

I rode down the gradual slope toward downtown, pedaling and thinking and pedaling and thinking. The more I thought about it all, the more I realized that Jen and Hutch had a lot in common. Both of them had divorced parents, both were living with their moms now someplace new and not really home. And they both had buttcap dads—or at least jerky, selfish dads. I wondered if they knew they had so much in common.

I slowed down as I got closer to the address. There it was, a small but cute little house with a few potted flowers by the front door. I could hear the twangy bounce of a basketball on concrete. I hopped off my bike and pushed it into the short driveway. Hutch was shooting baskets near the carport. I watched, waiting for him to see me.

He took a few shots with his good hand, then, chasing the ball toward me, stopped in his tracks. He looked surprised. The basketball bounced toward me. I trapped it with my foot.

"Thought you were calling at noon," he said, sounding annoyed.

"Oh. Sorry. No, I don't have my phone." I pushed the ball back to him, soccer style.

He picked it up, wiping his forehead against his sleeve. "How'd you get this address?" He took a shot. Swish.

"Your stepmother. Oh, Sheila says hi." I hesitated. "And they really miss you."

He looked at me like he had a bad taste in his mouth. "Yeah, I'll bet."

Hutch took a few more shots, then passed me the ball. I dribbled it a few times, then I took a shot. The ball bounced off the backboard like a brick, hit the rim hard, popped up, then somehow miraculously rolled halfway around the rim and went in.

"Good shot."

"You mean lucky."

"Hey, sorry about your lip." He took another shot.

I reached up and touched it. It was a little sore and bruised. "It's okay."

"Wanna play some one-on-one?"

I fake chuckled. "I don't think so. But thanks."

"Come on. It'll be fun."

"Hutch, I didn't come here to play basketball with you. You wanted to talk?"

"Well, maybe I don't feel like talking anymore."

"What?" I sighed. Wait, was he flirting with me? "Hutch, that's the whole reason I came over, the only reason."

He gave me a quick sideways smirk. "Okay, whatever you say. How about a game of HORSE while we talk?"

I sighed again. It's not that I can't play basketball. Actually I can. But I was totally out of practice since it was soccer season. I was starting to think this was going to be a big waste of time—that Hutch wasn't going to tell me anything. So I took a gamble.

"I have a better idea. How about a game of TRUTH?"

"What?"

"T-R-U-T-H. Just like H-O-R-S-E. But whoever misses the shot gets a letter *and* has to answer a question—truthfully."

"For real?"

I nodded. I know this probably sounded like Q & A suicide. But I'd actually played a lot of HORSE with my dad and my brother. And that cast had to throw off Hutch's game, right?

Hutch broke out into a big grin. "Okay. You're on! I'll start easy," he said, making a dumb face at me.

He took a shot from the free-throw line. Swish. Crap.

I lined up and took my time, concentrating. Legs, arms, full extension through the fingers. I took the shot. The ball hit the side of the rim and bounced off.

"Ooh! Unfortunate, Hanover. Unfortunate!" He looked at me, holding the ball. "T. So, did you put all those notes in my locker?" I looked at him. Uh-oh. He pointed at me. "Truth!"

I was about to say *yes*, when I caught myself. "No." He twisted up his face and tilted his head like a dog trying to understand. "I put *one* of the notes in your locker."

He looked at me suspiciously, then he took a quick jump shot from the side. It hit the back of the rim, popped up and went in. Oh man. Even with one hand in a cast, he was still pretty good.

But my jump shot hit nothing but net! Unfortunately, it was net below the rim, not through the rim.

Hutch smiled. "This is gonna be too easy. R. Did you *write* all those notes and get someone else to put them in my locker?"

I sighed. "Yes."

He grinned. "I knew it! Okay, easy one. Left-handed." He held up his yellow cast, then did a simple layup. Silent library scream! Thank God. It didn't go in.

I followed with a back-sided layup. It was a Hanover family special that requires a little backspin to go in. Mine did. Hutch's didn't. Ha!

I draped my arm over the ball holding it against my hip, thinking. This might be the only question I get to ask. Hm. Jen and the sext? Or Charlie's nose?

Hutch tossed up his arms, like *come on*.

I poked at my lip trying to decide while Hutch dribbled with his good hand. Help Jen or help myself? I didn't have to think long. "Did you break your hand when you hit Charlie Dodd in the face?"

Hutch whipped his head around and glared at me, blinking, like he couldn't believe I actually asked that. His upper lip curled slightly and his eyes were flickering mad. I took a step back.

Hutch stepped toward me. "I don't care what that scrawny little parasite said, I'll deny it." I swallowed. Hutch was so mad his voice sounded hoarse. Then he turned away and started dribbling the ball again and tried to laugh it off. "Come on, Hanover." He smiled a little too hard. "You can do better than that. Give me a real question." He bounce-passed me the ball. "You can get personal if you want."

That was a little scary-weird. "Okay." I took a deep breath, trying to figure out the best way to phrase my question so Hutch couldn't wiggle around the truth. "What exactly did you do to Jen before, during, and after that photo was taken and why is someone sending it around?"

"*That's* your next question?" He looked at me, disappointed. I nodded. He dropped his head and kneeled to retie one of his shoelaces. Finally, he stood up. "That's two questions—at least."

"Okay, okay. Forget the last part."

"You really think I *did* something to her?" He sounded indignant.

"Everyone does!" I sounded indignant back. "Isn't that the whole point of sending it around?"

"What did I do to her?" Hutch crossed his arms, giving me this you-asked-for-it face. "Your perfect friend Jen was drunk in the hot tub. So drunk, she passed out. Then some moron untied her bikini top and swung it around over her head. You wanna know exactly what horrible thing I *did* to Jen? I lifted her outta the hot tub and got her into some clothes so she could sleep it off on the couch! That's what I did before, during, and after that photo! You satisfied, Hanover?"

I slowly closed my mouth. I didn't know what to say. I just stood there trying to remember the details of what Jen had told me that first night during Code Pink. I was totally caught off guard, but it kind of made sense. "Truth?" I asked. "Really?"

"Yes, truth! Jeez, why does everyone think I'm such a friggin' screwup?!"

"Wow. Jen's gonna be *so* relieved nothing happened. Hutch, you gotta tell her—you gotta tell everyone nothing happened."

"Why? Why?! Because I'm not good enough for *Jen Sweetland*?"

"No! Because . . . because she has a boyfriend! And . . . and because it's the truth. And because now her reputation is trashed and she's totally depressed!"

He grabbed the ball away from me. "Sorry. Not my problem. I've got my own depressing crap to deal with."

"Hutch, you have to!"

"No, actually, I don't. Maybe you should ask the moron who

took that stupid photo and started sending it around to un-trash her reputation!"

"Okay. Fine. I will. What's his name?"

"*His* name? What's HIS name?" Hutch looked at me all disgusted. His face was red and sweaty—and not just from shooting baskets. "*His* name is Carreyn."

"What?!" My mouth fell open. Wait. No way. I put my hands on my hips. "Ha. Ha. Nice try. Come on, who is it? Really?"

"You don't even believe me!" He slammed the basketball on the driveway and stormed off toward the side door of the house. The ball bounced a few times and rolled into the bushes. But then Hutch stopped and turned around and pointed at me. "Truth. Do you like me at all or were you just playing me to get your stupid answers?"

I didn't say anything—with words at least. But this cold splash of guilt hit me in the face. I guess it showed.

"Yeah. That's what I thought. By the way, I *am* sensitive. Thanks for noticing." He walked inside and slammed the door.

pillow of strength

I think I was more depressed now than Jen.

We were lying on her bed, toe-to-head, eating poor-me-me's right out of the pan and thinking. I'd just told her what Hutch had told me—except for the Carreyn part. I mean, it couldn't be Carreyn. That's just . . . Could it? What if it was? What if Hutch *was* actually telling the truth? The more I thought about it the more I got this ick-to-my-stomach feeling about Carreyn. She was at that party. OMG. Maybe it really was her. I decided to keep my mouth shut for a little longer. I couldn't be 100 percent sure until I checked Jen's phone the next morning. And I really didn't want anyone else's life to get ruined because of this sexting mess.

"Your feet stink," said Jen like it was a compliment.

"Yep." I smiled. "Did it special. Just for you."

"Thanks. You're so sweet."

I tried to smile. Not really. Then I let out a big long sigh and ate another poor-me-me. Even though Hutch was a total shidiot and a bully, he was right. I played him. I totally took advantage of his feelings. *I* was the shidiot. I don't know why, but for some reason, I never thought of guys like that as even *having* feelings. It sounded totally ridiculous, I know, but . . . I mean, they're always acting so dumb and tough. I didn't get guys at all. I should probably never talk to another guy ever again. My mouth was like guy repellent. I thought about Clint and Eric and that kiss and . . . Maybe I should just date a vampire. I reached for another gooey square of depression delight and shoved the whole thing in my mouth.

"You're sure?" Jen asked out of nowhere. She lifted her head off her pillow. "You're sure Hutch was telling the truth?"

I nodded, chewing. "Think so. Yeah. I mean, why would he lie to me about it?"

She sat up. "Oh my God. Clint Bedard? Eric Sobel? 'Cause you're a hotness monster, and Hutch likes you and wants *you* to like *him*."

I snorted. "Um. Don't think so, actually. Not anymore. You should've seen his face." I tugged at a loose thread on Jen's com-

SIDEBRA

Poor-Me-Me's (a Jen & Paisley invention going back to sixth grade):
Follow the directions for your fave chocolate chip cookie recipe. Add two small bags of peanut M&M'S. (If you have a nut allergy, then substitute Junior Mints.) Mix up a separate batch of fudge brownies. Fold brownie mix into cookie mix. Plop poor me-me's onto cookie sheets and bake. Best with a glass of cold milk and a warm blanket curled up on the couch. Serves two.

Pity Pockets (a Paisley invention going back to last summer when Jen was like totally blowing me off, and we were all out of cookie and brownie mix):
Cut the tops off two pita bread pockets and warm in the toaster. Fill pockets with sliced banana, whipped cream, and chocolate syrup. Top with crumbled bacon and/or smashed potato chips. (If you're a vegetarian or health freak, feel free to substitute Bac-O-Bits for bacon.)

forter, but I just made it worse and quickly let go. I looked back at her. "Where did you wake up that night at the party? Do you remember?"

She thought about it for a few seconds. "Bodie woke me up— after he finished off a six-pack and had some qual time with BS1 and BS2 in the hot tub." She cringed. "Carreyn told me."

Holy shiitake mushrooms. Carreyn really *was* there when it happened.

Jen shook her head like it wasn't a pretty picture. "Ick. When I woke up I felt like I'd been run over a few times by a tequila truck. That part I remember." She slowly clicked two fingernails against her teeth, trying to remember more. "I *was* on the couch inside. Yeah. And I was wrapped in a blanket, wearing Hutch's sweatshirt—it smelled funny—and . . ." She cringed again. "Nothing else on top."

"That's good! I mean, horribly embarrassing, but it fits with what Hutch told me."

Jen and I smiled at each other. Then she burst into tears. I wasn't sure why, so I just handed her the box of tissues, and another poor-me-me.

"Thank you, God! Thank you, Hutch! Thank you, Paisley!" She wiped her cheeks with both hands. "God, I'm so, *so* relieved. I'll never get drunk like that ever again. Ever! I promise." Then she started sobbing even harder. I'd expected her to feel relieved, but not like this. Finally, she blew her nose a few times. "Pais, you have no idea. I've barely been keeping it together the past few weeks knowing that picture was out there."

I crawled down to her end of the bed and threw my arm around her.

"I mean, it's still embarrassing but at least it's not"—she hesitated—"at least it wasn't . . . *that*. God, that would've killed me. *Killed* me." I nodded. She cried a little more, then she got this funny wicked smirk on her face. "Okay, so, the whole school has seen one of my boobs. Big deal. I'll get over it. They'll get over it. Besides, I have great boobs." She stuck out her chest proudly, with a cocky grin. "Am I right? Am I right?"

I had to laugh. This was the Jen I loved. "Yep. You're right!" I yelled just before I smashed her in the face with a pillow.

She was laughing now too. "God, I feel . . . So. Much. Better. Now I just have to work things out with Bodie. This info will definitely help." She wasn't laughing anymore. "But I don't know how

I'm gonna get him to trust me again." She stroked the pillow on her lap like it was a cat. Then she looked at me. "I'm gonna call him. I'm gonna call him right now and tell him every—"

I winced, watching her remember the no phone thing.

She shook her head at me. "You're so lucky I was totally depressed this weekend, or else I would have killed you." She hit me in the face with a pillow.

I pulled it away. "Hey. Jeez, Bodie can wait one day!" I shook my head in her face. "I've waited for you for like six weeks!" She pushed the pillow into my face again, smothering me. I pretended to die, and we both laughed.

Then my mom pulled up in front of Jen's house. I know because she started honking wildly and yelling out the car window like a crazy lady.

"Paisley Hanover! Paisleeeey!"

Uh-oh. Was I in big trouble? What had I done now? Jen and I popped up and ran to the front door. Jen opened it, and my mom was standing right there jumping up and down like her underwear was on fire.

"Paisley!" Mom squealed. "You didn't tell me you saved Candy Esposito's life! Oh, I love you. I'm so proud of you!" Mom gave me a long and embarrassing hug.

I cringed. "It wasn't that big of a deal. And I didn't do anything really. It was all Charlie," I wheezed, mid-hug. Mom finally let go, and I could breathe again.

Jen turned to me with this no-way face. "Wait. You saved Candy's life?"

"No, no. Really. Charlie did it. I only got him and dragged him onto the stage. He did the Heimlich on her."

"Come on girls, we've gotta go! Kimmie Esposito called and

asked me to pick up toilet paper and margarita mix for their Life Is Beautiful barbeque. Paisley, Candy can't wait to see you."

Oh God.

Jen acted all horrified. "Ride in the wardrobe-malfunction vehicle? I don't think so, Mrs. H."

"Mom, Jen can't go. She's grounded. And I probably shouldn't go either. I should stay here and keep her company."

Jen turned to me with her devil-girl smirk, pushing her hair out of her face. "Well, here's the thing, Pais. I'm not really grounded. I just *really* didn't want to go anywhere or have to talk to anyone this weekend."

"Really?" I tried not to smile. Devious! "Okay, then you're definitely coming with me." I pulled her by the hand. "I'm so not doing this alone."

What was I going to say to Candy? And more to the soon-to-be-painful point, what was Candy going to say to me? Well, at least one thing was clear. The old Jen was officially back. I had hers, and she had mine.

chapter thirty-six
gazeb-uh-oh!

We pulled up in front of the Esposito house and had to park on the street. The driveway was already jammed with bikes and cars, which, interestingly, were almost all owned by *Proud Parents of Horny Students*. I kept pointing them out to Jen behind Mom's back as we walked up the driveway and making her laugh. But just seeing those stickers made my heart ache.

"The Uns are awesome," Jen whispered. "How did Cate and Clint come up with this?"

Full-body groan. I so didn't want to think about Clint. I so didn't want to think about Eric either. Clearly, that part of my life was a total disaster. And totally over. Okay, so I might have caused Candy to choke—but she lived. And I didn't do it on purpose, at least not consciously. Now I had bigger fish to fly. I tried to focus on the here and now. I looked up at her house.

"Holy shiitake mushrooms."

I'd never been to Candy's house before. It was . . . how should I say this? Nuevo-Groovo. It was huge and new and kind of a Modern Tropical Tuscan villa, kind of what you'd expect from a former pro baseball player and three-time All-Star-Game MVP and current Burger-King-franchise owner and his family.

I could hear happy playground voices flying over the fence from the backyard. We headed toward a cluster of white helium balloons tied to a side gate. There was a big glitter-pen sign on the gate.

Life Is Beautiful And so Are You! Git on in Here!

We pushed through the gate, down this stone path past the garage, carrying a jumbo-pack of toilet paper and two jugs of margarita mix. Yes, I made Mom carry the toilet paper!

Wow. There was a full-size basketball court behind the garage. I spotted Amy shooting hoops with some guys from school and Candy's younger brothers—and Hutch. Cringe. I quickly looked down, suddenly very interested in the type of stone used to make the path. I kept walking.

Candy reclined glamorously on a chaise longue beside the pool surrounded by friends and family, laughing and making jokes. Lying there under a cream-colored cashmere throw blanket, Candy looked more beautiful than ever. Her cheeks were smooth and rosy, her big brown eyes sparkled, and her sun-kissed honey hair glistened, reflecting the warm afternoon sun.

I was doomed.

"Paisleeeeeeey!"

I turned just in time to see Kimmie Esposito do an excited mom-jump that sent her long blond hair and the skirt on her short tight little tennis dress flying up. She speed-walked across the patio right at me like an overexcited woman at a semi-annual clothing sale.

She threw open her arms. "Paisley, life is beautiful, and so are yuew!" she screamed, giving me a kiss on the cheek and a big ole Texas-style hug. Ouch.

"Paisley honey, thank queeew! Thank queeew!" Mrs. Esposito's eyes started to tear up as she kissed me again, cupping my cheeks in her warm French-manicured hands. "Charlie told us everything. Hon, your quick thinkin' saved the day. Thank quew so so very much."

I got all hot and red in the face. "You're . . . so . . . so very welcome." Yes, it felt weird to be thanked for saving Candy from something I kinda-sorta-totally-maybe caused. But if Candy hadn't told her mom that I'd almost killed her, I sure wasn't going to.

"Hey, Pais!" Charlie Dodd waved. He was wearing his Nut King sash and crown, surrounded by his new fans. "Howdy, life-saving partner!" he called.

Oh, God. He'd better be kidding. We were so not going there. I did a quick micro-wave, then looked away. How was I going to get him and his nose alone and convince him to tell me the name of that *pole* that hit him?

Candy gracefully got up from her chaise and walked toward us with her arms outstretched. She glowed more than usual and seemed to be floating a few inches above the ground. "Hello, beautiful Paisley! Hello, beautiful Jen!"

"Hi . . ." Jen and I exchanged glances. Was Candy on medication? "Beautiful . . . Candy," I added.

Mom and Kimmie headed off to the margarita bar, arm in arm and sniffling.

"Jen, I've been thinking about you so much lately," said Candy. "And feeling your hideous pain." She gave Jen a long hug.

"Thanks. It *has* been pretty hideously painful," Jen said. "It sucks to have enemies." Jen raised her eyebrows, but Candy just stood there smiling. Jen put one hand on her hip. "Luckily, Paisley got the truth out of Hutch. It turns out nothing happened."

"Thank God." Candy turned to me, shining her perfect movie-star-teeth smile. She squeezed my wrist. "Paisley, you are such a good friend."

Why was she acting so weird? Does almost choking to death do something to your brain?

"You guys, let's go over to the gazebo and talk." Candy looked at me and smiled. "Paisley, we have a lot to discuss." Oh no. Oh no! Candy led us across the lawn toward this raised giant birdcage thing with a roof.

As we walked, Jen poked me in the side and looked at me like *What is going on here?* I had a bad feeling, but I was too curious to turn back now. Either Candy was going to totally torture me about yelling "Queen of Mean" and almost killing her, or . . . her body had been invaded by aliens. Either way, our talk was going to hurt.

The three of us sat down on the cushioned chairs in the gazebo and took in the scene.

"Isn't this beautiful," said Candy, looking out at her backyard and all the people in it. "Isn't *life* beautiful?"

Jen and I just nodded.

Candy put her hand on my knee and looked me in the eye. I had to fight the urge to look away and, frankly, run away. I would totally understand if Candy was mad about the protest and the choking, but hey, she definitely started it with that whole UnDatable thing. That was just mean, telling everyone like that. Even if it turns out it was completely, totally true.

"Look, I get it," said Candy.

What? I looked at Jen, then back to Candy. "Get what?"

"I understand what you were doing—and, yeah, it felt awful, really, really horrible. It scared me to death almost."

"Candy, I'm so so sorry about that. I didn't mean to. I . . ."

"It's okay," she said in this really calm serene voice. "It was meant to be. It was my path, my life's path. I had to learn something, something really important, and Miss UnPleasant was my teacher. *You* were my teacher. Maybe you still are."

Wait. Was I having a really long flash fantasy? I looked at Jen. Jen seemed real. And real confused. What was Candy talking about?

"Paisley, no one has ever picked on me before." She nodded

thoughtfully. "No one has ever teased me. No one has ever humiliated me in front of a crowd. I get it." She looked at me solemnly,
strands of her sun-kissed-honey hair blowing softly in the breeze.
"I get what it feels like to be an *Un*."

Huh? An *Un*? This was the last thing I expected Candy to say. So
she wasn't even mad at me . . . ? Then why was I so mad at her?

"Wait." Jen looked at both of us, confused. "Why am I here?"

"To be my witness, to witness my pledge to Paisley." Candy
leaned into me. "As of today, I'm devoting my life, well, my free
time at least, to service—service to others at our school who are
less fortunate than I am."

"Isn't that just about everybody?" Jen asked.

"No, no. I mean the *Uns*—the UnPopulars, the UnBeautifuls, the
UnFashionables. Paisley, you are such an inspiration. You've inspired
me with your selfless dedication to improving the lives of others."

The *UnBeautifuls*? I never called anybody that.

Candy paused, taking my hands.

"I want to follow in your footsteps," she said über-earnestly. "I
want to work with you to reach out and send love and beauty and
confidence to the UnPops."

"Really." I sat back folding my arms. I thought of the ad and
that creepy Pleasant Hill patriot sign-off. "Well, if I'm such an
inspiration to you, Candy, then why'd you run that nasty 'Boycott
Paisley' ad in *The Fly*?" The words were out of my mouth before I
could think.

"Yeah," Jen echoed, shooting me a *What was that?* look. Ah yeah, I
kind of took a more direct approach than I'd planned.

Candy looked puzzled. "What?" She looked from me to Jen and
Jen to me. "I didn't."

"Come on, Candy. Look, I'm super-happy you're alive, but that
doesn't mean you suddenly get to be all *Touched by an Angel* perfect."

"What makes you think I had anything to do with that ad? Seriously. I can't believe you thought I did that. I mean, that picture was so unflattering. Your nostrils were huuuge! God, you must hate me!"

I stood up. "Look. I don't want to get ugly here. Er. Uglier, I guess. But I know you're lying. I know the ad was paid for with a pink panda check with *your* signature on it."

She stood up too. Her face was crunched into an angry exclamation point. "That's impossible!"

Jen just sat there with big eyes, like she was watching an Olympic Ping-Pong match.

"Not according to Logan Adler, *The Fly*'s assistant editor." Ha! Gotcha!

Candy looked completely confused. Then she turned to Jen, shaking her head.

"Jen, I would never . . ."

She stopped abruptly. Impossible, huh? Candy tilted her head, staring at something in mid-air, thinking. Then she blinked a few times like little flashbulb memories were going off inside her head. "No. No way," she said, turning back to me. "I cannot believe they did that."

"Who?" Jen asked, jumping to her feet.

The wind blew really hard, rustling the leaves on the trees around us. I suddenly got a chill—and not the good kind.

"A couple of weeks ago, I lost my checkbook. And then . . . then a few days later it mysteriously appeared on the floor of my car after . . ." She put one hand to her lips and closed her eyes like she was actually feeling pain. Candy was either telling the truth or she was a really good actress. Then she shook her head like she still couldn't believe it. "After I drove them home from frozen yogurt and Yogilates."

"Who?" I asked.

Candy's nostrils flared with every breath and her eyes kept blinking fast. "Paisley, I'm really sorry about that revolting ad but I . . . I didn't write the check. I hope you know that if I had something to say to you, I'd say it to your face."

"Who did, then?" Jen and I asked at the exact same time.

Candy clenched her jaw, took a deep breath, and pointed out across the lawn. Jen and I turned.

Candy was pointing at three girls sitting around a big brick planter, laughing—BS1, BS2, and Carreyn.

OMG. Jen and I looked at each other. I suddenly felt like I'd been walking around all weekend with my clothes on backwards. Everything was crazy. If Carreyn could do *this*, then Hutch was right. She was totally capable of sending that sext.

"I'm going to kill them," said Candy calmly. "All three of them."

"Wait, wait. There's got to be some explanation, don't you think?" Jen asked. "I mean, they wouldn't steal a check. They're your friends. And Carreyn's *our* friend."

Oops. Maybe I should have told Jen by now. But everything was going in fast-forward!

They saw us looking at them and waved. Holy shiitake mushrooms. How come I didn't notice this before? Carreyn wasn't dressed like a discount version of Jen—she was dressed like . . . like a *BS3*! All three of them stood up and started walking across the lawn toward the gazebo. "Um, you guys," I said quickly. "Jen, there's something else I should probably tell you." I took a deep breath. "Hutch also told me who took the photo, the one of you and him together." Candy and Jen turned to me. "I didn't believe him at first. It was too crazy. But now it all makes sense." Jen leaned forward like *well?* "It was . . . It was Carreyn."

Jen's mouth fell open. Then her face clenched up like she'd just been kicked hard in the stomach. "What?! No."

Candy looked at me, tilting her head.

"Are you sure? Really sure?" Jen asked, clearly not wanting to believe it.

I nodded, talking fast. "That's what he said, but I wasn't sure I believed him. I was waiting to tell you until I could check your phone and be one hundred percent—"

"Hello, beautiful people!" called BS1, waving from halfway across the lawn. What nerve. She had a big smile on her face. Carreyn and BS2 followed a few steps behind, looking happy and innocent as could be. Obviously, they thought they'd gotten away with it all.

Jen took a deep breath. Her disappointment quickly morphed into full-on anger management. "And I know the first two people she sent it to. I'm so going to kill them too."

"No," breathed Candy. "Don't say anything now. I have an idea, a much better idea."

chapter thirty-seven
late-breaking news

After a brief exchange of breezy gazebo chit-chat with BS1, BS2, and Carreyn, where Jen, Candy, and I pretended that life was *all* beautiful, I bolted for the taco bar. When I spotted Charlie going up for seconds alone, I decided to make my move.

I jogged up behind him. "Hey, Charlie. How's the nose?"

"Hey. Did you see me on the news last night? Yeah. *Me* on TV! But as cruel fate would have it, this is how I looked." He pointed to his nose-saddle with a big grin.

His black eyes had settled into a nice eggplant-chartreuse blend. Perfect colors for fall. "Yeah, but . . . It wasn't really cruel *fate* that broke your nose, was it?"

He looked at me suspiciously. "What do you mean?" Then he looked over both shoulders.

"Look." I pulled him away from the table where I was sure no one would overhear us. "Bean told me about *the pole* that hit you in the face—three times."

Charlie winced and looked up at the sky like he was saying a quick prayer. "Oh, never put your face in a beautiful woman's bosom."

"Okay." I nodded. "I won't."

"I'm serious. The strangest things—like the truth—come out of your mouth," he whimpered, looking around all nervous.

"Yeah. That's what I wanted to talk to you about," I whispered. "The truth." He blinked away a look of dread. I put my hand on his shoulder. "Charlie, you gotta tell someone. You gotta report it."

"I can't. I can't report it." Charlie shook his head like a crazy man. "He'll kill me. Really. He said so. He'll kill me. Very slowly and very painfully."

"He's not gonna kill you. He's just a bully—he wants you to be afraid."

"Yeah. Well, it's working."

"Oh, come on. What did he say?"

Charlie shook his head. "I don't want you to have nightmares. It's a guy thing, involving . . ." He cringed. "Tweezers . . . and a wrench." He made a very scary face.

"That's ridiculous. He's just trying to keep you quiet."

He smiled a little sadly. "I like quiet. It's peaceful."

"Charlie, you cannot let him get away with this! He'll just do it again, to you or to some other scrawny little guy." OMG. Did I just say that out loud? I winced. "Sorry. I didn't mean to—"

"Hey, I've gained eight pounds since the beginning of the school year." He flexed his arm for me. "I'm lifting. I'm getting stronger."

"Good. Stronger is good." I hesitated, not sure where to go next with my apparently not-so-compelling argument. Then it came to me. "If you don't report Hutch, then he *wins*, Charlie—and not just as class president." Charlie let out this huge sigh, gazing out across the yard. He looked a little sad. "You gotta be fearless," I urged.

"Don't you understand?" Charlie looked down at his plate of

now cold tacos for a few seconds, then up at me. "Don't you under-stand what every day is like for me? I don't want to be honest. I want to be Nut King. I want to be popular, even if it's just for a few days."

I didn't say anything. I just looked at him. And I kind of knew what I had to do. I wasn't sure how I'd pull it off, or even if I could. But I needed to be fearless.

chapter thirty-eight
write on!

Later that night, I sat in my beanbag chair, staring at a blank screen. Well, not totally blank. I'd managed to type, yet again, *Teen Scene*. Genius. But I still couldn't figure out where to start. I kept flipping my topic over and over in my head like a new CD wrapped in plastic, searching for the loose end and a way in. I'd been thinking so hard my brain hurt. Even worse, I had nothing to show for it. I leaned back and threw my arms behind my head. It was hopeless.

Then I just closed my eyes and pointed my index finger at my laptop and dropped it on the keyboard. I looked at it. My finger had landed on *J*.

I stared at it for a few seconds. Then I sat up and typed *Justice*.

And I typed some more. And some more. And then I moved over to my desk and kept thinking and typing and thinking and typing—not necessarily in that order—for a really long time. It actually wasn't that hard to channel Miss UnPleasant's charm and personality and her fearless honesty. But it took me forever to figure out what I really wanted to say, and even longer to figure out what *not* to say. I didn't want anyone to choke or get arrested, or fired, or killed by tweezers and a wrench.

I just wanted to get the truth out, the truth about what the quote-unquote Teen Scene is really like at Pleasant Hill High. And it came out all right, I think. But around 4:00 a.m., I kind of lost it. I got this serious surge of self-doubt. It might have been my conscience, but it was more likely my exhaustion and an overdose of peanut M&M'S. I suddenly couldn't stop thinking about Hutch. I mean, his life seemed kind of messed up under the surface. I didn't want to make it messed up *on* the surface too. But then I thought about Jen and Charlie and all the Uns whose votes weren't counted—and how Hutch had messed up so many other people's lives, on *and* under the surface. If I didn't stand up to him, then who would? By about 4:10, I was totally over it and typing again.

I typed and typed and typed. And then I looked up and noticed the sky getting light. Crap. I checked my clock. It was 6:03 a.m., Monday morning. My eyeballs burned, my stomach felt queasy, and my mouth tasted like belly button lint. (Does that even exist? I don't know. But it sounds like it would taste really gross. Not that I would ever stick my tongue in anyone's belly button to find out! OMG. I'm so punchy.) Anyway, my Teen Scene sample article was finally finished!

I propped my head on my elbows and read it over for like the tenth time, checking for typos and my usual creative spelling. Then I sat back and smiled. I thought it was pretty good—it was definitely fearless and honest. And, the best part, it was written by *me*. I proudly typed "By Paisley Hanover, Slowest Writer on the Whole Planet."

Then I added one more line at the bottom of the article, Miss UnPleasant's signature sign-off. *Big kiss, class dismissed!*

I hit SAVE and then PRINT.

I wanted to show it to Miriam Goldfarb, the editor of *The Fly*, and get her feedback before I actually submitted it. I was calculating how much time I'd have to make any last-minute changes before the noon deadline when I put my head down to rest for just a second. My mom woke me up like an hour later. I had a keyboard imprint across my left cheek and just enough time to brush my teeth, grab my printout, and run for carpool.

chapter thirty-nine
mea gulpa

When I got to school, everything and everyone was crazy. Crazy!

The Uns were still in silent-protest mode. It was officially day three, not counting some time off over the weekend. Due to a rash (ha ha!) of skin irritation, duct tape and greasepaint over the mouths had been replaced by wax Halloween lips—mostly blue lips with big buck teeth, classic red lady lips, and the most popular, red lips with long vampire fangs.

Cate and Bean and LG Wong were leading dozens of wax-lipped Uns, running up and down the front of the school swarming students as they arrived, passing out a fresh round of flyers.

Election Do-Over or Die!
UnPopular? Maybe. UnImportant? No way.
UnDefeated? Never!
Count our votes for Miss UnPleasant
for Sophomore Class President!

And if swarming mobs of wax lips weren't weird enough . . . a lot of people were hugging.

The news about Candy's near-death experience at the Nut Festival had spread fast, but what had also spread and stuck like chunky peanut butter was Candy's reaction to her near-death experience. Suddenly, life was beautiful for a lot of people, which was really weird for a Monday morning.

I was standing there waiting for Jen when I heard a *honk! honk!* Candy, behind the wheel of her white Beetle convertible, zipped into her parking spot right in front without even slowing down. BS1 and BS2 were in the backseat. Ooh! Candy was good. Keep your friends close and your frenemies closer. And—holy shiitake mushrooms!—you'll never guess who was riding shotgun. Charlie Dodd!

They all spilled out, and Candy and Charlie were mobbed like they were rock stars or something. It was insane.

"Hello, beautiful people!" Candy called out a few times as she hugged her way through the crowd. "Thank you. I'm relieved to be alive too. Thank you! I love you guys!"

Carreyn rushed right up to her and gave her a hug. *Un-friggin'-believable!* For a second Candy seemed startled, but then she just smiled and said, "Carreyn, life is beautiful, and so are you."

Carreyn smiled big, until she saw Charlie getting mobbed by a horde of girls.

Charlie pointed at a few freshman girls like a slick game-show host. "I love you guys too!" He winked at them. Had he gotten taller since yesterday or was it just my imagination?

Candy spotted me and waved. "Hello, beautiful Paisley!" She gave me a knowing look and a quick nod. She must've found the canceled check.

"Hello, beautiful Candy!" I waved back, shrugging like I didn't know for sure, because I didn't. I hadn't gotten Jen's phone back yet. Candy nodded.

As she and Charlie walked past the protesting Uns, she gestured to them all. "Life is beautiful and so are you!" Candy touched her heart and smiled lovingly. "I want you all to know that I see you. I feel you. You've all touched me. I get it. I feel your pain!"

Some of the protesters looked totally confused behind their wax lips. Was Candy Esposito talking to them? Wait. Candy Esposito had pain? Hey, wait. Was Candy Esposito trying to steal *my* UnPop popularity?

Mandy approached her, holding a stack of flyers and looking a little nervous. She took off her big red lady lips. "Candy? Excuse me, Candy?"

Candy turned around and smiled warmly. "Hi . . ." She hesitated.

"Mandy."

"Right. Hi Mandy." Candy gave her a big, long hug. Almost everyone around them stopped talking and stared. Mandy looked really surprised, but she also seemed to glow afterward, like something of Candy had rubbed off on her.

Mandy looked at her flyers and took a big breath. "On behalf of the protesting Uns, I want to apologize for what we did on Saturday night. Our message was really . . . Well, it was mean. Sorry."

Candy smiled. "Thanks. But you don't have to apologize. It was part of a bigger message, a message I needed to get." Mandy seemed a little confused. "Hey," Candy said, "have you ever considered bangs?" She reached for a few wisps of Mandy's flat, shapeless brown hair. "And some layering. I think it'd be really cute. Your eyes are so pretty." Mandy seemed *really* confused, but then she couldn't hold back her smile. "And what about conditioner? Let's discuss, okay?" Mandy just nodded as Candy grabbed a bunch of flyers from her, waved, and headed up the main hall.

Cate and Bean and Amy and LG and I all exchanged glances. Then they all swiveled and looked at me. What was up with Candy?

I just smiled at them. It was way too much to explain. Still, I had to wonder if Candy had more up her fab designer sleeve than I knew.

Mr. Canfield fought his way around Candy's entourage, emerging from the main hall with his bullhorn and Dan the security guard. He started barking at the Uns as he fast-waddled after them along the front of the school.

"Listen up! Stop passing out flyers. Now!" Canfield yelled. He stopped and turned up the volume on his bullhorn. "The election results are final! There will be no do-over. I repeat—there will be NO ELECTION DO-OVER!"

The protesters basically ignored him. Except for Cate. She waved at Canfield and kept passing out more flyers, including slipping them right into open car windows as parents dropped off their kids. Dan just stood there watching the show, amused. So Canfield did the only thing he could do.

"Detention!" he yelled, pointing at Cate. "Detention! Detention! Detention!" he yelled up and down the swarming mob, pointing at every Un. It was hard to tell behind their wax lips, but I'm pretty sure they were all smiling.

Then Mandy—her big red lips were back—handed Canfield an envelope. He ripped it open, read it, and turned eggplant mad like his head was going to explode. Was that the letter from the *Proud Parents Club*? It had to be. I looked around for Clint. I felt this pinch of pain. There he was, leaning casually against a pole near the big gym, watching Canfield freak out. And yes, Clint still managed to look hot, even wearing red wax lady lips.

I watched him from a distance, feeling this heavy motorcycle boot on my chest right over my heart. Three cute perky freshmen bounced up to him and each gave him a hug. Wow. Candy's love machine was on fire. Or maybe it was Clint's post-Bouncy-House-Party love machine. I knew I had to say something to him—but I didn't know what. So I stood there twisting up the flyer into a tight paper swizzle stick, trying to work up the guts to go over and apologize. Luckily Jen showed up and grabbed my arm before I could open my big mouth and probably make things worse.

"Morning, sunshine!" Jen looked relaxed for the first time in like weeks. "Time to confirm the terrible truth about Carreyn."

"Oh, right!" We could finally get our phones back!

We started speed walking for the hall, but for some reason I slowed for a second, turning to take one last look at Clint, and— OMG. Eric was talking to him. I stopped and did this like huge *mea gulpa*, swallowing hard. "Look."

The acid in my stomach launched into a rapid spin cycle.

Jen squinted in their direction. "Pais, you knew they were gonna talk, right?" I nodded, trying to read their body language. "Well, at least they're talking, not trying to kill each other. Pais, come on!" Jen grabbed my hand and started running.

We raced all the way to Mrs. Hollet's room. Jen was going to win, but she slowed down at the very end so it was a tie.

Mrs. Hollet pulled our phones out of her desk drawer and handed them to us like they were covered with something sticky and gross. Jen turned on her phone, and we ran back out into the hall. I watched her scrolling through all her sent texts from the past month as I ran my tongue over and over the cut on my lip. I really didn't want it to be Carreyn, but I *did* want to know the truth.

SIDEBRA

mea culpa
[**mey**-uh **kuhl**-puh]
—*noun*
a Latin phrase meaning "my fault" or "my bad" (great to use when wanting to sound smart while apologizing).

mea gulpa *n*
[**mey**-uh **guhl**-puh]
—*noun*
a Paisleyfied phrase describing what happens when you swallow hard, realizing that you totally owe someone (or two) a *mea culpa*.

"Getting close, getting close," said Jen, concentrating hard on her phone. "The week after Labor Day." I waited, watching her face. The warning bell for first period sounded. "Here it . . ." She blinked a few times like her eyes wouldn't quite focus. "Here it is."

She slowly shook her head, and her whole body sighed, then she looked at me. "Yep. Apparently, I sent a topless photo of myself to Carreyn that night while I was passed out on the couch."

I grabbed her phone and looked at it. Oh man. "I'm sorry. That sucks."

"Why would Carreyn do that?" Jen asked as we walked back down to sophomore hall.

"I don't know. She's desperate, I guess. She just wants it so bad."

"What?"

"What you have just naturally, without even trying." Jen looked at me like she had no idea what I was talking about. "To be liked. To be popular. People do really stupid things when they're desperate. Carreyn was probably just trying to impress someone and it got out of control, and now she's afraid to say anything."

Jen shook her head. "Wow. That *is* desperate."

"Yeah. Well, Carreyn's hair may be evil, but she's not."

We snort-laughed as we maneuvered through the morning rush.

I turned to Jen. "Do you think we should give her at least a chance to confess and save herself?"

Jen thought for a second. "Yes. Definitely. Wait. No! Definitely not."

"You sure? It's my new specialty—shining the light of justice and badgering people with questions until they cough up the truth and never want to talk to me again."

"I'm sure. She's had every day since that stupid party to confess."

I nodded. That was true. Jen was right. Right?

As we turned the corner into sophomore hall, I almost bumped into Charlie Dodd, who was surrounded by a small crowd of mostly small guys, looking awed and pelting him with questions.

"Did you feel her spirit leave her body?"

"What does she smell like?"

"You actually touched Candy Esposito? You're a god."

Jen and I exchanged looks and kept walking. If my Teen Scene article ever ran in *The Herald*, Charlie might need bodyguards.

A few yards away from our lockers, Jen stopped suddenly. Her shoulders fell.

"What?"

She pointed at her locker. Someone had scrawled "HO" across the front in big black letters. Groan. Not again! I took a deep breath and slowly blew it out.

"Is this ever gonna end?" She sounded totally annoyed—which is a lot better than totally depressed.

I shook my head, staring at "HO" and twisting up my mouth.

"Hey you guys!" said Carreyn, bounding up to us all perky. OMG. Jen and I exchanged quick glances. "Isn't Candy awesome! I just love her energy." We stared at her silently. Then Carreyn's mouth dropped as she took in the new addition to Jen's locker. "God, that totally sucks."

"Yeah." I nodded. Jen didn't move a muscle. "So Carreyn . . . I was wondering. Is there anything you want to tell us?" I know, I know. But I couldn't resist.

Carreyn's eyes swelled with a delicious blend of fear and guilt. Then she did a quick *mea gulpa*. "No. Um, I mean . . . What do you mean?" she asked, looking from Jen to me.

"I dunno." I shrugged casually. "Just thought maybe there was something you wanted to say."

For a second, Carreyn looked like she was about to puke, but then she had this miraculous transformation and instantly any signs of guilt were gone. OMG! BS1 and BS2 had totally body-snatched her.

She smiled all faux real and gushed, "Yeah, actually. Jen, I so love your new top! It's the cutest. Where'd you get it?" Neither of us said a word. "You should totally come into the salon this weekend. Brandi just got a huge shipment of product from Color Girl. It's new. From Japan. For you, Jen, The Beauty Bar is always open. You too, Paisley." She flashed a big forced grin at me.

Jen smiled with a twinge of sadness. "Cool. Thanks, Carreyn. Sounds like fun."

I stood there for a second, feeling this unexpected full-body wilt of disappointment as Carreyn took a few steps backward.

"Um. Yeah. Fun!" Carreyn tried to sound normal. "I have to . . . have to get ready for a big test." She raced off down the hall.

Jen and I looked at each other. Yeah. If she only knew.

Well, Carreyn had had her chance. I wasn't going to pull it out of her with tweezers and a wrench. So I started digging through my bag for my good ol' black Sharpie.

I bit off the cap, turned to Jen's locker, and stylishly transformed "HO" into "PONCHOS RULE!"

Amy jogged up to us just as I was dotting the exclamation point. She golf-clapped and gave me two thumbs up from behind her blue bucktooth wax lips. Jen and I stepped back to admire my smart fashion statement.

Jen smiled. "Very fashion forward." She spit out her gum and smashed it onto the bottom of the exclamation point. "Cinnamon." We all smiled.

"Congratulations, Paisley!" I whipped around. Mr. Canfield was speed-waddling past us. "That's vandalism!" he barked without slowing down. "That's a detention!"

"Come on," I yelled after him. "Let me explain. It's anything but!"

He stopped suddenly and turned around with his jaw jutting out, looking enraged. "What did you say? Did you just call me *elephant butt*?!"

"No!" But that was a really good one. I tried not to laugh. It was hopeless.

Jen and Amy were already doubled over.

Canfield looked at them, then back to me, pointing with his furry index finger. "Make that two detentions, young lady!" He turned and speed-waddled off.

"You guys! Crap."

We were all still laughing when I saw Eric walking down the hall. I stopped laughing suddenly and smiled at him. He smiled back. As he got closer and closer, I got butterflies in my stomach, but they were shy butterflies and really confused and . . . "Hi," I said softly, remembering the way he'd said hi to me after we'd kissed.

"Hey, Paisley." He waved all friendly, but he didn't even slow down.

He walked right past me—just like nothing had ever happened. I turned and watched him until he disappeared around the corner. Ouch. My heart felt way more sore than my lip.

Jen and Amy stood there staring, looking sorry for me.

"What can I say?" I shrugged. "Guys love me."

Amy spit out her wax lips. "Oh, Pais . . . Want me to talk to him for you?"

"Thanks. But there's nothing to say really. Till I . . . Till I figure it out."

"Well, we love you." Amy gave me a hug.

"Yes, beautiful Paisley, we totally love you! Group hug!" Jen threw open her arms, pretending to be all weepy. "I love you guys!"

chapter forty
tough love

In homeroom, I couldn't concentrate at all. I spent the entire period planning out my apology to Clint. I waited for him outside of Drama, going over and over it in my head, hoping I was rehearsing a scene for a romantic comedy—not another tragedy. Every two seconds, someone wearing wax lips was hugging me and congratulating me on the killer Un protest at the Nut Festival. I couldn't help feeling a little guilty. I mean, I didn't really do anything but be kind of bossy—and nearly kill Candy Esposito, of course.

Cate and Bean and Mandy came running toward me from down the hall. They were all still wearing their wax lips. But not for long.

Cate popped hers out first. "Paisley, help. Candy Esposito keeps hugging me. It's really freaking me out. She's hot."

"She keeps hugging me too!" Bean squealed. "Guilt. I'm burning inside."

"You guys, we don't have to feel guilty," said Mandy. "I apologized to her. Remember? I think she's fine."

"Well actually . . ." I hesitated, wincing. "I found out yesterday that Candy didn't actually have anything to do with the boycott-me ad."

"What?" Cate blurted.

Bean put her hand over her mouth. "No way."

I nodded.

"Oops," said Mandy.

"Oh crap," said Cate, obviously replaying the Boycott Candy protest in her head. "Now even *I* feel guilty."

"Hello beautiful people!" Charlie strutted up with a bounce in his step and a trying-to-be-suave face. "Just wanted to let you know I'll be dining in *the quad* today at noon—with my new lady friend, Candy Esposito. Feel free to swing by and say hello."

We were all speechless. LG was right. We were never going to hear the end of this. The bell for third period rang, and Mandy and Charlie raced in. I looked up and down the hall. Still no sign of Clint.

"Hey, have you guys talked to Clint today? How's he doing?" I asked, a little afraid of the answer.

"Yeah, yeah. We just talked to him." Bean nodded.

"Oh wait." Cate jumped in. "He asked me to tell you something. It was weird. Something like . . ." She tucked a piece of dark hair behind one ear, trying to remember. "Something about Bermuda shorts. He lost something in his Bermuda shorts? I dunno. He said you'd understand."

My heart winced, and my shoulders dropped. Oh no. The Bermuda Love Triangle.

"Clint wears Bermuda shorts?" Bean asked. "He is so cool. Nobody else could pull that off."

Clint never showed up for Drama. Not even late. I knew this time he was totally avoiding me. He had to be. And I didn't really blame him. I kind of wanted to avoid me too.

For the rest of the class, I really tried to follow Mr. E.'s lecture on the dramatic power of the soliloquy, but the only thing keeping me awake was Clint. I kept thinking about our romantic night at the water tower and the Bermuda Love Triangle, aka the BLT. I so hoped he wasn't planning on disappearing without a trace. I was starting to get the feeling that for the rest of sophomore year my heart was going to be really, really lonely.

By morning break, everyone was hugging. Everyone! Everyone but Clint and me and Eric and me. It was like this campus-wide hug-edemic. Candy's newfound appreciation and love of life had spread faster than our love of fried mac and cheese bites, which were now available at lunch *and* breakfast. Everyone's soon-to-be-clogged heart was open and full of love—just like Candy's—and, suddenly, everyone at Pleasant Hill High was beautiful.

I ran toward the headquarters of *The Fly*, stopping along the way for a few quick hugs from people I didn't even know. I had to find Miriam Goldfarb, get her to read my Teen Scene article, and get her opinion fast.

Miriam was sitting cross-legged on a desk, playing the bongos, calling out directions to the staff. They were this colorful mix of bohemians, smarty radicals, and smarty radical partiers, basically, the under-the-counter culture at our school.

"Our headlines on this protest action need to pop, peoples!" Miriam called out, punctuating her comment with a quick flurry on the bongos. "No pun intended."

She saw me standing in the doorway and smiled. And then she started clapping. Everyone turned and stared at me.

"Well hello, Miss UnPleasant!" She waved me over. "We were just talking about you. Nice protest work at"—pause—"the Nut Festival. Way to keep the pressure on those shiny"—pause—"happy, clean-scrubbed oppressors." Miriam spoke in this strange singsongy rhythm, pausing at the weirdest times like she had no idea what she was going to say next, although she always did.

"Thanks." I shrugged. "But it wasn't *my* protest. I just helped. Sort of."

"Got any more incendiary, popularity-offending pieces for me?"

"Well actually, yeah. I was kinda hoping you'd read this." I held up my Teen Scene article. "Can I get your opinion? I'm submitting it to *The Herald* for the Teen Scene columnist job. It has to be in by noon today."

"Tough competition, Hanover. Hand it"—pause—"over."

She sat there, quickly scanning my article.

"Interesting. Short little stories, perfect for our short little"—pause—"attention spans. It's a verbal mosaic, Hanover." She looked at me over the frames of her smudged-up glasses. "A not-so-pretty picture"—pause—"of paradise."

Uh-oh. Was that a good thing or a bad thing?

Then she started speed-reading and blurting out lines:

"'Double-crossers, double standards, and double daters make life teen-obscene for students at PH High.'" She looked at me. "Nice! Zing zing."

She kept reading. Logan Adler ambled over and started reading over her shoulder. His dark roots were starting to grow out under his peroxide bleached hair. I looked around the room anxiously, wondering how many other real student journalists had already submitted their Teen Scene writing samples.

"'But it's not justice for *just us*—it's justice for all.'" Miriam read out loud. "Ooh, good one, Hanover. That's language that pops, peoples!"

And then her face got suddenly serious as she kept reading and reading and reading. Logan Adler was shaking his head slightly. Finally, Miriam looked up at me. "Is this true?" she whispered, an eyebrow arched above her glasses. "Did you check your sources?"

I nodded.

"Holy shiitake mushrooms. Canfield is gonna crap in a hat."

Hey, I started that one! Both of those, actually.

"So what do you think?" I asked. "I mean, as a writing sample?"

Miriam hopped off the desk and started pacing back and forth, all excited. She paused and leaned into me. "Paisley, this is news. Big news!" Then she started pacing again. "What do I think? What do I think?" She stopped cold and looked at me. "I think we need to run this. Are you cool with that?"

What? "Um, yeah, I guess. Just double-check my spelling, okay?"

"I'm not changing a letter. Your typos? Some of your best work."

Typos? I cringed. Uh-oh.

"Peoples! We're doing a special edition!" Miriam called out. Everyone looked up at her and groaned. "Finish dotting your i's and crossing your t's A-SAP. We're putting this puppy to bed"—pause—"tonight!"

OMG.

She waved the printout of my article. "We gotta get this out in time for that CPR awareness assembly tomorrow morning. The entire student body will be under one roof." She licked her chapped lips and smiled with delight. "Dying of boredom—and dying for something to read.

"Now get outta here, Hanover." She pushed me toward the door. "We got a paper to publish! And write me another"—pause— "scandalous column!"

chapter forty-one
not so n.i.c.e.

While some people had been depressed or saving lives or finding their life's purpose over the weekend, others had been rewiring Mr. Canfield's phone. In fourth period, a strange series of announcements came over the school intercom.

"*Glen Canfield here.*" Long pause. Mr. Yamaguchi stopped writing on the board and looked up. "*No, ma'am. I did not authorize any such stickers!*" Pause. "*Absolutely not!*"

I glanced around the room, trying to figure out what was going on. But everyone seemed just as baffled as I was—everyone but Pyroman. Elliott smiled at me, innocently twirling a pair of needle-nose pliers. Snip. Snip. I smiled back. Clearly, he wasn't just good with lighters.

"*Yes. Of course, I'll get this sorted out right away!*"

But just as we got back to work, another weird announcement crackled through the intercom.

"*This is Glen Canfield.*" Pause. Mr. Yamaguchi stared up at the intercom speaker, confused and now a little concerned. "*No. No. No! I'm outraged as well. This must be a prank. We will find the perpetrators! Absolutely. Yes, sir.*"

We couldn't get any work done in class because the intercom kept sounding off.

"*Hi, I'd like to place an order for delivery at eleven forty-five. Canfield.*

Yes, Pleasant Hill High. Pot stickers. Kung Pao Chicken, and . . . and . . . I know I shouldn't, but Buddha's Belly Pudding. Thanks! Sayonara!"

By then, everyone in class was in hysterics—except for Mr. Yamaguchi. He was pissed, probably rethinking for the hundredth time that day his decision to leave corporate law for a relaxing, intellectually rewarding career in the public schools. He pulled a chair over to the intercom speaker and climbed up on it, frantically trying to tape a folder over the big round speaker.

"Canfield here." Long pause. All of us stared at the speaker, gleefully waiting for the next hilarious installment of Canfield's tragic life. *"No, ma'am, this school is not a den of iniquity. I certainly do not endorse or reward a student's sexual activity."* He sounded exhausted.

Suddenly, there was the sound of shuffling and then a woman's voice in the background.

"What? WHAT?! You're kidding me. Aahg!" Canfield made this loud grunt like he was lifting up his desk or something. *"Rotten! They're all rotten to the core!"* Then the intercom went dead. I looked over at Elliott. He was grinning proudly.

When the bell for lunch rang, I didn't even go to my locker. I wasn't hungry. I jogged straight to the flagpole on the front lawn. Jen and Candy and I had agreed to have a quick meet up to compare notes and make a decision about Candy's plan.

Candy handed us a piece of paper. "I downloaded the image of the canceled check," said Candy, not sounding happy. "It's definitely not my signature." Jen and I examined it, nodding grimly. "And, by the way, I was very insulted. Look at the amount. I would *never* pay full price for an ad in *The Fly!*"

I eyed her a little suspiciously. Jen passed Candy her phone, confirming the identity of Sexter Zero—Jen's good friend Carreyn.

We sat there silently for a minute, reflecting on the many disappointing terrible truths of high school life.

I picked at the tiny pebbles in the cement around the flagpole. "Are you guys sure we're doing the right thing?" I asked.

"I am," said Jen without any hesitation. "I want them to suffer. I've been suffering for weeks."

"The only other option, Paisley, is to call the police," said Candy like a good citizen. "And I really don't want to do that. Yeah." She nodded. "We're doing the right thing. And just think about how many other *un*fortunate people will benefit from our plan."

Wait. I thought it was *her* plan. And now it's *our* plan? Jen and I glanced at each other and did our subtle eye-smile. Okay. We were all systems go on Candy's payback plan, even if I didn't totally agree with her philosophy.

I stood up and walked over to Cate and Bean and Amy. They were sitting cross-legged in the middle of the front lawn, surrounded by Uns, leading a silent lunch protest and mindful-eating meditation. I waved them over and quickly explained the assignment, and that they had to make it happen *today*.

"You're serious?" asked Cate with one penciled eyebrow arched high. I nodded.

"Yes, yes, yes, yes yes!" Bean squealed, clapping her hands under her chin. She jumped a little, and her glasses went askew.

Amy just smiled. "I get to go thrifting?"

Cate threw her head back and laughed. "Shopping well is the best revenge."

They were in. Not that I had any doubts about them.

Candy took out her notebook and walked straight into the wonderful weirdness of the lunchtime front lawn as if she were on a fact-finding mission in a third-world country. Jen and I trailed behind her as she wandered around the various groups of Uns, observing their behavior, taking detailed notes, and giving out big hugs to all sorts of hair-impaired guys and girls—people she'd probably never even looked at before, much less touched. Behind her, she left this trail of smiling, glowing geeks.

Part of me couldn't believe that I'd ever thought Candy had anything to do with that ad. She really *was* nice. At least I think she was nice. I eyed her carefully as she maneuvered through the various groups of Uns, chatting and hugging. She seemed sincere, even if she didn't completely understand the life of an Un.

She gave Teddy a long hug. Uh-oh. Pants tent! I looked away. Maybe I didn't completely understand the life of a Pop. Hm. If I'd spent even a minute getting to know her for real instead of just deciding she was some hate-worthy perfect Pop, then . . . Well, then you wouldn't be reading this book. Never mind!

Candy waved to the Uns like an adoring celebrity showering her fans with love. And then she dashed off to meet Charlie in the quad for lunch. Charlie hanging in the quad? This I really wanted to see. But first, I had to sprint to the library so I could e-mail my Teen Scene article before the deadline at noon. OMG! I had like four minutes!

I raced through the halls, dancing and spinning my way around people. When I pushed through the library doors, I was panting and . . . Crap. The library was packed! Ms. Whit was doing one of her lunchtime digital research seminars on . . . I grabbed a flyer off the checkout counter.

The Ten Best Kissing Scenes in Literature. Double crap in a hat! Every single computer was in use and there were clumps of guys and girls—and not just Library Girls—gathered around.

I checked the clock on the wall as I speed walked over to the bank of computers. Yikes—11:57. I walked along the clumps, searching for an opening. Nothing. I couldn't believe it! I finally wrote this awesome article and stayed up all night and . . . This couldn't be happening. I was desperate.

"Excuse me!" I said really loud to no one in particular. "Can I get on for a sec? I really need to send an e-mail!"

Everyone turned and looked at me like I was a brainless buttcap. And Ms. Whit gave me her scariest *library-voices* face.

"There's a waiting list," said some officious (new vocab word!) freshman Library Girl in training.

"And it's really long." Hutch stood up and glared at me. Holy shiitake mushrooms. My stomach did a quick flutter kick. It was karma! I had to warn Hutch about the article—as soon as I submitted it, of course.

I turned to Ms. Whit, who was leaning over a keyboard helping some kid spell *libidinous* correctly.

"Ms. Whit, can you help, please? I wrote my Teen Scene article all last night. It's really good. And the deadline is in . . ." I checked the clock again. "*Two* minutes. Please?"

She looked conflicted for a second, but then she looked like someone determined to do the right thing. "I'm sorry, Paisley. These students have all been waiting for a long time. I'm glad you wrote your article and I'm sure it *is* good. But I'm sorry you waited, literally, until the last minute." She smiled like she was really sorry, then looked back down at the computer screen. "*French-kissing* is capitalized."

Ergh! I was so frustrated, but she was so right. Silent library scream!

And then I had a total brain sneeze. "Hey, you guys!" The computer clumps turned and looked at me. OMG. I'm going straight to writers' hell. "Candy Esposito and . . . Eric Sobel are giving out free hugs in the quad!"

SIDEBRA

brain sneeze
[breyn] [sneez]
—*noun*
a sudden, involuntary, spasmodic idea that you blurt out really loud, causing everyone to stare at you. Not to be confused with a **brain freeze** (a sudden headache caused by the quick consumption of something really cold) or a **brain fart** (when suddenly your brain doesn't work at all).

The clumps rustled with excitement and chatter. Ms. Whit tried
to shoot me a stern face but her librarian's instinct was overpowered
by her inner hellion. She barely concealed a smile as she shook her
head at me. And just like that, half of the computers were suddenly
available.

"You're *un*believable, Hanover," Hutch snarled, but I think there
was a microscopic bit of admiration in there too. No? Okay, well
maybe not.

I sat down and started typing as fast as I could, which is not so
fast. "Hey, don't go," I said as Hutch got up. "I really need to talk
to you."

"Not my problem," he said coldly as he walked off.

I kept typing, popped in my flash drive and made the deadline
by a fraction of a second. Yes! Teen Scene gig here I come! I leaned
back and exhaled, feeling really good for a second. And then my
next locker note to Hutch started writing itself in my head.

> Hutch,
>   Be prepared for the T-R-U-T-H. It's all
> coming out tomorrow in The Fly. Sorry, but
> I had to do it—for Charlie and all the other
> Uns.
>   Paisley
>   PS: I'm *not* playing you. Now that I know
> you a little more, I'm actually on your
> team. Sorry for being a buttcap.

Instead of going to the quad, I went to Hutch's locker, slipped
it into one of the vents, and hoped for the best.

Canfield appeared to be crumpling under the pressure from the
Uns' official protest and *un*official pranks. I almost felt sorry for

the guy. Irate, unhappy parents were coming and going from his office all during lunch. He probably never even got to eat his pot stickers. In the afternoon, there were multiple sightings of him speed-waddling up and down the halls carrying an armload of confiscated cell phones. By seventh period, he seemed to have completely lost it.

On my way out of class, I saw an angry mob gathered in front of the bulletin board in sophomore hall. There was a huge handwritten sign taped up. It looked like the work of a hungry madman in a big hurry to save his job.

PLEASANT HILL HIGH IS NOW A N.I.C.E. CAMPUS!

New Campus-wide policy:
No Inappropriate Contact Ever.
That means no kissing, no lap-sitting,
no hand-holding, no hugging!
Anyone caught violating this policy will get an automatic
detention. Two-time offenders
will be in detention for a month.
THIS SCHOOL WILL NOT BE TURNED INTO A SAFE HAVEN FOR DIGITALLY TRANSMITTED STUDENT TERRORISTS OR SEXUAL PRANKSTER PREDATORS.
All honor students, please stop by my office to pick up a
new Proud Parent sticker.

No *hugging*? OMG. Canfield had totally lost it.

chapter forty-two
b.l.t. on a roll

After practice, I went home and well, kind of moped. I should've been really happy about my article and about how Miriam was going to run it in *The Fly*. I was, I guess. But I was totally stressed about how Hutch was going to take it. What if my note got jammed between two books or just lost in his piggy locker and he never found it? Or what if he found it and went ballistic and tried to break my nose? I tried to focus on something positive—our payback plan. That should've made me really happy, right? But it didn't. What kept bubbling up to the top of my brain foam—Clint and Eric.

Eric had downgraded me to casual-friend status until I figured out what was going on with Clint. But Clint wasn't talking to me! I couldn't even apologize to him, much less begin to figure out what—if anything—was going on between us. Was he hurt? Was he disgusted? Was he totally over me? Did he want me to choose too? Because if he did, I think I was ready to choose. Really.

OMG. Did I just think that out loud? I totally did.

I sighed. I didn't know what to do or what to say to make it better. And I sure didn't want to make it worse. I couldn't really talk to Bean or Cate—they would so side with Clint. And I couldn't really talk to Jen or Amy—they were definitely in the Eric camp. So I called my brother Parker. But, as usual, it went straight to voicemail.

"Hey Park. Parsley Hamburger here. How's college? High school's crazy. I miss you. I think Mom and Dad are getting weirder but, I don't know, maybe it's just me. Hey, I almost killed Candy Esposito over the weekend but now we're kind of like really good friends! Call me, okay? Really. I need some serious guy advice. I kinda screwed up. Call me soon! Okay. Love you!"

At dinner, I poked at my food. I had no appetite for anything and definitely not for brown rice, steamed fish, and broccoli. Was Mom trying to kill me? I checked my phone. Parker hadn't called back.

"Paisley, hon, tell us more about the Nut Festival," said Mom, all cheery. "Tell Dad all the details about how you saved Candy Esposito's life."

This was a good excuse to put my fork down. "Mom, it wasn't like that," I said, doing my best imitation of patient.

"Well, what was it like?" Dad asked. "It all looked very exciting on the news."

I cringed. "I don't want to talk about it, okay? I'm like too depressed or whatever."

"Depressed?" Mom looked at me like I was crazy. "That's silly. You're a lovely, popular young lady. And you're a hero!"

"Mom, please. I'm not a hero." I picked up my fork again and pushed broccoli spears around my plate, making a little barricade between the brown rice and the fish. "I'm a bossy choking hazard. And . . . and I'm totally UnDatable."

"Undatable?" Dad chuckled like a dork. "That's not what I read on Clint Bedard's MyFace wall," he said, trying to sound all dialed-in.

I looked at him, then closed my eyes for a second. "Thanks, Dad. But Clint doesn't have a *MyFace* wall. He's way too cool for that."

Then Mom looked at me, really looked. "Honey, what's going on?" she asked, suddenly in sensitive-mom mode, which always makes me melt into a big blob of mush.

Before I could stop myself, I'd explained what had happened after the Bouncy House party. The kiss with Eric. And Clint seeing the whole thing. Mom was on the edge of her chair, seeming way more excited for me than concerned by my depressing guy drama. But Dad nodded thoughtfully.

I slumped back in my chair. "I'm kinda . . . I mean, I really, really like these guys, both of them, and . . . and they're like friends, and now I have to choose." I twisted my napkin up. I couldn't believe I was actually admitting this to both of my parents. I must have been totally desperate. Anyway, I looked at my mom and actually said, "I don't know what to do. I mean, I know a lot of girls would think I was lucky. *I* thought I was lucky. But that was before I realized how hard it would be to choose. God, I'm such an idiot." I tilted my head back and draped my napkin over my face.

Mom reached out, lifting the napkin off my face, and stroked the back of my head. "Oh honey, you're not an idiot—you're fifteen. You don't have to choose. You should be having fun now. When I was your age, I had three boyfriends."

"You did? No you didn't." I scrunched up my nose.

Dad looked at Mom. "You had three boyfriends? When you were fifteen?"

"Yes. Sure. Everyone did." Mom poured herself a little more wine. "Doug, things were different then."

"*Three* boyfriends?" Dad asked.

"Oh, come on." Mom leaned in toward him. "Your mother had three *fiancés*."

"I think they were her suitors, not fiancés," Dad said.

"Grambo had three fiancés?" I asked. This was getting good.

"No." Dad shook his head. "But men liked her, and she liked to keep her options open. She was very smart and very beautiful and she was a terrific dancer. She took the time to find the right man, the right man for *her*," said Dad, trying to sound all dad-like.

"Grambo was a hottie?" I couldn't really picture it.

"Oh yes. Quite the hottie." Mom laughed, leaning back in her chair. "She kept one *suitor* waiting for hours, driving around and around the block, while she finished up a date with another *suitor* inside."

"Really?" I asked. "Which one was Grampa H.?"

Dad looked at Mom like she had revealed some deep, dark family secret.

"The one in the car," said Mom. "It was a very nice car."

"Hey, hey," said Dad. "He had much more to offer than a nice car."

"Wow," I said. "Grambo *was* a hottie."

Mom and Dad looked at each other, exchanging the I-love-you-honey hairy eyeball.

Then Mom said, "Paisley, really. You're fifteen. You don't have to decide anything right now. If you like both of them, then you should just tell them—both of them. Tell them how you're feeling. Tell them you're not sure what to do."

I looked at Dad. He nodded. "You can all talk it out. And then they can fight over you." He smiled.

Fight over me? I liked the sound of that.

"Guys love a little competition," he assured me.

Mom turned to him. "You didn't, as I recall."

"Can we not go there, please, when I'm being the helpful wise father?"

"Oooh, Dougie." Mom gave him a quick kiss. "You're *always* the helpful wise father."

They both came over and gave me a hug, and Mom gave me a big bowl of ice cream to make up for the brown rice and broccoli. Then Dad turned on some really bad music, and they did their dancing-while-doing-the-dishes routine. I know. It's tragic. Thank God they found each other.

I went up to my room, flopped onto my bed, and threw one arm over my face. Tell them? Tell them both? The idea terrified me. And how could I tell them what I was feeling if *I* didn't even know what I was feeling? But what if I suddenly did know what I was feeling—but it was the wrong choice? Or what if I did choose and it was the right choice, but the guy I didn't choose never talked to me again? I heaved a big, long horizontal sigh.

Dyson jumped up and pushed his head against my arm. I scratched his little cheeks with my thumbs, and then he curled up in my armpit and went to sleep. I lay there for a while, feeling totally exhausted but too tired to sleep. I wished I could just curl up in someone's armpit.

And then I had the strangest thought. Maybe my parents were actually right. Ooh, I hate it when that happens! I sat up. Maybe I *should* just tell Clint and Eric that I liked them both and I didn't know what to do about it. And then just sit back, fasten my emotional seat belt, and see what happens . . .

I hopped up off my bed and opened my laptop and my e-mail. I sat there for a minute, thinking. Wait. Could this totally backfire on me? No. Yes! I'm Paisley Hanover. This could definitely backfire on me. But what did I have to lose at this point? Nothing. So I went for it.

To: ClintBedard@PHmail.net; EricSobel@PHmail.net
Subject: Our Bermuda Love Triangle—aka, the BLT
Hey you guys,

I'm writing this to both of you because there's something I need to tell both of you and I don't have the guts to say it in person. So, before I can change my mind, here goes.

I kissed both of you last week.

Okay, that sounds really bad. Or maybe it's not even the hugest deal. But the hugest deal is—I really, really, really like both of you and I so don't know what to do about it. You are the two coolest guys I've ever known.

Apparently, I come from a long line of women with numerous boyfriends. It's a Hanover family tradition or a genetic flaw or something. Not that I'm saying you guys are my boyfriends. I mean, I want you to be my boyfriends, just not both of you, at least not at the same time. OMG. Am I totally making this worse?

I feel horrible about what happened at the Nut Festival. I didn't mean to hurt either of you. But (yay me!) I ended up hurting both of you—and, yeah, myself. I know that you guys are friends now and it's all gotten weird because of me. I want you to know that I'm really sorry.

I have a serious heartache that needs immediate attention. So I'll be in the nurse's office tomorrow at the beginning of third period if you guys want to talk about this.

And I hope you do. But if you don't, I'll understand. And thanks for reading this. I just hope we can all be friends again.

Paisley

Dyson jumped up on my lap. I scratched his head while I read quickly through the e-mail. Then before I could have a rare moment of clarity and delete the whole thing, I pushed SEND with Dyson's paw, just in case. Hey, if the e-mail was a total disaster, I could always just tell them my cat sent it.

chapter forty-three
beauty without borders

The next morning, there was this mandatory campus-wide CPR awareness assembly second period. We all filed into the small gym like sleepy, happy ants who hadn't studied for their quizzes and were really relieved to be anywhere but in class. I scanned the gym for Clint or Eric or Clint and Eric, but I didn't see them.

And then I looked around for Hutch. My stomach acid was popping mini popcorn. I really hoped he was having an okay day—so far—and that he would understand.

I sat down on the bleachers next to Jen and Cate and Bean and Amy, jiggling my knee all nervo-excited. And not because of what I knew was about to happen—more because of what I *didn't* know was about to happen.

I kept looking around for copies of the special edition of *The Fly*, but there was nothing. Maybe they didn't get it done in time. The idea totally freaked me out. I suddenly realized just how badly I wanted Miriam to publish my piece. My knee went into crazy jiggling overdrive. Cate put her hand on it and gave me this look like *be cool*. But it was too late for that. The group of us all looked back and forth at each other down the row, barely containing our excitement.

And then, just as the doors were closing, the staff of *The Fly* rushed in carrying huge stacks of white paper. Gulp. They all looked haggard. Some of them were even wearing the same clothes they'd been wearing yesterday. They fanned out across the gym to the sides of the bleachers and started passing big stacks down the rows.

When all of the students had crammed into their seats and were starting to settle down, Mr. Canfield stepped up behind the podium and stacked his notes a few times. He cleared his throat. "Good morning, students and faculty. This assembly is a celebration of Candy!"

People cheered. Then somebody tossed fistfuls of candy out over the bleachers. Tons of people squealed and laughed and cheered even more. Hey, who doesn't want to celebrate candy for breakfast?

"As most of you know, over the weekend, we nearly lost one of Pleasant Hill High's most treasured students, Candy Esposito. Were it not for the quick thinking of Paisley Hanover and the skilled expertise of CPR-certified Charlie Dodd, Candy might have choked on a nut and expired at the Walnut Festival."

People cheered and clapped and whistled. A few more fistfuls of candy cascaded over our heads. I looked around. Who was throwing candy?

Mr. Canfield nodded to us. "Paisley and Charlie, please stand up!"

Charlie jumped to his feet and waved. Bean and Jen patted me on the back, pushing me to my feet. I stood there and did this lame little wave as another blast of candy went up into the air.

OMG. It was Clint! I smiled at him, then quickly dropped my head back down. OMG. OMG! He was sitting next to Eric. Wait. Had they gotten my e-mail? Oh, crap in a hat! Were they already talking about me? I mean, us? Weren't we supposed to talk about this *together* in the nurse's office?

Canfield cleared his throat. "The Esposito family has generously sponsored a series of CPR awareness classes after school for all interested students. But before I explain the details and pass out the sign-up sheets, Candy has asked to say a few words."

Everybody clapped as Candy approached the podium. She caught my eye and winked wickedly.

"Thank you, beautiful people!" The whole student body cheered. "I am so happy to be alive and even happier to be alive here at Pleasant Hill High." She looked down at the podium and composed her thoughts.

"I too want to thank Paisley Hanover and Charlie Dodd." She touched her heart. "Thank you guys. Seriously. If it weren't for you two, I'd be a choking-hazard statistic. Thank you. Thank you. Thank you."

Everyone clapped politely.

"After my near-death experience Saturday, I saw the light. I had an epiphany." Candy pulled the mic out of its stand and began to walk around the gym floor like some evangelical preacher. "I realize why I am here, why I have been given a second chance," she said passionately. "It's to be of service, of service to others. I am here to share my gifts and skills and talents with others at this school."

Silence. No one knew what she was talking about.

I was all of a sudden distracted by fluttering white paper and whispering voices. I could see copies of *The Fly* being passed down the rows of bleachers on the other side of the gym.

"With this in mind, I am pleased to introduce my new Unfor-Profit program, *Beauty Without Borders*. I will be devoting all of my free time to improving the looks and the lives of the Uns at this school, offering makeovers and hair, beauty, and fashion tips at lunch every day."

The audience was getting restless, or maybe just waking up. There were a few claps, then laughs, and a lot of twitters. (No. Not that kind. The old-school kind.)

Candy waited until everyone had quieted down. "And I want to introduce to you three very special people. These fine ladies have volunteered to assist me and devote their lives to Beauty Without Borders for the rest of the school year."

Carreyn and BS1 and BS2 trudged out of the girls' locker room wearing these gray, baggy, totally shapeless long-sleeved coveralls, pink baseball caps, and clunky work boots. They were trying to smile but it was pretty clear, as they lugged their pink toolboxes, they were doing a shameful, painful perp walk.

I whispered down the row to Bean and Cate and Amy. "Nice thrifting!"

They all nodded proudly, nudging each other.

"Yeah," said Bean. "And we didn't even wash them!"

Onstage, Candy went on. "As a sign of their devotion to the less-fortunate—but no less valuable—students, these three fine humanitarians and Pleasant Hill High *Patriots* have committed to wearing their Beauty Without Borders uniforms to school every single day until winter break!"

Candy nodded enthusiastically and everyone else went wild, laughing and hooting and cheering.

Candy raised her hand to quiet the crowd. "*And* they have generously donated all of their personal makeup and hair products to Beauty Without Borders and promised to take a vow of natural-ness and gossip silence until the end of the year. Isn't that beautiful?" Candy asked the crowd, nodding her head. "What an inspiration!"

Candy began to clap for her three miserable quote-unquote volunteer assistants. The audience enthusiastically joined in, clapping and whistling. Carreyn looked ill—and that was before she sniffed at the armpit of her coveralls and swayed a little like she was about to pass out. I couldn't tell if everyone was cheering because of their selfless volunteerism or because everyone was psyched to see poor

Carreyn and these two notorious meanies totally humiliated and stripped of their popularity props. I guess it didn't really matter— payback is Pleasant Hell!

I turned to whisper something to Cate just as a thin stack of copies of *The Fly* landed on my lap. Holy shiitake mushrooms. My article was on the front page! And the headline was *huge!!!*

VARSITY POP PUNCHES PUNY PAL!

After reading the headline, the first thing I did, of course, was look for my name. It said *By Paisley Hanover, ace reporter*. I smiled. I love Miriam Goldfarb and her peoples.

I looked over at Jen, who was staring hard, reading *The Fly*, then back down at Candy just in time to see Miriam handing Mr. Canfield the special edition of *The Fly*.

"Please join us on the front lawn every day at lunch for a complimentary mini makeover or haircut. And don't miss our Plucking and Tweezing seminar every Friday! Thank you! Thank you all!" Candy shouted. "Life is beautiful and so are all of you!"

The audience clapped for Candy, and Candy clapped for the audience as she stepped away from the podium. Everyone was awake now, and in a total love fest.

Well, almost everyone. Carreyn, BS1, and BS2 tried to clap for Candy, but I could tell it hurt. Obviously, they were seeing their formerly Pop lives pass before their puffy un-mascara'd eyes. Meanwhile, Canfield was seeing red.

He was standing near the podium, staring at *The Fly* in his white-knuckled hand, getting redder and redder and redder.

Jen grabbed my hand and squeezed it. She had this amazed and totally relieved look on her face. "Thanks," she said, smiling big.

Then she held the paper up and read like some kind of scholar. "'In further Teen-Obscene news, Peter Hutchison and Jen Sweetland: Just bosom buddies—spread the word!'" She scanned the page for a second before continuing. "'*Some moron untied her bikini top and swung it over her head,* explained Peter Hutchison, an athlete and a sometimes gentleman. *So I lifted her out of the hot tub and got her into some clothes.*'" Jen dropped the paper to her side and smiled at me, placing her hand goofily on her heart and looking like she was about to cry—but in a good way, for a change. Cate and Bean and Amy were all watching us with these übery-goobery grins.

"It's all good, Sweets," said Cate. "But, sorry, you're out of our trash-talk club."

Jen giggled, pointing to a word in my article. "Pais, who's *popaganda?*"

What?! I stared at it. Oh man, not again.

"Is that like Grambo's new boyfriend? He sounds foxy."

I rolled my eyes and shook my head.

"Thanks, Pais," Jen whispered. I just smiled and squeezed her hand back. What could I say that I hadn't already said?

Then I grabbed Cate's hand and held it, and she grabbed Amy's hand, and Amy grabbed Bean's. And then we all smiled at each other, holding on tight. Jen stood up first. Then we all stood up, raising our hands. Screw Canfield's N.I.C.E. policy! If we were going to detention, then we were all going together.

And yeah, we were all going to detention.

chapter forty-four
school rules!

After Canfield explained that the CPR sign-up sheets would be in homeroom classes tomorrow and *not* passed out today, he yelled into the microphone, "This assembly is officially over! Return to your regularly scheduled second period class immediately or I'll see you in detention." Everyone groaned, especially the teachers. "And remember, this is a NICE campus. No inappropriate contact ever!"

Everyone jumped up and went totally nuts scrambling for the exits. I looked around, searching for Clint and Eric. I spotted them talking near one of the exits and tried to make my way in their direction, but I could hardly get down the bleachers. People kept coming up to me and congratulating me on my article. By the time I made it down to the gym floor, I was smiling so hard, my cheeks hurt. And—ergh!—Clint and Eric were gone.

Amy and Jen and Cate and Bean and I finally found our way outside. We were all standing in a group with Candy, enjoying everyone's sudden interest in helping others and Beauty Without Borders, when Carreyn clomped up to Jen in her heavy work boots.

Everyone stopped talking and turned to her.

Carreyn stood there just staring at Jen. She looked younger and sweeter without any makeup on or mayonnaise in her hair. And then her lower lip started to quiver. "I'm sorry," she said softly, blinking back tears. Jen folded her arms, not exactly softening. "I'm sorry," she said again. "They gave me their cell phone numbers and told me to send it to them and I thought it was just gonna be a joke. I thought we were all gonna be like friends. I didn't know any of this would happen." She mashed her lips together and wiped her nose. "And I thought . . . I just thought . . . if I did it, Candy would really like me."

Candy's head tilted at that one. "Excuse me? Carreyn, why would I possibly like you for sending that photo around?"

Carreyn looked a little confused, like she wasn't sure if she should say any more.

"Carreyn, answer her," said Jen coolly. "I'd kinda like to know too." Amy and Cate and Bean and I all gave each other the uh-oh face.

Carreyn did another big mea gulpa. "Um . . . So Bodie would see it and break up with Jen and get back together with you." Holy shiitake mushrooms! Candy and Jen exchanged glances. "At least that was their plan. That's what they told me . . ." Both Candy and Jen were fuming, which just made Carreyn blab on faster. "Candy, don't be mad! They're your friends. Really. They were just looking out for you. Everyone knows you want to get back together with Bodie!"

Candy stepped toward her. "Let me be perfectly clear—to you and everyone else at this school. Those two are *not* my friends. Anyone who operates like that . . ." She shook her head looking totally disgusted. "Not a friend anymore—and probably not a real friend ever. Got it? And I do *not* want to get back together with Bodie. Bodie and I are just friends, okay? Bodie's with Jen now." She looked pointedly around the group. "And Jen is my friend."

Wow. Candy was really good at the tasteful verbal smackdown.

I watched her throw her arm around Jen. I may have a lot to learn from Candy Esposito.

Poor Carreyn seemed to shrink like a turtle into her stinky coveralls.

"Sorry Candy," she practically whispered. And then she looked at me, blinking away tears.

I felt pretty awful for Carreyn. BS1 and BS2 had totally used her. But then, I guess she let herself be used, which is almost as bad. I shook my head. If only she'd just told Jen the truth like weeks ago. If only we'd *all* just told the truth.

"I'm sorry too, Carreyn." Candy gave her a hug but quickly pulled back to avoid the stench. Candy brushed her perfect nose with her fingertips. "Don't worry. I'll talk to them. And they will not enjoy it."

That's when Charlie Dodd pushed his way through the crowd, almost knocking Carreyn over. Fortunately, she was wearing those steel-toed boots.

He waved a copy of *The Fly* at me, looking truly terrified, and totally pissed off. "Paisley, how could you do this to me?" He looked over his shoulder nervously. "How could you?!"

"Charlie, I had to."

"She didn't do it *to* you," Jen added. "She did it *for* you."

"But I'm a dead man. I'm a total dead man! Paisley, I can't believe you!"

"You're kidding, right?" I laughed. "You *do* remember selling me out for Hutch, right? And then how did he thank you?" I waved my hand in front of Charlie's black-eyed, saddle-nosed face. "You're not a dead man. You'll be fine." I put my hand on his shoulder. "But just in case, I've ordered a little protection for you." I made a quick call. "Snip. Snip," I whispered into my cell phone.

In no time, Elliott, Split Ends, and the Future Prison Inmates of America walked up to us looking huge, scary, and hairy as ever. Well, except for Split Ends, but she still looked dangerous. "Charlie, meet your new bodyguards."

He looked at them, then he looked at me. "Really?" I nodded. Charlie's face relaxed into a huge grin. "Cool. What do you say, guys, lunch in the quad today?" Charlie was about to walk off with his new entourage, when he gave me a quick spontaneous hug. "Oops, sorry!"

"Paisley Hanover!" barked Canfield. "I want to see you in my office. Right now!"

Perfect. I smiled faux real, watching him speed-waddle off in a rage, clutching a copy of *The Fly* in his clenched fist. I waved to my friends, all of my friends, and followed Canfield to his office.

When I got there, Hutch was slumped in a chair with his arms folded, looking royally pissed. I smiled at him. He sneered at me.

Then without even hesitating, I plopped into the Fink Fast chair, leaning hard on my left knee. Hutch looked at me all . . . I don't know. It was complicated. And his face was red and sweaty—but not as red and sweaty as Canfield's. I kept smiling, but it wasn't easy.

Canfield closed his office door and sat down in his chair. Holy shiitake mushrooms. Did I just imagine that or did he lean back and almost . . . OMG. Cate must have like sawed a little off one of the back legs of Canfield's chair. Genius!

Canfield waved *The Fly* in the air like he was calling for the check at a restaurant with really bad service. Then he leaned forward on his elbows, looking at me with bulging eyeballs. "Why? Why did you do this?" he asked, gritting his teeth. "You should've just come to me!"

Yikes. I had never seen Canfield so mad before. My smile wilted. I glanced at Hutch, who was staring at his lap, and I swallowed hard. "But I tried that before, Mr. Canfield, remember? And you didn't—"

"Writing this sensationalized pack of lies was completely unnecessary," he growled, wiping sweat off the side of his head. "*The Fly* is not *The National Enquirer!*"

My butt was starting to sweat. I sat there looking at my knees, not sure what to say next.

"Mr. Canfield, it's not a pack of lies."

What? I turned to Hutch so fast I wobbled in the Fink Fast chair.

Hutch took a deep breath. "It's . . . it's true."

OMG.

Canfield stared at Hutch with big bulging eyes and flaring hairy nostrils. I swear I could see his blood pressure shooting up. Then Canfield looked at me with this freaky mix of disgust and defeat. Like he couldn't stand me—or what he was about to do.

Canfield popped to his feet and started pacing back and forth, shaking his head and muttering to himself. "Miss UnPleasant . . . (Hrmf!) . . . We're educators, not agitators . . ." He looked like he had hot coal in his mouth. "I can't even make this school a safe place for . . . (Grunt!) . . . for you rotten kids."

Hutch and I exchanged glances. I gave him this look like *What is happening?*

Then Canfield stopped and turned to us, suddenly composed. It was kind of weird. "Well Peter, as we all know, violence on campus is grounds for suspension. And no class officer is permitted to stay in office once suspended, for any reason. I'm sorry. But I don't have any choice in this matter."

"I know," said Hutch glumly, picking at his dirty yellow cast.

Canfield went on, trying to sound positive and professional. "So. I have some good news and some bad news. The good news—

Peter will be in a soft cast by next week and back in school in time to play in next Friday's football game. The bad news—for me at least—Paisley, you're now sophomore class president."

OMG! I popped up in the Fink Fast chair. It wobbled back, and so did I. What?

"Can I go now?" asked Hutch, sounding totally bummed.

I leaned down on my left knee again, watching Hutch remove his baseball cap a few times and put it back on, pulling it down low. I felt bad for Hutch. But also, good for me. But also guilty. But also justified. I *had* to write that article. Right? And sometimes . . . well, sometimes the truth hurts. I knew that as well as anyone.

Canfield nodded. "I'll make an announcement later today."

After Hutch left, Canfield walked around his desk and got in my face. "And I expect you to be a student leader!" He was so close I could smell his gross coffee breath. "And you *will* play by my rules! Do you understand me, young lady? I don't want any more trouble from you. Got it? No more detentions, no more hugging, no more protests! And. No. More. Writing! Is that clear?"

I nodded. I mean, what else could I do? But as I was getting up to leave, I spotted Canfield's paper shredder behind his desk. And it hit me. What was I thinking? What was I *doing*? I couldn't play by Mr. Canfield's rules. They were wrong. They were totally *unfair*. I decided that from now on, I'd tell Canfield what he wanted to hear—but I was going to do things my way.

I was surprised to see Hutch waiting for me outside Canfield's office. We walked a little down the main hall without saying a word. Then all of a sudden he stopped.

"Hey." He shifted his backpack uncomfortably. "Just wanted to say thanks for clearing my name about the sext thing at least. I didn't want anyone to think that I'd . . ." He shrugged. "You know."

I looked at Hutch. Really looked at him. And I realized that I might never figure him out. He was a shidiot and a bully, a decent guy, and an emotionally stunted ten-year-old boy, all wrapped up in an oversized varsity letterman's jacket. So I just nodded. "Sure. And hey, thanks for telling the truth in there."

"Yeah, well . . ." He looked away. "I figured I'd try it out and see how it went. Oh, and thanks for the heads-up." He gave me the head nod and walked off down the hall. But then he turned. "Hey Hanover! Can you score me some of those horny student car stickers?"

I smiled. "I'll try." As I watched him walking away toward the quad, I got an idea—like the most brilliant idea of my life. Believe it or not, I went back into Canfield's office and closed the door.

chapter forty-five
pain mismanagement

Instead of going to Drama, I went to the nurse's office.
I told her I had a pain in my cheeks. Yeah, I know. I'd started to say
a pain in my *chest,* but I didn't want her to call an ambulance, and
cheeks just came out.

The nurse looked at me suspiciously. "Your *cheeks?*"

I nodded, holding my face.

"Lie down on the cot."

She pulled a thermometer out of the sterilizing canister, slid it
into a plastic sleeve, and put it in my mouth, then folded her beefy
arms and stared at me, shaking her head. I smiled, gently biting the
thermometer, but then I remembered to be in pain and grimaced.

She looked a little disappointed in me. "I'll be back in a few
minutes. Rest your *cheeks.*" She walked off to her cubicle in the back
of the office.

I lay there staring up at the ceiling and counted three pencils
hanging out of the foam ceiling tiles, making a big lopsided triangle. There it was right above my head, the BLT constellation. I
closed my eyes. My heartache was this dull throbbing, but my ner-
vousness was like a wild pack of kamikaze moths in my stomach.

If only one of them showed up, I decided I'd automatically
choose him because, obviously, he cared enough about me to cut

class. Yes! Keep it simple. Wait. That doesn't make any sense. Clint would cut class for no reason at all, and Eric . . . ? I clutched the edges of the plastic-covered mattress. *Just be fearless and go with your heart.*

I tried to listen carefully to my heart but all I could hear was the fluorescent light buzzing and crackling above me. Would anyone show up? I checked the clock on the wall. Wait. What if *no one* showed up? *Oh mighty Crisis.*

I closed my eyes again and tried to breath normally. It smelled like industrial-strength teen cleaning solution. And then I heard the door open. I popped open an eye. Eric hopped in on one foot and propped himself against the doorjamb. I smiled—inside and out.

The nurse rushed over to him.

"I turned my ankle," said Eric, hopping into the middle of the room. "Do you have any ice?"

"Oh you poor thing! Lie down. Lie down." The nurse stuck her head into the freezer and pulled out an ice pack. She went to work making him comfortable, propping up his ankle with pillows. "Should I call your parents?" she asked.

He looked a little embarrassed. "Um . . . No. I don't think so. I'll just ice it for a while."

She reached over and pulled the thermometer out of my mouth and gave it a hard stare. "You're normal, kid." Yeah right. If only that were true. She opened her mouth, and I could tell she was going to kick me out, so I gave her a pleading look, like *Don't make me go!*

She sighed. "All right, you two. Keep to your cots."

She was about to head back to her cubicle when the door swung open.

"Aaah! It burns. It burns!" Clint busted into the room with a big grin on his face.

"What, honey? What?" The nurse ran to his side and helped him in.

Clint grabbed his butt, looking totally in pain. "It burns! I think it's hemorrhoids!"

Eric and I tried not to laugh as the nurse recoiled, looking a little grossed out. "Oh. I'll have to look that up. Have a seat. No. No! Don't sit. Lie down on the cot."

She helped him get settled facedown on the third cot and then she rushed back to her cubicle. I could hear her tapping away on her computer doing, I'm sure, a search for a new career.

We lay there on the three cots in a row. It was a Paisley sandwich, me in the middle and a guy on either side.

Clint sat up. "Hello. Is this the meeting of the Pleasant Hill High BLT club?"

"Yep," said Eric, sounding a little cold.

Clint examined me from head to toe. "So, Red, what's your mystery injury?"

I hesitated for a second. "My cheeks hurt," I whispered, trying not to sound like a total idiot.

Both guys laughed.

"Hey, what a coincidence." Clint grabbed his butt again. "Me too!" Hey! Was he saying I was a pain in his butt?

"Lower your voices, please!" the nurse shouted from her cubicle. "No one is sick with loud voices."

We all got very quiet. Then Eric and Clint both turned to look at me like *Okay, so why are we here?* I suddenly couldn't remember a single thing I had planned to say. I just lay there holding my now-burning cheeks. OMG. This was a bad idea. A very bad idea.

"Uh, Paisley," Eric whispered. "Can we get this going? This ice is freezing my foot off."

I sat up slowly on my knees and turned so I could face both of them. Clint's dark hair was messy and sexy. He looked like he hadn't shaved in a few days—and he looked a little bored. Eric's jaw muscle flexed and unflexed under his smooth, tan cheeks. I could only see one of his eyes, and then he pushed his dirty-blond bangs to one side.

Oh God. The kamikaze moths in my stomach took things up a notch. I thought I'd made a decision. I thought I had it together. I thought . . .

I took a deep breath and swallowed hard. "I guess . . . I guess I just really wanted to apologize to you guys in person," I said lamely.

Eric looked confused. "Wait. So you haven't made a decision?"

I shook my head miserably.

Eric and Clint exchanged annoyed glances. Eric dropped his ice on the floor and looked away while Clint played the finger drums on the edge of his cot.

Then Clint sat up. "No worries, Red. *I've* made a decision." He flashed his grin but it wasn't flirty. "I choose you, Eric," he said all fake googley.

Clint laughed, but Eric didn't. And neither did I.

And then Clint rolled his eyes. "Lighten up, kids."

This so wasn't how I thought it would go. Clint looked like he couldn't care less, and Eric looked miserable. Everything I said just made it worse. I suddenly felt so tired. I had to fight the urge to slip into an emotional coma right there on the plastic-covered mattress.

I closed my eyes and took a deep breath, gulping down the lump in my throat. "I'm really sorry. But . . . I don't know what to do," I whispered, leaning toward them. They both looked like I was freaking them out. My eyes were starting to get all teary. *You will not cry.*

You will not cry! "It's just . . . I've never been in this situation before and I . . . I was just hoping . . ."

And then it was like my whole body did the wave—but it was like this wave of uncontrolled emotion, everything I'd been holding in came up and out. I rolled off the cot and lunged for the door. I so didn't want them to see me burst into tears like a stupid girl. I ran down the main hall and out into the parking lot, and *then* I burst into tears. I walked to the far end and sat on a car bumper, sobbing, trying to understand how I had gotten myself into such a mess.

chapter forty-six
and justice for all

By morning break, I had pulled myself together—thanks to the support of four friends and two bags of mac and cheese bites. Amy and Jen and Bean and Cate and I sat on our bench in sophomore hall, talking. We vowed never to let a guy—or in Cate's case, a girl—get in the way of our friendship. And then we looked around for Canfield and all hugged really quickly.

Jeez, we already had like twenty detentions between us. The first one was at lunch. I sat there, tapping my pencil eraser against the table, staring at a blank page in my notebook.

I should have been writing about what I had done wrong and who it had hurt and why I had done it and what I would do differently next time. But the problem was—I didn't have that many pages in my notebook.

I looked around the library.

After Canfield's ridiculous no-hugging rule, practically everyone I knew was in detention. My new good *friend* Eric Sobel sat a few tables away, across from Bodie, who got busted hugging Jen during their big public makeup in the quad. I waved at Eric. But he had his nose in his camera, probably capturing all the detention drama for Yearbook.

I turned to Amy, Bean, Cate, and Jen all sitting together in the back row and whispered, *"Vive la résistance!"*

Ms. Whit walked out from behind the library checkout counter, frowning. She shh'd us all. I pretended to be writing my detention essay until she disappeared back into her office.

I peeked over my other shoulder. Mandy Mindel and Teddy Baedeker and LG Wong were sitting happily between Bodie and Candy like they were all riding together on the homecoming float. Yep, even Candy Esposito was in detention for hugging. Apparently, this was the very first detention of her life. She was smiling like she was living the Un dream.

Charlie, surrounded by his new bodyguards, sat next to Candy, his new lady friend. Whatever that meant. Charlie and Bean kept passing notes back and forth.

And there was Clint, my new *not* friend, in the far back row. I tried to catch his eye but he was busy texting and whispering back and forth with Split Ends and Elliott, who by the way, looked kind of foxy after his Beauty Without Borders haircut, I had to admit.

I glanced up at the clock. Groan. Sixteen minutes to go. I sighed, looking back down at my blank page. I knew the people I'd hurt. That was easy. I ticked them off on one hand. Well, okay, both hands. But I honestly didn't know what I would've or could've done differently—except maybe get a personality transplant.

I turned to look back at Clint. OMG. I think he might have just been looking at *me*. I kept staring at him smiling, waiting, hoping. Nothing. I sighed and looked back at the blank page of my notebook.

Suddenly, this crackling sound drifted out of the intercom speaker above us. Then Canfield cleared his voice. I popped up in my chair, all nervo-excited.

"Good afternoon, NICE students of Pleasant Hill High! This is your vice principal, Mr. Canfield, with a quick announcement."

A wave of groans and snickers followed. I held my breath.

"Due to unfortunate circumstances beyond my control, Peter Hutchison is no longer eligible to be sophomore class president."

There was a sudden echo of disbelief and even a few cheers. I tried not to smile too hard. SHHH!

Canfield took a deep breath and exhaled into the mic. It sounded like a jet taking off—we all covered our ears.

"Therefore, I have no choice but to name Paisley Hanover as the new sopho-more class president."

Everyone around me started cheering and whooping and whis-tling. I turned around and casually waved to all of my fellow deten-tion mates like it was no big deal. Eric snapped a bunch of pictures while Cate and Bean jumped up and down hugging and squealing, totally ecstatic. Watching them, I got a little lump of cotton-candy luv fuzz stuck in my throat.

Amy was on her feet, pointing at me, yelling, "You! You! You!" And a bunch of other people joined in until Ms. Whit came march-ing out of her office looking pissed. Everyone quickly shut up.

"As we all know, Paisley Hanover is a . . . a . . . a rather unusual girl. Her first official act as class president was to resign."

There was dead silence.

Then everyone around me freaked.

"What?"

"NO way!"

Are you crazy?"

I just smiled. I couldn't help it.

"Her second official act was to name her successor, which according to the school bylaws is the right and privilege of a no-fault resigning class officer."

Pause.

"Effective today and through the end of the year, the new sophomore class officer is . . ."

Canfield sounded like he was about to cry.

"Cate Maduro."

The intercom went silent.

There was this eruption of sounds and surprise all around me. I looked right at Cate. Her mouth was hanging open and it kind of looked like she was having her very first flash fantasy! And then she got this huge grin on her face, like she was so going to kill me.

Eric hopped up on a table and snapped a bunch more photos. Of me. Of Cate. Of all the celebrating Uns.

Suddenly, my phone in my pocket started to vibrate, and I jumped a few inches out of my seat. Jeez! I'll never get used to that. I looked up. That was weird. Phones all around me were vibrating, buzzing, and skittering on the tabletops.

I opened mine under the table, careful that Ms. Whit couldn't see me. OMG. It was a text from Clint. But I had to read it twice before I actually believed it.

GROUP HUG 50-yd-lin 2-day @ 12:23

I checked the clock. It was 12:21. Trying to be super-cool and casual, I turned around to look at Clint.

But of course he was gone.

My heart sighed and my shoulders fell. I studied his text again. Wait. Was this a flash mob thing? Or a cruel joke? I'd just have to be fearless and find out.

The minute hand clicked. Everyone in detention, basically every person in the whole library, glanced around at each other all excited like *Are we going? Are we going?*

I stood up. There was no way I was playing by Canfield's rotten rules. And no way was I done with protests. "Come on, people!"

I yelled. "Canfield can't keep the entire student body in detention. Let's roll!"

Then everyone else jumped up and followed me to the door.

Ms. Whit waved with a sly smile on her face. "See you all back here soon!" But she didn't try to stop us.

I walked out of the library and down the hall, bobbing and weaving, leading the way through the lunchtime traffic. And then I started to run. I couldn't help myself. I jogged into the football stadium, panting, and slowed to a walk. Clint was standing alone in the middle of the field. He smiled at me. I tried to be cool, but I totally wasn't. I started jogging toward him.

"Hey, Red." He smirked. "Man, you are fast."

I slowed to a walk again, mashing my lips together as I tried to read his face. I had butterflies in my butt and my heart and my brain and I couldn't stop smiling. I stood a few feet away from him, breathing hard, trying to catch my breath.

"Hey there," I said between breaths. People were starting to stream onto the football field from all sides. I looked him in the eye. "Hey, are we okay?"

He flashed me his flirty sexy grin. "Yeah. Yeah, I think so. I am. Red, come on. I *love* a good BLT."

I laughed. "Me too! Easy on the mayo, or whatever. Never mind." OMG. Did I just say that out loud? I blushed.

He opened his arms. "Sure you wanna do this?" he asked, raising one eyebrow. "It's a whole month of detentions."

"Yeah, I'm sure."

I stepped into his arms, and we hugged—and my whole body did the wave. How does he do that?

Clint lifted me up off the ground and dramatically spun me around. I had this full-body smile going on, and that was before I saw all of my friends and practically the whole school rushing out onto the football field to join us. Clint lowered me to the ground.

And there was Cate, looking exasperated but smiling at me. "What did you do?" she asked like I was totally bonkers. "Are you nuts?!"

"Congratulations!" I gave her a big hug too. Bean, Amy, and Jen jogged up to us.

"But Paisley, I want to fight the authority," Cate said. "I don't want to *be* the authority!"

"What better way to fight?" I asked.

"You gotta admit," said Bean, all excited. "Infiltrating the establishment? Very underground."

"*Oui*," said Amy like an old French man.

"Besides, you earned it. You really get stuff done."

"Really?" Cate asked. "Are you really okay with this?"

"Are *you*?"

"I dunno? Maybe." She made this uh-oh face. "But I already put the tarantula in Canfield's suggestion box."

"I love you!" said Bean, all goobery, giving Cate a hug.

"Me too," said Amy.

"Me three!" Jen joined in, throwing her arms around them. "I love you guys!"

Then Cate and Jen hugged, and Clint and Bean hugged, and Candy and Teddy hugged, and Clint and Mandy hugged—and she almost fainted. It was all kind of amazing.

Then someone tapped me on the shoulder. I turned around. Eric was smiling at me, his intense green eyes sparkling with . . . I wasn't sure what.

"Hi," I said, totally happy to see him there.

"Hi," he said. Then he smiled bigger, nodding. "Hey, it's not the *listening spot*, but . . ." Eric shrugged. "It'll play. For today."

I reached out and gave him a long hug. And yeah, he hugged me back. And—I'm not sure—but I don't think it was just a *friend* hug. Oh man. Here we go again.

Then Cate hugged Clint, and Bean hugged Amy, and Candy hugged Charlie, and Charlie hugged Bean, totally blushing as his nose saddle mashed up against her boobs. Bodie hugged Jen, then Jen considered hugging Hutch. But she couldn't do it. I didn't blame her one bit—but I hugged him. Don't worry. It was a really quick one. It just seemed like the right thing to do.

I smelled something totally disgusto and turned around just as Carreyn trudged up to us in her work boots and stinky, shapeless coveralls. Her eyes looked a little red and puffy. Jen and I exchanged glances. Then Jen took a huge breath and gave Carreyn a huge hug. I told you Jen was great. I watched them for a few seconds. But I started to get this big lump of cotton candy luv fuzz in my throat, so I quickly looked away. Clint was giving Eric a dude hug. I smiled, feeling puppies-under-rainbows happy. Suddenly, all of us got smooshed together into this big giant hug as more and more people joined in.

The group hug was *un*real. It spread and spread and spread until it almost filled the whole football field, growing into this gigantic tight bouquet of all different shapes and sizes and colors and styles and smiles.

And life was beautiful—even in detention for the whole next month.

The UnEnd

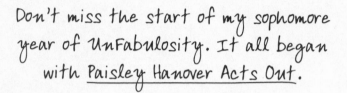

Don't miss the start of my sophomore year of UnFabulosity. It all began with Paisley Hanover Acts Out.

paisley hanover
acts out

cameron tuttle • author of The Bad Girl's Guide

always one of the

popular kids, stylish and quirky sophomore Paisley Hanover gets a rude
awakening when she's booted out
of Yearbook and into the badlands
of Drama class. Out of her element
but only momentarily out of ideas,
Paisley takes action—and an un-
expected liking to her Drama buddies. The result?
An undercover crusade that could bring down the
Pleasant Hill popularity pecking order, and Paisley along with it. Take a page or two from Paisley's
book, as she discovers how to be UnPopular, and
accidentally becomes UnForgettable.

OMG, making a website is really hard. Fortunately, mine turned out kind of fabulous.

Wait, am I allowed to say that about my own website? Whoops!

www.PaisleyHanover.com

Hello? Why are you still here? That's it! The story's over! Well at least until book three . . . Keep your eye out for _Paisley Hanover Crosses Her Heart_. You're so going to love it—I promise.